The Fake Zone

Mariah Dietz

MD Publishing, LLC

The Fake Zone

Also by Mariah Dietz

Tangled in Tinsel, A Christmas Novella

Content Editing: Nicole McCurdy, with Emerald Edits

Cover Design by: Laura Hidalgo, Spellbinding Design

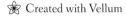 Created with Vellum

THE FAKE ZONE

The Fake Zone

A Frienemies-to-Lovers / Fake Dating / Suspenseful / Sports Romance

A romance that will keep you on the edge of your seat by USA Today Bestselling Author Mariah Dietz.

Greyson Meyers can't afford the distraction of a relationship. His focus is football and earning his degree to ensure his mom never has to work another day.

Mila Atwool has it all together—at least, that's what everyone thinks. But after an incident fractured her safety and trust last year, Mila's been struggling to maintain appearances.

The two strike a deal: Mila will pose as his girlfriend to make his life appear better balanced so he can earn a sponsorship, and in turn, Grey will train her in self-defense to help her rebuild a sense of security.

Two and a half years of friendship ensured their fake relationship would be a safe bet—or so they thought. But what was a simmering tension quickly boils over, and both are terrified of getting burned.

They realize this new zone may be impossible to escape unscathed.

Content Warning

This is not a dark romance nor is it a romcom. While reading, you will likely laugh and snicker, feel angst, frustration, suspense, lust, and likely even a little heartbreak. The story contains explicit sexual content, profanity, and topics that may be sensitive to some readers including mental health, childhood neglect, and child death (which does not occur in the book but is mentioned).

Your mental health matters greatly to me so if you have questions or concerns, please feel welcome to email me at mariah@mariahdietz.com and I'm happy to answer any questions you may have.

XO,
   Mariah

For every Mila. Remember, you are strong. You are beautiful. And you are loved.

And for Miss Nadia. Thank you for looking at so many dots of my pointillism painting with so much care, love, and compassion.

Chapter 1

Mila

I take another sip of my hot tea, hoping it will settle the unease churning through my stomach and muscles. Who knew going to a restaurant alone would be so uncomfortable? My server has given me no less than a dozen tight-lipped pitying smiles despite my assurance I'm here alone on purpose, not because I was stood up.

It's the dress, I'm sure.

I was told to dress up and take myself somewhere nice on this self-date experiment, and I did so without considering what others would think when I sat alone at a table with my hair curled, makeup pristine, and wearing a dress worthy of attending a movie premiere. This evening is supposed to promote independence and self-worth. Instead, my confidence is dropping faster than the late December temperature. And it's not solely attributed to the pitying and curious looks I keep receiving but because sitting alone while surrounded by conversation is uncomfortable and has me green with envy.

I want to sit across from someone and hear about their day and then tell them about the book I'm reading for book club

1

that has a hero I'm torn between loving and hating because he won't kiss the heroine even though I think she wants it nearly as bad as I do. I want to discuss the menu and desserts. At this point, I'd be willing to discuss something as mundane as the weather.

I straighten my silverware and try not to check my phone for the twentieth time. I'm not supposed to look at my phone or a book.

Be with my thoughts.

My thoughts are boring.

As a couple passes, the man glances over my gorgeous dress and then my table set for one before glancing at my face. His eyebrows jump, and he gives a bemused expression as though trying to understand why I'm here alone. I straighten my shoulders and brush off the residual judgment that swims in my thoughts like bloodthirsty sharks.

His thoughts don't matter. He doesn't know me.

My self-worth drops a couple more degrees, regardless.

I take another sip of tea.

I only ordered it because a book I recently read had a heroine who loved tea. I'd connected with her so deeply I thought I might love it, too. Three sugar packets later, I realize if tea is the prerequisite for heroine roles, I may be bound forever to supporting roles.

Thankfully the waiter appears with my soup.

I slide my silverware over to make room for the steaming bowl, wishing I'd thought to ask him to bring my meal at the same time to get this night over with sooner. "Thank you."

"Absolutely. Would you like anything else? More tea? Anything else to drink?" He has a stark widow's peak and thick eyebrows that move when he talks.

"No. This is great. Thank you."

He nods. "Are you having a good night?" His eyebrows dance.

I want to go on a tirade and tell him that I'm not, that I struggled with the holidays even more this year than usual, and I'm the only person who's ready for winter break to end, and how uncomfortable I am eating alone. But I swallow the words, paste on a demure smile and nod. "I am."

He nods. "It's beautiful out tonight. Do you have any plans after this?"

"I'm taking a friend to the movies." He doesn't need to know that I'm that friend.

He smiles, appearing relieved on my behalf. "Let me know if you need anything." He tucks his serving tray under his arm and walks away.

I feel the weight of another curious stare as I break the thick layer of Gruyère cheese covering my soup. I'm so distracted trying to ignore the onlooker and pretend I don't care that I ignore the billowing steam and scald my tongue with the first taste. My spoon clatters against the bowl in my haste to drop it. I grab the glass of ice water, feeling prickles of curious stares from nearby tables, but that doesn't slow me from draining half the glass like I'm at my first college party with something to prove.

My attention is tugged toward the front, where broad shoulders wrapped in a white button-down demand notice. I take in the trim waist and large hand, the jacket folded over his forearm, before climbing back to those impressive shoulders and higher to see his face, forgetting about everyone and everything else.

A strong squared jaw, the hint of a scowl, a straight nose, piercing blue eyes, and dishwater blond hair send a wave of panic coursing through me as recognition and shame tell me I've just ogled—publicly—the wrong person.

For a split second, I consider slinking under the small table and crawling toward the nearest exit to escape, but Greyson Meyers smells blood in the water—my blood—and his eyes flick to mine. He skirts his gaze over me and the empty seat at my table for two.

Greyson, or Grey, is teammates with my oldest and best friend, Hudson McKinley, who is like a brother to me. Hudson is the only reason that Grey-I-only-glower Meyers and I know each other and sometimes spend time in the same building.

Luck arrives in the form of another server stopping to refill my water.

"Are you off soon?" I ask her, my voice caught between a plea and a whisper.

Her caramel-colored eyes fall to me, wide with alarm. "Uh ... sorry?"

"I'll buy you a drink or dessert. Both. Anything you want. A kidney?"

Her eyebrows tip higher with confusion and a hint of amusement. "I'm closing."

I sigh, shifting so I can hide more of myself behind her.

She tilts her head, her amusement vanishing. "Is someone bothering you?"

"I'm just trying to avoid someone."

She glances over her shoulder, destroying any semblance of a cover. Grey is the only guy standing at the front, his six-foot-five frame a beacon. "Your ex?"

"God, no. We can't stand each other. And I don't date blonds."

She chuckles. "Why do we hate him?"

I'm enamored with her call to girl code. It's not me hating Grey—it's we. "Because..." My reasoning is a blank space, slow to fill, because my dislike for him is largely based on his dislike of me. I know that's prideful and spiteful and probably a half-dozen more words that end in -ful, so I stick to the poster reasons.

"He's bossy and stubborn and a terrible conversationalist. And his grumpy ass is judgy as fuck." My eyes flare as I glance at the nearby tables, hoping they didn't hear me swear in this full-service restaurant filled with class and money. People come here for wedding anniversaries and proposals. I have no idea what I was thinking when making a reservation here for a self-date.

"I think I'd enjoy being bossed around by him," the server tells me, her eyes bright with lust. "And while I'm with you on blonds, there are always exceptions—Charlie Hunnam, Chris Evans, Chris Hemsworth..."

"We don't focus on the exceptions," I inform her, trying not to stare at Grey and his date, but questions are firing off in my head—the loudest being, who is she? Who has broken Grey's two-and-a-half-year record of being single? She's stunning with long dark hair, round, sunny eyes, and plump lips.

The server grins as she faces me. "Well, I hate to tell you this, but exception or not, he's coming this way."

"Of course he is," I mutter and take a sip of my refilled water, still trying to ease my raw tongue and floundering nerves.

The hostess leads them closer, and Grey says something quietly before pointing directly at me. I'm frozen, glued to my chair as he walks to my side and swoops down, perfuming the air with his cologne, cedar, pine, and a faint trace of orange, before kissing my cheek. "There you are," he says. "Sorry I'm late. Did our wires get crossed? I thought I reserved a table for three?"

The server looks at me in bewilderment. I stare back at her in shock.

"We can get you to a table for three," the hostess says.

Grey nods, already pulling my chair back from the table and offering me his hand.

His date—or whoever he came with—stares daggers at me.

"Let me just get my things."

The hostess nods to a nearby table. "I'll just have you all sit right over here." She leads Grey's apparent non-date to the table, and I can't help but admire the short, dusty rose silk dress she's wearing that would be obscene on me due to my height. It's ruffled and flouncy, showing off her toned legs and modest hints of her cleavage. Sometimes I really wish I were short or at least shorter than my five-foot-ten frame so I could wear mini dresses like that, not to mention her towering heels that would earn me a few dozen Sasquatch comments.

When my gaze returns to Grey, he scowls at me.

I glare back. "What are you doing?" I whisper.

"I need your help. I need you to pretend to be my girlfriend."

"Did you hit your head?"

His glare deepens. "You're here alone, right?" He glances at the empty spot across from me, cleared of utensils and glasses.

"What if I'm not?"

"Mila..." His voice is impatient. "I need your help."

"You are going to owe me..." I say, grabbing my purse as he takes my jacket and crosses to my new table.

"His hair's definitely more brown than blond," the server says quietly.

It is, but I'm not about to admit it.

The server grabs the plate my bowl of soup is balanced on along with my unused silverware and strides the twenty feet to deposit them right in the hot seat I'm intended to fill.

So much for girl code.

"I'll pay you a hundred dollars cash to fake an allergic reaction," I whisper in a rushed voice as the server returns.

"He asked you to sit with him," she whispers back. "When someone like that asks you to join them, you say yes."

"Not when you're the third wheel," I hiss.

The server winces, and I know I've scored a point in this heinous game of reasoning. "But he asked you to come. Clearly, he doesn't like her. You have to find out for all of us."

I wait to see if fate will open the ground and let me escape this hell for another, but as the ground remains firmly intact, I grab my soup spoon and napkin and follow the server to Grey's table.

I'm never going on a self-date again.

More curious gazes follow me as I slink into the chair and try to smile at Grey's non-date, who looks as uncomfortable as I do based on her slackened jaw and round gaze.

"Hi. Nice to meet you," I say, offering my hand because my Southern charm and manners are a habitual response even under duress.

"Mila, this is Emma Kemp. Emma, this is my girlfriend, Mila Atwool."

"Girlfriend? I didn't know you were dating anyone," Emma says.

"Me either," I say.

A kick to my shin has me wincing. "She's kidding," Grey says.

Emma looks between us.

"That's me. I'm a jokester." I take a long drink of my tea, wishing it were coffee, and glance back at my table longingly, only to be kicked in the shin again. I sit up straighter, shooting Grey an accusatory glare. "Nervous twitch?"

"Emma's here because her dad, Linus Kemp, the booster club member we were supposed to meet for dinner, had something come up. She's standing in for him."

7

I know little about the booster club or its members, only that their influence is steeped in the team.

Emma glances at my soup. "Do you always order before the rest of your party arrives?"

I've always wanted to stand by the philosophy that women should stick together. That we should share our crowns and privately straighten each other's if one slips. After all, we've been stepped on, forgotten, and silenced for too long. But Emma reminds me how men aren't the only ones to blame. Sometimes women are, too. I've received a multitude of cruel remarks regarding my hair or makeup, clothes, or body aimed at making me feel less about myself, and they were almost always coming from other women.

Grey clears his throat. "It's my fault. I got the time wrong." He grabs his napkin, draping it across his lap. "Emma's a junior at Camden, too."

"I was telling him how much we have in common," Emma says, giving Grey a look of longing and sheer hunger. Of course she likes him. Most women are attracted to Grey for his base masculinity, devastating handsome features, and stacks of chiseled muscles, all capitalized by his broody personality. However, his recognition as one of the best wide receivers in college football has doubled his fan base in recent months.

"Oh yeah? Like what?" I don't mean for my words to sound like a challenge or spark a war, certainly not over Grey. I'm not jealous, and I'm definitely not trying to prove anything. However, I don't take back the words and revel a little too much in watching Emma shift uncomfortably in her chair.

"Well, for starters, we both love football," she says, looking flustered and ready to slash me with her perfectly pink manicured nails.

I think of my best friend Evelyn, of my newly found book

club comprised of girls who are genuinely remarkable and kind women.

I wonder if Emma and I met under different circumstances, would we be friends? I imagine an invisible crown on her head and swallow my snark with a drink of water and start over. "Are you attending the bowl game this weekend in Orlando?" It's Camden's final game of the season.

Emma nods. "I wouldn't pass up the chance to watch Grey play." She gives him a smoldering look—a come and bang my brains out, please, look—that reminds me of one of a dozen reasons why I'd never date a guy on the team.

"Mila loves football, too," Grey says.

"Really?" Emma asks, matching the same level of challenge I posed. "Who's your favorite team?"

I hold my chin up a little higher. "Camden, of course." I paste on a smile.

Chapter 2

Grey

I f I'd had any idea this night would bear any semblance to a blind date, I would have canceled. Linus Kemp is a booster I've been working to impress for the better part of a year since he told me he was interested in offering me a paid sponsorship, promoting the car lots he owns here in Oleander Springs, North Carolina. I thought we were going to sit down with a contract. Instead, ten minutes ago, I was blindsided by a text that informed me his daughter, Emma, would be taking his place because he had to work late.

I never expected to walk inside and find Mila here, certainly not alone. Mila Atwool is all confidence and grace wrapped in jaw-dropping beauty and an impenetrable wall of sarcasm that catches the eye of every man. Seeing her alone sparked a plan of desperation and prayer. I knew I was being catfished—or something too damn similar—and having Mila pretend to be my girlfriend is the perfect ruse. At least it will be if she maintains the role. The only problem is Mila can be as prickly and challenging as a trapped raccoon.

A waiter stops beside me, and his smile and greeting falter

as he peers from Emma to me and then at Mila before glancing at the table I convinced Mila to abandon. "You..." the waiter says, pointing at Mila, "moved." He tries to save face, but it's too late. His tone is laden with disappointment. The poor schmuck couldn't be more obvious.

Mila sweeps her long blonde hair over a shoulder, revealing a large pearl earring. "I hope that's not a problem." She blinds him with a smile.

"Not a problem at all," he says.

Mila's smile somehow turns more radiant. I've seen her pull a similar look when a police officer stopped us for jaywalking two years ago while we were at the beach and again when telling a bartender she'd forgotten her ID, though she was only eighteen. It's deceptive and highly impactful.

The waiter smiles back, blissfully unaware. I wouldn't be surprised if he brings us complimentary appetizers or desserts.

Emma clears her throat, sitting forward, her back ramrod straight. "Could I have a rum and diet, please?"

The waiter's smile wanes, and he nods, trying to tear his attention from Mila's bright red lips, wide blue eyes, and flawless cheekbones.

"Of course, and for you, sir?"

"I'm good with water, thanks," I tell him.

The waiter nods again. "Would you care for any appetizers?"

Emma looks at me expectantly. "Grey? Would we like any appetizers?" God, those words sound too date-like.

Mila quietly drums her short, bare nails along the edge of the table. "The arancini here is amazing."

The price of everything on the menu is criminal.

"I don't eat carbs," Emma says.

"I think we'll pass, thanks," I tell the waiter.

He nods. "Have you decided what you'd like to order?"

11

Emma nods and orders a salad with a dozen modifications as I turn to Mila, setting my hand on hers to gain her attention.

Mila's eyes flash to mine. They're the color of steel, and tonight they look even wider and more striking than usual. I haven't seen her in two weeks, not since my close friend and teammate Nolan Payne pulled off creating a new tradition for Camden by turning a library into a dance floor for his girlfriend to celebrate her birthday. Mila had mentioned then that she was leaving for California and was planning to decorate a palm tree for the holidays.

"And for you, sir," the waiter says, interrupting my mental thanks for Mila for being here.

I order the roasted bass and try not to wince at the price tag. Boosters like to show off their wealth by taking us to the nicest restaurants, working to impress us while offering paid and unpaid sponsorships: attending a grand opening or company event, golfing, and more. I need this sponsorship far more than the dent to my shrinking bank account this dinner will leave me.

The waiter nods and turns to Mila. "Would you like anything else? More tea?"

"No, thank you."

He nods. "I'll have them wait on your dinner until theirs is ready."

Mila's smile turns tight. "Thanks."

His reluctance to leave is visible in the way he sways and keeps his pen firmly pressed against his ordering pad before he gives a wistful sigh and turns to a nearby table.

"How was your Christmas, Grey?" Emma takes a sip of her water, her eyes trained on me.

"It was nice. And yours?" I ask.

She smiles. "It was pretty amazing. My dad rented several

snow machines and had the entire yard looking like a scene out of a movie."

Mila's eyes soften and her lips part. "I love the snow."

Emma looks at Mila with uncertainty, like she doesn't know whether to trust the sincerity in her words or tone. I silently chuckle, wishing her luck. I've been trying to figure out Mila for the past two and a half years, despite Hudson's many attempts to assure me she's the most genuine and kind person I'll ever meet.

"How did you two meet?" Emma asks.

Mila raises one eyebrow, promising trouble.

I give her an exasperated look, waiting for her to make up a tall tale that will make Emma even more suspicious.

Mila rolls her eyes at me, and I hear her silent admonishment that I'm boring and ruining her fun before she sighs and folds her hands in her lap. "A mutual friend introduced us at a party at the beginning of Grey's freshman year."

"Actually, we met at Hudson's. While you were painting his wall black."

Recognition sparks in her gaze. "That's right. You asked if I was painting it to match the color of my soul ... He's a romantic." She shucks her thumb at me.

I chuckle. *She* had told *me* she was painting the wall to match the color of *her* soul when I asked why she chose black. From day one, Mila Atwool has been an enigma with wit and sharp remarks that make her difficult to read and impossible to ignore.

Emma leans back with a predator's gaze as she sets her mark on me. "Is that so?"

Thankfully, our waiter appears then with our meal, distributing plates with scarce food artfully stacked in the middle of large plates. My biggest complaint when attending one of these dinners is that I always leave hungry.

Emma eyes the steaming plate of pasta the waiter sets in front of Mila like a ticking time bomb. "Cheat day?"

Mila glances from the pasta to Emma twice before flashing a tiger's smile—all teeth. "No."

Emma shakes her head and looks at me from under her lashes with a flirtatious grin. If she knew my truck was twenty-five years old and my bank account held less than four-hundred dollars, I doubt she'd give me the time of day.

"Are you looking forward to having some downtime since football season is coming to an end?" Emma asks.

I nod, but the reality is college athletes don't get an off-season. Even the early months of summer are devoted to football. The following two months will be packed with unofficial practices I'll have to attend to maintain my position as a starter.

Emma licks her lips. "I imagine it's crucial for you to surround yourself with people who understand the responsibility and politics of the game. People who will take care of you."

"Have you seen how many trainers and personal chefs the team has?" Mila asks. "Trust me. They're well taken care of."

Emma laughs mirthlessly. "That wasn't the kind of care I was referring to..." She keeps her gaze on me, unabashed by the insinuation.

I grapple, trying to find a response to turn her down without offending her.

Mila clears her throat and pushes her seat back. "Please excuse me a moment. I need to find the ladies' room."

I tap her with my foot and shoot her a look that pleads for her to stay and change the subject. Stat.

Mila winces and then scowls, pushing her chair back farther before she stands.

"I should, too. We've been hydrating all week, preparing for the bowl game."

Mila furrows her brow, a silent, *What in the hell are you doing?*

"We'll be right back," I tell Emma.

Mila leads the way to a hallway at the rear of the restaurant and spins to face me. "What are you doing, weirdo? Guys don't follow women to the restroom unless they plan to hook up. And why do you keep kicking me?" She swats at my biceps.

"I need this sponsorship deal from her father."

"I don't understand why you can't just tell her you're not interested and leave me out of this. I was having a perfectly good night until you showed up."

"Perfectly good night? You got stood up. I hardly made your night worse."

"I wasn't stood up," she growls. "I was here on a self-date."

"A self-what?"

"*Date*," she says again, but before I can clarify, she turns on her heel and heads into the women's restroom.

I should think better of it, but I follow.

Mila's at the mirror, her eyes growing round as she looks at me in the reflection. "Have you lost your mind?"

"Look, I'm sorry I'm ruining your night, and I'm sorry she's being a bitch to you."

Mila stops and stares at me for several seconds before closing the space between us and placing a hand to my forehead.

I brush her hand away. "What are you doing?"

"You just apologized. Twice. I was checking to make sure you don't have a fever."

I clamp my molars to keep from saying something that will rescind my apology. "I had no idea she was coming. I don't know her and don't want to lead her on. But I also don't want her telling her dad that I'm an asshole, and we both know that if

I sit through dinner alone with her, that will happen because I'm terrible at small talk."

She sighs, and her shoulders drop a full inch. "You're the worst at small talk."

I nod. "Exactly."

Mila purses her lips as I take the wind from her sails with my self-deprecating remark. "You're going to have to go out there, so it doesn't look like we just did the nasty in here. Talk to her about Camden. Classes. Anything that isn't personal."

I nod.

"I'll be out in a few minutes and dazzle her with my charms."

An older woman steps into the restroom and gasps at the sight of me.

"Sorry. He was..." Mila grabs a tissue and dabs her eyes, "just checking on me."

The woman's bewildered expression calms, and she loosens the tight grip on her purse.

"I'm okay," Mila says, blotting her eyes. "Or I will be. I just need another minute." She shoves me toward the door with a meaningful look.

I duck out, straighten my shirt, and return to the table where Emma's picking through her salad.

She looks at me and then over my shoulder before checking each button along my dress shirt, ensuring nothing is amiss before smiling, her relief palpable.

I take my seat. "How has school been this year?"

"Great. How has yours been?" She captures a piece of steak with her fork and brings it to her lips, drawing her tongue over the tines before pulling the bite free with her teeth.

"Busy."

I glance toward the hall, wondering how long Mila plans to wait. "Was Camden your first choice?"

"How long have you two been together?"

"About a month."

"That's not very long," she says.

I swallow. "I've known her for two and a half years."

"That's a long time to know someone and not be sure if you're interested."

Mila appears before I can respond. Her dress casts a red glow across my glass as she takes her seat. I wonder if she was supposed to meet the same asshole she dated in October that Hudson was ready to punch in the face after standing her up a third time.

"You're going to school to become a financial manager, is that correct?" Emma asks, ensuring this is less of a coincidence than it was painted to be. She's done her homework.

I swallow my bite of fish and nod. "Have you declared a major?"

"Human resources," she says. "I plan to work for my father's company when I graduate."

"What about you?" she addresses Mila without saying her name.

"Criminal justice."

"What does one do with a criminal justice degree?" Emma asks.

Mila tucks her napkin on her lap. "Hopefully, reform some archaic laws." She gives a charming smile. "Emma, are you looking forward to going to Orlando? I looked at the weather report, and we should have great weather."

"Oh... You're going, as well?"

Mila nods but doesn't offer more.

"Maybe we'll all have to go out," Emma says, looking at me as she extends the invitation.

Mila gives a waning smile. "We'll be pretty busy. But please, tell me more about yourself."

Chapter 3

Mila

Emma summarizes her childhood, detailing awards received with equestrianism, her years spent dancing, and how she continues working out six days a week before she compares workouts with Grey. All the while, she flirts shamelessly with him.

I could warn her that she won't impress him, that I've witnessed girls flash their bare breasts at Grey and sneak up to his hotel room, and he still hasn't broken his rule to remain single. But a cruel and vengeful part of me enjoys watching her try to impress him, and the casual way he ignores and deflects her every effort.

"Would y'all care for some dessert?" the waiter asks, returning to our table and positioning himself between Grey and me.

This restaurant has the best chocolate mousse I've tasted outside of France, but I swallow my inclination to say yes and look at Grey and Emma for their responses.

"I can't take another bite," Emma says, glancing at her barely touched salad.

"I'm full, too," I say. "Could I get the rest of this to go?" I extend the shiny gold credit card I'd slipped from my purse while half-listening to Emma list off her credentials like this was an interview for her to be Grey's girlfriend, hoping to move things along.

"Of course." The waiter takes my plate and credit card.

Grey drains the rest of his water, his face marred with a new scowl.

I ignore him and feign interest as I turn to Emma. "When are you leaving for Florida?"

"We're flying out first thing Friday morning." She doesn't reciprocate the question, and for the first time since she began talking to us about her equestrian accomplishments and details of her life, we lapse into awkward silence. I kind of hope she has another horse or dance story for us as we wait for my credit card to be returned.

"Grey, do you have any siblings?" Emma asks.

Grey shakes his head. "I don't."

Emma gapes. "You're lucky. I have two younger sisters, and we constantly fight."

She goes on about a decade-long feud between her and her middle sister as the waiter drops off the leather folder with my credit card and receipt.

It's still not the worst date I've been on, but it nears the top.

I grab my jacket and purse, scoop up my leftovers, and am prepared to run for the doors when Grey steps in front of me, forcing me to continue the charade.

"Jesus. You're huge," Emma says, moving to stand beside us. Her tone ensures her words are an insult before she laughs like a bully on the playground. I'm easily six inches taller than her.

"You're not even wearing heels!" Emma exclaims. "How tall are you? And your feet! They're enormous."

I level her with a glare before gaining my composure. "Nearly as tall as Taylor Swift."

Grey steps closer to me, setting a hand between my shoulder blades. His touch is so slight and gentle it's a whisper against my skin, yet I feel it all the way to my toes. "I love that you're tall."

Emma says nothing.

As we step outside, the cold night air hits my face and bare shins like a slap, clearing the haze caused by his words.

We follow Emma to her car, where Grey lowers his hand from my back and opens her door. "Thanks for a nice evening. Please give your father our regards."

Emma flashes him a pageant smile. "I'll see you in Orlando."

I wait until she slips into her seat and then pull my coat tighter, my knuckles turning white as I move to cross the parking lot.

"You couldn't wait for one minute?" Grey asks, jogging to catch up with me.

"My giant feet and I are perfectly capable of walking to my car."

He narrows his eyes on me but doesn't say more. It's one of the reasons we manage to stand each other. We don't ask questions, knowing neither of us wants to exchange truths or realities.

As we pass a large truck, a couple steps out. The surprise has me gasping and pulling back like an alligator's snuck up on us.

Grey wraps his hand around my waist, steadying me before I lose my balance.

"Are you okay?" the man who surprised me asks, taking in my reaction as he wraps an arm around his date's shoulder.

"Sorry. You startled me. I'm fine."

The couple smiles and moves away as Grey places his hand between my shoulder blades again, firmer this time.

"What was that?" Grey asks as we stop at my car.

"What was what?" I ask.

His gaze sweeps over me, his lips pursed as though he's working to recall the rules of our acquaintanceship that keep discussions like this off the table. "Thank you again for doing that. I appreciate it, and I owe you."

"I'll bet you a cupcake she tries sneaking into your hotel room in Orlando."

His lips fall into a frown. He never accepts a bet from me.

I open my door before Grey can, and slide into my seat. The cold leather seat stings the back of my thighs, causing goose bumps to dance across my flesh. "Do you want a ride to your truck?" I start the engine and press buttons to warm up my seat and steering wheel.

He runs a hand through his hair, his jaw is locked with impatience. "I'm right there." He points at his red truck.

"Okay, well, see you."

The night clings to him as he gives a barely perceptible nod and closes my door.

I wait until he's in his truck, the door closed and engine started, before I back out of my spot and drive home.

"Hey. You're back early," Evelyn Watts, my best friend and roommate, says from where she's cuddled up to her boyfriend and my other best friend, Hudson, on the couch. The three of us grew up together. Hudson and I were neighbors, and Evelyn visited every summer. The two began dating in August, an inevitable conclusion to the feelings they've harbored for each other since we were kids. They are my foundation, my sanity, and their dating has hardly changed a thing in our dynamic aside from the fact I now walk in on them actually making out rather than just staring at each other and imagining making out. "How was your self-date?"

"Self-date?" Hudson asks, lifting a brow in a similar reaction to Grey's.

"I took myself on a date, or I intended to, but I ended up being pulled into a third-wheel nightmare where I posed as Grey's fake girlfriend."

"Oh, I need details." Evelyn sits forward.

Hudson raises a brow. "Fake girlfriend?"

Evelyn shushes him.

I'm not about to admit it might have been better than sitting alone, definitely less awkward. "He got catfished."

"By Kemp? I warned him," Hudson says, a grin staining his lips.

"What happened? What does a fake girlfriend look like?" She stares at me intently, and I know her real question is whether we kissed? Since May, Evelyn has been praying for the impossible—Grey and me to become a couple.

I shake my head. "We just ate together and learned her life story. I now know too much about horses. Grey owes me big time."

Hudson chuckles.

"Did you miss your movie?" Evelyn asks, checking the time.

"I skipped it."

"You're welcome to join us," Evelyn pats the empty seat beside her. They often extend invites to prevent me from feeling left out, and I accept more than I should.

"I appreciate it, but my self-date is resuming upstairs in my sweatpants with a movie or book. I haven't decided yet. Either way, I plan to pass out early so I'm bright-eyed and bushy-tailed for our flight to Orlando tomorrow."

"Night, Mila," Hudson calls.

I wave to them and head upstairs to my bedroom, where my imagination creeps into my subconscious, warning of imaginary dangers and noises as I flip on every light and check every corner. Some habits are hard to break—fears are even harder.

I take a breath, noting my curtain, the old brown stuffed bear tucked on a shelf, my miniature pink Christmas tree adorned with ivory ribbons and clear lights, and my TV. Then I listen for three sounds: the TV downstairs, Evelyn's laughter, and the deepness of Hudson's voice.

I walk to my dresser, pluck a bottle of perfume off the small metal tray, and pull off the cap to smell it. It's floral and rich, taking me back to Hawaii, and then a second bottle made of twisted glass. This perfume is lighter, reminding me of the streets of Salzburg, where I purchased it.

Four items, three sounds, and two scents.

Four, three, two.

My heartbeat slows, and my shoulders relax as I strip off my coat and the red formfitting dress. I catch my reflection as I hang them in my closet, noting where my thighs meet, and cellulite reaffirms my imperfections as Emma's judgment rings in my head. I tug on an oversized sweatshirt and sweatpants before heading into the bathroom to scrub my face clean and brush my teeth. Once ready for bed, I bury myself in the warmth and weight of blankets and lose myself in the pages of my current book, waiting to see if the hero finally kisses the heroine.

Chapter 4

Grey

The house I grew up in looks borderline depressing during the winter months. The beige exterior of the doublewide trailer is dull, and the roof is becoming more orange than gray as the rust spreads in angry, greedy splotches. The yard is well tended, though; come spring, dozens of flowerpots will be filled with brightly colored blooms.

Mom opens the front door before I get out of my truck. "I told you not to stop by today. You're supposed to be getting ready for your game." She's already dressed in navy blue scrubs for her job as a medical assistant, her blonde hair pulled back in a ponytail.

"Glad to see you, too," I say, climbing the stairs I rebuilt two summers ago. Inside, the scent of coffee lingers.

She smiles smugly and then leans up on her toes to hug me. "I'm always glad to see you. I've told you before if I had it my way, I'd buy a duplex, so you'd never be more than a few feet away."

I love my mom more than life, but sharing walls with her is a little too close. "We'll get a giant plot of land, and we'll each

24

have a big old house," I say, following her inside. Though the outside looks rundown, the inside is clean and homey. Gramps and I painted and replaced nearly every part of the mobile home, including the floors, shower, faucets, and the entire kitchen.

"I don't know what I'd do with all that space. All I need is something to cover my tomatoes to stop the damn hornworms."

"You'll have a greenhouse twice the size of this place."

Mom laughs. "I don't know that I need *that many* tomatoes."

It doesn't matter. For the first time in her life, I want my mom to live in excess, even if it's something as simple as plants, which she has always loved.

"How are you? I haven't seen you since Christmas," she says.

I want to tell her that was just a couple of days ago but quickly realize it's already been ten. "Football's been crazy."

"Did you do anything fun for New Year's?"

"Drank too much and rode a sled off some dude's roof."

She crosses her arms, feigning a look of disappointment, but she can't fight the grin that pulls at the right side of her mouth, knowing I'm lying. She flashed the same defiant smile any time I got in trouble for doing something she was secretly proud of but was supposed to be mad at me for, like in the sixth grade when a kid made it a habit to steal my best friend, Cole's, free school lunch, claiming his father's taxes were paying for it. I finally got him to stop by adding laxatives to the chocolate milk before the asshole took it. He spent the rest of the day in the bathroom.

The school warned our parents if they found out what we did, we'd be suspended. Mom splurged and bought pizza that night, telling me to always stick up for the underdogs because that's what we were—underdogs.

"Sounds boring. You could have at least done something exciting."

"Nolan and Hadley threw a party."

"Oh, she's already back? That was a quick trip home. She must really like him."

I tell my mom too much shit about my personal life. I always have. Mom was only eighteen when I was born, and as a single parent who couldn't afford much, time was usually her gift. We've always been close. "She was probably worried he'd get bored and try something stupid with Lenny," I say, referring to our tight end, known for his bad ideas and worse judgment.

Mom quirks a brow. "Like sledding off a roof?"

"Or getting so drunk they don't know where they are for three days." Again.

Mom shakes her head. "What are you guys going to do after you win your game Friday?" Her blue eyes spark with excitement and the promise of our team's victory like it's a sure thing.

"The university worked out some kind of a deal, and we all got free tickets to Disney World on Saturday."

Mom points at me. "You're not turning that down. You better ride every damn roller coaster. I'm expecting photographic evidence." Her face softens. "Deb, that lady I work with, goes to Disney World twice a year with her husband. I think we should go when I retire."

"You're only thirty-nine," I remind her.

She grimaces. "I've decided I'm staying thirty-nine. We're just going to keep celebrating the anniversary of me turning thirty-nine."

I roll my eyes. She doesn't have a vain bone in her body, but age freaks my mother out. "Which faucet is leaking, the kitchen or the bathroom?"

"You have a big game tomorrow. You don't need to be worrying about this right now."

26

"Your water bill's going to be ridiculous if we don't fix it." She points at the kitchen faucet.

I circle around the counter and pull open the cupboards below the sink, finding a pot with an inch of water at the bottom.

Mom tells me about work, how bad traffic has been in town, and then about my Aunt Rita as I take apart the sink.

"It's the O-rings," I tell her. "Let me run up to the hardware store."

"I can go," she says. "Just tell me what you need."

I'd argue, but determination has formed a hard line between her brows, warning me I won't win this argument. I tell her what we'll need, and she reads the details back twice before heading to the store. While she's gone, I slide the forty dollars cash I brought with me into the old coffee tin where she keeps her rainy-day cash. We never had enough money to take trips to the beach or mountains. Still, Mom scraped and saved and crafted, making every holiday special and splurging when she could after a particularly hard test or game, and sometimes for no reason at all by ordering pizzas or taking us to the movies, our pockets filled with candy we brought with us.

I check around the house, ensuring problem areas aren't causing issues, and take out the trash before she returns.

"Okay. I think I got the right ones," Mom says, opening the front door.

We change the rings and get everything put back together in under thirty minutes.

I'm testing to ensure it's fixed when she grabs the old coffee can I added cash to and pops the lid off. "Busted," she says, withdrawing the small wad of cash and fixing me with a stare. "I don't need your money, Grey. I'm the parent, remember?"

"It's so you can do something nice this weekend. Go to the movies or dinner. Go buy something besides more work clothes or shoes that won't make your feet hurt." I wish I had enough to buy her tickets to come and watch the game in person.

Mom shakes her head and shoves the money at me. "I have the best job I've ever had. I've got things covered. You know me."

I do, which is why I tried to slip the money in while she wasn't here. She'll never ask for help—or accept it. "I'm making close to twenty bucks an hour," she assures me. "I'm good. You work too hard for your money. Spend it on something stupid and fun at Disney World."

"You've wanted to try that new pizza place for months."

"They're almost forty bucks a pizza. We'll wait for a coupon and order it for my birthday."

"When you turn thirty-nine?"

She cracks a smile. "Exactly." She shoves the bills into my palm. "Thanks for coming by and fixing my sink. Don't get hurt tomorrow. Okay? And don't forget, photographic evidence." She gives me a knowing glance before wrapping her arms around my waist and squeezing me tightly.

"Keep the pot down there another day or two, just to make sure the O-rings were the only problem."

"You underestimate yourself," she says, giving me another tight squeeze. "I already know you fixed it."

Her arms loosen as she takes a step back. "I've got to get to work." She pulls on her coat and hitches her purse over a shoulder. "Where's your jacket?"

I pull at my hoodie. "It was sixty when I left."

"It's supposed to get cold next week," Mom says, locking the door to the trailer and following me down to the driveway. I hope to buy her a house with a garage one day, so her car will never be too warm or cold. "Have a great game and an amazing time. I love you."

"I love you too, Mom."

I head to Cole's, knowing he's already awake and training.

His parents live just five minutes from my mom in one of the dozen trailer parks that make up much of Highgrove. I pull up behind his dad's Suburban that is currently sitting up on jacks with the back left tire off.

I slam my truck door shut and circle around to their backyard, the neighbor's pit bull barking at me through the five-foot chain-link fence that separates their properties. Rock music confirms Cole is inside.

I knock twice on the shed door before pulling it open. Cole looks at me from where he's doing biceps curls and grins. "About time you showed up."

I grab a dumbbell and take a seat.

"I'm pissed things didn't work out, and I can't make it to Florida to see your game tomorrow," Cole says, completing his set.

"Don't worry about it." I try to brush off his guilt.

I lower the dumbbell, the warped mirror in front of me, making my biceps look too short and then too long, like a fun house mirror. Like everything else in here, it was something we salvaged.

Highgrove, my tiny hometown located thirty minutes south of Oleander Springs, was built on old money and influence and continues running that way today. A handful of families who live here are filthy rich while everyone else is poor and works for them.

That small group holds the wealth and runs this town, looking at families like ours as though we choose to be poor, choose to not have enough money to pay both the electric and gas bills some months, and choose to live in trailers that don't have adequate insulation or air conditioning when the North Carolina sun threatens to melt everything in its path. They don't care that my mom juggled three jobs for most of my childhood or that Cole's dad had seizures that prevented him from working while his mom picked up every shift she could at the café, earning too much money to ever get on state insurance and too little to afford their own healthcare. We were stuck living in a vicious cycle of poverty that our parents and grandparents struggled through. Cole and I have been determined to break that cycle since we were kids.

I imagined myself living in a high rise, driving a new, fully loaded truck to an office, and wearing a suit tailored to fit me. I was committed to the college route, believing good grades and a prestigious degree would get me there, but Cole pointed out how many other kids had the same dream—the same path. We realized the only way we could break out of these patterns was to excel in ways that allowed us to stand out. For me, that was football, and for Cole, it was fighting.

We turned his parents' shed into a gym and have been training and studying our crafts together and separately for the past decade.

"What do you know about this guy you're fighting tomorrow?" I ask, grabbing my water bottle. My coaches and trainers would lose their shit if they learned I was working out hours before our flight. But sitting around would only lead to Cole razzing me, and I don't have the energy to put up with his shit when all my attention and time has been focused on tomorrow's game. "You said it's a big pot."

Cole nods. "He's from Staten Island or something. Abe says he's stacked but doesn't know how to use his weak side." Abe is Cole's younger brother, and if he could control his temper, he'd be one hell of a fighter because he reads the defense better than anyone we know.

"If he's seeking you out, he knows something about his weak side."

Cole chuckles. "It sounds like he goes one hundred percent

and burns out quickly. I've just got to keep him moving and wear him down." He lies back on the bench press. "What about you and tomorrow's game?" he asks, gripping the straight barbell. "Are you still feeling confident?"

Our game is against Cal State, and if I were allowed to bet, I'd put every cent I own on the game. "Without a doubt."

"Good. I bet on you."

"Guaranteed money," I tell him.

"You haven't changed your mind on the draft?"

Until a couple of weeks ago, I had intended to enter the draft, but then our head coach shafted us, benching two of our best players that cost us a win and our chance at playing at the final game. My closest friends on the team—including Hudson McKinley, Corey Bishop, Zack Palmer, and Nolan Payne—and I decided to wait one more season, allowing me to earn my degree and a better season to place higher in the draft.

I've got it all mapped out, but once again, Cole's reminding me of contingency plans.

"I mean, you were a beast this year. You made national TV reels. This is huge. How could they not draft you?"

"A lower draft pick could mean I won't get any minutes." For me, it's the long game. When the average NFL player's career is a mere three years, if I don't have a degree to fall back on or any endorsements, even the large signing bonus won't last me but a few years. It certainly won't give me a way to get my mom into an early retirement or help Cole and his family.

Cole hefts the bar up. "I hear you," he says, knowing these concerns I've listed a dozen times prior. "Are you worried about sticking around another year and going up against some of the guys on your own team? Payne was flexing in the last game, and Palmer isn't exactly someone to sneeze at."

"If we go undefeated next year, it's going to help all of us get what we want. That's the point."

31

Cole blows out a sound caught between a scoff and a laugh. "If you ask me, they need you more than you need them. You make them look good. Even in that game you guys lost, you looked good."

This is one of the stark differences in our sports. As an individual athlete, all decisions are based solely on him rather than a team. "Hudson's the best damn quarterback I've played with, and these routes aren't something I can do alone."

Cole heaves a breath of exhaustion. "Are you going to spot me or sit there and collect dust?"

I stand and meander over to him. "Depends. How much weight did you put on the bar? Is it enough to choke on your own words?"

He chuckles.

"Hey, assholes," Abe steps into the shed with Dustin two steps behind him.

Dustin grew up with us and has been working out with us and training in fighting for nearly as long as we have.

Our buddy Bryant used to hang out with us most days. Like Dustin, he's never had the same desperation to get out of Highgrove. His parents, grandparents, cousins, aunts, and uncles all live here, and though he did well in high school, he didn't want to go to college and never gave a shit about having a career with a pension or health insurance. He's content working for one of the mechanics in town and married his longtime girlfriend the summer after graduating high school. They already have two kids, so we don't see him often.

Abe, like Cole, wants to get into the fighting scene. He's worked hard to try and get into the circuit, but his temper flares and takes control. Both brothers have a switch in them, but when Cole's is flipped, he becomes focused, animalistic, and unstoppable whereas Abe loses control and focus.

"Didn't expect to see you here," Dustin says, wrapping me

in a side hug. "How's it going? You missed the barbecue last week."

I nod. "I know, man. I'm sorry. I've had a shit ton of meetings and additional practices to prepare for tomorrow's game."

Cole nods, clapping a hand on my shoulder. "We know. And we'll be gathered around my living room, cheering you on and toasting to you for making me an easy grand."

Dustin laughs, and Abe winks.

I fucking hope he's right. "I've got to head out."

"Go get on your fancy jet?" Abe's voice hints at contempt.

"Hell yes," Cole says. "Once we start rolling in the money, that will be us, jet-setting across the country for Vegas, renting out the biggest suites, private everything..."

"You get to stay in a suite?" Dustin asks, turning to me.

I scoff. "No." I don't mention it's still a four-star hotel or that we're staying through the weekend, despite the game's outcome, to celebrate the season.

"Give them hell," Cole tells me, pulling me into a hug.

I head for my truck. It won't be the first game my friends or mom haven't been able to attend, and in some selfish way, not having them be there makes things easier. These two parts of my life are so wildly different that keeping them separate is usually simplest.

Chapter 5

Mila

I sip my iced coffee and stare down at the football field. The crowd is already loud, filled with banners and colorful shirts to represent their chosen teams though the bowl game isn't scheduled to start for another thirty minutes.

I wish Hudson could experience this part of the game and see how devoted and excited so many are to watch him play.

Pride blossoms in my chest, knowing how hard he's worked to get here today, and I'm grateful I can be here to watch.

Evelyn's gaze flicks to the row in front of us, and then back to me as she leans closer. "A guy one row down keeps staring at you."

Curiosity gets the better of me—as it usually does. A group of guys sit in front of us, and for a second I think I'll have to show my hand and ask Evelyn which one she was referring to when a guy with dark curly hair and green eyes gives me a second and then third glance before a wide grin covers his face. He's cute. Heart palpitations cute, and I'd bet money he knows it.

I stare at him a few extra seconds—long enough to let him know I've noticed him—before turning my gaze to the field.

Anticipation thrums in my veins as possibilities take flight in my thoughts. This is where my father's career as a producer for popular romance movies becomes my greatest weakness—and fault. I'm waiting for the meet-cute, already imagining what story I'll be sharing at our wedding, our ten-year anniversary, our twentieth anniversary. Will he have the jumbotron confess his interest in me? Or will he ask the stranger beside me to trade him seats because he needs to know my name? And will it be today or later when he leans in close and whispers something sweet and poetic in my ear—his voice a perfect, gravelly baritone—telling me of his intentions to sweep me off my feet with romance and the promise of toe-curling ecstasy?

"I'm going to get something to drink. Do you want anything?" I ask, needing to move before my hopes can sweep me off my feet.

Evelyn's brow tangles with thoughts. "The game's going to start any minute."

I shake my head. "They'll drag this out as long as they can. This is the perfect time to go because everyone is rushing back to their seats, making the lines shorter."

Evelyn glances at the field and then at me before reaching for her purse.

"You don't have to come," I tell her.

Her only reply is to stand and tuck her purse over one shoulder. "I need some snacks." She leads the way, apologizing to everyone we pass as they move and fold their legs in the impossibly narrow aisles. Multiple times a guy slows to stare at her. A few note me a step behind, and don't try to hide their fantasies as their bright gazes jog between us.

"Is your seat next to mine?" a guy with shaggy brown hair

asks me, hooking his hand around my shoulder to gain my attention.

I glance from his heavily chewed and bloodied nailbeds, where his fingers brutishly dig into my flesh, to his muddy brown eyes, bright with innuendos. This is definitely not the meet-cute situation I've overthought too many times, and the pleasure he's considering right now certainly doesn't include my own as his gaze falls to my chest.

I brush his hand away and keep moving without a reply.

"You can sit on my lap," he calls to my back.

"Less tempting than measles," I tell him.

One of his friends howls out a laugh, and another mocks him ruthlessly as Evelyn turns around to ensure I'm okay. A third friend looks from me to Evelyn, cruel sarcasm sizing us up.

I set a hand on Evelyn's back and urge her forward. I hate feeling like I'm running from someone and loathe that he might realize how bothered I am. Guys who are loud and aggressive are equally as creepy as the quiet ones who stare too long.

"Are you all right?" Evelyn asks as we hit the center aisle, pausing as someone moves past us carrying a tray filled with beer.

I nod.

"What did he say to you?"

"Nothing. He was just trying to flirt with my boobs."

Her gaze hardens. "He seemed like a perv."

"Probably because he is one."

With a smirk, Evelyn climbs the stairs that take us to the concessions.

We order frozen lemonades and a bucket of seasoned potato wedges that smell flavorful and spicy.

"Let's go this way," Evelyn nods in the opposite direction from where we came, requiring us to walk in front of even more people to reach our seats. Pride wants me to square my shoulders and object. I hate the idea of cowering or backing down to a jerk, but I hesitate a second too long before making my claim, and Evelyn hooks her arm with mine and leads me to the opposite stairs.

Just as we slide into our seats, the announcer yells Camden's name, and we're instantly back on our feet, unwanted attention from strange guys and warm potato wedges forgotten as we cheer. The energy is palpable, a buzz that feels stronger than any alcohol or adrenaline I've experienced. Pride swells again in my chest as Hudson's name is announced. Hudson and his younger brother Griffin are like family—compensation or maybe an assurance from the universe not to seal myself away from others. They and Evelyn helped pave the path that led straight to my heart, where the three have lived ever since. Hudson has dreamed of this moment—being the starting quarterback and playing in a big game like this—his entire life.

I wrap my arm around Evelyn's shoulders and squeeze her close.

As more names are announced, the weight of a heavy stare draws my gaze to the row in front of us where the guy Evelyn had pointed out earlier is looking at me rather than the field. Those faint wings of hope brush against my stomach, opening the gates for hope and an epic meet-cute to slink back into my thoughts.

"Sorry, we're late!" Hadley Foster says, appearing on my other side with Hannah Owens and Katie Payne. The three are roommates and close friends who have begun spending more time with Evelyn and me. We had a Friendsgiving, formed a book club, and have a shared group text.

"Getting a ride was next to impossible." Hadley pulls off her coat, her cheeks flushed.

Hadley dates Nolan Payne, Katie's older brother and one of Hudson's closest friends on the team. I still question if it's all too convenient and we're setting ourselves up for a record fallout if things go awry, but Evelyn swears it's kismet, knowing and liking Hadley even before she learned of her relationship with Nolan.

Green-eyes distract me once again. His smile tips, becoming broader and more brazen.

If this were a movie my father was producing, the heroine would tear her gaze away and play hard to get, and the hero would rise to the trivial challenge to prove he's worthy of her time and attention, but my nearly twenty-one years have taught me the male ego is far more fragile than Hollywood portrays. Instead, I respond by giving Green-eyes a half smile, to show I might be interested.

I might be.

I think.

I lower my hopes and expectations, realizing I don't need—or want—anything serious, nothing that would involve the start of a long-distance relationship that would fizzle out in a few weeks after he realizes I'm horrible at talking on the phone and worse at replying to texts. Still, a single night of bliss that would invite us to sink into pleasure and not look back or carry regrets into the next day is perfect for my current state of mind.

Green-eyes raises his eyebrows as though asking if I permit him to flirt with me.

For fuck's sake, does he need written instructions?

Evelyn's laughter draws my attention to where she's watching Camden's mascot, a knight in shining armor—how fitting—chasing the opposing team's squirrel mascot, sword drawn to show how Camden plans to destroy our opponent. She glances at me, recognizing my distraction, and then at

Green-eyes. "Maybe you should invite him to go out with us tonight."

I shrug, not half as interested as I should be—as I want to be. "We'll see," I say noncommittally and turn my focus back to the field, not wanting to miss a moment of this game since I know the significance it has to Hudson's future as well as Evelyn's and maybe even my own.

I know too much about football. Hudson has always watched games and talked about the sport with as much passion as my father discusses movie scripts and art connoisseurs talk about their favorite artists.

Evelyn gently bumps me with her elbow to gain my attention again. "I'm glad we came."

I wrap my arm around her shoulders. "You mean you're glad you stayed?"

Evelyn didn't grow up in Oleander Springs like Hudson and me. Instead, she spent her summers at her grandma's, who lived behind Hudson's house, and returned to New Mexico every autumn. She returned to Oleander Springs eight months ago, at the beginning of May, uncertain if she wanted to attend college at Camden.

While Hudson is like a brother to me, something hits differently with having a girl best friend. She understands and battles the same emotions and expectations. I've never been very good at making friends or trusting women, but Evelyn is my rock. My confidante. I'm eternally grateful she decided to stay and become my roommate as we had imagined since childhood.

Evelyn grins as she wraps an arm around my shoulders, squeezing me tightly. "I was referring to the warmer weather and these potato wedges," she says, grabbing a fry with her free hand and smiling around the bite she takes. "You already know you're stuck with me." Her hand tightens around my shoulder as the ball is hiked and the play starts.

I'm licking the last of the frozen lemonade from the spoon when Green-eyes clears his throat. It's nearly half-time, and though he's looked back at me a few dozen times, he hasn't made a single attempt to talk to me.

I play hard to get. I can't help myself, keeping my eyes trained on the field and making him try a little harder than the subtle gesture to catch my attention.

Camden is up by twelve and currently has possession. They're huddled at midfield, where Hudson is leaning close to Grey.

"You're a Camden fan?"

I glance down at him and note a beer cupped in one hand. Evelyn, Hadley, Hannah, Katie, and I are all wearing blue Camden tees, making it clear who we're cheering for. Still, I know how difficult it can be to start a conversation. While this isn't as suave as most of the love stories my dad has worked on, in plenty of them the audience sees his side and is aware of all he worked to be there to give them their chance meeting. Maybe Green-eyes wasn't supposed to be here. Maybe he won tickets that landed him here, right in front of me. Perhaps fate is still at work, and our meet-cute will grow and flourish.

I nod. "What about you?"

"We're here for California." Our opposition. He looks like he's from California, his skin golden with an air of careless optimism that assures me he's always looking for a good time and doesn't have a closet filled with enough skeletons.

His whole persona is wholesome and ridiculously attractive. His gaze skirts over my body, his eyes glinting with appreciation before he takes another swallow of his beer. I know he sees exactly what he wants to—what most people see when they look at me—an affluent woman with clothes that emphasize my best features and a carefree smile that hides my messiest and most unforgiving broken pieces.

"Do you have plans for after the game?" he asks.

I glance at Evelyn, catching her slight grin that's telling me to invite him out with us. "We're going out to celebrate beating your team." I flash him the hint of a smile, just enough to tease him.

He laughs good-naturedly, as I knew he would, and runs a hand through his hair. I'm interested in two types of men, and they're polar opposites. Those who are sweet and innocent, naive and untouched by the harshness of this world, and those who have not only faced but inflicted that harshness. Neither asks questions—one because they don't know better and the latter because they're too afraid the questions might be reciprocated.

They're the only types of guys I date—the only types I've ever dated.

Green-eyes snickers and then laughs. He is, without a doubt, the sweet and naive type. A total Ken Doll. "Can we join you?"

"Only if you're up for having a good time."

His smile flashes broader. I'm sure if someone were to ask, he'd think he's wooed me when, in reality, I'm dropping breadcrumbs for him to follow. But we're only here for two nights, and if everyone else is going to be celebrating and having fun, I sure as hell am, too.

Chapter 6

Grey

Sweat drips down my neck, soaking my pads and jersey as the final whistle blows.

Palmer whoops and slings an arm around my shoulders. "We won, baby!"

Adrenaline chases my exhaustion and the pains I'll feel tomorrow as I laugh and stare at the filled stadium. It's larger than Bia Stadium, Camden's home field, and packed with fans from both teams. The flashes of navy blue and gold point out the Camden fans.

I allow myself a solid minute to soak in all the sounds and the posters with our names. I wonder if NFL players feel this same hit of adrenaline and joy when realizing everyone wants to prop them on their shoulders or if the excitement eventually wanes.

I give a final pass before turning off these thoughts and focusing on what needs to happen for us to get into the playoff next year to participate—and win—the biggest game in college football. I stand a chance of making it into the draft without it, but damn, that game would be an insurance policy.

Palmer grips my jersey. "Smile, goddammit. We won!"

I grin.

He shakes his head, laughing before he pulls me into a rough hug.

Nolan sprints toward us, gripping both of us. "We fucking slayed." He drops his head back, soaking up the energy and sun as I had as his grip tightens, seconds before Hudson and Corey join our circle. The press and interviews will separate us in a few minutes, but for a moment, we're just celebrating the unthinkable.

"Captain!" Palmer calls out to Hudson.

"We did it," Hudson says, dazed and proud.

I want to remind him that we have an entirely new mountain—a new beast—to slay that comes in the form of another full year of practices and games, but instead, I clap him on the shoulder. No way would this journey have been half as good without him. He's my closest friend on the team and at Camden.

"We're getting fucking wasted tonight!" Lenny, one of our tight ends, yells. Lenny's a good guy with a good heart, but he's absolute shit when it comes to making decisions or avoiding peer pressure, and he's the first to suggest a bad idea.

The media descends before we can confirm our plans, pulling us in separate directions with Hudson forced to remain on the field.

It's hours before we're showered, and I'm giving the Orlando stadium a final glance over my shoulder, feeling equal amounts of relief and disappointment that our season is officially over.

I don't bother asking about the where we're going. I don't care. I hop in a Lyft with Hudson and Corey. Nolan and Palmer are in a second car ahead of us.

During the regular season, parties are far and few between

with our strict curfew and stricter morning practices. Tonight's different, not only because we're in a foreign city in a foreign state, but we have the next two months off from official practices, which has everyone lowering their guard and ready to have a good time.

Instead of pulling up to a bar, we stop in front of a generic nightclub downtown. Inside, music pulses through the darkened space as lights trail over faces and writhing bodies. If I had my choice, we'd be at a bar with pool tables and a dozen TVs following sports and reliving the game, but most of the team is looking to celebrate with a girl tonight and after this win.

A girl with short blue hair smiles invitingly to us, and Hudson pats my shoulder before continuing in the direction of a table, where I catch sight of Evelyn and Katie. I do a quick double glance, noting Hannah and Hadley as well. Mila is the only one missing.

"Want to dance?" the blue-haired woman asks, tugging her bottom lip between her teeth. It's likely rehearsed, but that doesn't diminish the effect, regardless of how much it should. I hate dancing. Give me a football, and I don't care if a million people are watching me, but put on some music and ask me to move, and suddenly I can't remember what rhythm is or how to move my own limbs.

"How about a drink?" I ask.

She flashes a grin. "Sounds perfect."

I gaze over faces as we pass through crowds, crossing to the bar on the other end of the club.

The blue-haired woman sets one hand on the bar to reserve her place and looks back at me. She's wearing a dark dress that drops low between her large breasts and barely has a back, exposing a trail of tattoos down her spine. "What's your name, handsome?"

I consider not telling her. Names don't really matter—not

44

here, not tonight. But she flutters her long lashes and tilts her head patiently.

"Grey."

"Like the color of my dress?"

I nod.

"I'm Courtney. Are you from around here?"

"North Carolina," I tell her.

Her smile broadens. "I'm local."

A smile catches my attention at the end of the bar. The reason it garners my attention isn't attraction but familiarity, I realize, when spotting Mila. Her long blonde hair shimmers in the lights, and her dark pink dress stands out in a sea of black.

Mila's gaze slowly drifts to mine, and her disarming smile fades into a look of indifference. We stare at each other, something we've never been good at avoiding. If I were closer, she'd likely congratulate me and then say something cunning and sarcastic. It's how we interact—how we've always interacted. Her gaze shifts to the blue-haired woman at my side. Courtney, I remind myself. Mila blinks and then shakes her head.

Mila's judgment is a cold blade to my chest. I shouldn't care what she thinks, who she was smiling at, or what she plans to do tonight, but each of those details consumes my thoughts. Mila Atwool has always commanded my full attention.

My molars ache as I grind my teeth. A second later, Evelyn appears beside her. Mila gives me another cursory glance and then whispers something in Evelyn's ear.

"How long are you staying in Orlando?" Courtney asks, drawing my attention back to her.

"Tonight's my last night." She doesn't need to know we're staying through Monday.

She runs her fingers up my chest, her eyes dilated with desire.

"There you are." Mila appears beside me, close enough to touch, though she doesn't, as if a thin barrier exists between us.

I lower my brow, confusion not even close to describing my feelings.

Mila inclines her head as if instructing me to follow her, and I'm left questioning every hit tonight, suspecting I'm suffering from a concussion.

Her gaze turns sharp when I don't move.

"Sorry, do you know each other?" Courtney asks.

Mila turns to Courtney. "Please, tell me he didn't tell you he was a surgeon." She looks at me, raises a hand to shield her mouth as though she's going to tell a secret, and says, "He's not. He's not even a doctor. And let me tell you, if you've ever gone fishing and baited a hook, you know exactly what you'll find if he convinces you to follow him into a dark corner. He doesn't last long enough to take you to bed..."

Courtney's gaze skitters to mine, and then lower, sawing her jaw to the left.

I had no intention of sleeping with Courtney, but that does little to lessen Mila's words.

"He also told me he was clean," Mila continues.

Courtney's eyes round as she pulls away from me, sinking into the bar and strangers beside her.

"Thankfully, some antibiotics were able to take care of the worst of it, but I—"

I hook an arm around Mila's waist and drag her away from the bar before she can finish the sentence.

"What in hell are you doing?" I barely get the words out before Mila's working to disentangle herself from me.

"You're welcome," she says.

"Welcome?" Outrage fills my tone.

"I tried to take the subtle route, but you stared at me like I grew a third eyeball in the middle of my forehead." She stabs a finger there, emphasizing the point.

"That was subtle?" I shake my head, rage the devil on both my shoulders. "You just cockblocked me by saying I gave you an STD!"

She shrugs. "I inclined my head and told you to follow me."

"I thought something was in your eye."

Mila scowls. "Then go tell her I'm crazy and hook up with a married woman. I'll give zero fucks."

I don't tell Mila it was only going to be a drink. Instead, I challenge her, working to understand why she'd care. "How do you know she's married?"

"She and her friend are at the table next to ours, and they tucked their wedding rings into their purses before having a round of shots. I couldn't hear them, but I had a pretty good idea of her plan when I saw you with her." She lifts a shoulder. "I tried to get Evelyn to warn you because I knew you'd listen to her, but she stole my drink and walked away."

My buzz from winning is forgotten as I scrub my fingers across my forehead and consider the easiest and fastest way back to the hotel.

Mila makes an annoyed sound, something between a growl and a sigh. "Don't let this ruin your night. The only three people who heard our conversation were you, the married chick, and me. Plenty of women here are interested in you." She extends a hand to the dance floor behind us. "They're all looking at you, praying that we're fighting so they can swoop in and mend your heart." She takes a step back, her matching pink heels laced up her ankles, effectively distracting me from refuting her words before she gives me a pointed look, and disappears into the crowds.

I head back to the bar, undeterred by the thought Courtney might still be there, and slip into an empty spot.

"What can I get you?" the bartender asks. She's all business, with a polite and friendly smile to ensure a tip and nothing more.

"What do you have on tap?"

She lists half a dozen beers before I choose one.

I accept the beer and take a long drink, prepared to wipe the past twenty minutes from my memory. But as I take another gulp, the memory of my arm around Mila's waist, the sweet, floral scent of her perfume, the warmth of her skin, and the shock in her gaze burns every damn thought until she's all I can think about.

Chapter 7

Mila

I dance, smile, and laugh until I forget about Green-eyes and the faint scratch left by him standing me up. It doesn't matter. It was only going to be one night. I wasn't that interested in him. Eventually, the songs start to bleed together, and we're breathless and sweating.

"I don't know if I'll be able to walk tomorrow," Hannah says, slumping into a chair as we finally take a break. "Why did I wear these shoes?" She stares accusingly at her elegant peep-toe shoes. For the past hour, she's been my partner in crime. We don't know each other super well, but the combination of alcohol and being single created a uniform bond that we were mutually happy to fulfill, especially when someone got too close or touchy.

"Those shoes deserve an award or a glass case. They're gorgeous."

She stretches her feet in front of her, admiring them. "Why does beauty hurt so much?"

Evelyn and Hudson appear, their arms wrapped around each other's waists with smiles staining their features. "We're going to head back to the hotel. Do you want to catch a ride with us?" Hudson asks.

"The night's still early!" Hannah objects.

It's past midnight. Hadley, Nolan, and Katie have already left.

"Your feet are killing you," I remind her.

Hannah frowns at the reminder. "They are. Let me finish my drink, and then I'll be ready." Her gaze turns to the dance floor that hasn't thinned since we arrived.

"I'll stay with her. You guys can head back."

"Are you sure?" Evelyn asks. "We don't mind waiting. It's getting kind of crazy." The club is at capacity and hasn't allowed anyone to come in for the past hour.

I nod. "Yeah. I'll text you when we leave."

Evelyn hooks the back of my neck with her elbow, pulling me in for a hug. "Corey and Palmer are still here if you need anything."

"I'll keep my eye out for them."

We watch them walk away.

"He's cute." Hannah points, but with so many people, I don't know who she's referring to. "Maybe we should have one more drink."

"Maybe we should take a rain check?"

Hannah frowns, but her exhaustion is apparent with her sunken shoulders and long blinks. "I haven't gone out since my ex drugged me with a disgusting pumpkin cookie. I'm not ready for a one-night stand, but I want to wake up feeling a little dehydrated to remember I had fun tonight."

Guilt lances through me, reminding me why trust is so fragile and becoming obsolete. "Let's get one final drink."

She beams, climbing to her feet before grimacing. "Damn, my feet hurt. Okay, maybe we go back to the hotel and have a final drink there. They have a martini bar."

Her optimism is contagious.

We don't have to request a car because a line of them is outside, waiting to take people home.

"Where are we heading, ladies?" a bald man asks. His car smells strongly of men's cologne, and his stereo's too loud, but I keep those details to myself and recite the hotel's name and address.

"Have you finished the book for book club?" Hannah asks as we pull away from the curb.

"I finished it in two days," I admit. I mastered small talk at a young age, thrown into situations with strangers that required me to acclimate quickly. Still, there's a point when I start to know someone, and we're no longer only acquaintances but not quite friends when small talk becomes a chore, where I'm afraid I'll say something that offends them, or they'll reveal something to me that makes me want to return to the safe place where we're friends of friends. That's the middle ground where Hannah and I are currently. "What about you?"

She shakes her head. "I just got back to Oleander Springs from visiting family. You picked the title, right? Hadley was raving about it."

"I'm a sucker for the dark and broody types."

Hannah tinkers a laugh. "Same. I love nothing more than a hero who hates everyone, but the heroine is his soft spot. They don't cheat. They don't drug you with edibles. They don't lie. They just treat you like a princess and growl at everyone who dares to look at you."

I nod emphatically. "Exactly."

Hannah sighs wistfully. "If only."

I chuckle as we pull up to the hotel, the lights emanating warmth and comfort as the night air blows against my bare skin. It's not as cold as Oleander Springs, but uncomfortable enough to make us hurry inside.

"Should we change first?" I ask.

"I don't know. If I sit down, I may not be able to get back up."

I blow out a knowing laugh and turn to familiarize myself with the hotel before pointing to the rear corner. "I'm pretty sure it's over there."

Hannah links her arm with mine, and we cross the shining tiled floor to the back, discovering a closed sign hanging on the door.

"No..." Hannah groans, throwing her head back. "Is it that late?" she looks around, trying to confirm the time.

"We still have another day and full night for bad decisions and dehydration."

She smirks. "I'll wear flats."

I grin, clutching her arm as we approach the bank of gold elevators. We ride to the third floor, where I walk Hannah to her room, positive she's tipsier than she's letting on.

"Thanks for tonight. Even if I didn't get that last drink, this was the most fun I've had in a while."

I hate her ex a little more as I smile. "We'll do it again tomorrow. Bigger and better."

She tinkers out a laugh. "I'll text you tomorrow."

I return to the elevator and get into an empty car, where I lean back, watching the lights along the top highlight the next two floors before stopping. The doors open, and my heart stalls as the guy who grabbed my arm earlier at the game appears. Ire has his lips twisting with a cruel smirk. "Decided measles might be worse?"

I'm frozen for a second, debating if he's waiting for the elevator or me. Did he know I was coming?

He couldn't.

My heart hammers too loudly to hear my thoughts as I try to smother my fear and debate if it would be better to get out or press the doors to close and ride back down to the lobby. I step out, my cell phone still in my hand from paying the Lyft driver, and curse fate who has the creepy guy staying at my hotel rather than Green-eyes. Not that I'd be inviting Green-eyes over after standing me up, but at least my mind wouldn't be racing with perceived threats.

"What? Now you're mute?" he asks, taking a step back and making no attempt to get into the empty elevator. "Where's that attitude you showed me at the game?" His eyes are rimmed red, and his breath stinks of whiskey and stale cigarette smoke. Either is enough to churn my stomach. Together they make me physically ill.

"You're not as hot as you think you are," he continues. "In fact, I bet once you remove all your makeup, guys want to slip a bag over your face before they bang you." He takes a step closer to me, his gaze sharp and predatory, watching his hateful words cut something much deeper than my skin.

I step back at the same time a door opens at the end of the hall. A familiar form steps out. It's Grey, wearing sweatpants, his chest bare and an ice bucket in hand.

"Grey," I say his name. "Sorry, that took me so long." I pass super creep and head toward him, trying to calm my nerves and not look over my shoulder to ensure the stranger isn't following me as I count my steps that bring me closer to Grey.

His blue eyes are inquisitive. "What's going on?"

I shake my head. "Nothing. I just forgot what floor we were on."

He looks past me to the elevator and then at me again. "Did he say something?"

"Are we out of ice?"

Grey cuts his eyes over me.

"I hope you have a bag," the stranger calls.

Grey looks at me for clarification.

I plaster a smile on my face and hold my chin a little higher. "He's drunk. Mind if I stay in your room until he leaves."

Grey's frozen. I'm not sure he's even breathing as he stares beyond me for a long minute and then slowly slips his hand into his pocket and withdraws the hotel key.

I nearly sigh with relief, glancing back as I turn to his door.

"Don't scrub too hard," the stranger calls before flipping me off.

"What the fuck does that mean? Did you sleep with him?"

Offense stings on my skin. "What?"

"Did you bring him back from the club?"

He still hasn't opened his door. "You don't have a girl in here. Do you?"

Grey rolls his eyes and shoves the door open. The lights by the bed are on, the bedding is pulled back, and the TV is on. I step into the space that smells more like the hotel's notes of vanilla and less like Grey.

"I'll be right back," he says, closing me inside.

Awkwardness swallows me whole, not sparing enough sense for me to consider what to do as I catch sight of my reflection in the floor-length mirror across from the bathroom.

I'm pale, and my hair is flat, my eyes dull. It's from dancing too long, but I can see why Grey mistook my look for post-sex.

When Grey returns, my heart stutters like a mouse about to be trapped. "I didn't know people used their ice buckets at hotels," I say.

His only response is a slightly arched brow before he walks past me to the small round table where his duffle bag is open. He pulls out a plastic freezer bag, pours the contents of the ice bucket inside before sealing it, and then grabs a hand towel and wraps it around the homemade ice pack.

A small part of me wants to ask him why he doesn't call one of the trainers on the team, who I know would come with supplies and medications and anything else he might need. But I remain silent because moments like now when it's just the two of us, our relationship—or lack thereof—becomes glaringly obvious. We don't know each other and don't spend time together, which creates a downright awkward tension.

"Thanks for the ... um... Thanks. Have a good night." I move toward the door.

"That's it?"

"What? Did you want to accuse me of sleeping with someone else?"

"I'm sorry. I shouldn't have ... it just looked like—"

"Like what?" My voice is an icy challenge, daring him to accuse me again. "Like he was in my space? Like he was trying to intimidate me with his size? Like he was trying to be a total asshat?"

The ice pack crunches as Grey's fist clenches around it. "Who is he?" His voice is a quiet growl, and once again, he's so still that I question if he's breathing.

"I have no idea, and I don't care." I try and match his same level of aloofness with a parting look and then turn to the door.

"Mila," he calls my name, his voice deep but less growly and more pleading, like he's trying to apologize without actually saying anything.

I grab the door lever but pause, looking over my shoulder at Grey. His jaw is clenched, and every visible muscle in his arms and chest appears flexed. "Don't worry. My skin's thicker than an insinuation, even from you."

He swallows. "Let me grab my shoes and a shirt. I'll walk you—"

"Don't worry about it. I'll be fine." I slip out before he can offer or feel obligated and sigh with an ounce of relief that the hall is empty.

I walk down the maze of halls, rounding a final corner

when the hairs on the back of my neck and arms stand erect. I glance over my shoulder, my lungs frozen, but I see nothing more than an empty hall. I walk faster, practically running to my door where I have to dig for my hotel key and then scan it three times before it flashes green and the lock releases.

I slam the door and flip the deadbolt, breathing entirely too hard as I lean against it as though prepared to hold it closed.

Every one of my muscles and tendons is tense—even my bones and organs feel heavy as I remain stuck in place for several long minutes before I can finally pull in a full breath and ease myself away from the door and into the room. I flip on every light, checking in the closet and bathroom before I untie my shoes and dig through my suitcase to find my pajamas. I get changed and am preparing to brush my teeth when a gentle thump against the door makes my heart and lungs stall again. I'm too warm and too cold. I glance at the door, the lock still in place.

I turn on the tap, brush my teeth and wash my face before examining my reflection again, seeing myself through the stranger's lens and scrutinizing every flaw until it's all I can see.

I flip off the light and head back into the bedroom. A loud noise has me jumping higher than a cat, and I somehow find the wherewithal to look around and realize it was just my bag slipping from the edge of the bed and onto the floor.

My fears are beginning to feel like paranoia—a fact I despise. I bend down to gather the items that fell out when a noise comes from the connecting room, and the door between my room and the one next door rattles.

I scramble for my phone. Gripped between white knuckles, I scroll through my contacts stopping on the last person I want to see but the only person I know is still awake and alone—Grey. Grey and I never text or call each other. I don't even know how to begin this conversation without sounding crazy, which I might be—or desperate, which I am.

The connecting door jiggles again, making my decision for me. I grab my purse, slip on some flip-flops, and check the peephole to ensure no one's outside my door. Then I run like the dogs of hell are chasing me. I can't call Grey, but apparently, I can arrive at his door unannounced.

I raise my fist and knock before I can second-guess myself and nerves get the best of me.

Chapter 8

Grey

I debate ignoring the door, positive I'll find Lenny or some other idiot from the team who's had too much to drink and can't remember their room number. Another rap of knuckles has me dropping my ice pack to the nightstand and heading for the door. Mila stands outside, her cheeks red and hair pulled back as she looks over her shoulder like someone's following her. Instinct has me pulling her into the room and peering down either hall, assuring it's clear before closing the door.

"What's going on?" I ask. "Did something happen?"

She swallows, appearing so nervous and fragile I'm nearly convinced it's Mila's doppelganger rather than the fiercely confident and sarcastic woman I've harbored feelings for that expand far beyond platonic.

"Mila?"

"I need to preface this with I'm not trying to come on to you, and I'm not looking to be a damsel in distress, but at the risk of sounding crazy, can I sleep on your couch?"

I shake my head, working to articulate all the points she just made that don't seem capable of fitting into a single sentence. "What happened?"

"I promise I don't snore. I don't sleepwalk. I don't talk. I will lie there, be silent as a mouse, and leave by sunrise."

"First, I need some answers."

She shakes her head. "The couch is all I came to bargain for."

"Great. Then let's bargain."

Mila winces, clearly regretting her words, but she doesn't object or renege on the deal. "You owe me."

"Just tell me, did something happen?"

She shakes her head, but relief is the last thing I feel because she's still too nervous, too tense. "The room next to mine was just being really loud."

I know she's lying, and I'm pretty sure she knows that as she stares at me with pleading eyes, begging me to leave well enough alone.

"You're too tall for the couch."

She shakes her head. "I don't mind. I curl up like a cat when I sleep."

I glance at her pastel purple shorts and Camden tee, a dozen more questions on my lips.

"Just pretend I'm not here. Watch TV or do whatever you do before bed." She sets her purse down and goes to the couch, where she lies down and curls on her side.

I wrench open the closet and grab the spare pillow and blankets.

"I don't..." she starts.

I set the pillow above her head, shake the blanket, and drape it over her. "You can sleep on the bed with me. It's a king. We can build a wall between us if it makes you feel better."

Mila shoves the pillow I brought over under her head and lies back down. "I'm fine."

"What would you have done if I didn't answer?"

Mila's eyes flick back to mine, reluctance in her gaze. "You're supposed to pretend I'm not here."

"Was it that guy from the elevator? Did he follow you?" I don't know what I'm hoping for. Answers? An assurance that everything is okay? A clarification that she's not mad at me for insinuating she slept with the fuckwad? Maybe all of it.

Mila pulls in a shallow breath. "Do you remember last spring when I stayed at Hudson's for a few weeks?"

I nod slowly. I do because her staying at the dorms had all of us doubting their claim as only friends. Neither offered an explanation, only that Mila was staying there and that we needed to keep our mouths shut because it wasn't allowed.

She nods, too, and I wonder if she recalls the rumors and jokes that spread about her dating Hudson as clearly as I am. "Someone had broken into my apartment, and now, I get a little paranoid when I hear things, especially when I'm alone and since Evelyn's staying with Hudson..."

"Someone broke into your apartment?" Rage sluices through my restraint. "Were you home? What happened?"

Her eyes train on mine for a fraction of a second before she shakes her head. "Nothing. I called the police."

"You were home when they broke in?" Revenge pulses through my veins, considering every nightmare she may have endured.

Her gaze darkens, not with lust but malevolence. "I was fine."

We can recover from a whole hell of a lot, but surviving does not mean we're fine. "Mila, I'm—"

"Nothing happened," she insists. "I just get spooked. That's all."

"Someone breaking in isn't nothing."

Defiance has her lips pursing.

"And that guy from the elevator?"

"Was drunk and stupid. Let's go to sleep. I'm sure you're exhausted, and tomorrow will be another long day."

She closes her eyes, effectively ending the conversation.

I sit on the edge of the bed, uncomfortable with this arrangement. "Your back and neck will hate you. It's not even a couch. It's half of a couch."

Mila opens her eyes where humor dances with a look that isn't contrived or guarded. "It's a chaise, and I'll be fine. Believe me. This is a thousand times better than..." She shakes her head and grabs the pillow, shifting it higher on the seat.

"Better than what?"

Mila clears her throat. "It's a thousand times quieter than my room." She tucks both hands under her pillow and closes her eyes again.

"Has anyone ever told you you're stubborn?"

She smirks. "Only on good days."

When I open my eyes, Mila's still curled on the couch, her hands and legs tucked up to her chest.

I grab my phone and check for any messages from Cole to see how his fight went, but I only have two messages, one from my mom, a picture of waffles—the breakfast she always makes after every game—with a note that she's proud of me. And the second is from Emma, congratulating me and asking if I want to hang out today.

This is the sixth text I've received from her since going to dinner with her where Mila posed as my girlfriend. I need the paid sponsorship her dad's been promising me, and I have a sinking feeling that if I turn her down, his offer will be rescinded.

The moment I roll out of bed, Mila's eyes flash open, and she sits up. She scans the room and stops on me, her shoulders sagging with what I can only believe is relief. She rubs a hand across her face, looking more tired than last night. The blanket slides lower, revealing her thin tee, and I note her nipples before pulling my gaze away, knowing she'll skewer me if she catches me.

"Morning, sunshine."

She flips me off and lies back down.

"We're supposed to meet the others in the lobby for breakfast in fifteen minutes," I warn her.

"Five more minutes." Mila closes her eyes.

"I'm going to get in the shower."

She gives me a thumbs up.

As I wash my hair, my thoughts return to last night and then back to last spring, working to recall if she had any bruises or cuts and if Hudson had mentioned anything that might have hinted at what occurred.

I question if he would tell me the details my brain demands to know as I wrap a towel around my waist on the off-case Mila didn't leave.

I find her asleep again, the blanket pulled up to her chin. I take the stolen second to study her, something I can't do when she's awake. She's always stunning, drawing attention wherever we go.

She shifts, and I turn away, grabbing some clothes that I carry into the bathroom to get dressed. I brush my teeth with the door open and the light on, hoping it will wake her up.

It does. The window shade slides open with a whir of the tracks, and sunlight fills the room. Mila's sitting up, knees folded against her chest with the blanket draped around her shoulders as she wipes the sleep from her eyes for a second time. She's not a morning person.

"Do you have a sweatshirt I can borrow?"

To cover her breasts that her thin tee reveals too much of without a bra.

I nod and cross over to my bag, grabbing the one I'd worn on travel day.

Mila catches it and pulls it over her head, surprised when the sleeves cover her hands.

"You're short compared to me," I remind her.

Mila unfolds slowly, rolling her shoulders and neck like they might be sore from sleeping on the too-small and too-hard surface all night. Guilt leaves me feeling annoyed, and I wait for her to make a snappy comment about not waking her up or a dozen other things, but instead, she turns and refolds the blanket before stacking the pillow on it.

"Thanks again for last night," she says, her voice quiet but sincere as she looks at me and then quickly away.

"It's not a problem."

She gives a tight-lipped smile, slides her shoes on, and grabs her purse. "How much do you think Katie will freak out if I go to breakfast before getting ready?" Katie has a reputation for being an unforgiving hardass.

"Someone else will be there in their pajamas."

She shakes her head. "But no one from our group."

"Nolan might."

Mila shakes her head again. "Not likely. Not with Hadley here." She seems to weigh her options for half a minute. "Maybe I should go get ready before coffee."

"We both know you can't function before coffee," I say, pulling the door open.

"Preferably two coffees," Mila says, holding up two fingers as she follows me into the hall.

I start to grin, but the reaction slips away as I notice Emma approaching us, wearing denim cutoffs and a shirt that shows most of her midriff. She looks past me at Mila and narrows her eyes.

Mila will be the first person to tell me she doesn't need my help, but I intervene, wrapping an arm around her waist before stepping in front of her and blocking her from Emma's glare.

She tilts her chin a little higher and arches a brow as she stops. "I thought players had to double in rooms?"

Some universities require it, but like our large dorms, single rooms are one of the perks Camden uses to attract talent.

I try to think of a suitable response, but Mila slips her arms around my waist and leans into me. "After all their hard work and sacrifice, it's a small perk." She places a hand against my chest that feels nearly as protective and intentional as my grip on her. "Hi again, by the way."

Emma's gaze is filled with disdain. "Way to flaunt it."

Mila's fingers fist around my shirt, and she leans further into me. "Can you blame me?"

Emma raises her eyebrows with judgment. "Have a nice day." She passes us and stabs the elevator button.

Neither of us moves until the doors slide shut, and then Mila peels away from me, making the boundary that always exists between us even wider. "We should probably fake a breakup over breakfast."

"Why would we do that?"

"Because fake dating me isn't going to do you any favors. She hates me, if you didn't notice during our fun little threesome."

A couple carrying a car seat stares at us as they pass, the man coughing in an attempt to hide his laughter while the woman can't hide her shock as she stares at us.

"I didn't mean it like that!" Mila calls. "It was just a conversation. Not an invitation. Not even ... a trio. We were talking as a trio!" She smacks a hand across her face, her cheeks flushed with embarrassment. I think this might be the most off-kilter I've ever seen her, and I am beyond amused.

"Stop smirking." She tries to make the words sound like a threat, but exhaustion and humiliation soften them.

"Trust me, you're not deterring Emma enough. She's sent me several texts inviting me to hang out."

Mila's jaw drops. "She's texting you even though she thinks we're dating? What a..." She doesn't finish her sentence. "I need coffee." She turns for the elevators.

"Grey! Mila!" Nolan calls, waving a hand as we enter the lobby. He and the rest of our group are crowded around two tables they've pushed together.

Mila doesn't say anything before peeling off toward the food. I make my way to the group, taking the empty seat next to Corey.

"Perfect timing. We were just discussing Hannah's love for pickles and sausages," Palmer says, spearing a breakfast sausage.

Hannah's cheeks flame pink, promising the conversation wasn't meant to be embarrassing but turned south quickly.

Hadley cackles, leaning into Nolan, who dips his face to hers and kisses her hairline. Evelyn tries to muffle her laughter.

Hannah shakes her head and stabs a bite of breakfast with her fork. "Finish eating so we can get going. I haven't been to Disney World since I was ten."

"We used to go twice a year. My parents still go all the time," Corey says.

"You can be our Disney guide," Evelyn says. "I've never been."

Most of our friend circle comes from wealth. Attending Camden and receiving things like free tickets to Disney World, flights on private jets, and catered meals has me sampling what my life could be like—what I would love to provide for my mom after years of her working so damn hard to make ends meet.

"You have ten minutes to eat, or we're leaving without you," Katie says, looking at me.

"She's ruthless," Hadley says.

I grin as I stand. "We could use her on the team."

"Want some more sausages?" Palmer asks Hannah as he stands to join me.

Evelyn grins, coming along as well.

Several guys from the team are filling plates, talking about their days, and making plans. I fill two plates and find Mila gripping a coffee and plate filled with food as she locates Evelyn and waves off whatever question that has Mila glancing down at my sweatshirt and shaking her head.

As we eat, Katie keeps track of time, and only a little steam releases from her ears when Evelyn tells her that Mila took her breakfast upstairs so she can get ready.

Thirty minutes later than Katie ordered, we're outside, the sun and anticipation of the theme parks sparking in my veins and making each step up onto the bus lighter.

I don't know what I was expecting, but as we step into Disney World, it's like stepping into another world, complete with theme music and costumes.

Evelyn stops beside me, turning to take in all the angles and sights, the sweet scents from a nearby bakery, the jovial music streaming over invisible speakers, and more people than I've ever seen in a single place apart from a football stadium.

"Okay," Corey says. "We'll meet together at two for lunch?"

I cut my attention to him, realizing I should have paid more attention to what Hannah and Katie were planning while on the bus over here.

"Text if you're going to be late," Katie says, slapping on a pair of sunglasses and checking her watch.

I know how the groups will break apart before they do, Nolan with Hadley, Hannah and Katie, and Corey with Palmer.

"Grey, do you want to stick with us?" Evelyn asks. She, Mila, and Hudson are the final group.

Mila raises a brow at me before inclining her head in the direction of where Corey and Palmer are heading. "Aren't roller coasters and bad decisions your thing?"

Hudson grins. "Where should we start?"

Evelyn shakes her head. "I don't even know where to start."

Mila points. "We have to go down Main Street, regardless." It doesn't surprise me that she's familiar with the park. She's one of the wealthiest in our group.

"How many times have you been here?" Evelyn asks, looking around as we cross by storefronts and vendors with giant bouquets of colorful balloons.

Mila blows out a breath and shakes her head. "More times than I can count."

Hudson grins. "Alex is a Disney fanatic. He finds every excuse to come down here."

Mila's smile is the opposite of Corey's dismissive shrug when mentioning how often he's been here. Instead, her face is serene, as though seeing this place holds significance for her.

"Have you been here many times?" I ask Hudson.

"Just once when I was ten. My grandparents took me for my birthday. It's too loud and full for Griff," he says. "Have you?"

I shake my head.

"Maybe we start off jumping into the deep end," Evelyn says, her eyes bright, filled with determination.

Chapter 9

Mila

Splash Mountain was Evelyn's first choice—a solid decision, spoiled only by the long wait time. During the seventy-five-minute queue, I make small talk with strangers, compliment a woman's gorgeous curls, pretend to play Buzz Lightyear with a little boy dressed as Woody, and discuss the weather with a mom who looks overwhelmed and exhausted. Then Evelyn rescues me by giving me the task of planning our day. I want her to experience everything the park has to offer. I'm considering the best snacks, rides, and adventures when a cast member asks Hudson how many are in our party and waves us forward. I realize a crucial detail about this particular ride. You sit in pairs.

Hudson tucks into the seat beside Evelyn, and I sit behind them. Grey sits beside me, his shoulders, hips, and thighs pressing against me. It's the closest we've ever been, aside from the night he walked me to my car when I nearly tripped over my own fears until he caught me. We haven't exchanged a single word since the elevator on our way to breakfast, and the tension is eating at me from the inside out.

I glance over at him, and he appears completely at ease, making the tension inside me growl a protest. He's barely acknowledged me, which isn't like us. We generally spar and poke. He criticizes my poor eating choices and addiction to coffee, and I prod him for being too serious and grouchy. Then we avoid each other and roll our eyes—or I roll my eyes—and we each go on our merry little way. I need the universe to return us to this norm.

"You don't get motion sickness, right?" The question pops out of me, hoping to find something to heckle and tease him for.

Grey lowers the lap bar as instructed, widening his legs to pull it lower so it also hits my thighs. His knee is now touching mine. We would have managed less contact if I had slept in the bed with him last night than we do now, strapped down to a pseudo log preparing to fall down a giant waterfall. Twice.

"No, but you're looking a little pale. You aren't going to faint, are you?" he asks.

I'm pale because he's pressed against me, and I smell the spice and hint of citrus from his cologne which is annoyingly perfect. Because Emma is hitting on him, and it shouldn't bother me half as much as it does.

I manage to shake my head.

The music starts, and the ride has us moving through a cave. Evelyn echoes words of amazement and wonder that replace my discomfort. Excitement grows in my stomach before we go down a small decline that causes nervous laughter from the couple behind us. My anticipation grows, as does my smile, triggering fourteen years of banked memories and making me recall how many times my stomach shot up to my throat at the same spot.

I grip the bar across my lap, recalling how this safety measure wasn't here the first several years. I'd felt equal measures of relief and anger when it was installed because as much change as I've endured, sometimes I particularly resent it. Though the lap belt made my fear of this ride drop by ninety percent, I didn't want it to be changed. I wanted to face this fear because safely arriving at the end of the ride symbolized something far greater and bigger, and the lap belts removed that small gamble and allowance.

Grey turns, breaking my thoughts from the unwanted memory, and I glance over to make sure he's not lying about what his stomach can tolerate. He's looking around, soaking in every magical detail with an expression I don't recognize or understand. He lowers his gaze to me. "What?"

I shake my head and turn my attention forward. "Nothing."

"Is this it?" Evelyn asks, craning her neck to look back at me as we ascend a hill, the tracks clicking like a timer.

"Maybe," I taunt her.

She belts out a laugh and grips the bar before we coast down another small drop that elicits more of the nervous laughter that has my smile broadening again.

The ride cruises around a bend, and then we fall without warning, screams piercing the air. The wind brushes my hair and face, welcoming me back to where I first experienced this crazy and wonderful space, openly defying not only gravity but the first seven years of my life.

As we coast into the mountain part of the ride, Grey sits back, his smile wide and bright and so damn carefree it kicks me in the teeth. The only time he flashes this smile is when they win a game, and even then, it's reserved for the toughest games when he's made plays that are guaranteed to circulate on the highlight reels.

I want to laugh with him and tell him all the other rides that will give him the same stomach-pitching feeling but don't because that's not a condition of our relationship.

"That was amazing!" Evelyn says, her dark eyes bright as a

smile consumes her features. "That just ruined every future roller coaster." She links her arm with mine. "Where should we go next?"

"Haunted Mansion or Pirates of the Caribbean," I tell them.

"Haunted Mansion," Hudson says. "It was closed the last time I was here."

Evelyn walks beside me, the Florida sun warm on our skin. It feels like November in Oleander Springs, where the weather makes you yearn to spend every moment outside, dry and warm, with an artist's sky.

Evelyn brushes her elbow against my side to catch my attention as we move around a large group. "Is everything okay?" she asks quietly.

Evelyn has always had the uncanny ability to read people, like me and most empaths, it's because she's been exposed to too many unstable situations that required her to be perceptive of people's moods and rely on instinct.

I nod absently and then with intention as her gaze becomes scrutinizing. "Yeah." I clutch her arm a little tighter and point out the boat that can take us to Tom Sawyer's Island.

She studies me a beat. The past several months of living together have given her the ability to read me like a book, recognizing my attempt to deflect.

"I'm just tired." It's not a lie. I didn't sleep well, and it had nothing to do with the chaise. Telling Grey that Julian Holloway, the maintenance man at the apartment building I lived in last year, had broken into my apartment opened the door of past fears just enough to let them flood into the recesses of my mind. I ignore the additional distractions that include Emma and Grey.

Evelyn doesn't prod me for more as we approach the infamous ride that used to terrify me as a child.

We walk through the iron gates before finding the end of the line.

"You have to stick together, or you get stuck riding with a stranger," I warn them. "The ride starts with us as a large crowd."

"Can all four of us ride together?" Evelyn asks.

I shake my head, hating the answer, before I tell her, "We'll have to pair off again." I'm almost tempted to pull out a best friend card and ask Evelyn to ride with me. She would without hesitation or complaint, but one of the worst parts of having your best friends date is that you care about their feelings and happiness more than your own, hence last night and why I'm already coming to terms that I'm going to sit by a random stranger or Grey.

"I'll ride with you," Evelyn says, likely knowing I won't ask her.

I shake my head. "Just promise to ride It's a Small World with me, and I'll be happy."

Evelyn side-eyes Grey. "Are you sure?"

I nod. "Think about what you want for your first snack, a cinnamon roll the size of your head, a Dole Whip, a turkey leg bigger than Hudson's biceps, funnel cake, corn dog, a huge fruit and chocolate filled waffle..."

"I'm never leaving," she says wistfully.

I chuckle and focus on being present. When the line moves us into the mansion, the temperature drops considerably, chilling me after the Florida sun had me feeling too warm. My eyes are still adjusting to the muted lighting when Evelyn gives me a final questioning glance. I squeeze her hand. "I'm okay. I swear." I will my residual bad mood to leave.

She offers a supportive smile as we follow the crowd into the small room, forced to stand a little closer. The iconic voice welcomes us to the Haunted Mansion, marking the beginning of the ride.

The same nervous chuckles that people emitted on the small drops of the roller coaster fill the small space as jokes about our safety are announced. Evelyn's fascination and surprise as the paintings and walls grow has me feeling like it's my first time on the ride.

When the doors open, we follow the crowd to the small cars, Grey a step behind me.

"How many?" the cast member asks when I hit the walking conveyer belt.

I start to lift a hand when Grey answers, "Two."

She waves us forward.

I slip into the empty car, and Grey climbs in beside me, taking every free inch of space. I've never felt like the cars were too small when riding with my dads, Alex or Jon, but as Grey presses against every part of me once again, I hear Emma calling me ginormous. I try to force myself to be smaller, tucking in my legs and arms and pressing against the hard plastic of the car before the lap bar is snugly lowered into our laps by a girl who takes a few extra seconds to stare appreciatively at Grey.

I'm inclined to ask her if she wants to switch positions. I'd gladly dawn her hat and heavy dress to get out of this appropriately titled Doom Buggy.

The ride starts, and Evelyn leans forward to wave at us, just as I used to when riding it with one parent while the other rode behind us.

I glance at Grey, nearly missing the library and the busted statues with eyes that follow us, wanting to see his reactions to each part of the ride.

He glances at me from the corner of his eyes but says nothing.

We pass by the grand piano and enter the darkened tunnel, where eyes flash in bright colors. They never scared me. It was always the dark that made me dislike this ride so vehemently I refused to ride on it for years.

Without warning, we come to a stop. Grey looks at me. "Is this part of the ride?"

I shake my head, the hard plastic of the seat biting into my spine from the slight incline that has us leaning backward. "Sometimes they have to stop the ride so someone can get off or on."

A minute later, they ask everyone to remain seated, assuring us we'll move again shortly.

"What happened last night at the elevator? What did that guy say to you? The comments about the bag ... the scrubbing?"

"Better question, why did you assume I slept with him?"

"Because I assume most guys want to sleep with you."

I stare at him, wondering what kind of dimension we've fallen into that has him saying something like that and debating whether I should be offended. My heart pounds a traitorous beat. "I don't know what you mean by that or if I'm offended," I tell him, filters forgotten.

Grey smirks, but it's too dark for me to fully appreciate how his lips tilt higher to the left or how a small dimple stamps into his right cheek.

"I don't know what I'm saying either."

I scoff.

"Did you see him again? Is that why you came back and stayed?"

My heart thumps so hard, I swear it's hitting against my ribs, making each beat audible.

I shake my head. "The neighbor in the adjoining room was messing with the door, and it freaked me out."

He nods, accepting my answer. "Will you just tell me what he said?"

Pride shakes her head adamantly. "Why?"

"I need to know if I should punch him if I see him again."

Nolan, Corey, and Palmer would say the same thing, I remind myself.

"But seriously? A bag?" he asks.

"So you could put it over my head, so you didn't have to look at me while we had sex." The words come tumbling out of me like a dare as I stare at him with raised brows, waiting to take his reaction without flinching.

Grey stares back, eyes searching mine.

I wonder if he's going to laugh. I want him to make a joke. It would be kinder than him agreeing and so much easier to accept than the flicker of regret I see in his gaze.

"What a bastard."

It's a neutral sentiment—neither supporting nor rejecting the bag claim.

It stings.

It shouldn't.

"Exactly." I lean back, appreciating how the seat bites into my shoulder blades, and send a silent plea for the ride to start again soon. This sharing bubble is too small, and the darkness has me considering other things I might share or ask Grey, like why he's always disliked me.

Thankfully, the ride starts before I can do either.

Chapter 10

Grey

"**M**y feet still hurt, and I don't even regret that we didn't get drunk and waste the night avoiding guys at a bar," Hannah says as we pile into the hotel.

"This was the best day ever," Hadley says.

Evelyn flashes a smile. "It really was."

"Remind me, what time are you girls flying out tomorrow?" Nolan asks.

"Eleven. The van is coming to pick us up at eight." Katie cuts her eyes over the entire group. "Be down here for breakfast at seven."

Hadley looks at her phone and whimpers. "How about seven thirty?"

"*Seven*," Katie says.

Mila's the only one who doesn't comment. We pile into two elevators, stopping three times before we hit the fifth floor, where only Mila and I get off.

I eye the Disney bag in her hand and tilt my head. "You can stay again if you want..."

She shakes her head. "I need to pack."

I follow her down the opposite hall toward her room.

"You really don't have to walk me."

"I know."

"You're going to anyway. Aren't you?"

I nod.

Mila's shoulders slump, but she doesn't object, continuing to her room.

"What did you get?" I ask, pointing at the gift bag.

"Just something for my dad, Jon." She shrugs.

"What is it?"

Mila releases a breath. "A Stitch ornament. Jon gets something Stich themed every time we come to Disney. It's kind of our thing." Her voice is a singsong, as though she's trying to lighten the mood or the significance of her words.

"Why Stitch?"

We take five more steps before she rubs her lips together. "Because I was adopted." She swallows. "Kind of like Stitch."

I've only heard Mila mention being adopted once before, and that was after Palmer asked her outright when learning she had two fathers.

"I've tried to convince him to switch to Hercules, you know, God instead of alien, but..." She shrugs her tone light again, the same playful notes from earlier.

"How old were you when you were adopted?"

"Seven."

The number feels like a gut punch, but as I consider it, I'm not sure any age would feel easier—better.

Mila stops at her door before I can consider a question that doesn't sound either intrusive or thoughtless, like why she was adopted or if it was a difficult adjustment.

She waves her key across the keypad and presses down on the door lever as soon as it flashes green. With one foot inside, she looks over her shoulder at me. "Thanks... I'll... see you around."

If I were any of the other guys in our friend circle, she'd be hugging me. I try not to think about it as I take a step back. "If you need anything—text me, or call, or whatever."

She smirks like she assumes the words are an obligation and disappears into her room.

The blackout shades make it appear like its midnight when I wake up, but the digital clock confirms it's six-forty-five, two hours before I need to be awake.

I roll to my side and close my eyes. I had a hell of a time falling asleep last night, checking and rechecking my phone to ensure Mila hadn't messaged me. I even got up twice, convinced I heard footsteps in the hall and thinking she might be waiting outside my door, worried about disturbing me.

Someone yells, a toilet flushes, a shower turns on. I shove a pillow over my head and close my eyes.

My phone vibrates across the nightstand.

I swear.

"Yeah?" I answer.

"What are you doing, asshole?" Cole asks.

"Sleeping," I mumble.

He chuckles. "Not anymore. You won your game, and you won me a grand!"

"You're welcome," I murmur.

He laughs again. "Guess who called and wants to set up a fight? Scooter," he answers before I have the chance to say anything.

I sit up.

"When does he want to schedule it?" It's not an if but a when. Scooter Williams is one of the most followed fighters in the MMA. Going up against him—beating him—would be a golden ticket.

"He wants to fight the second week of March. This is my chance, Grey."

"You have a fight the week before," I remind him. "Schedule it for April."

"Did you not hear me? Scooter Williams. You don't say no to this kind of opportunity."

I don't know if he's talking about his fight or my decision not to enter the draft.

"He reached out to you," I remind him. "Baxter will be a tough fight. You don't want to fight Williams if you're bruised or still sporting a swollen eye."

"Baxter doesn't stand a chance. The fight won't last thirty minutes."

I scoff. Confidence aside, we both know that's a lie.

"I can do this. I'll beat the shit out of Baxter and then take on Williams. This will define my career. I thought you'd be happy for me."

I roll to my back and peel the pillow off my face. "Scooter wants to fight you because you're gaining recognition. Don't let him start with the upper hand."

"And turn away this money? I haven't even told you how much they're offering me yet."

I pull in a breath through my nose and close my eyes. "What did Mackey say?" Mackey is Cole's trainer, a gym rat who pushes Cole and the only one with a free pass to insult him, which he takes full advantage of.

"He thinks I can do it. I'd be putting in the hours, working my ass off, regardless. Might as well make it worth it."

Scooter has gained recognition because he's one of the toughest competitors, known for his speed and strength. I don't tell Cole this, though, because reminding him of his weaknesses is what the people of Highgrove have been doing for the past twenty-two years.

"You'll do it. We'll get in extra training."

"Hell yes. Abe's fighting tomorrow against Preston. You gonna show?"

"What time?"

"Nine over at Billie's."

"Yeah. I'll be there."

"Well get up. You're wasting daylight. Get those miles and reps in. What in the hell are you doing asleep, anyway?"

It would be a dick move to tell him I'm exhausted from a thirteen-hour day at Disney World. I grumble a response that makes Cole chuckle before he hangs up.

I shower and pack the last of my things before heading down to the lobby.

"Hey," Evelyn greets me with a smile as she steps behind me at the buffet. "You're up early."

I hand her a plate and gesture for her to go first.

She blushes but obliges. Evelyn's one of the most genuinely good and kind people I've met. She reminds me of my mom: hardworking, honest, and always looking out for others, which makes her one of the people whose opinions I care about.

We pile our plates full, Evelyn carrying two because she leaves wide gaps between her food to prevent them from touching. I catch sight of Mila at the end of the table, nursing another coffee before Evelyn leads us over to her.

"You need more than just melon," Evelyn says, pushing a plate I realize now was intended for Mila in front of her with a pancake, scrambled eggs, and bacon.

Mila looks up from her coffee, her eyes puffy from exhaustion. She looks at me without a reaction and then pushes the plate away. "I ate my weight in snacks yesterday."

Evelyn nudges the plate closer to Mila, but not as far as she had the first time. "No one says no to pancakes." She bites into a slice of bacon.

Mila glances at the food, spears a piece of honeydew and pops it into her mouth before turning her attention to her phone for half a second before setting it in front of Evelyn. "I wouldn't respond."

Evelyn shakes her head. "I can't just ignore her. That would be rude."

Mila takes another drink of coffee. "Her message is snotty. She's mad at you for not coming home for Christmas and is telling you she returned your gift because of it."

"Who?" I ask.

Mila's eyes flash with malice.

"My best friend from New Mexico. She feels like I'm putting Hudson in front of everyone else."

"In other words, she's bitter as fuck," Mila says, taking another bite of cantaloupe.

"I forgot my coffee," Evelyn says, pushing back from the table. "Do you guys need anything to drink?"

We both shake our heads before Evelyn leaves us with a heavy cloud of silence falling over the table.

"Why are you staring at me?" Mila asks.

"You look tired."

"You don't tell women that," she says shaking her head. "It's basically code for saying we look like shit."

"No, that's only what you take it to mean."

Mila shakes her head. "It's like telling us to smile, or to eat, or not to curse."

"Wait..." I pull my phone out of my pocket. "Tell me that list again."

Evelyn returns with coffee and a glass of orange juice before I can poke hard enough to see if Mila will bite. She looks between us, reading the tension as she plasters a smile on her face. "They have pretty decent coffee here and good creamer choices."

Mila nods, taking a sip from her own cup.

"What are you doing for the rest of break, Grey?" Evelyn asks, cutting into her pancakes.

"The gym and going home to Highgrove," Mila answers for me.

Evelyn waits for me to clarify or add something as she takes a bite of her pancakes. When I don't, she looks between us. "We should all do something."

Mila's smile teeters between being smug and amused. I'm waiting for Evelyn to call her out on it and ask what in the hell she's thinking, but Hudson drops into the chair next to Evelyn with a full plate, kissing her on the temple before greeting Mila and me.

"Where have you been?" I ask.

"Talking to Griff," he says. "He—"

"Greyson!"

I turn in my seat to see who's called my name and spot Emma Kemp striding toward us, tucking a pair of sunglasses on top of her head.

"Oh god," Mila mutters.

Our table has three empty seats, but Emma takes the one beside me. "I was hoping to run into you!" She places her Starbucks cup on the table and smiles warmly. "Did you get my text?"

I did. I ignored all eleven messages until we returned to the hotel late last night. They varied from apologizing for being rude yesterday to understanding my attraction to Mila and insisting she knew how persistent fans could be before making it clear she'd still like to hang out.

It took turning off my phone and completing a hundred

pushups to soothe my annoyance and keep myself from responding.

"Yeah, sorry. Mila and I were at Disney World, celebrating."

Emma pulls her chin back. "You went to Disney World?"

I take a bite of biscuits and gravy and stare at her.

"I mean, don't get me wrong, I love Disney, but ... I don't know. I just can't picture you with the matching shirts and ears."

I glance at Mila, hoping to find annoyance or maybe jealousy, but all that's visible are the traces of humor and surprise before she tips back her coffee.

I point at Hudson. "Emma, have you met Hudson and his girlfriend Evelyn? Guys, this is Emma Kemp. Her father is Linus Kemp, one of our team's boosters."

"It's so nice to meet you. I don't think we've met." She extends her hand to Hudson and Evelyn, ignoring Mila.

Mila's expression reveals only bland indifference aside from her arched brows.

Blood pumps through my veins, fighting every instinct to react and tell Emma to take a long walk off a very short pier.

"I heard you decided to stay at Camden another year rather than enter the draft."

I nod, lacking the same skills of diplomacy Hudson has mastered. It's one of the many things Krueger reminds me I must hone.

Emma smiles encouragingly. "I have no doubt you would have been a high pick, but Camden's lucky to have you stick around." She tucks her elbows to her sides. "Well, I should get going. I'll see you Saturday at the party." She slips out of her seat and waves before disappearing, reminding me I need to ask Mila for another big favor.

Chapter 11

Mila

"You don't mention Grey very often," Briggs says, looking up at me from the notes resting on his folded legs. He slides his glasses up the bridge of his nose as I recount my trip to Florida and my triggered moment that led me to Grey's room.

I try not to roll my eyes. "For good reason."

"What's the good reason?" Briggs is a master of turning my words around on me without sounding accusatory or flippant.

I pause, knowing now is not the time to mention how obnoxious Grey is or how my best friend chose the grumpiest, most difficult-to-read person who tolerates me on his best days and ignores me every other day. "We're just acquaintances." I shrug, ignoring the way those thoughts feel like lies after Florida.

"*Just* acquaintances? But you trusted him enough to seek him out and stay overnight with him..." He raises his graying eyebrows at me.

"He's Hudson's best friend on the team. I know he's trust-worthy. We're just not friends."

"Why's that?"

"Because he doesn't like me."

Briggs leans back in his chair, studying me for a moment as he does every time he finds access to an anthill in our discussions and rushes to scribble down notes. "Why do you think he doesn't like you?"

I started seeing my therapist, Briggs, five years ago after my maternal uncle contacted me, and I didn't know how to process the storm of emotions that his unsuspecting letter brought. He was the fourth therapist my parents helped me find and the first I felt comfortable with since I was young. For the first six months, we talked about surface topics, and though it didn't make a lot of sense to me, I didn't complain because I was a sophomore in high school with a guy best friend and sometimes talking about gossip and bullies with someone else felt surprisingly good.

Little did I know that during those months of me rambling about things I found funny, annoying, or destructive to society, Briggs was studying me, learning my cues, moods, and fears without me ever vocalizing them. I was resentful and confused initially, but I'd already grown used to our meetings and telling him things I didn't trust with others, things I needed to get off my chest and out of my thoughts that weren't always important but somehow managed to take real estate in my head.

Over time, we began dissecting my life, looking at it like a pointillism painting. Examining small bits and pieces that were sometimes significant and other times benign until more dots were uncovered.

I want to tell him Grey isn't even a full dot, but I know that will lead to more questions, so I try my best to answer him honestly—as I do most times with Briggs.

"He just ... avoids me. I think he assumes I'm just a spoiled rich kid who doesn't care about anything."

Briggs rubs a thumb over his tongue, working to turn the page in his notebook before looking at me with lowered eyebrows that portray his offense on my behalf. I both hate and love when he does this because it makes me feel validated, and all too often, it makes my eyes burn and my throat grow tight. "Why would he think that about you?"

"I can just tell by the way he looks at me."

Briggs holds his pen, working to read the situation and me. "I can see that it bothers you that he thinks this about you."

Impulsively I want to say *no*, but a part of me wants to say it does and have Briggs verify for me that I care about more than just superficial things and have experienced more than just a princess's life. But doing so entails us visiting dots in the painting of my life that I don't care to look at or discuss today.

"I think he's had a hard life, and he struggles to trust people. I get it."

"Sometimes, when someone has their guard up, we have to share a secret to earn their trust."

"I don't really need his trust. Grey cares about football, and that's about it."

Briggs's pen races across the paper. I used to worry about what he wrote about me and if he thought I was a terrible person for some of my thoughts and views or small-minded for my opinions, but now I take the seconds as a reprieve to gather my thoughts and think of a safer subject to discuss.

"I took myself on a date as you suggested."

I swear he smirks, though he doesn't show it. He knows how much I hated the idea. "How did it go?"

"Terrible."

He chuckles. "We discussed that it would feel awkward the first time. Where did you take yourself?"

"To the Italian restaurant downtown, *Buona*."

Briggs raises his eyebrows. "I've heard they're good."

"It was delicious, but that didn't make it any less weird. Everyone stared at me like I'd been stood up. I endured constant looks of sympathy and assumption."

More laughter bubbles out of Briggs. "You were out taking care of yourself, reminding yourself what you deserve and want, and enjoying your own company." He points at me. When Briggs isn't scribbling down my innermost secrets, he's often making gestures with his hands that include lots of pointing.

"I can't say I'd be inclined to accept a second date with myself."

"Things aren't always going to come easy. That doesn't mean we give up. Maybe you dove a little too deep on the first try. Maybe a trip to a bookstore by yourself or to get coffee."

"But you said I can't read."

"You're supposed to be with your thoughts, not lost in someone else's story."

"I'm with my thoughts all the time." Though the words are authentic, I'm goading him, hoping we can stretch this topic until the end of our session.

He gives me a leveling stare. "We've talked about this, Mila."

"I'm kidding," I say before he can start in on the importance of these dates again. "I'll try it again—just not to a nice restaurant."

"It wasn't a bad choice. Remember, you're deciding how you deserve to be treated." I don't know if his words or the long stare he delivers them with is more unsettling.

I glance at my watch to see it's a couple of minutes shy of our hour being complete, acceptable as an ending point. I lean down to gather my purse. "It's supposed to get cold this week."

Briggs grins a genuine smile that flashes his white teeth. "I'm hoping it snows." He moved here from New York, and though he claims to be happy to have left the city and cold, his entire being lights up at the mention of snow every year. It's one of our shared loves.

I slip my arms into my coat, pulling it closed with a fist. "I could use a snow day."

He chuckles, knowing how the city closes down the moment snow appears in the forecast. "I'll see you next Wednesday, Mila."

I smile at him. Some days I leave here so emotionally drained, I'm physically exhausted, but today isn't one of those times. Our conversation was easy, our uncovered dots mostly colorful and bright. "Bye, Briggs."

The wind burns my cheeks as I step outside of the large brick building, working to recall where I parked. His office is on the outskirts of downtown, not far from where Hadley and Nolan live, situated among a dozen more professional buildings that make parking sometimes a sport. The wind slices across my cheek, so cold I flinch and turn my head away.

My heart catches and stops at the sight of an old white Ford truck with a rusted fender, the exhaust a plume of white smoke that distorts the license plate. The maintenance man at my old apartment drove the same make and model. Recognition has me turning to measure how far I am from Briggs's office and my car to see which I can reach faster.

I hurry to my car and slip into the cold interior, nearly hitting myself with the door in my rush to get it shut and locked.

My heart pounds so loud it's hard to think, harder to move.

I press the ignition button and reach for my phone as I turn to look at the truck again, but it's gone. Fear digs its claws into my spine.

I drive home, checking my mirrors for the same white truck as I chase the memory of Briggs's words, *You decide how you want to be treated,* until arriving at our apartment. I remain in the car for a couple of extra minutes, waiting another minute to ensure no one followed me.

Gates. I remind myself.

We have gates at the entrance with an armed guard who's there all day. It's one of the reasons this complex was so high on my list.

It was just a truck.

I'm safe.

It wasn't him.

I'm safe.

I repeat the words half a dozen times, recalling all the assurances Briggs helped me construct until my muscles slowly comply and relax enough that I can unbuckle my seat belt and head for the front door of our apartment.

"It's freezing," I announce to Evelyn as I rush to close the front door behind me. "You might get your first snowfall!" Knowing her aversion to the cold, I say the words with enthusiasm and the promise of fun.

"I literally can't get warm," Evelyn says, from where she's sitting on the couch wrapped in multiple blankets. "I don't want to insult our fortress because this place is insanely nice, but it's drafty. I don't think it was made to withstand this cold of temperatures." She snuggles back further into the confines of her blanket fort.

"Maybe we should check your iron levels?"

"My iron's fine. It's just freezing. Literally."

I kick off my shoes and pad into the living room, forcing myself into her blanket cave. "You were made for California. It never gets too hot or too cold."

"Fires and floods kind of freak me out, too. Maybe we should aim for Arizona?"

"Not New Mexico?"

Evelyn lifts a shoulder. "I don't know. The longer I'm here, the less Albuquerque feels like home."

"Does Oleander Springs feel like home?"

Evelyn releases a breath. "I'm slowly realizing home isn't really a place but a feeling."

"Orgasmic feelings?" I tease.

Evelyn hits me in the chest with a throw pillow. "You're included. Living here, moving in with you, I'm so grateful that things worked out this way rather than how I'd planned."

I grin as I pull my knees to my chest, huddling closer to Evelyn and her nest of blankets.

"Oh! I almost forgot that the neighbor in building C stopped by to return our immersion blender and looked particularly disappointed when I told him you weren't here."

"Sounds like I dodged a bullet."

Evelyn grins. "He's actually kind of cute."

"He's so smiley."

Laughter belts out of her. "You say that like it's a bad thing. Those dimples definitely aren't a bad thing. Plus, he fills out a suit pretty damn well..."

"Should I warn Hudson he might have competition?"

She rolls her eyes, but they turn sympathetic with her next breath. "You haven't dated anyone since stupid Will."

Will was a cute senior I met in September with a flashy smile and a penchant for a good time. We had the perfect meet-cute, meeting in line at a bistro near campus. He had pretended to be able to read my palm and told me I'd fall for a cute guy with brown eyes very soon—referring, of course, to himself. And I did. Or I wanted to. It took four weeks before I realized all he wanted to do was to party and have sex—the same things most guys want—without the labels of a relationship.

"He was the first guy I really wanted to like in over a year," I admit with a sigh. The same level of honesty I've established with Briggs was born with Evelyn. I don't know if it's her willingness to look ridiculous with me or the fact she's never judged me or treated me like an outsider, even when I first moved here and was steeped in the feeling.

"He was a jerk who didn't deserve you." Evelyn shakes her head. She read the warning signs that I happily overlooked and bet me that he wouldn't ask about my family, try to meet our friends, or invite me on a date that didn't include a keg. Unable to refuse a bet, I accepted with the stipulation I couldn't sleep with him until he did one of those three challenges.

Evelyn won, and Will lost interest.

"I don't know if I'm relationship material," I admit.

"What are you talking about?"

"I'm afraid of my own shadow, and I have a complex fear of abandonment paired with serious trust issues." I wave a hand over my face. "I'm every guy's nightmare."

Every ounce of humor leaves her as her eyes turn solemn. "A nightmare? Mila, you're hilarious, gorgeous, smart, independent, and the best damn friend a person could have. Don't let Will or any other undeserving jerkwad let you believe anything different."

The lock clicks open, and Griffin, Hudson's younger brother, yells out a greeting.

Evelyn holds my gaze for another second. "Will didn't deserve you, and that doesn't mean you should date hot neighbor, but don't think for a second that Will's idiocy is a reflection of you."

Griffin bounds toward us with his backpack in hand and a permanent smile on his face. "Hi, Mila! Hi, Evelyn!"

I'm barely able to stand before Griffin wraps me in a hug and smacks a cold, wet kiss on my cheek. He releases me to do the same to Evelyn.

Growing up next door to Hudson and Griffin had me

seeing the brothers nearly every day of my childhood. We became integral parts of each other's lives. They offered me consistency, acceptance, and reliability that I'd only ever experienced in short bouts. It also gave me a sense of pride and purpose when I became one of Griffin's most trusted and favorite individuals, titles I never take advantage of. Being autistic, people often focus on all his differences, overlooking the many amazing gifts and joys he brings to every situation.

Hudson kicks off his shoes and hangs his coat in the closet.

"I learned a new chess move," Griffin says, shrugging out of his coat and straightening both sleeves before hanging it beside Hudson's and launching into the details of the offensive maneuver like a war tactic.

"Want to set up the chessboard?" I ask him. "I thought we could either make grilled cheese sandwiches and soup or order pizza for dinner."

"Grilled cheese," he says, walking farther into the living room where our chessboard awaits him.

Hudson winks at me as Evelyn slides her arm around his waist. "We'll make dinner," he says.

My phone vibrates with a message as I sit across from Griff.

Grey: I need to ask you for a favor...

I read the text twice, unsure how to respond. We don't text, hence why I didn't text him while at the hotel.

Me: Ominous...

Grey: I'm nearby. Can I stop by?

Once again, I'm rereading the message several times, searching for meaning or sense in the words. Grey doesn't randomly stop by. We don't hang out. In fact, I'm a little surprised he even remembers my address because, apart from helping us move in along with ten other teammates, it's the only time I recall him having come over.

Pride stirs in my chest as I debate a response. I'm still reeling from the weekend, knowing I should have told Briggs about how a stranger's words stripped my confidence and self-worth so easily and completely, but I'd focused on how I'd been triggered, fearing for my safety because someone jiggled the doorhandle because it felt like a much safer topic than admitting the hurtful words.

> Me: Sorry, I'm not home right now. What's the favor?

I tuck my phone between the couch and the cushion and sit forward in my seat, prepared to make my first move as Griff reminds me that he's waiting.

I should be a chess champion for how many games I've played, but Griffin cleans the floor with me every single game without fail, and as we move our pieces across the board, I'm already preparing for my loss when the doorbell rings.

Hudson wipes his hands and goes to answer the door as Griffin explains the plays I should have considered with my last move.

"Hey," Hudson says. "Come on in."

I look up as Grey steps into our apartment, one eyebrow raised with question as our gazes clash, and I'm reminded this is definitely not how things go in the movies.

Chapter 12

Grey

Embarrassment or maybe shock flits across Mila's face as she stares at me with wide blue eyes.

"Hey, Grey!" Evelyn wraps her arms around my shoulders in a hug as Mila turns away, studying the chessboard between her and Griffin. "Want to stay for dinner? It's nothing fancy, just grilled cheese and tomato soup."

"Yeah," Hudson says, backing up, encouraging me farther into the apartment.

"Hi! Hi, Grey," Griffin says, standing. He crosses the room with his arms spread, awaiting a hug.

Mila's gaze drifts after him, watching our interaction with a hint of curiosity before she slips out of her seat to joins us, stopping at Evelyn's side as Griffin pulls me into a firm hug.

"Want to see a new chess move?" Griffin asks, taking a step back.

"Why don't we pause the game?" Hudson suggests. "You guys can finish after dinner."

Griff looks bereft for half a minute before Evelyn asks him to help her make the sandwiches.

"You got home fast," I say, turning to Mila.

She doesn't react except for a slight shrug. "I was playing chess with Griff."

Hudson messes up Mila's hair by rubbing his palm over her scalp. She winces and ducks before shoving him toward the kitchen and looking at me. "What are you doing here?" She absently smooths the strands that Hudson displaced.

I step back to prevent myself from reaching forward to run my fingers through her hair and offer an assurance that would make her roll her eyes. "I called Hudson, and he mentioned he was over here with you guys, so I asked if I could stop by. I have a favor to ask you." I give her a pointed look, intended to point out I'd asked her first.

"You'd get further making a bet with her," Hudson taunts.

Mila cuts her eyes to him with a silent warning that Hudson laughs off. Slowly, she turns back to me, hesitation heavy on her brow. "What kind of a favor?"

"The booster club is hosting a party this Saturday for the team, and Linus Kemp and Emma will be there. I would appreciate it if you'd come as my date."

Mila's eyes flare just slightly before she schools her features. "No one is going to believe I'm your date."

I scoff. "They might if you can pretend to lower your standards for two hours."

Steely eyes snap to mine. "It has nothing to do with *my* standards. You look at me like I'm diseased when we're near each other. Have you considered what this will entail? The whole team is going to be there. Nolan. Palmer. Freaking Lenny." She waves a hand. "There's no way this would work."

"Diseased? You insisted on sleeping on the couch so you wouldn't have to be close to me."

"Because I knew you didn't want me there."

"I'm the one who offered for you to sleep beside me."

She doesn't say anything. She doesn't have to. Doubt is etched across her face.

"The team won't say shit. Trust me. If anyone understands the power of our boosters, it's Palmer and Nolan. And Lenny will fall into line because as much as he likes to raise hell, he knows the team comes first."

"They're going to have a full dessert bar," Hudson adds.

Mila bites low on the inside of her lip, making them almost look pursed. The expression drags my thoughts back to the hotel this weekend when she had done the same subtle action. And like a key turning in a lock, I realize I've seen her do this before, hiding her vulnerability behind those squared shoulders and sharp eyes.

"You love cake." My comment is too quiet for the others to hear, intended to be a joke before promising her I'll be on my best behavior to make this easier for her.

She sputters. "I can't wait to hear Emma's insults." She bites the inside of her cheek, surprising me almost as much as it confuses me. Mila is pure confidence and swagger.

"If she tries to insult you, I'll deal with it."

Mila's eyes flash with another steely look. "I don't need you to defend me."

I give her a sardonic look. "I wouldn't dream of it."

Her gaze sharpens, preparing to parry my words and land her own blow.

"It would be kind of fun for you to come Saturday," Evelyn says. "We can eat all the desserts together, and if Emma says one word to you, I'll accidentally set my plate on her seat before she sits down."

Mila chuckles, not admonishing her for offering to stick up for her.

"Make sure they're all chocolate," Hudson adds.

Evelyn grins at him, a look that verifies he's said the right words.

"Should we start the sandwiches, or does the soup need to be warmer?" Griffin asks, turning from where he's finished buttering a tray filled with slices of bread.

"Let's wait until it's a little warmer," Hudson says.

Mila turns to me. "How long are we going to carry on this charade?"

"This is the last time. After this, the boosters will only be interested in meeting with us to offer sponsorships."

She releases a breath, and her shoulders slowly round. "You're lucky two-thirds of my social life is already attending the party."

I realize that's the closest thing to an agreement I'll receive. "I'll be here at seven."

She nods her acknowledgment before moving into the kitchen, where she leans against the counter, her back to me as she faces Griffin.

"Grey, what can I get you to drink?" Evelyn asks, opening the fridge and listing off a dozen beverages.

"I'm good with water," I tell her. "How can I help?"

"You can help Hudson set the table if you want."

Hudson opens the cupboard beside the sink, withdrawing a stack of plates as Evelyn offers me the glass of cold water.

Mila's voice is animated but too soft to hear over the clang of the plates Hudson sets out and the fan over the stove where the steam curls off the soup.

Griffin belts out a laugh that has Mila grinning. Her eyes are a warmer, darker hue. I've learned that Mila, like her eyes, is comprised of multiple shades. She shines the brightest when she's around Evelyn, Griffin, and Hudson, specifically during times when she doesn't realize anyone's paying attention.

"What are you two laughing about?" Evelyn asks.

"I was telling Griff about the icy patch I nearly broke my butt on after your sage advice," Mila tells her.

Evelyn laughs, turning to look at Hudson. The two share a look that has jealousy slinking into my chest with so much intensity it's a sharp breath. The way they often look at one another like they're each other's reason for breathing—existing —nearly eclipses my reasons for putting the entirety of my focus on school and football.

"No! No! No!" Evelyn protests, shaking her head before giggling, shaking me from my thoughts. "I warned you. I said it was slick."

"You said I should have worn different shoes," Mila objects.

Evelyn bends as a second wave of laughter hits her. "Because it was slippery!"

"Saying I should have worn different shoes doesn't translate to: *Watch out. It's slippery.*"

Tears have Evelyn wiping her cheeks with the back of her hands as she continues laughing.

Hudson shakes his head and turns to me. "Did you tell Krueger about Emma Kemp?" he asks, referring to our temporary head coach.

I shake my head. "I figured the fewer people involved, the better. I don't want Krueger or anyone else to think I influenced Kemp. I didn't know Emma and had never met her before that damned date."

"She's been around a few times. You probably didn't notice."

"I'm wondering if that was the only reason he offered me the sponsorship."

Hudson grimaces. Despite his ease with politics, he still loathes them. "Bringing Mila is a solid choice."

It was his suggestion. While flying home from Orlando, Krueger shared he's encouraging the boosters to offer more paid sponsorships and to see us as more than just athletes. He insisted we needed to show the boosters other sides of ourselves, balanced, real people with families, relationships, and dreams.

I had already planned to ask Mila, hoping she'd ride out this lie a little farther with me when Hudson suggested I invite her. His reasons had been her understanding of the game, familiarity with politics and wealth, and how she wouldn't be distracted by the team or the event because she'd been on red carpets in Hollywood as her father's date.

My reasons weren't half as illustrious.

"I asked around, and Emma sounds like the vengeful type. Don't let Mila get caught in the crosshairs."

"She's jealous of Mila."

Hudson raises his brows. "I can guarantee you that's not what Mila thinks."

"Did she say something?" I glance to where they're assembling and cooking the sandwiches and then at Hudson as he shakes his head.

"No, and she won't."

The memory of her expression when that stranger yelled lewd and hateful comments have my fists clenching with regret.

"And Silva. Avoid Silva. I saw him yesterday when I met Krueger, and he is bitter as hell."

Bitter doesn't come close to describing the man Krueger has been working to find a way to ban from all booster events due to the reckless and rude comments he's become trademarked for.

"I avoid him like a damn cornerback. Have you heard anything about Peters?" I ask.

Hudson grips the back of a dining room chair and shakes his head. "Krueger says he wouldn't be shocked if he shows up to the event, but so far, he hasn't shared anything about his intentions or whether he'll be well enough to return to the head coach position come spring."

I sigh. "I hope he takes an early retirement." The shift of the team without Peters being on the field or in the locker room has been a complete one-eighty. If anyone doubted Peters' lack of skill and leadership before, they have to notice a difference now that he's gone. It's as though we replaced the weak link.

"This Saturday, we have to be a unified front and talk about how well Krueger is doing. How the team is happy and thriving, but we need to tread carefully. If it looks like a coup, the boosters could turn on us, and we have one more year."

I nod. I'd already considered the risk. My background didn't teach me how to maneuver the system, though, only that I should keep my head down and my nose clean.

Griffin carries a plate piled high with sandwiches to the table while Mila and Evelyn follow him with bowls of soup.

I sit across from Hudson, and Mila sits beside me without so much as a glance.

"Okay, dinner question," Griffin says, reaching for a small red box from the buffet table behind him.

"Why don't we wait since we have company," Mila says. "We can do it tomorrow before breakfast since you're sleeping over."

"It's for three *or more* people," Griffin says.

"Dinner question?" I ask.

"Griff got them in his stocking for Christmas," Hudson says, taking one of the sandwiches before serving Griffin and passing me the dish. "They're like icebreaker questions to get to know each other. Things like biggest fear, what animal would you be, what meal would you eat every day, that kind of thing."

Griffin opens the box and withdraws a small white square. "What's the scariest thing you've ever done? And why did you do it?"

"I'll go first," Evelyn says. "Moving to Oleander Springs. Hands down."

"Over quitting volleyball?" Mila asks.

"I mean, quitting was hard, but it wasn't as scary as leaving almost everything I knew behind."

"And why did you do it?" Griff asks.

Evelyn's cheeks flush as she glances at Hudson, then Mila, and Griff before returning to Hudson with another private look. "Because home isn't a place. It's a person—*people*. And you guys are my people."

Mila scoffs, and Evelyn's cheeks flash red as she glares at her.

"You want to go next, Griff?" Hudson asks.

"Moving to that place." He nods several times as he shifts forward and then back with a slow rocking motion. The place was an assisted living facility that Griffin had moved into during our freshman year that nearly led to Hudson quitting football because having his brother living so far away and being unhappy made him miserable. "I had to move there. Dad thought it would help me."

"That was hard, huh?" Hudson asks, setting his hand on Griffin's. "But you were so brave to try making it work and telling us that you weren't happy."

Griffin nods, still rocking.

"Who's next?" Hudson asks. "Grey?"

"Playing football for Camden."

Evelyn balks, even Hudson looks surprised.

"I was a backup option. My high school team was pretty terrible. No one knew about us. I was recruited because my mom won tickets to a Camden game and gave them to my buddy and me. His seat was chosen for the halftime drawing, and he let me go down in his place. They had the field set up with one of those gauntlet scenes they do. I guess the athletic director was impressed because he gave my name to the coaches. They came out and scouted me a couple of times but didn't recruit me until a kid out of Minnesota turned down the scholarship last minute. I didn't know if I'd live up to the potential."

"And now you're being scouted by the NFL," Hudson says. "I suddenly hate our athletic director a little less."

"Hate isn't a nice word," Griffin tells him.

Hudson nods. "Dislike."

Griffin turns to Mila. "Your turn."

She blinks and looks away from me. "Um, do you remember how hard it was to pick an apartment this summer?"

Griffin's shoulders slump. "Do you want to reread the rules?"

She grins. "I remember." Mila releases a sigh. "Adoption court was the scariest thing I've ever done." She clears her throat. "Like you, Griff, I did it because I had to."

"What's adoption court?" Griffin asks.

"It was when Jon and Alex adopted me, and I legally became their daughter."

Griffin stares at her. "You had to go to court?"

She nods.

"Why was it scary?" Griffin asks.

Mila bites that low spot on her bottom lip. "Because I didn't want to leave."

"Leave?" Griffin looks perplexed. "Where would you have gone?"

Mila licks her lips. "Back to Oklahoma."

"But..." Griffin looks from Mila to Hudson. "I didn't know you were from Oklahoma."

"You were only six when I moved in." Mila leans back in her chair, her voice soft and patient as it is every time she interacts with Griffin.

He blinks at her, trying to process the onslaught of information. "Who would you have lived with in Oklahoma? Your old family?"

"I'm pretty sure that question isn't on the card," Hudson says.

Griffin shakes his head. "But I don't understand."

"It's complicated," Mila says.

"Griff," Hudson says. "That's enough."

"But..." Griff begins.

"Just one question, bud," Hudson says. "She answered. It's my turn."

Griffin turns a pleading gaze to Mila and begins rocking again in his seat.

Mila rubs her lips together and then gently tilts her head to the side and swallows, her eyes bright with unshed tears that cause an ache in my chest to form and expand faster than I can blink. "I wanted to live with Jon and Alex," she says. "It was just ... intense."

Hudson looks at Mila, wearing his captain's face as he surveys the situation and how to respond just like he does on the field.

"What are we going to do tonight after dinner?" Hudson asks.

Mila points at Griffin. "Griff hasn't finished beating me at chess. I'm waiting to see the new move, and maybe we can watch *The Santa Clause*." It's Griffin's favorite movie. Hudson jokes he can recite it.

"And make hot chocolate?" Griffin asks.

"A hot chocolate bar," Mila tells him. "I picked up four kinds of marshmallows and three flavors of hot chocolate." She looks at Evelyn. "I think Hadley's corrupted me."

Evelyn grins, but I notice a residual sadness in her eyes.

"Griff, did you hear how many flavors of cheesecake

Hadley made before New Year's? I think there were six varieties."

"Eight," Hudson says.

The conversation turns to cheesecake and the holidays before jogging to their shared childhood. Stories about their attempts to beat world records, peppered with memories that keep the conversation light and constant. I'm sure it's to prevent questions from returning to Mila's childhood where my own thoughts are stuck as I once again imagine Mila as a child facing uncertainty and inconsistency rather than the confident and independent woman she is, surrounded by wealth and comfort.

Chapter 13

Mila

"My bra isn't showing, is it?" Evelyn asks, craning to see her back in the mirror.

I cap my mascara and thoroughly inspect her lavender dress covered in intricate lace patterns that looks like it came from the pages of a fantasy romance novel. It's stunning, and on her it's even more gorgeous. "Nope. It's perfect. You're perfect. Hudson's going to make an excuse to cut out early tonight."

She grins. "I already told him we're not leaving until you and Grey do."

I look at my reflection again. "Do I look okay?" Cruel words are still at the forefront of my thoughts as I question if my blush is too dark or my mascara too heavy.

"Better than okay. You look like you stepped out of a fashion magazine," Evelyn assures me, taking in my emerald green gown that has intricately woven beads patterning the bodice and front panel of the skirt and then flows into solid matte for the rest of the skirt.

My lungs feel tight, and though I want to blame it on the

weight and constriction of the bodice, I know that has nothing to do with the dress. I'm nervous, and I can't put my finger on why. Is it because pretending to date Grey feels like a minefield, or am I simply dreading seeing Emma again?

"I'm here!" Hudson yells up the stairs.

My stomach falls to my knees, realizing it's nearly time to leave.

Evelyn smiles. "You look a little nervous..."

"I don't know how to act or what to do. The last time I went on a formal date was prom, and this isn't a real date."

"It's Grey. Just be you."

"Am I supposed to hold his hand? Are we going to have to dance? What about small talk? When you make small talk with a couple, they always share bits of their history. One talks about the beginning, the other mentions a funny detail, and then the initial one corrects them ... Grey and I will fail epically at small talk. We have no stories."

Evelyn raises her eyebrows as a smile forms on her face. "You guys have known each other for two and a half years. You have stories."

"I've never been someone's fake girlfriend. I don't have much experience being a *real* girlfriend."

She laughs as the doorbell rings again.

I turn off the bathroom lights and follow Evelyn downstairs, veering toward the kitchen with the excuse of needing a glass of water to avoid answering the door. I peek around the wall in time to catch Hudson's eyes grow wide as he takes in Evelyn with adoration and a heavy dose of lust that leaves me smiling and ready to mock them both. I swallow the quips, though, and resume getting my water.

"Hey, man," Hudson says as I take a drink.

I turn, my mouth still full, and find Hudson and Evelyn with Grey close behind, dressed in a black suit that enunciates the width of his shoulders and a light blue dress shirt that makes his sapphire eyes stand out like the first stars in the night sky as they stop on me. He looks even better than he did the night he crashed my self-date.

Emma's going to hate me.

Grey slides his hands into his pant pockets and turns to face me. His gaze locks on mine, and for a second, that pressure in my lung grows in intensity. It feels as though he recognizes every one of my nerves, fears, and insecurities yet isn't avoiding or placating any of them as he maintains my stare, sharing his own with me.

It reminds me of being five while living with a foster care family that had their mother living with them. She was a mean, no-nonsense kind of woman who made us eat every crumb from our plates and didn't tolerate any noise after eight. She was Polish and would watch movies in the living room every night in Polish, and we were forced to sit still and listen silently.

I marveled how, despite not knowing what they were saying at different points in the films, I could still understand what was happening. That's how I feel now like Grey is a foreign film without any closed captions, and still, I'm able to recognize his nerves, hope, and the hint of an apology.

I smile, which breaks the spell and has Grey returning the look before his gaze lowers, taking in the full length of my gown before tracking back to my face.

"Do I look like a Christmas tree?" I ask, my voice teasing and light.

Humor doesn't hit his features, though, as he slowly takes me in again, like an expensive bourbon meant to be sipped and appreciated. "You look ... stunning."

My stomach does something unrecognizable as my nerves roll to a new side, like sunbathing in the summer, exposing new nerves as I try and remind myself this is fake, a proposition, a deal. He's Hudson's friend.

I pull in a shallow breath.

All day, I imagined the jokes the other guys on the team would be ribbing me with and the glares and offensive words Emma would deliver with a smile. I didn't consider these new nerves born from being attracted to him.

My heart beats unsteadily, and though fear isn't crawling over my skin, threatening to encapsulate me, I feel the need to ground myself as I take in the sight of Hudson and Evelyn, my favorite red coat, and the chess board in the distance with a game still waiting to be finished. I latch on to the sounds of Evelyn chuckling, a car engine outside, and the clip of Hudson's shoes against the floors. Then I raise the inside of my wrist to my nose, smelling the floral scent of my perfume, and move back into the kitchen, pouring cranberry juice into a glass so I can lift it to my nose and take in the bittersweet scent.

My heartbeat slows, and my chest feels lighter.

"Looking sharp, Atwool," Hudson says, winking at me as he turns to open our coat closet.

I remain still, reminding myself to stay present and in the moment for another second as I watch Evelyn dig through the closet for something to wear over her dress. She hasn't acclimated to our colder winters.

"Evelyn, wear the long black pea coat with the clasps in the front. It's heavy and will keep you warm."

"I can't borrow your coat. You should wear it. It's cold tonight."

"I'm wearing a gray coat, with my Grey date."

Hudson and Evelyn laugh. Grey flashes me an amused expression before Evelyn gives me an appreciative smile and reaches for the heavy wool coat. Hudson helps her thread her arms into it.

"You guys know where you're going?" Hudson asks.

"I'm pretty sure the directions you sent said Gates to Hell. Is that right?" I set my empty glass beside the sink.

Grey rolls his eyes and talks about the fastest routes while Evelyn giggles.

There's a reason we're best friends.

"Remember cake," she assures me. "They've had excellent catered food at the events I've been to."

"Want gloves?" I ask her, reaching for my dark gray tweed coat.

She shakes her head. "No. I'll be okay."

I hand Hudson a pair of gloves to put in his pocket, anyway. Evelyn shakes her head.

"Ready?" Hudson looks across at us as a collective group, and we all nod and follow him to the entryway, where I set the alarm and lock the front door.

"We'll see you guys there," Evelyn calls before following Hudson to his Jeep.

I slip my keys into my purse and pull my jacket tighter, casting a glance at the night sky. It's clear, stars studding the black expanse. We still haven't received any of the snow the news has teased.

The cold mutes the smell of the trees and grass in the distance as Grey moves beside me and offers his arm. The scents of sandalwood and cedar greet me, making me draw in a long breath through my nose as a citrus undertone tickles my senses.

God, he smells even better than he looks.

Grey always smells good; I just forget because we've made it a habit of keeping an invisible yardstick between us. "It's icy out."

I swallow, and my heart forgets to remain calm, colliding with my ribs as I slip my hand into the crook of his arm. The warmth of his body tricks me into feeling frigid and wanting to slide closer to him. I lightly grip his biceps, and through the layers of his pristine suit, I feel his muscles contract, another tease to my senses.

I clear my throat as we walk to the parking lot, reminding myself this isn't weird. I've hung out with Grey and the other guys hundreds of times. We've gone on trips and vacations together. I slept in his hotel room. He's seen me in a bathing suit and first thing in the morning when I'm bleary-eyed and on the hunt for coffee. This only feels weird because we're trying to imitate something we're not—a couple.

"I've never been to one of these booster events," I say as we stop at his truck. It's red and probably older than me. I've never been inside of it. My aversion to Grey—his aversion to me—has existed since we first met.

"A lot of people will be in attendance. The entire team, full coaching staff, along with many alums, the boosters, and their families." He opens the passenger door for me.

I gather the skirts of my dress in my right hand and climb into the cab. The swaths of fabric threaten to tangle as I smooth them into place. The truck's interior smells like Grey, and as he closes me inside, I take a single deep breath before he opens the driver's side door.

"Most of the boosters will drink too much, and then they'll ask for photos and autographs to give to people they know."

"Is that weird?" I ask.

A faint smile forms as he nods and starts the engine. "Much weirder this year when they actually know who I am. Previous years, I could bleed into the background." He looks at me.

"Eat the cake?" I ask.

He bestows me with a grin. "Exactly."

We're silent as Grey navigates us to the highway. We're heading for Eastmont, a county Northwest of Oleander

Springs. There isn't a giant screen in the middle of the dash dictating directions or flashy lights. It's dark in the cab, offering a sense of anonymity and comfort that has me settling into my seat.

"Did you go to California for Christmas?" Grey asks.

I clear my throat. "No. My dad's work schedule changed, and I couldn't find a flight that would get me there before Christmas. With Evelyn staying, it just made sense to stay," I explain, feeling like I should attach a dozen excuses for why it was okay to miss going before recalling this is Grey, and he doesn't care. "Did you spend Christmas here?"

A nod of confirmation is his only response.

I clear my throat again, the silence growing uncomfortable. "Is there anything I should know? I mean, any details or questions I should have a good answer for, so I don't come across as the world's worst fake date?" Nerves have me overexplaining and rambling. "Any special awards I need to say you worked hard for? Or accomplishments you want me to mention when I'm scavenging the dessert table?"

"I've never brought a date, so I don't know what to expect."

I should feel relieved that he doesn't have any expectations. Instead, panic feels like a mountain. I'm his first date.

First *fake* date, I remind myself.

I asked Evelyn a hundred questions to prepare because I hate the unknown. She assured me it's mostly a lot of shaking hands, small talk, and eating. I was feeling confident until yesterday when she mentioned with their head coach not running the event, there would be some changes but wasn't sure what they were.

"Any specific objectives for tonight?"

He glances at me, his eyes glittering under the glow of a streetlamp. "Just the sponsorship with Linus Kemp I told you about."

I want to tell him to befriend Emma and play the same games so many others do—will be playing tonight—in the attempt to network and seek the right contacts to reach their goals. Alex has assured me these political games make up all facets of life, but they also make my skin feel stretched and pulled inside out, so I don't try and advise Grey except to point out the obvious.

"Maybe we shouldn't be doing this? You'd probably have a better chance of landing this sponsorship if you go alone."

"It's a little late for that," he says. "Besides, Linus loves Hudson, and you're Hudson's best friend."

I blink through my surprise, realizing Grey doesn't need my advice. He's already playing the game.

We ride the rest of the way in silence, arriving at the address located on the outskirts of downtown. I'm glad Evelyn accepted the heavier coat because there's no valet.

Once Grey parks, I open my door and hop out. The cold night air races up my legs and across my exposed skin. The terrain is flat here, paved for what will likely be commercial space as Oleander Springs continues to price people out, forcing them into other nearby towns. I glance skyward again at the vast openness, the cold stinging my eyes for a second as I take in the stars shimmering in thick clusters, so much denser and brighter here than at my apartment. The sight steals my breath and reminds me just how tiny my existence is in this vast space.

Grey appears next to me, close enough to block the breeze but far enough that he doesn't radiate warmth.

"Ready?" I ask.

His only response is to offer his arm once more, and I take it, walking with him to the gates of hell.

Chapter 14

Mila

Our early arrival is painfully apparent by the emptiness of the room. Thankfully, it allows me to find Evelyn and Hudson with barely a glance. They're talking to an older couple, Hudson's arm secured around Evelyn's lower back.

Unease floods me for just a second, enough to remind me of the stars outside and the gravitational forces that keep them shining. The constant push of gravity while fusion and convection expand the star, pushing against gravity.

I remember learning about the balance from one of the first therapists Jon and Alex had me meet before my adoption was finalized. She had a wall filled with posters of constellations with words I didn't know how to read and an office full of toys she'd invited me to play with. The stars caught my attention. In an office—a state—full of new things, I'd realized the sky was the same. It offered me a comfort I didn't realize I'd needed before I tried to navigate answering her questions to prove I wasn't too defective or damaged as so many openly discussed about children like me who had been in the foster care beyond the nine-to-twelve-month average and had seen too much.

She noticed my nerves and the way my attention kept straying to those posters, so she explained the delicate balance of a star's existence and how we sometimes feel that same way —the desire to fall apart and the constant maintenance required to keep ourselves together.

Tonight, that pressure to fall apart is a fraction of what it had been that day. I've had years to perfect and polish my shine, and as we stop at coat check, the beads on my dress shimmer as brightly as my smile.

My shoulders, arms, and most of my back are exposed, the air set to cool for a crowd as I follow Grey farther inside, hoping that, like me, he plans to make a direct route to Hudson and Evelyn.

"Meyers."

We stop as Coach Krueger approaches us, dressed in a dark navy suit, his hand secured around a gorgeous woman with black hair, flawless dark skin, electric red lips, and a stunning gold dress.

Coach Krueger extends his hand to me. "Hi. Mila, right?"

I nod, shaking his hand. I'm surprised he knows who I am but also not. As the acting head coach, he's spent an exorbitant amount of time with Hudson, drawing up new plays and changing the team dynamics. "Nice to see you."

He straightens. "This is my girlfriend, Kat."

"I'm obsessed with your dress," Kat tells me, shaking my hand.

I grin. "I'm obsessed with yours and your lipstick."

Her smile grows.

"Vogel's here," Coach Krueger says quietly. "He's got about ten friends here, including Barnhardt, who owns twenty restaurants in the state. He's been looking for someone to feature in his ads." He looks sideways as though ensuring no one's overhearing our conversation. "He'd be a good one to make friends with. Not only would it help the program, but it would be lucrative. He's a big fan of yours. I hear he likes to golf."

"How long have you been dating?" Kat asks me as the two continue discussing those in attendance.

My first question and I'm already caught off guard. "It's pretty new. We've known each other for a couple of years, though."

She smiles. "Phil and I were friends for three years before we began dating. Friends first is always best."

I want to ask her what her thoughts are on acquaintances that don't always like each other but paste on another shiny smile. "Are you from the area?"

She shakes her head. "New York. What about you?"

"Local," I say. I took on the role of native North Carolinian before reaching middle school. "Do you miss the city?"

"I miss the energy, but this place has grown on me." She clutches Coach Krueger's arm, staring up at him reverently. He gives her a secret smile that looks a little too forced—a Hollywood smile meant to be genuine. I wonder if it's because having an audience makes him uneasy or if he's not nearly as convinced as she is, and that's why it took them three years to begin dating.

"Mingle. Be sure to say hi to Cathy. She always feels like she's ignored for being one of the only female boosters. And if you see any of the guys drinking too much, find me." Coach Krueger moves his attention to me again and clasps his hand on my shoulder. "Nice seeing you again, Mila."

Kat waves goodbye.

The party has doubled in size in just a few minutes, and more are streaming inside. I look to see if I recognize anyone before turning to Grey. "Want to find this Barnhardt guy?"

His blue gaze meets mine, filled with conflict. "I don't know a damn thing about golf."

I shrug. "But you know a hell of a lot about football."

Grey's eyes dance across the room, searching the crowds. "He'll be looking for someone to impress him."

Across from us, I spot Emma with a tall, balding man with a silver beard that I presume is her father. I point them out to Grey. "You should talk to them. I'll go find Evelyn."

Grey curls a hand around my waist, heat seeping into me though a shiver slips down my spine, stopping me. "They're coming this way."

A glance confirms Emma and her father are heading straight toward us.

"Greyson," someone says with a nod as they pass.

"Maybe I should call you Greyson," I muse.

His eyes glitter with humor. "You can call me whatever you want."

The words shouldn't sound like an innuendo, but paired with the intensity of his gaze, they send heat flushing down my neck.

"In that case," I say, "I might need to get a little more creative with my nicknames."

"I thought we were retracting the claws for tonight?"

"Claws? That was my teeth." I snap my jaws together. "Good luck impressing Kemp," I say, sending him a wink as I turn. Before I can move, Grey's hand constricts, reeling me in with so much gentleness it defies the firmness of his hold. His gaze tangles with mine.

"How far are you willing to take this?" he asks, stepping closer, his chest brushing mine. He moves his hand from my waist to my shoulder and trails his fingers to my elbow, leaving a trail of goose bumps.

His gaze shifts, acknowledging my response to him. His

116

fingers caress my forearm, the back of my hand, and my fingers. His touch is intimate, so gentle it leaves me restless, wanting —*needing*—more. More pressure, more touching, *more.*

His eyes track across my face, attempting to read me as though I'm asking a cryptic question, and then Grey tilts his head and slides his hand around to my lower back, pulling me closer. My stomach becomes weightless and my thoughts fuzzy as I realize he intends to kiss me.

My heart falls to somewhere near my knees again, or maybe it's in my throat, and that's why I can't breathe as I stare at him, realizing how badly I want him to kiss me and how conflicting that desire is.

Humor dances in his sapphire eyes, reveling in my confusion or maybe my shock as I race to recall the steps of kissing. It's been months since I kissed anyone. I'm trying to remember the moves like a dance, calling on every movie and scene when Grey closes the space between us and presses his lips against mine. His mouth is warm and surprisingly tender, lacking the force I was expecting that might prove this is familiar to both of us. Instead, he kisses me slowly, his hand gathering me closer as he explores my mouth, my reactions, me.

Restlessness rolls through my veins like a tank engine, contracting every muscle, making me fight the impulse to gather his jacket in my fists, lean into him, slacken my jaw, and deepen the kiss. I force myself to remain still, my heart thumping painfully in my chest as my breathing grows heavier.

His lips open fractionally, and his fingers press more firmly against me, two of his fingers against the swell of my backside. My nerves are carried away by desire and instinct as I part my lips, the scent of cedar and sandalwood fresh in my nose. His tongue sweeps over mine, the taste of him filling my mouth as temptation crackles through every nerve ending, desperate to feel and taste more of him, feel the warmth and strength of his body against mine.

The reminder that we shouldn't be doing this, that I'll regret this, is a raindrop, the ripples teasing my senses and keeping me from arching against him and threading my fingers into his hair as I want to. The ripples continue and grow. Consciousness and sense prompt me to take a step back, kiss him a final time, and end things.

Grey misses the cue, his other hand coming to my jaw, skimming the pad of his thumb across the expanse of my cheek, gentle and sweet while his hand at my back presses even harder, inviting me to stay under this tide. Reason doesn't stand a fighting chance, and I slip deeper into the kiss, into Grey. He kisses me fuller, no longer an exploration but a crusade, pummeling my mouth and making my muscles feel both tight and loose.

I grasp his waist, convinced I need the support to remain upright. The cool crispness of his shirt and the hard expanse of Grey slowly warming under my fingers has me thinking of bed sheets as I hold on to him tighter.

He makes a sound then, something deep in his throat, a growl or maybe a groan, that has an ache pulsing between my legs. I want to forget the ripples that warn against the thoughts racing through my mind that are becoming filthy, consisting of clawing every piece of clothes from his body and feeling him against all of me, inside of me, stretching me, consuming me until I lose that balance that keeps me together.

I'm slipping, the balance shrinking. I recall how stars that run out of fuel become either a neutron star or a black hole, bending and destroying everything around them—and realize with absolute certainty that I'd do the same, namely to those closest to me.

The ripples become waves that have me slowly releasing Grey's jacket and leaning back.

Grey's hand slips from my face, and without his mouth and body against me, the room feels cold. Goose bumps dance across my flesh, rejecting every inch I move away from him.

The sight of Grey's dilated pupils and slightly labored breathing has confusion twisting with something in my gut that makes it difficult to breathe or look away.

"Greyson," a man says as he swaggers closer, wearing a grey suit and a scowl. "Nice to see you."

Grey steps closer to me, his jaw strained as he places a hand on my hip and leans closer. "Why don't you go get some cake," he says.

The man looks at me below thick, bushy brows. "Is this your girlfriend?" he asks, lowering his gaze over me with shrewd, appraising eyes.

"This is Mila Atwool," Grey says. "Mila, this is George Silva."

I'm still suffering whiplash, or something similar, the heat and ice of Grey a confounding culmination of emotions. "It's a pleasure to meet you," I say.

Mr. Silva frowns, turning his attention to Grey. "After this last season, I bet you can't keep them away. Can you?" He takes a drink of the amber liquid in the tumbler he holds in one hand.

Grey's fingers constrict on my waist as he grins, and I suddenly want to reduce our titles from acquaintance to enemies. "Actually, I'm still trying to win her over."

Mr. Silva appears taken aback for a beat.

I'm stunned into silence.

Fake. Fake. Fake.

The word repeats in my head like a mantra as the taste of Grey lies heavy on my tongue, contradictory to my mental chant.

Grey clears his throat, inclining his head toward the buffet and encouraging me to go as his hand relaxes and falls to his side.

Mr. Silva's gaze focuses on the spot Grey was touching me, and then he studies my face before his smile turns calculating and borderline skeevy. "Well, young man, you had quite the season. I hope the rumors are true and you will stick around for a final season. By next year, you'll be beating women off with a stick. There's a long list of worthy women who will be more than impressed with you. May I recommend you not waste time on unrequited conquests?" His gaze shifts to mine for a second before he moves past us.

I'm immune to the strange insults and praises that the team receives. Maybe it's a product of Alex working in Hollywood and his indifference toward seeing his name across the movie screen, instead introducing himself as Jon's husband or my father as though both are more significant. However, a ghost could appear before me, and I'd likely feel less shocked than I do now, reeling from kissing Grey and his words.

"That..." Grey says. "He's such a fucking asshole. I'm sorry." He shakes his head, his jaw gritted.

I blink, trying to recall the conversation and if I'm the one who should be offended or Grey. Who was he insulting? I'm stuck in a haze.

"You guys look like you could use these," Nolan appears with Hadley. She's wearing a gorgeous royal blue dress that looks like it was designed for her. Nolan passes Grey and me each a beer, and I ignore that I don't like the taste of beer or that I'm not twenty-one and drink half the glass in a single gulp.

"Was that Silva I saw talking to you?" Nolan asks.

I wince, hoping that's all he saw as I debate who might have witnessed me making out with Grey. I wonder if he's feeling the same sharp edge of panic.

Grey takes a drink. "I didn't even see him coming."

Nolan grimaces.

Hadley moves closer to me. "Gents, we're going to check out the buffet. We'll be back." She weaves her arm with mine and leads me halfway across the room before I realize I'm moving.

If I weren't drowning in my thoughts, I'd be appreciating the beauty of the buffet that's split in two with canapes on one side and desserts on the other, artfully decorated with foliage and tiny fake flames that flicker warmly.

Hadley grabs two plates, forcing one into my hands. "Are you okay?" Her voice is soft, barely a whisper so as not to draw attention from anyone nearby.

I nod. "Yeah. No. I'm fine. I'm just..." I blink too fast, trying to recall the conversation again. "He was saying I wasn't worthy of Grey, but the joke's on him because I'm just here as Grey's friend."

Hadley gives me a consoling look. "I'm sorry." She searches the crowd that has gotten significantly fuller since we arrived, the floor nearly filled with guys in suits and women in gowns. "Nolan warned me about Silva before we arrived and pointed him out, so I'd avoid him. He sounds like the scum that grows on scum."

"The program would definitely benefit from a little more estrogen," I say.

She grins. "Everything in this world would benefit from more women's influence."

I move to grab something that looks cheesy and delicious, and Hadley follows me.

"What do you think that is?" I ask, pointing at one of the dishes.

Hadley takes one and discreetly lowers her nose to smell it. "Brie and thyme, I think." She examines it a little closer. "They should have added some cranberry. It would have been a good balance." Hadley loves food and cooking, and everything I've tried has been delicious.

I follow her, listening to her analyze each dish and make best guesses about what each is, only taking a couple because my stomach is full of butterflies.

"You and Grey make a cute couple," Hadley muses as we peruse the dessert side, where she becomes picky, and I want to try everything.

"I'm only here to keep him safe from one of the booster's daughters."

She snickers. "Like a hot bodyguard?"

I beam. "Exactly. And thanks for the compliment. My ego needed that." I pull in a breath and stop myself from reaching for another mini chocolate something that I know will stick to my hips.

Hadley grins as she looks toward Grey and Nolan. "Are you sure he sees you as just his hot bodyguard?"

I nod. "It's Grey. He doesn't date."

"You did notice that he was contemplating ten ways of tackling Silva when we got there, right? You saw the flexed jaw? The fists?"

I take another pull from the beer because I did, and it's not the first time or even the second time he's stood up for me recently.

"I'm sure Grey is like Nolan and hates being here. I think most of them do, except for the disgusting jerks—like Hannah's ex. The good guys, the ones who recognize Silva and his opinions are absolute shit, are only here out of obligation and the chance to make money. Nolan said they can't get jobs except in short stints because they have so many practices, even in the off-season, so the sponsorships are the only way most of them can earn money."

I think of how the coach mentioned things to Grey, realizing he was doing that as a favor. I don't know the details of Grey's financial situation, but I know he doesn't come from money or have much disposable income.

Hadley's assertion has me seeing the event as one of the hundreds of games of chess I've played with Griff.

"Is my being here going to help Grey? Or will it hinder the situation? What will make him stand out and make them like him more?" I'm trusting her more than my comfort levels permit, but her feelings for Nolan and his best interest—which includes the team—make this question an exception.

"They want to know the players and learn about their lives. Not to sound like I'm supporting these archaic and sexist customs, but you look like a model, Mila. You'll make Grey look good. Like he's successful and well-rounded in all realms of his life, though this is one of the few nights they actually care about it." Hadley smiles grimly.

I glance toward Nolan and Grey again, catching Grey's stern face and Nolan's easy grin. "Should we bring them something?" I ask.

She nods, and we go through the buffet a second time.

"I have to say, this is quickly becoming a second fear of mine. Talking to strangers who have influence over my boyfriend's future is way too similar to public speaking," Hadley confides.

"Spin the conversation," I tell her. "When a booster talks to you, ask them what their greatest achievement or current goals are. Most of these people eat and breathe business. They want to talk about themselves."

Hadley's eyes grow. "That's genius." She leans closer. "I have a tube of red lipstick in my purse. If we find out what Silva drives, we can leave a warning to others..." she whispers.

I find myself smiling without thought, feeling that same niggling feeling that says I want to like her—want to trust her.

It seemed too convenient for a friendship to form between us when I was introduced to her a few months ago. I know how fleeting and shallow most relationships on the team are, but Hadley defies those perceptions, and Nolan has changed in ways I never expected. He went from being one of the most flirtatious guys on the team to not even noticing other women. I'm rooting for them.

Nolan and Grey are where we left them, only now, Palmer has joined them along with his date, a girl with dark hair, a slender nose, and pink pouty lips.

Grey's eyes meet mine as I pass him the plate of canapes and desserts. I see appreciation and a hint of question that I avoid by turning my attention to Palmer, who's surveying my plate. He grins as he lifts his gaze to my face.

"Hey, Mila. Hey, Hadley," he says, looking between us. "You two look beautiful as always." Zack Palmer is a couple of inches taller than me—when he's standing straight and has shoes on—with curly blond hair and a friendly smile that he wears like my favorite accessory. And like a golden retriever, he's loyal, filled with energy, and makes it his mission to ensure everyone feels included and happy. He's a flirt with enough confidence for three people, but he's also one of the sincerest and most genuine people I've ever known. "This is Scarlett. Scarlett, this is Grey's date, Mila, and Nolan's girlfriend, Hadley."

I juggle my food and glass again to shake her hand. "Nice to meet you."

Her smile is warm, and she doesn't look even a little nervous, though I know this is their first date. I wish I could borrow her confidence for the rest of the night.

"I see Carrie," Nolan says quietly, tracking someone in the

crowd. "I need to go talk to her. Remind her how fucking awesome our last couple of games were."

Hadley gives me a meaningful look. "Red lipstick," she whispers.

I grin before they disappear.

"And there's Barker," Palmer says. "Good luck with Linus. We'll catch you cats later." He winks at me, not making a single joke about my reason for being here. Apparently, Grey was right.

"Did I mention I owe you?" Grey asks as a man in a rich suit sets his gaze on us from a few yards away.

"Don't worry. I'll remember."

Chapter 15

Grey

"Greyson!" Mr. Potter, another booster, approaches me with his wife at his side. They own a jewelry store in Oleander Springs, and I whisper the fact to Mila to ensure she feels included. I want to whisper more things to her—brush my mouth against her ear, breathe in her perfume's light scent, and study how she leans closer as though feeling the same damn pull that I do—but I straighten my shoulders and smile in greeting.

I kissed Mila.

I kissed her, and she kissed me back, and now all I can think about is how damn badly I want to do it again.

"So glad to see you," Mr. Potter says, shaking my hand.

I nod. "You as well. This is my date, Mila Atwool."

Mr. Potter smiles warmly at her. "It's so nice to meet you. My name's Al, and this is my lovely wife, Therese."

Mila beams in response, taking his hand and then Mrs. Potter's.

"What a final game," Mrs. Potter says. "We weren't able to make it down because we had a conference in Michigan, but we recorded it and have watched it twice. It was a great way to end an amazing season."

"Thank you. I really appreciate your support. We all do," I say, placing a hand on Mila's back, feeling the curve of her spine, the gentle cadence of her breaths, and the warmth of her radiating through my palm.

"Were you able to watch the game?" Mr. Potter asks Mila.

She nods. "I went to Florida to watch."

"*Oh*," Mr. Potter says, exchanging a look with his wife and then me. "So, not *just a date*."

I should probably clarify, but I probably shouldn't have kissed her, either. There are no rules tonight, only exceptions, and I'm taking full advantage.

"Brenda, where's Scott?" Mr. Potter says, greeting another couple. "Come. Let me introduce you to Greyson Meyers and his girlfriend, Mila Atwool. In a couple of years, we'll be watching this guy on Sunday night football, telling our friends we met him."

I pose for pictures and sign a couple of autographs before they continue, and another booster, Mr. Wheeler, a local architect, greets us, striking a pose that I think is supposed to be of me from our recent bowl game.

"You had a phenomenal season, son. Is this your girlfriend? What a handsome couple you make. What's your name? Do you attend Camden?" He offers his hand to Mila.

She smiles, all grace as she fields his barrage of questions, every bit the affluent, cultured bombshell I was introduced to two and a half years ago at Hudson's dorm.

I wait for her to make a cutting or sarcastic comment about me, point out my obsessive workouts or lack of a personal life, but instead, she has him eating out of the palm of her hand. He accepts each of her smiles like tokens at an arcade, which has him telling her more stories of his life and business. When she interrupts to tell him how ads with my face would help his business, he begins prospecting all the ways he can market the idea, planning an entire year of goals that include me and all the ways our new "partnership" will take off.

Twenty minutes later, he parts with us after exchanging contact information and plans to meet next week.

I turn to Mila. Since meeting her, I've known she was an enigma, but tonight confirms as much. "I appreciate what you did there, but you don't have to do that. You don't have to sell me."

Those incredible blue-grey eyes flash to me. "You don't talk yourself up at all."

I don't have a chance to say more before another booster greets us, and then another, each time Mila is flawless, orchestrating every conversation to the tune set by our audience.

"Let's get something to drink," I say, setting my hand on Mila's back as a party of ten parts from us. They're all smiling, dazzled by Mila's charms, and we've set up a meeting with Mr. Barnhardt to play Topgolf with Mila next week.

"I don't want to sound unappreciative because I am, but this isn't why I asked you to come," I say, trying to keep my voice quiet.

She turns, looking mildly offended. "All you're doing is talking about Krueger and how great of a coach he is. You're missing opportunities to promote yourself."

"Because Krueger staying as our head coach is the priority."

"We can achieve both." Her voice is a hushed whisper.

"Greyson. You're just the person I was looking for." Linus Kemp's eyes spark with recognition as he and Emma appear in front of us.

I place a hand on Mila's back, hearing Hudson's warning.

"Nice to see you, Mr. Kemp. Emma. Please, meet my girlfriend, Mila Atwool."

"Pleasure to meet you," Mr. Kemps says, shaking her hand. "Have you two had a chance to try the food? Every time I look up, people are surrounding you."

Mila's chin notches up. "A lot of people are interested in Grey representing their businesses. He had a stellar season. Everyone knows and wants him." Her gaze slides to Emma.

"Isn't that the truth?" he says. "You've become quite the hot commodity. Oh, before I forget, I have to ask. Did I see you downtown this week at the arena for the fight between Stephens and Ford?" His gaze sparks with something as he looks at me.

The question comes out of left field. "I was only there as a spectator. I didn't participate." The guarded response makes me sound guilty as fuck, but besides having a difficult time getting employed, participating in other sports could get me kicked off of the team.

"Of course. But that was you, right? Down in Stephens's corner. Down with his trainers."

I nod. "We grew up together."

"What a small world," Linus says. "That was quite a loss."

Abe held his own far longer than I expected. For a short while, I even thought he might win. "It was a tough loss."

"Do you know how to fight? Did you train?" His eyes gleam. I'm sure he's about to share a story about his days in college.

"I did train, but I don't fight." It's a lie, but I have a feeling if I tell Mr. Kemp the entire truth, this conversation will become a scatter play.

"Of course." He looks bereft. "And Stephens has a brother. Cole Stephens, is that correct?"

I nod, uncomfortable by the bridge he's building between the two halves of my life with Mila here to pay witness.

Mr. Kemp nods. "I've heard he's quite the fighter. That he has a left roundhouse that's unstoppable."

I nod. "He's going places."

Mr. Kemp nods. "I can't wait to see it." He grins and steps forward, placing a hand on my shoulder. "But back to business. Florida was great. Wasn't it? I mean, that game couldn't have gone better."

"Coach Krueger was a huge asset. I was telling Mr. Potter how instrumental and effective he is as a coach."

Mr. Kemp's face is almost grim as he nods, forced to accept the reality.

"If they had made it to the final game, they would have won," Mila says, letting the words hang in the space between us —allowing Mr. Kemp to draw conclusions about what prevented us from the opportunity. All of us know Peters benching two of our starting players caused us to lose a critical game.

We continue making small talk, Mila dazzling him and then acting impressed as he explains his company's ventures and accomplishments. She recalls details that she peppers into the conversation to keep him talking, guiding him toward the topic of sponsorships. Once again, it's as though she's tricked him into thinking it's his idea when she laid out the vision and details pertinent to the plan. She doesn't stop at the blueprints, ensuring I'm on his calendar—at his office—to finalize the deal.

"I'll be there," Emma says, smiling.

Mila carries the conversation back to football and Camden, how amazing both are, how much Mr. Kemp benefits the school, and how excited we are for spring ball.

I realize the very worst place to be would to be on Mila's bad side because she's a mastermind.

Mr. Kemp parts, noting how late the hour is. He's smiling

wider than he had when greeting us as Emma follows him with a growing frown.

Mila turns to me, and I don't recognize her expression, only that she's nervous as she bites that spot low on the inside of her lip again. I'm about to launch into an apology, try to explain that I had been debating inviting her even before Emma because these events are unsettling and ruthless, and I'd wanted someone who'd join in making jokes and heckling the night that often felt like a cattle show.

"You lied to him. You know how to fight." Her words take me by surprise. "You're a terrible liar," she adds as an explanation. "What kind of fighting?"

My attention focuses on her and her barely apparent nerves. "Why?"

"I just want to know are we talking like karate or street fighting?"

"Street fighting?" I wince. "No. It's MMA."

Her steel eyes flash. "Could you teach me?"

"To fight?" I shake my head. "No." There's no way in hell I'd consider training Mila to get into an MMA Octagon ring and fight.

"Why?" the single word is a demand that has adrenaline spiking my blood.

"Why do you want to learn to fight?"

"Not fight. I just want you to teach me how to hit someone, to punch someone hard enough to give pause."

"Why? What happened?" I take a step closer to Mila. "Who do you want to punch?"

She rolls her eyes, attempting to deflect. "You, if you keep asking so many questions."

I don't respond with sarcasm or ignore the quip as she wants me to. "Why do you need to learn to hit someone?"

"It's not a singular person or reason." She crosses her arms over her chest.

I shake my head and turn toward the buffet, where half the team is gathered as things wind down. "I'm not training you."

Mila moves with me, stopping me. "You owe me."

"Hey!" Evelyn calls, closing the distance between us. Her smile wanes as she looks between us. "How did the night go?"

Mila's brow smooths, and she manages a half-hearted smile. "It was fine. How was yours?"

"This was nothing like the other events I've been to," Evelyn says, the apology thick in her tone. "The others all included a lot more downtime and speeches. I feel terrible that I told you we could hang back and stuff ourselves with cake, and then I didn't see you at all."

"I think it's because Peters was out," I tell them. I was never a big fan of the events that involved the mic being passed around for hours, with everyone feeling obliged to tell Peters how well he'd done. Tonight didn't allow us to hang out, but I have a feeling Krueger architected it to be like this, knowing the pain points we face because he lived them as a college athlete less than a decade ago.

Evelyn raises a brow. "But everything was okay? We don't need to grab the leftover mousse and find Emma?"

Hudson slides in behind Evelyn, a glass of water in hand as he loosens his tie, proof that tonight was exhausting.

Mila grins, a genuine smile no less stunning than the ones she flashed when impressing everyone but different all the same. This one is less rehearsed, her front teeth digging into her bottom lip rather than showing both rows of perfectly straight teeth. "I only saw her for a second," Mila says.

"Silva caught up with us, though," I say, directing my words to Hudson.

132

Hudson's gaze roves to Mila, knowing his reputation. "What did he say? I told Krueger he needs to be dealt with."

"He told me I'd be a ten if I were five inches shorter," Evelyn says. "Hudson told him he should grow a foot." She shakes her head, flashing an amused expression before taking a bite of a chocolate tart.

Mila laughs, the sound rich and full. "I hope you stared down at him."

"That man's a rattlesnake. He bites back," Evelyn says. "We had to step outside for a moment to take a little breather after that conversation to ensure Hudson didn't lose his place as captain."

Hudson silently seethes, assuring me he was ready to sacrifice more than just his position as captain.

"His divorce has turned him into a bitter asshole," I say.

"Hey," Corey says, joining us with a redhead on his arm. Palmer and his date follow with Nolan and Hadley a few steps behind.

"What a night. I barely saw you assholes," Nolan says, flashing a smile and wrapping an arm securely around Hadley. "I think Cathy got a little suspicious. I was playing Krueger up a little strong."

"Like an espresso shot," Hadley says.

Laughter spreads from those of us who know, which is everyone but Palmer's and Corey's dates.

"I might have been a little too blatant, too," Hudson says.

"So was Grey," Mila says.

"It was a good night," Palmer says, and we collectively nod, hearing the words he can't say in our mixed company. The last thing we need is rumors that we're trying to overthrow our head coach—not that we can, just that we're doing everything to influence those who could.

"We should get going so the staff can get this cleaned up," I say, thinking of my mom and all the nights she got home late due to stragglers while working at the diner in Highgrove for over a decade.

The others move, though their actions are slow with silent protests, wanting to spend time together. We've seen less of each other than usual without school and regular practices.

"I'm going to need you guys to come over soon to try some recipes because that sweet onion tart was insanely good, and that bruschetta..." Hadley says. "I think if I kick the acidity up a little, the bruschetta could be even better, but those onion tarts were perfection. I might email the catering company and see if they'll divulge their secrets."

"That would be fun," Evelyn says. "Text me and let me know what we can bring."

We finally reach the doors leading us outside. The icy wind has everyone kicking it into gear, forgetting about plans or small talk as we exchange a quick round of goodbyes and part ways, heading for the warmth of our own vehicles.

Hudson and Evelyn are the only ones in our direction. The girls huddle together as we cross the parking lot. "Think it will snow?" Evelyn asks.

Mila glances at the sky as she shakes her head. "It's too clear."

"We have to stop at the dorm because I need to grab laundry," Hudson says. "We'll be at the apartment later."

"And, I promise, we'll gorge on cake this weekend," Evelyn adds.

Mila smiles. "Don't worry about the cake. Drive safely!" She waves as they veer off, heading for Hudson's Jeep.

I unlock the passenger side of my truck and pull open the door for Mila, offering her my hand, which she eyes like a bear trap before gingerly taking it and climbing inside.

"Who do you want to hit?" I ask once settled in the driver's seat, the engine running.

"Whoever deserves to be hit."

"So you're planning a vigilante movement? Have you figured out a name? A costume?"

"Don't be an asshole. Regardless of what society says, it's not a good look on anyone, even you."

"But if I wasn't a dick, you might learn to tolerate me."

"Unlikely."

"I didn't invite you to impress everyone."

"I don't care why you invited me. You said you owed me, and I want you to teach me how to hit someone."

I grip the steering wheel, waiting for the engine to warm. "Hitting someone isn't as simple as forming a fist and punching. There are other things you need to consider."

"Like what?"

"Like their height, your angle, how close they are. Nine times out of ten, you're better off walking away."

"I don't need it to be perfect. I'm not looking to be scored."

"Why in the hell do you want to learn to hit someone?"

Mila

I shake my head and debate dropping the subject of Grey teaching me how to throw a punch. "I just want to be able to feel safe. That's all."

I expect him to laugh, maybe even mock me, but Grey's eyes seem to darken as we stare at one another for a silent moment.

"From whom?"

"Do you remember when I told you someone broke into my apartment?"

He nods.

"I *was* home when they broke in."

He stops breathing.

"Why do you do that? I swear..." I poke him in the side. He doesn't even flinch, but he catches my hand in his much warmer one, and memories from our kiss flood my mind—his hands on my skin, and his mouth devouring me. I convince myself the shock, the lack of food, and the fact I haven't kissed anyone in months made that kiss seem different as I pull my hand away. "Are you part vampire or something? Why do you hold your breath and go completely still?"

"What happened?"

"Nothing," is my automatic response.

"Mila..."

I pull in a breath and let it sit in my chest as I draw on the memories. "I was still awake. I hadn't been able to sleep and had this weird gut feeling." I shake my head. "I heard the lock click and hid in my closet, where I pulled a bunch of clothes over myself."

I pinch my forefinger and thumb together, using the familiarity of the five-finger relaxation technique I was taught over a decade ago to calm my nerves. I don't often think of what each finger is meant to represent as I subtly pinch each fingertip to my thumb. I've been doing it so long that the motion lends the comfort I'm seeking.

Grey stares at my hands but doesn't say anything.

I clear my throat. "He turned on the lights and dug through my things. I thought he was there to rob me, but then he started talking to me, like he knew I was hiding, telling me he saw my car and wanted to talk to me."

"Did you know who he was?"

"He was the maintenance guy of the apartment building."

Grey's eyes grow round, and I see the questions he wants to ask—is afraid to ask—as he stares at me.

I shake my head. "I texted the police, and they came and arrested him while he was still in my apartment."

"Tell me he's in jail."

"His only crime was trespassing. He claimed he'd taken too many painkillers and was confused about the time, so he'd just come to check on the faucet he'd replaced the week before."

Grey clenches his jaw so hard I'm unsure how his teeth remain intact. "Does he try and contact you? Have you seen him again?"

I shake my head. "No, but stupid things trigger me, like someone trying to open the connecting door at the hotel that leads me to do embarrassing things like beg my best friend's teammate to sleep on their couch." I try to lighten the mood with a smirk.

Grey doesn't crack even the hint of a smile.

"I'm not looking for vengeance or a fight. I just don't want to be afraid. I hate feeling helpless." Blood drains from my face as I pinch my fingertips again, trying to calm my racing heart.

Grey's eyes dance over me, and I can't read his thoughts for what feels like the hundredth time tonight. The man is and always has been a giant question mark, which makes keeping him at arm's length so much easier.

"We'll meet tomorrow."

"Tomorrow?"

He nods. "We'll need an hour."

Relief is a warm breeze on my face, the first snowflakes falling, the crisp perfection of clean sheets.

"I'll be by at seven."

"Do I need anything?"

"Dress warmly."

I stare at Grey and wait for more instruction, but he reaches for his tie, loosening the knot instead of saying anything. He raises his chin and releases the top couple of buttons with one hand, using a practiced grace that's hard to look away from. He sighs, a deep rumbling noise that pulls too many questions to the forefront of my thoughts, recalling the way it felt to swallow a similar sound, the way his arm and hand had tightened, pulling me closer as he kissed me.

"That's why you moved back home," Grey says, popping my thoughts like soap bubbles as he shakes his head. "How did he not get charged?"

I turn my gaze to the windshield and take a steadying breath. "My parents tried to get something more done, and I think the police wanted to, but he didn't do anything except come in uninvited and rummage through my stuff."

Grey pulls in a breath, drumming his thumb against the steering wheel to a silent beat.

I consider admitting the sight of old white Ford trucks always has a sense of cold dread flushing through my veins. How my memories are unstable like hydrogen, easily bonding with other past nightmares and making my fears sometimes feel like a handicap. Instead, I try my best to assure us both. "I haven't seen him since."

Grey doesn't appear even slightly appeased, but he drives me home without question or a single mention of our shared kiss.

Chapter 16

Mila

Grey knocks five minutes before seven. I've already drunk three coffees, and as I reach for the door with a trembling hand, I realize I probably should have eaten something to soak up some of the caffeine and residual nerves that kept me awake into the early morning.

He stands on the front doorstep wearing a pair of gray sweatpants and a dark blue Camden sweatshirt, the morning fog a soft background behind him.

His gaze crosses over my tennis shoes, joggers, and zip-up sweatshirt before meeting my gaze. "Ready?"

"Are we going outside?"

He nods.

I grab my keys and set the alarm. "There's a gym here or a large green space," I motion to the left, where the field is usually empty.

"Today, we're just going to run and do some stretches."

"*Today?*"

"If you want to be able to hit someone, you're going to need to train, and that begins with conditioning."

My shoes become leaden as I shake my head, betrayal and anger bitter in my mouth. "We had a deal."

Grey lifts his chin, his hair isn't styled this morning, but somehow looking even better than last night. "And I'm here, honoring it."

I shake my head, wanting to glare at him and withdraw— old habits I had to break through and overcome years ago with the help of multiple therapists. I find myself once again pinching my fingers, searching for a sense of calmness that allows me to breathe through my annoyance. "I just want to learn to punch someone in the face."

"And what do you think will happen if you hit someone?"

"If I do it right, I'm hoping they'll bleed."

"They hit you back," he says. "If you want to take your fear back from this asshole, you'll have to learn more than just how to hit someone. You need to know when and where to hit them and be sure you can get away."

I press both index fingers to the inner corners of my eyes. "Can't you just teach me how to do some kind of fighter move that debilitates them long enough for me to call the cops?"

"What if you lose your phone or they take it from you?"

"And what happens if aliens from outer space abduct me? There will always be a dozen scenarios, but at least being able to hit someone hard enough to stun them would be a good starting point."

He crosses his arms over his chest, the image of stubbornness as I imagine stakes in his heels digging into the ground. "If you want to learn how to fight, we're doing it my way."

"Who said anything about fighting? I want to learn some self-defense maneuvers."

"Then join a class at the Y."

My gaze narrows, accusing him of going back on his word. "You said you'd teach me."

"And I will."

I grind my teeth together to stop the flood of annoyance that carries accusations aimed straight at Grey.

"Afraid you can't do it?" Challenge flares in his eyes, shoving me though he doesn't move.

"Are you seriously goading me?"

He unfolds his arms, reaches into his pocket, and pulls out his cell phone. "You have two minutes to decide."

"Decide on what?"

"If we're going to do this or not. If not, I've got better things to do than argue with you about technique over strength."

Better things to do.

His words feel like a rejection with every second that ticks by, making me yearn to cancel and forget the deal, forget that he owes me, and more specifically, why, but pride plants its flag.

"Good. If you're going to waste my time, it only seems fair that I waste yours."

I turn and start running, following the path connecting to the nearby greenway, like a giant spiderweb of interconnecting trails across Oleander Springs.

"You need to stretch first," Grey calls.

I flip him off, refusing to do this entirely his way.

"You're going to regret it," he warns, but he doesn't insist we stop or slow down as he matches my pace.

With pride in the driver's seat, boredom and pain quickly shove into the passenger side as I push myself to continue, ignoring how my muscles protest, and the stitch in my side becomes a second pulse. I hate running. I joke with Evelyn that the only thing I'll ever chase is Henry Cavill or a sale on a pair of Manolo Blahnik heels. I feel too big and awkward, my strides are somehow both too short and too long, and that doesn't even cover the discomfort in my breasts.

Grey says nothing.

I'm not sure how long we run for, only that sheer will prevents me from stopping or complaining. When we return to my apartment, sweat has my clothes feeling sticky and uncomfortable, and my hair is plastered to the back of my neck. My breaths are literal heaves, and my ears ache from the cold, combined with my internal temperature being too hot.

"Let's stretch," Grey says.

"Now?" I ask, through heavy breaths.

He nods, stopping near the edge of the field where he bends at the waist, touching his palms to the grassy space.

I bend over and barely touch the tops of my ankles. As if that run or my heavy breathing wasn't enough to prove I'm out of shape, this confirms it.

Thankfully, Grey doesn't comment, but I know he notices. He notices everything.

We continue doing a series of stretches, moves I haven't done in years, some ever, and like the basic stretch to touch the ground, I fail at each of them.

"You need to make sure you're stretching your hamstrings more," Grey says.

I shift my gaze to him as he moves closer to me. Grey in a tux is something to celebrate, but Grey in sweatpants, his sleeves pushed up to his elbows to reveal the ropes of muscles down both arms paired with a fresh gleam of sweat, is a thirst trap.

Once again, I have to swallow my objections and tell him I can do it myself. Independence has always been my greatest strength and weakness.

Maybe he sees my reluctance or is beginning to realize just how hard it is for me to trust because his gaze softens fractionally.

"It will prevent your muscles from getting sore and cramping."

I give a brief nod of acquiescence.

"Lie on your back."

If I weren't already sweaty and gross, I'd grumble about lying on the wet grass that will be filled with fire ants come spring. Grey squats near my legs, close enough that I smell cedar and sandalwood.

My heartbeats quicken as he leans closer.

"Extend both arms and place your palms face down at your sides." He moves even closer, his knee brushing my thigh. "Now, keep this leg straight," he moves to straddle my right leg, "and lift your left leg." He's already lifting my leg, though, crawling up my body on his freaking knees.

If I weren't already battling filthy thoughts thanks to our kiss last night, I would be now.

My thighs clench and heat blooms low in my belly, growing as he runs one large hand along the outside of my knee.

"Keep both legs straight." He props my foot against his shoulder. His knee is inches away from the apex of my thighs, and I can barely even think about it because he runs his hand over my leg again, instructing me to relax as he leans over me, his broad shoulders eclipsing the sky entirely.

After a few moments, he tells me to switch legs, and he moves to straddle my opposite leg and prop the other against his shoulder. He wraps a hand around my thigh as he inches forward. I can't breathe. I can't stop imagining him naked.

Grey glances down at me, his fingers constricting against my thigh. "Try and relax."

The thought of him thrusting inside of me does anything but make my muscles relax.

When he moves away, I'm hit by a sudden wave of disappointment that makes everything feel unfamiliar.

"What next?" I ask.

Grey shakes his head. "We do it again tomorrow."

I sputter. "What?"

"We have to start with cardio. In a few weeks, you'll be ready to start shadowboxing."

"*Weeks?*"

He raises a brow. "You're out of shape." Obviously. His assessment still stings, like being told my favorite pair of jeans makes my butt look big. "It's going to be a few weeks until you're ready."

I staple my hands to my sides so my knuckles don't drag across the ground—not that they could. I've already proven I'm not flexible enough for that, but every muscle in me is so fatigued it feels plausible.

"If you pick up and do some extra training on your own, it'll go faster."

If my brain weren't so addled with exhaustion, I'd like to believe I'd be returning a snappy comeback that would prevent my pride from feeling so bruised. "I'm going to hate you if you make me do this daily."

He raises one sweat-free brow, his hair still dry and his face not even pink. "I thought you already did?"

"If you're gaslighting me, I swear, I'm—"

He shakes his head. "This is how it works. Drink plenty of water," he tells me, and then he turns, moving toward the parking lot without another word.

I unlock the apartment and disarm the alarm before kicking off my shoes, a chill running through me as my heart rate slows and my damp clothes settle against my skin.

I head up to my room, where my gaze locks on my reflection for two horrified seconds. I take in the extreme redness of my cheeks and the whisps of hair clinging to me before I tear myself away so I don't continue to scrutinize myself.

I turn the shower past hot straight to scalding and stand under the spray, debating if training with Grey is what I really want or if it's actually a terrible idea wrapped with good intent like other grand ideas I've had. I have examples of these bad ideas in my copy of *The Guinness Book of World Records*, where I've marked every record I thought we should try—imagined us winning—and never did.

I pull on a clean pair of sweats and head back downstairs, questioning whether another coffee would be a bad idea with my heart currently feeling so off rhythm from the exertion.

I eat a bowl of cereal instead and devote the rest of my Sunday to the confines of my room with a book.

I'm still lost in the pages of a book when Evelyn knocks on my bedroom door.

"Are you still hibernating?" She had come by earlier, asking if I wanted to hang out with her and Hudson, but I declined, knowing how little time Hudson has before the weight of responsibilities as team captain return.

"It was a good day for it," I say, hearing the rain dance across the roof. "How has your day been?"

"Good. We were thinking about getting Chinese food. You want to come?"

"Well, if you're going to twist my arm..." I tease, moving to stand. My thighs and shins burn a protest before I can get upright.

"Are you okay?" Evelyn asks.

"No," I gasp. "How do you run every day? *Why* do you run every day?" Evelyn ran every morning during the summer and most of autumn. She's recently taken to running in the afternoon or sometimes in the gym here at the apartment. "And why do I hurt so bad?"

Evelyn looks confused. "You were running?"

"Yes," I croak, finally standing.

"Was someone chasing you?"

"Ha-ha," I say mirthlessly.

145

"You hate running."

"I know."

"When did you go running?"

"This morning."

Her gaze narrows with a fresh set of confusion. "Where was I?"

"Sleeping."

She shakes her head. "Why are you being so cryptic? I need details."

I heave a long sigh as I consider where and *how* to start this conversation. "As restitution for that fake date, Grey agreed to teach me how to hit someone so that when we eventually run across the next skeevy jerk at a game or bar, I can punch him in the face. *But* he failed to mention cardio being a part of this plan until showing up this morning with little more instruction than to run."

Evelyn's eyes slam open. "He's teaching you how to hit someone?"

"He has a friend in the MMA scene and apparently trained with him."

"Seriously?" She shares my bewilderment.

I shrug. "News to me, too." I wince with every step I take to my closet.

"How far did you run?" she asks.

"Too far."

"Did you stretch?"

"Afterward."

She flinches. "How long are you doing this? Like once a week?"

"Daily?"

Her lips slip apart with surprise. "Every day?"

"Don't."

"What?" Her voice rises, feigning innocence, but I see how her eyes shine with hope and intention.

"I know where your thoughts are going, and you need to reel that shit in because it's not happening." Evelyn has been hoping that Grey and I will become something since she arrived this summer.

"It might happen."

I give her a severe look of warning. "It's not."

"He wants to see you every day."

I shake my head. "Grey and I will never happen. We are the definition of acquaintances, two people who get along for the benefit of others who matter to us."

"You like Grey, and you trust him."

"Because he's Hudson's closest friend on the team. We're doing this because he owes me for going with him to that booster event. It's a transaction."

Evelyn sits on the edge of my bed, her hands resting on her thighs. "I can show you some stretches that might help while you go through the worst of the muscle pains. The first week will be the worst. If you stretch before and after, it will help, and so will hydrating—water, not coffee."

"This just keeps getting less and less enticing."

Chapter 17

Grey

Mila is wincing and stiff as she follows me to the field beside her apartment, but she doesn't say anything.

I knew she'd be sore from running yesterday. "Want to stretch today?"

She stares daggers at me before she bends to try and touch her toes.

I grin, pulling my foot up to stretch my quad.

"How do you not have an accent?"

That steel in her gaze fractures as she sits, bending her knees and pressing the soles of her shoes together. "You don't have much of one, either."

"I do when I drink," I admit.

"Alex is from New York, and Jon is from Colorado."

"But you lived in Oklahoma for seven years."

She stares at me for a minute before moving to the next stretch, extending a leg in front of her and looking at the gap between her fingers and toe, making me believe she's not going to respond.

"I had a lot of tutors after I was adopted. One was a stickler for speech."

"They made you lose your accent?"

Mila scoffs. "Don't try and twist it into something ugly. I couldn't read or do basic math when I moved here. I didn't know anything about science, space, or geography. Believe me when I say I wasn't sad to leave any part of my past behind, accent included." She stands, reaching an arm across her body.

Once again, the image of Mila as a child transforms slightly as I try to piece together these hints of her past. A dozen new questions percolate in my thoughts, wondering what happened with her parents and what a seven-year-old Mila with a Southern accent and no formal education was like? Was she just as stubborn? Just as willful? Did she stare down grown men even then?

"Are you done?" Mila asks, swinging her arms to her sides.

I should insist she stretches more, knowing how sore she is, but before I can respond, she turns and starts running, taking the same path we did yesterday.

* * *

"There he is!" Mr. Potter beams.

Days ago, I thought my only chance of getting a sponsorship was at the mercy of Linus Kemp—or potentially his daughter Emma. Never, did I expect so many emails and calls from boosters vying for my time and offering contracts and paid sponsorships.

I've never been to one of the jewelry stores Mr. Potter and his wife own. They have three locations, and I'm at the original today. It's pure class. Bright, warm lights shine all around the store, making it feel like the sun is in here. Glass cases line the walls, and several more form an island in the middle of the floor. A glint catches my eye, and I stare at a pool of diamonds. I think of Cole, adding this to our list of experiences right up there with Vegas suites and private jets. I want to be able to walk in here, have my mom pick out a birthday present, and buy it with cash.

"How are you, Greyson?" Mr. Potter asks. "Can I get you something to drink?"

I shake my head. "No thanks, Mr. Potter. This is quite the place you have here."

He raises his chin with pride. I like Mr. Potter. Of all our boosters, he's one of the friendliest and easiest to get along with, constantly bragging about his wife, Therese. They've been married for thirty years, and he thinks the world begins and ends with her.

"My wife did most of the designing. Lovely, isn't it? She hoped to make it, but she's at one of our other locations today." He glances around the store with a similar note of adoration that he gives Mrs. Potter, as though enough memories have been made here that he senses her even when she's not here.

"Are we ready?" A woman with magenta-colored hair and deep purple eyeshadow steps forward with a camera in her hands.

"We should probably sign the contract really quickly and be sure to get this in your hands." Mr. Potter slips a folded check from his breast pocket and places it in my hand.

It's my first paycheck associated with football, and damn, does it feel good.

"You're late," Cole yells as I step into the small gym located between Highgrove and Oleander Springs. This is where Cole met Mackey and where we trained for three months. We worked to convince Mackey to take him on because he wasn't looking for any trainees, knowing how few make it beyond the first year.

"I had that sponsorship thing. I texted you." I let my bag hit the floor before grabbing a jump rope to get warmed up, despite my morning workout with Mila. It's our fifth day working out, and like during the summer months when the team begins our strenuous workouts to prepare for the season, the results are slow.

"What sponsorship thing?" Dustin asks, applying a fresh layer of tape to his knuckles.

"A photoshoot," Cole tells him.

Mackey scoffs and shakes his head. "Don't get soft on us."

"Our boy is going to be famous." Cole punches his gloves together.

"Work out his bad mood." Mackey shucks a thumb at Cole. "He came in with a hangover and has been bitching about everything this morning." He runs a hand over his bald head before slipping his hat back on and running a hand over his goatee. He moved here twenty years ago from New Jersey, though his thick accent makes most assume it was more recent. My thoughts briefly veer to what Mila had told me when I brought up her lack of an accent.

I wasn't sad to leave any part of my past behind.

The words have followed me all week.

I turn raised brows to Cole. It's not judgment but a question. Normally, he only drinks after a fight.

He shrugs, but the agitation on his face says there was a reason. Cole flips Mackey off. "Come on, old man, I'll remind you how slow you are." He taps his gloves again.

I have no idea how old Mackey is, but if I were pressed to guess, I'd say mid to upper fifties. Regardless, he's yoked—a life-long gym rat I'd never cross or dare to sneak up on despite him being a foot shorter than me.

Mackey waves a hand at Cole as proof of said bad mood. "Straighten him out for me. Will you, Meyers?"

Cole's eyes blaze with a hunger for fighting, but before I can respond, Abe steps forward from where he's been working with a heavy bag and climbs into the ring. "Let's dance."

Mackey closes his eyes briefly, likely sending a silent prayer.

Dustin steps up beside me as I lower the jump rope, and we watch the brothers pull on gloves, my own palms itching to feel the material slide into place.

As always, Abe lunges, always the first one off the mark. He relies entirely on speed and strength, two things that have managed to get him farther than I would have imagined considering how his temper blinds him. He lands a hit and then a second before Cole goes on the offensive, knocking him off balance and striking fast and hard. Cole stuns Abe before he follows the impact with several more hits, quickly pushing Abe straight into a corner where his fight-or-flight instincts take over. His eyes glaze over with the same murderous rage he perfected before elementary school that used to make students and teachers alike fear him.

Cole isn't rattled by the stare or the crazed battle cry Abe makes around his mouthpiece before charging for Cole.

"Like a fucking bull," Mackey says, throwing up a hand.

Cole anticipates the move as quickly as we do, dancing out of his way and working on wearing him out as we've strategized will be the goal with his fight in March against Scooter.

Cole tires of the game first, clearly looking for someone to hit before he lands another series of hits to Abe that has him falling before Mackey calls it quits.

Abe spits out his mouthguard, blood and saliva following it. "You bastard. That was a cheap shot."

Mackey sets his hands on my shoulders. "Get Cole out while I go hang Abe up by his fucking toenails until some sense runs back into that brick he calls a brain."

Dustin and I don't try to stop Cole from prowling after his brother, knowing that will only make things worse. Instead, we don our sweatshirts and wait until Mackey yells at them both and forces Cole to take a walk.

Cole rips off his gloves, throwing them at Abe before spitting out his mouthguard and pulling a tee over his head. He pulls the door open, making the bells tied to it clang as Mackey swears again.

It's warm today, nearly seventy, making me regret my sweatshirt as we follow Cole down the sidewalk of the old strip mall. We round the corner where a couple of women step out of a shop, startled by Cole's proximity and then smile upon a closer inspection.

During the season, it's hard to make it out here as often as I'd like, but during breaks, I make the trip daily, to help Cole pursue his dreams just as he did mine when giving me the opportunity to step onto the field and impress our athletic director. That day, he gave me the keys to my future, and I'll be damned if I don't try and reciprocate.

Chapter 18

Mila

"Are you excited to go home to New Mexico?" I ask Evelyn as we take the same route Grey and I have been running every morning for the past six days.

It's the first time I've braved running a second run in the same day, and already I want to quit. I'm still not sure how Evelyn finds enjoyment or peace while running when all I can think about is how long until we can stop.

"I'm still undecided," Evelyn says as a man on a bicycle passes us. "My parents still refuse to be in a room together, and with classes starting the day after we get home, I kind of wish we canceled."

"It's going to be good for you guys, and if you start to feel stressed out, just remember you have three days of relaxation at the end of your trip while staying at an all-inclusive resort."

Hudson had been worried that the Christmas gift he gave to Evelyn would be misconstrued, but I assured him it was a good idea, reminding him how nervous Evelyn was to return home this year with her parents' recent divorce and the myriad of changes she was dreading.

Evelyn's face flushes, and a goofy grin crosses her features. It's her Hudson face.

"Besides, most of the professors will be exhausted after our six-week break and won't want to jump into anything, either. The first week or two will be slow, and come March, Hudson will be drowning in practices again, so this was a good idea."

I try my damnedest to sound convincing because inside, I'm curled in the fetal position, realizing my two best friends will be gone an entire week, and I won't even have classes to distract me. My parents being home is my silver lining.

We run a mile and a half down where the trail intercedes with Birch Park, home of the springs that Oleander Springs was named after. The popular park draws tourists hundreds of years later with the lore that the springs contain healing powers. It's one of the largest parks in the city, sprawling several acres with multiple playgrounds, walking trails, soccer fields, and more. I've been taking the same route with Grey every morning.

Evelyn coughs and slows to a stop. I had been worried I'd slow her down, but the cool afternoon has her asthma flaring.

"Want to sit?" I ask.

She shakes her head and places both hands above her head, prompting thoughts of Grey telling me to do the same, explaining that doing so would open my lungs.

A tightness forms in my stomach. I've been trying to forget how it felt to be kissed by Grey, but the memory slams into me sometimes, distracting me from all coherent thoughts.

Evelyn coughs again. The dry, high-pitched sound chills me. She's never been afraid of her asthma, but the condition has consumed my thoughts more than once. Sometimes her attacks can be so sudden and intense.

Evelyn pulls in a slow breath through her nose and blows it

out even slower through her lips. I strive to appear calm while watching her even though I'm not.

"My feet are killing me. Let's sit for just a minute."

Evelyn doesn't buy my story for even a second, her shoulders slumping. "I'm sorry. You're working so hard."

"I refuse your apology," I tell her, linking my sweatshirt-covered arm with hers. Evelyn is painfully independent, a perfectionist, and above all, loyal. I hate that she feels even an ounce of guilt for us stopping.

We cross the parking lot to reach the benches that line the park and sit across from a group of adults doing CrossFit. Evelyn's shoulder brushes mine as she reaches for her inhaler and pulls the medicine into her lungs. While we wait for it to work, I watch the class roll giant tires and lift heavy ropes. They're constantly releasing battle cries and groaning, their faces twisted with exertion. I wonder if this is how I look when I work out.

A man from the CrossFit class sets down a pair of ropes and walks to the edge of the field near us. He's tall and bulky, his long hair pulled back in a man bun. He shoots a snot rocket, adjusts himself, and then hocks a loogie before his gaze collides with us. Rather than appear sheepish, a wolfish smile crests his lips.

It's petty and vain that his attention makes me feel good about myself. Most mornings while working out with Grey, my ensemble of baggy sweats, messy bun, and no makeup have guys looking past me like I don't exist. Of course, it would be the guy who shoots snot rockets who doesn't find me completely unremarkable.

I look away before he considers coming closer.

Evelyn chuckles, but the sound is still too high.

A cooler with a handwritten dollar sign taped to the front catches my attention. I find a small handful of singles in my jacket. Thank goodness I never clean out my pockets. "They have water," I say, knowing hydration helps during her attacks. "I'll be right back."

I cross the damp grass to the cooler, shove a single into the crayon box marked "Cash," and fish out a water bottle.

As I stand, a feeling of unease crosses my shoulders and has my spine snapping straight. Audiences often joke about intuition in movies, whether a character possesses too much or not enough, which has always led me to question if my own instincts are faulty since they're always on high alert. Goose bumps pepper my skin, and adrenaline heats my blood as my gaze shoots to Evelyn, ensuring she's okay and conscious. She's still on the bench, but a man is beside her, offering her something.

Having lived with so many strangers over the years, faces and even builds and mannerisms can tickle at being familiar, and as I jog back across the field, something about this man niggles at my awareness, taunting me that I know him.

My heart beats faster and harder with every step I take to close the distance and see more than the stranger's back and dark curly hair.

He turns to walk away before I can reach Evelyn, a water bottle in her hand.

"Don't drink that," I call, raising my hand to catch Evelyn's attention.

The man stops and turns, his dark hair catching the single ray of sunshine in the muted afternoon. My heart feels like it stops as my feet speed up. His narrow frame, gaunt cheekbones, straight nose, and thin mouth are the same. But how? Why? If I were in a movie right now, I'd be the character everyone was rolling their eyes over because I'm refusing to believe it's him, though I know it is.

Julian Holloway, the man who broke into my apartment

last year, stares at me. "Mila," he says my name with a note of familiarity that shoots adrenaline through my bloodstream.

"What are you doing here?"

He raises both hands. "I work here." He slowly points at a riding lawnmower in the distance. "I was making sure she was okay."

Evelyn stands and comes to my side. "Should I call Hudson?"

I move, standing in front of her. "Leave us alone, or I'll call the police."

He cocks his head as though trying to process my warning. His eyes turn sinister, and he takes a step toward us. "What are you going to tell them? This is where I work now after you got me fired." Agitation lines each of his punctuated words.

"You got yourself fired," I snap back.

"I was just trying to talk to you."

I shake my head and take two steps back, shuffling Evelyn with me. "You broke into my apartment, psycho!" I regret the insult as soon as it leaves my lips.

I know from years of living with people whose tempers were as fragile as their egos that insults only escalate a tense situation, but thirteen and a half years of not having to worry about retaliation that came in the form of being beaten, starved, or stolen from has me forgetting the survival skills I honed at a young age.

Evelyn gasps as her hand grips the back of my sweatshirt, tugging me backward another step.

Rage contorts his features as he takes three steps toward us. "You ignored me for years, you bitch. What was I supposed to do?"

Three women and a man from the CrossFit group approach us. "Is there a problem?" a woman in her early forties with dark hair and shoulders that look like she could bench press me asks.

Julian once again raises both hands. "No problem. I was just trying to help."

The dark-haired woman looks at me for verification, but I can't respond because the word "years" is eddying in my thoughts.

"Years?"

Julian's expression turns savage, and then he turns toward the riding lawn mower across from us.

"Are you guys okay?" a woman with blonde pigtails asks us.

"No," Evelyn says.

My chest is tight, I'm sweating and shaking, and my mouth is dry. It's the beginning of a panic attack. I immediately think of the balance of stars and the analogy that first therapist helped me learn.

I blow out a breath as slowly as possible, searching for four things to lock my gaze upon, followed by three sounds and two scents, knowing I need to keep it together for both of us right now.

I wish I could call Jon and Alex and ask them to come and get us. They would. They'd drop everything and be here, but they're on a flight heading for us.

Unease crawls up my spine as I turn my attention to the strangers, realizing I need to ask for help outside my tiny circle. It makes me itch with discomfort. "Would you guys mind staying with us for a minute? I'm just going to see if we can get a ride."

"Is that guy bothering you? Should we call the cops?" a girl with black hair and friendly brown eyes asks, glancing toward Julian.

"Yes," Evelyn says. "We should."

"He was in a holding cell overnight for breaking into my

apartment," I remind her. "There's no way he'll get arrested for giving you a water bottle in a public park."

"He admitted to following you. For *years*."

Chills race down my arms.

The strangers stare at me. "That's serious shit," the brunette says.

Evelyn's uneven breaths are a taunt, threatening to overwhelm me.

"I'm going to get us a ride. You need to use your inhaler again."

I grip my phone, trying to stop myself from shaking as I, once again, push outside of the comfort zone that wants me to message only Hudson. I add Palmer, Nolan, Corey, Grey, Hannah, and Hadley and send a group text requesting a ride. It's vague. Hudson will be annoyed I lacked any sense of urgency, but it feels like taking a step on the moon as I wait to see if one of them replies.

> Hadley: I am checking out at Target now. I can be there in 25 minutes. Is that too long?

> Hannah: I'm home. I can be there in 15.

> Corey: We just got out of practice. If Hudson can't come, I'll leave here in 5.

> Hudson: I'm on my way now.

My chest warms, and I know later I'll feel particularly sappy about how fast they all volunteered to help. "Hudson's coming," I tell Evelyn.

I receive a separate text outside of the group message from Grey.

Grey: What's going on?

I hesitate, unsure what to say, unsure if I want to tell him that the guy who motivated me to learn how to defend myself is here now—and has been for years.

My pulse still gallops in my chest, recalling every white Ford pickup truck I've seen over the past few months. Past few years.

The strangers invite us to sit on a blanket placed in the middle of the field, surrounded by the CrossFit class. My thoughts are splintered in so many directions, my head aches, and I can't bring myself to care that I feel like a goldfish as curious and watchful eyes keep tabs on us.

Hudson pulls up twenty minutes later. I notice him immediately.

He jogs to the field, scanning the area. When his gaze stops on us, confusion pulls at his brow and has him sprinting in our direction. The three women who had come over to help with Julian move to our side with two others.

"We know him," I assure them as Hudson stops beside us.

Hudson looks from them to us. "What happened? Are you guys okay?"

Evelyn nods before glancing at me, inviting me to share the details.

Hudson stares at me. "Mila?" He turns to look at the fields, his jaw already strained as though anticipating a fight. He's likely imagining one of these CrossFit guys did or said something that explains our unease.

I don't want to be here for another second. I'm not sure when or if I'll ever be able to run this same path again or return to the park. "We should go," I tell him. I turn to the strangers who pulverized my suspicious tendencies and thank them for their time and help.

Hudson looks between us a final time and slowly nods before leading us to his Jeep. I scan the parking lot for what feels like the hundredth time, searching for a white Ford truck I don't find.

Not finding that small piece of certainty that allowed me to know it was him feels like losing something significant. Aside from the crawling feeling across my skin, his truck was the only definitive sign of him. I recognized it from seeing it around the apartment complex during the six months I lived there. I knew the rusted fender, the Phillies' bumper sticker, and the long scratch down the left side. Soon after he broke in, I realized he was around too frequently, driving by nearly every day when I'd leave for class.

"Did you have an asthma attack?" Hudson asks when we hit the main road.

"Julian Holloway was there," I say.

Hudson whips his head around to look at me in the back seat, his knuckles straining white. "What?"

"He works there."

"What happened?"

"I was having an asthma attack, and Mila went to grab me water. He came and talked to me while she was gone," Evelyn says.

Hudson turns to her for half a beat before focusing on the road. "What did he say? Exactly."

"He asked me if I was okay and if I needed to call anyone."

"That's it?"

"He gave me water."

"Did he see you, Mila? Did he recognize you? How do you know he works there?" Hudson fires off the questions as his gaze flicks to mine again in the rearview mirror.

"Yeah. He told me he works there." I work to recall what he said, but his expressions and tone are all I can think about.

Hudson pulls into our apartment complex, getting waved forward by the guards before he has to roll down the window. No one moves as Hudson turns off the engine.

"He was angry," Evelyn says. "He accused Mila of getting him fired and for ignoring him for *years*."

Hudson's eyes turn sharp. "Years? What the fuck does that mean?"

I shake my head, clinging to the numbness keeping me afloat. "I don't know."

"Let's go inside. We'll figure this out," Evelyn says, opening the passenger door.

Evelyn sits at the kitchen table while Hudson leans against the wall. Like me, he's too tense to sit.

I hear his silent questions as though they're in my own head, *Am I sure it was him? Why would he be looking for me? Why would he approach Evelyn? How concerned should we be?*

"It doesn't make any sense," I tell him.

"It's never made sense, Mila." He runs a hand down his face. "None of it. Why did he show up that night? How did he know you were home? How did he know you were alone?" He shakes his head. "How long has he been following you?"

I cross my arms to hide the fact my hands are shaking. "There's no way he's been following me. I would have noticed. You would have noticed."

He releases a heavy breath. I loathe the pity that softens his familiar gaze. "Do you still have that police officer's contact information?"

"What am I going to say? A guy offered my best friend water and then returned to work?"

Hudson leans his head back against the wall. "We have to at least try."

"Did you meet him before the apartment?" Evelyn asks.

I shake my head. "Never."

Hudson pulls in a long breath. "Mila, we need to tell the others. We need to tell your parents."

Griffin is a whiz at chess. One of his favorite pastimes is learning uncommon moves that can only be used under rare circumstances. Today—now—feels like one of those instances when the rules change entirely.

"If he's following you, we need to report it. Maybe it could bump up his charges."

I nod though my confidence for that happening is a sunken ship. Our system isn't set up to prevent most things. My childhood attests to this fact.

"Maybe we should cancel our trip," Evelyn says.

My attention snaps to her. "No. No way."

"What if he's stalking you?" she asks.

"I'll stay with my parents." I glance at the clock on the microwave. "Speaking of which, we're going to be late for dinner. We need to get ready."

Evelyn looks at Hudson, trying to gauge his thoughts.

"No way are you guys canceling your trip," I insist, refusing to allow Julian freaking Holloway to change one more damn thing in my life.

"Let's get ready," Hudson says.

"Let's have fun tonight. I don't want to talk about him. I'll tell my parents tomorrow. I haven't seen them since September. I just want to have fun and celebrate your last night here."

"Pack to stay the entire week. I don't think you should stay here while we're gone."

"I won't. I'll stay here tonight so I can drive you to the airport, and then I'll head straight there." A promise is unnecessary. After all, I moved in with him the following day because my parents were in Vancouver filming at the time of the incident.

Once in my room, I close the shades and turn on every

light. I can't help but wonder if I messed up fate, teased it for asking Grey to train me in an attempt to overcome my fears that have returned as a reality.

I quickly shower and dress before finding a text from Jon confirming they made it home. I pack a suitcase filled with clothes and the belated Christmas gifts while waiting for the others to get ready.

Since moving to Oleander Springs, Alex has always been gone for extended stretches due to work, but Jon previously split his time, staying two weeks wherever Alex was and then returning home with me for three weeks before leaving again. When I turned seventeen, he began swapping the stretches, going for three weeks, and staying home for two. By the middle of my senior year, he stayed with Alex, and they'd return home together between projects or on breaks. This is one of their brief breaks, a single week at home.

The drive to my parents' house is only twenty-five minutes, but it feels longer, anticipation a second pulse. Hudson fills the time discussing precautions, reminding me to contact the police and to call Grey, Corey, Nolan, or Palmer if I need anything.

The front door of my house swings open the moment Hudson pulls into the driveway, and Alex and Jon step out.

I don't bother with my purse or bag, closing the distance at a jog before being sandwiched between them in a hug.

"There's our girl," Alex says, kissing my temple. He pulls away, silently assessing my still-damp hair along with the jeans and sweatshirt I'd hastily pulled on before smiling a little wider. Last year when they got home, they obsessed over my living alone and spending so much time alone, and I know without him saying anything that he's relieved Evelyn moved here.

"How was your flight?" I ask as Evelyn and Hudson join us on the porch.

"Quick," Jon says. "We both fell asleep before hitting the Midwest, so we're ready to party." He swivels his hips in a two-step before hugging Evelyn and then Hudson. My parents love these two as much as I do.

"Let's go inside. Dinner was just delivered, and we got everyone's favorites," Alex says, pulling open the front door to invite us all inside.

The scents of different cuisines greet us. Ordering appetizers from multiple restaurants has always been my favorite treat and how we have spent every evening they return to Oleander Springs for as long as I can recall.

Chapter 19

Grey

I pull up to Mila's parents' and admire the mammoth of a house as my thoughts turn to my mom and the hope that I can someday afford to buy her a place half this nice. Mila had asked me yesterday if I'd mind meeting her here.

Mila's dad Alex answers the door wearing khakis, a blue sweater, and a Santa hat covering most of his graying hair. "Hi, Grey. Nice to see you." He takes a step back. "Please, come inside."

Wide-planked floors and light walls invite me inside where the ceilings span twelve feet, making the large room feel even bigger. An overstuffed sectional is positioned around a stone fireplace, and windows that stretch from floor to ceiling bring in extra light, lending to the rich feel of the house.

Jon joins us from the open kitchen, dressed in a T-shirt and jeans. He has dark hair, a short beard, and glasses.

"Jon, you remember Grey," Alex says.

I've met Mila's dads a few times over the years, usually for celebrations or holidays.

"Of course. How are you?" Jon asks, giving me a firm handshake.

I nod. "I'm well, thanks. How are you?"

Jon nods. "Glad to hear it. I'm doing great, thanks." He looks at Alex, brows furled as they share a look, and then he clears his throat. "So you're here to go running with Mila?"

Alex's smile hints at amusement as he slides his hands into his pockets and rocks back on his heels.

I nod. "We're going to take the trail around the lake. Hudson mentioned he takes it when he's home."

Alex nods. "That's right." His smile grows. "You know you should stay for brunch, Grey. We're having a belated Christmas today."

"Maybe we should wait until we have pizza night or—" Jon says, but Alex shakes his head.

"No. Today's perfect." Alex brushes his hands as though he's just completed a chore.

"I don't—" I start to object, but Alex shakes his head.

"You can. I know it will mean a lot to Mila, and we'd love to get to know you better." He looks at Jon, waiting for him to agree.

Jon gives him a panicked expression, one so damn similar to a look Mila makes that I know for certain not everything stems from genetics.

Mila jogs up the stairs then, a wince tightening her brow, revealing she's still sore as she looks between her parents and me. "You're early..." she says.

"Punctual is good," Alex says.

Jon cringes.

"Not a movie," Mila tells him.

"Where do you think screenwriters get their ideas?" he asks her.

Mila shakes her head, moving closer to me. She's wearing a

pair of skintight black leggings, tennis shoes, and a black tee that hugs her chest.

I swallow, trying to pull my attention away from her thighs, hips, and breasts. She's so damn perfect it hurts.

"You should wear a jacket," Jon says. "There's a light breeze, and being close to the water, you might get cold."

"I'll be okay," Mila says, shaking her head. "We won't be gone long."

"Oh, good. Maybe the four of us can play a game before dinner," Alex suggests.

"Sorry?" Mila asks.

"We invited Grey to stay for brunch since you didn't," Alex tells her.

Mila shakes her head. "We're just working out. He's helping me learn a new routine."

"A *new* routine?" Jon asks. "Since when did you have an *old* routine."

Mila drops her chin.

"We want to meet your friends. The only people we ever see are Hudson, Evelyn, and Griffin. Ease our parent guilt a little and let us hang out with him for a couple of hours. We swear we won't embarrass you," Alex says.

"*Much*," Jon tacks on.

Mila winces. "I'm pretty sure we've already surpassed much." She turns to me, her cheeks stained pink. "You really don't have to stay."

"He wants to," Alex says before I can reply. He steps forward and opens the door. "Are you sure you don't want a coat?"

"If we're keeping on script, shouldn't you be cleaning a shotgun or something, not inviting him over for dinner?"

Alex quirks a brow. "Maybe next time."

Mila steps outside, leading me halfway down the driveway

before she turns around to face me. "I told you to text me when you got here."

"If you're that embarrassed, I can say no." The truth is, I was entirely distracted.

Mila sighs. "Tell me we're going to do something besides run today."

"You're only on day seven."

"It feels like a month."

"You won't be this sore in a month," I tell her.

She huffs out a sigh. "Let's go."

Mila

I lead Grey to the side yard, where we stop and stretch. The air is deceivingly warm after our promised snow that never came—typical winter weather here in Oleander Springs.

I expect Grey to ask me how to get out of staying for dinner or complain about having to drive the extra ten minutes it takes from campus to get to my parents' house, or even about the prospect of having to work out with me for the seventh consecutive day that was met with my snarky comment, but he says nothing.

I stretch my hamstrings, which are beginning to burn less. I'm tired this morning both physically and mentally. After dinner last night, I'd rode home with Hudson and Evelyn, where we stayed up entirely too late, theorizing what Julian Holloway had meant when claiming I ignored him for years.

I didn't sleep well. Every bump and click had me sitting up in bed, checking our alarm and doorbell camera.

At four, I gave up on sleep, and decided to read until it was time to take Hudson and Evelyn to the airport. I dropped them off and returned to my parents' house to meet Grey.

I clear my throat and shove thoughts of Julian out of my head. "Who taught you how to fight?"

Grey lifts one long arm above his head and reaches for his opposite shoulder, the width of this biceps nearly wider than his head. My heart skips, defiantly recalling how hard those muscles are and how secure his touch had been.

That kiss—those few minutes—has become a forbidden thought, one I haven't discussed with even Evelyn, knowing she would read into it and imagine it signifying more than it did. Instead, I've locked the details up and thrown away the key.

Except for these specifics, which I quickly shove into the same stash as I turn my attention to the trees behind us. I sit down, stretching my legs out in front of me.

"We learned a lot of things on our own, and then, Cole's cornerman, or coach, picked him up after a few months and taught us the rest."

"Cole's your friend from Highgrove."

Grey nods once with confirmation.

"How long have you guys been friends?"

"My whole life."

"Why don't you ever bring your other friends around?"

Grey looks at me with pinched, cautious eyes. "What do you mean?"

"I mean, why don't you ever invite them to hang out with the rest of us?"

"Why don't you invite your other friends to hang out?"

"Because I don't have other friends."

He looks at me like I'm lying.

"I have other acquaintances, but I've always had a small friend circle," I clarify.

"Why's that?"

"Because I'm shit when it comes to trusting people." It's the absolute truth.

Grey swallows, and similar to when he asked about my forgotten accent, I see questions humming in his thoughts, ones he doesn't ask, maintaining the boundaries of our relationship. "They don't trust people, either," he says.

I stare at him, knowing he includes himself when he says "they." I wonder what he's like when he's around them. If he's less serious and laughs more. "Why?"

His eyes turn calculating as he runs his knuckles over the length of his chiseled jaw. Over the past few days, our conversations have been minimal, all business. My questions cross those lines we carefully constructed two and a half odd years ago. "Highgrove is a quintessential plutocracy."

I raise my brow. "A what?"

"It's run by the wealthy. A minority influence nearly everything. They've managed to stop competitors from opening businesses that would offer better job opportunities so they can be richer while everyone else struggles."

I think of some of the worst foster care homes I spent time in, where greed and strength equated to power and influence.

"Growing up and seeing how money can corrupt everything from school to police, it makes trusting others—especially others with money—difficult." Grey waves a hand toward my house. "People who have this in Highgrove are assholes who looked down on my friends and me and treated us like trash."

I think of the biting look Grey shot me a couple of weeks ago when I paid for dinner after my botched self-date, wondering if he took that as an insult. I know how desperation can lead to cruelty, and losing even a tiny bit of anything feels significant when you have so little.

"I can't really relate," I admit. "My mom was poor, but so

was every foster family I stayed with. I never knew anyone who had money until moving here, or if I did, I don't remember."

Grey swallows, his eyes stuck on mine. "I never in a million years imagined a rich kid with a dad who played in the fucking NFL would become one of my best friends."

I grin, but for some reason, my eyes feel wet with tears. "I still pinch myself, too." I glance at Hudson's. My love and loyalty for Hudson has nothing to do with his wealth or his father's status, and I know they mean nothing to Grey, either.

"I don't look at our Camden friend group as being less. It's just ... complicated."

I nod. "It's hard not to assume everyone will be like the person who hurt you."

Grey's gaze darkens, and his jaw locks. Before he can ask more questions, I dance back across the line of oversharing to comfortable with a playful grin. "But Palmer can befriend a rock, and I'm pretty sure, given a chance, Evelyn would make friends with the woodland creatures. It's impossible for people not to like them."

"Then why don't you include Palmer as one of your friends?"

I try and muster an eye roll, but I know it falls flat. "I never said I don't like Palmer, but it's not like he calls me to hang out or invites me to parties. We are, by definition, acquaintances."

"You're really sticking to that term."

"Because it fits."

"Cole would be cool. He's easy to get along with and likes most people, but his brother, Abe, is a loose cannon. He'd punch a fridge if he thought it looked at him wrong."

"Maybe we should invite Lenny..."

Grey huffs out a laugh. "The thing is, we're tight. One guy dives in, and the rest follow. That's how it's always been. So if I invited them to hang out with the others and Nolan makes a wisecrack or Palmer says something stupid, things would get tense real quick."

"And you're stuck in the middle."

He stares at me, his silence confirming he wouldn't be in the middle but on their side. Something in my stomach twists with unease.

"Are you done stretching?" I ask, already turning toward the trail that surrounds Lake Oleander. The lake is manufactured but vast, covering over forty miles. We live on the only section parceled for building. The rest is a county park with trails, sports courts, and green spaces. I'm pretty sure my need for nature and greenery was born here, where even in January, when most of the trees are barren, it's tranquil and beautiful.

Grey nods and follows me to the foot trail. On this side of the lake, it's unpaved and narrow, forcing me to run in front of Grey, which unlocks a new level of self-consciousness that makes this arrangement even stranger.

Why did I wear leggings? Leggings show every curve of my backside.

Why did I think running here was a good idea?

My frazzled thoughts wane as sweat pricks my brow and spine, and my insecurities steer me to fears as Julian's words about ignoring him ring in my ears.

Could Julian be watching me?

Ravens crow from nearby, giving me something to focus on. I find four things: the uneven path, the ferns still shamrock green, the dozen geese floating across the lake, and the glassy surface of the lake. I listen to the lap of the lake against the nearby shore, the whir of a boat engine in the distance, and the raven still crowing before picking out two scents.

When we reach the paved section where the path grows wider, Grey moves to run beside me without saying a word. The silence was easier when he was behind me, but I'm breathing too heavily to talk, and having him next to me is more comfortable, so I shove the discomfort aside and continue the pace.

I want to collapse when we return to my parents' yard, my lungs screaming and mouth parched, but I begin stretching without instruction, feeling my heart pounding in my ears as sweat trails down my back and temples.

"You're already finding a good stride," Grey says. "Are you still pretty sore?"

"Only when I move or breathe."

He flashes a surprised grin and chuckles but doesn't offer to help me stretch again. I work to ignore the stab of disappointment.

"I didn't know running would make my ribs ache."

Grey nods. "Next week, we'll start adding some calisthenics."

"Will I want to punch you?"

"If you don't, I won't be doing my job."

I bend over and try to touch my toes to hide my smirk.

"Are you guys done, or is there more?" Alex asks, leaning over the porch railing.

"We're done. We're just stretching. I'll be in shortly."

Alex leans closer. "You mean you'll both be in shortly. I set Grey a place at the table, and Jon's making him a mocktail, now."

"I'd tell you to fake sick, but he likely watched us through his bird-watching binoculars and knows you're fine."

Grey's eyes flare with alarm. I recall him asking me over to his table for dinner with Emma and the booster date, and my mortification is shelved.

"Don't worry. He'll probably wait until the next time he sees you to mention wedding dates and venues."

Grey goes entirely still. This time, I'm pretty sure even his heart has stopped.

"That can't be healthy," I tell him, shaking my head as I turn toward my house.

"Why does he look pale?" Alex whispers as I climb the stairs.

I look over my shoulder at Grey as he follows a dozen feet behind. "If you ask him to call you Dad or mention what you expect from a son-in-law, I swear, I will be the best child ever for all of eternity."

Alex steps closer, wrapping an arm around my shoulders. He's an inch shorter than I am, his eyes a dark brown, with impossibly long lashes I've always envied. "But I like him."

"You don't know him."

"I've met him at least five times. Plus, he makes you smile," he bumps his hip against mine. "I saw it."

"So does Jim Gaffigan."

Alex rolls his eyes and slips his arm free of my shoulders. "Grey, you can use the guestroom if you need a shower. We even have some spare clothes in there that I think will fit you because Jon's brother is cursed, and his bag gets lost every time he visits."

I breeze through the doorway as Alex tells Grey how he's made a habit of collecting shirts from every place they go to add to the closet. I find Jon mixing drinks in the kitchen.

"Should I put alcohol in his drink?" he whispers. "How old is he?"

"You should put alcohol in mine," I whisper back.

He glares. I giggle.

"He doesn't drink much. I wouldn't worry about it."

"Because of Hudson or because it doesn't mix well with steroids?" Jon glances toward the doorway where Grey is listening to Alex's tale of clothing. He's wearing a white tee that sculpts to his biceps and broad chest and a loose pair of black basketball shorts that reveal he doesn't skip leg days.

Laughter peels out of me, and I don't know if it's because it's been several months since I've seen my parents or because, for the first time, someone else isn't a hundred percent team Grey.

"Let's have a drink on the porch," Jon says, distributing tumblers filled with a bubbly and light red cocktail garnished with pieces of rosemary skewered with fresh cranberries.

Alex swoons. My parents are openly affectionate and ridiculously obsessed with each other.

Out on the sun porch—my favorite space except in the spring when everything turns yellow with pollen—I sit in one of the two wicker chairs.

"How were finals?" Jon asks, sitting next to Alex on one of the couches while Grey sits on the other couch, subtly inspecting his drink.

"A few were borderline brutal," I tell him.

Jon winces. "Sociology?"

I nod, taking a sip. The bubbles tickle my mouth and nose. "And that Shakespeare class Alex convinced me to take."

Alex's eyes grow wide. "You didn't like it?" Shakespeare is practically his god.

I cross my legs and lean forward. "My professor doesn't believe Shakespeare wrote his own plays."

Alex leans back, repulsion flickering across his features as he brings a hand to his chest like he's been wounded. "And he's allowed to teach?" He turns to Jon. "This is what happens when we allow our daughter to attend a liberal college."

Jon and I giggle as Alex takes a long drink to ease the sting.

"What about you, Grey? Are you relieved finals are over?" Alex asks.

Grey looks rigid and entirely uncomfortable, making the

glass look like a bomb about to detonate rather than a cranberry spritzer. "Very. Between football and finals, the month before the break was ruthless."

"Congratulations on your win at the bowl game," Jon says. "That was a great game."

Grey nods his appreciation.

"How have things been going at work?" I ask Alex. "Are things calming down?"

Alex leans back, sighing heavily. "We're still having some disagreements."

"Diva actors? Budget?" I ask, listing the common complaints.

Alex waves his hands. "Just business. You know how it gets."

I don't. My time spent in his world could be compared to sticking a toe into a pond.

"Is it something with the story?" I press.

Alex looks at me, his eyes bright with adoration and a familiar look I wish would eventually fade—one of pity that I used to mistake as shame. "Nothing to worry about. They always realize I'm right eventually." He brandishes a smile that has me laughing.

"So you two are running together?" Jon asks, raising his eyebrows. "How did that come about?"

"I pretended to be his date, and so he owes me." I lay out the facts as I usually do with my parents.

Grey swallows, his attention volleying between my parents. He's usually the epitome of calm and collected, but over the past couple of weeks, I've seen him uneasy a dozen times. Somehow, he wasn't even slightly nervous after kissing me, which still has me feeling a little bitter because I felt wholly unhinged afterward. Still do, any time I think about it.

I put that thought into the locked box as well.

"And for that, you want him to run with you?" Alex's voice reflects his confusion, likely for my long avoidance of organized sports or hobbies that included exercising.

"It was a black-tie event," I explain to mark the significance of the favor, omitting the largest part, which, of course, is the fact we kissed. I still remember the taste of him. Recall the weight of his hand against my spine when I'm trying to sleep. "I wore a gown."

Jon smirks.

"So you guys are—" Alex starts.

I shake my head before he can dive into tropes and plot-lines in an attempt to dissect what's going on between Grey and me. "It's just a deal we made."

"Or friendship..." Jon says. "Kind of like Hudson." He gives a pointed look at Alex, backing me up, only he's missed the mark.

"We're not friends," I regret saying the words as soon as they leave my mouth because they sound childish and cruel even before all three men look at me.

Alex's shoulders rise, and his demeanor switches from matchmaker to protector in a flash. I can see it, feel it in the way his gaze scrutinizes mine. I'm pretty sure I can even sense it in the air, as though the energy has changed.

"Grey's cool. He's a nice guy. I just mean that he's Hudson's friend. He's working out with me because he owes me. Nothing nefarious, romantic, or wherever you were going."

I swallow, looking at Grey and trying my damnedest to offer a silent apology.

Grey stares back at me, his blue gaze lacking the animosity I was expecting to discover. Instead, he looks almost perplexed with only a hint of bitterness.

"Mila," Alex says, pulling my gaze to him. His dark eyes are filled with tenderness that has me wondering if I'll always feel like a child, fragile and exposed, when he looks at me like this with so much love and compassion.

I swallow thickly as a rush of emotions tangles in my throat.

"Would you mind helping me with the charcuterie board?" he asks.

I clear my throat and stand, my knuckles white around the glass I'm gripping like a stress ball. I appreciate that it doesn't compress and falter under the pressure.

Inside, I lean against the kitchen countertop, pressing the fingers of my free hand together without thought, just habit. Alex stands across from me, allowing me a moment of time and space.

"I'm proud of you for trying something new."

"Did I embarrass him and make this really awkward?" I ask. "I didn't mean... It just came out. I feel like such a jerk."

"I think he was taken aback. I would guess if you asked him, he would have thought you were friends."

I shake my head. "He doesn't like me, and I'm not talking romantically." I hate the thin veil of tears that form in my eyes.

Alex steps closer, pulling me into a hug that feels forced and uncomfortable until I remind myself that it's not. Alex cares, wants to be here, and like the glass, won't break. I wrap my arms around him a little tighter and breathe in the calming scent of cypress that is so familiar until my tears recede and my breathing become even. Still, he holds me.

"I've missed you, my beautiful girl." He doesn't make this about Grey or my insecurities that some argue will never change or go away. Instead, he is again the glass, reassuring me of his presence, consistency, and love.

"I'm surprised Jon chose a charcuterie board. He seemed so adamantly against them when we spoke at Thanksgiving," I say, stepping back once my feelings are intact.

Alex gives a rueful smile. "You know him and how he hates

anything that gets trendy. I swear, it's like he's allergic to anything popular." He goes to the fridge and withdraws the wooden board filled with cheeses and fruits.

"Can you grab the crackers and nuts out of the pantry? He put them in a basket, so we'd know which ones to use."

I grab the wire basket and a bag of goldfish crackers I spot on the shelf beneath them and bring them to where Alex adds small ramekins for the different dips and nuts.

"Maybe running together will be good. Hudson's always been a good judge of character. I know my trainer wouldn't be willing to come over every day to work out with me in exchange for me dressing up for a couple of hours..."

"It's only been a few days."

"He was willing to meet you at your parents' house."

"You're in your producer's mind again."

"Am I?" he asks. "Or are you assuming he doesn't like you because you still sometimes struggle to remember that others see how amazing and awesome you are, just like Jon and I?"

I glance toward the back porch where Jon and Grey are talking, their expressions somber but amicable.

"He tolerates hanging out with me because of Hudson. We wouldn't be hanging out otherwise. In the two and a half years I've known him, do you want to know how many times we've texted or called each other before last week?" I make a goose egg with my hand. "Zero."

Alex fills the middle container with goldfish crackers. "Everything begins somewhere." With a meaningful look, he lifts the board and carries it out to the porch.

"Goldfish?" Jon squawks, raising accusing eyes at me. "Those weren't in the box."

I lean over and grab a small handful to set on one of the plates I brought out. "But they should have been." I wink.

He shakes his head. "Some of these cheeses are a hundred dollars a pound."

"For cheese?" I ask, shocked but not entirely surprised, feeling a twinge of guilt as my conversation with Grey floats to the top of my thoughts. I came to Oleander Springs with a half-filled garbage bag that fit all my belongings. I still remember walking into this house, amazed by the size and how nice everything was, and how hard I cried when they showed me my room. It was the first time I'd had my own bedroom, and it was made for a princess, filled with toys, clothes, and books that I struggled to accept.

"And these grapes are from France," Jon says, interrupting my trip down memory lane.

I grab a small bunch of the purple globes he's referring to. "Are you saying my crackers aren't fancy enough for your board?"

He frowns at me and the insinuation. "I'm saying these are all quality ingredients, and those are processed and high in sodium. How are they even in the pantry?" He turns his accusing stare to Alex.

"That's what happens when you send me to the grocery store alone. Things fall into the cart." Alex shrugs, grabbing a handful of the crackers.

I chuckle, passing a plate to Grey. "Eat the cheese or eat the crackers. Jon's a food snob but an excellent cook, so we don't hold it against him."

Grey accepts the plate with a broad smile. "I don't think I've ever eaten hundred-dollar cheese before."

"Please, help yourself. We have more of everything in the fridge." Jon sits forward, pointing to each cheese and telling him where they came from and how they taste. He turns to Alex as he finishes. "When we return to California, you're back on your diet. You heard what your cardiologist said."

My back straightens. "What did your cardiologist say?"

Alex waves a hand. "That I'm healthy as a horse."

Three years ago, Jon had a heart attack following his sixtieth birthday. The devastating and terrifying event changed what Jon cooks and buys.

Jon plucks a strawberry from the board. "As long as you avoid salt and saturated fats." He puts a handful of vegetables on Alex's plate, then grabs a celery stick and points to a hard white cheese, thinly sliced. "Try this one, Mila. It's going to remind you of Florence."

I take a small bit of it, and he smiles with satisfaction when I nod. "It really does."

Our conversation shifts as Jon asks Grey about his major and football before Jon tells me about the new condo they're considering buying.

"Do you need a coat, Mila?" Jon asks as I lean back in my chair. "There's a breeze."

"Yes. Why don't you get one and check on the timer for the potatoes, please? We need a minute to speak with Grey, anyway. Make sure I approve of his intentions." Alex crosses his legs and shoots me a wink.

I don't feel even a hint of guilt as I ignore Grey's stare and go inside.

Chapter 20

Grey

My thoughts drift to yesterday as I prepare to work out with Mila. Alex grilled me the entire twenty minutes Mila took to get a coat, asking me if I respected her, my future plans, what contribution I was planning to make to the world, and more. I didn't realize it was their own twisted brand of humor until Jon reached the bottom of his glass and couldn't hold back his laughter.

Mila returned within minutes, sporting a look of innocence until she realized the bit was up, and then her laughter was contagious. Alex practically rolled in his seat as he apologized, and I couldn't even be mad about it. Seeing Mila in that environment, so unfiltered and uninhibited, was addictive.

"Are you plotting your revenge for yesterday?" Mila asks, meeting me in the lobby of my dorm, dressed in a pair of navy leggings that threaten to kill me, a sweatshirt covered in a puffy vest, and her long hair already pulled up as it is most days. The lobby is practically barren with a final week of winter break left.

"Why would I be plotting revenge?" I ask, leading her

outside where the sidewalk is just as empty. Bia Stadium is a short distance away, but I spend enough time there, so I lead her past the turnoff.

Beside me, Mila rubs her hands over her arms. "Why are we meeting so early?" After the warm weather yesterday, the forty-degree morning feels particularly brutal and dark.

"Because I have other things I have to do today."

Mila looks at me as we continue walking, and I silently dare her to ask me what I need to do and where I'm going. I'm damn near catfishing her with my vague response, but over the time I've known Mila, one of our most pronounced unspoken rules is we don't ask each other questions. I thought it was because she wasn't interested, but hearing her say she doesn't think I like her as more than an acquaintance has me rethinking every damn one of our boundaries.

She swallows and turns her attention to the darkened sidewalk.

"What's your mom like?" Mila asks as we stop at a crosswalk, shoving her hands into her vest pockets and biting that spot on her lower lip.

It's one of the last questions I expected. "My mom's..." I shake my head, wishing there was a singular word significant enough to describe her. "She's the strongest person I know. Kind and always giving people the benefit of the doubt. Evelyn kind of reminds me of her."

Her smile grows. "I already like her."

"She's the reason I try so damn hard. Her entire life, she's worked so hard to give me everything, and I want to help her out. Ensure she can retire comfortably and just relax for once."

Mila taps the top of the sneaker against the sidewalk. "What about your dad?"

"He lives in Atlanta."

"Do you see him much?"

I shake my head.

Hesitancy flattens her brow. "Do you guys get along?"

"My mom was eighteen when she got pregnant with me. He was thirty-two, married, with two kids. He hid it all from my mom, promising her the world until she got pregnant."

Mila winces. "What happened?"

"He broke up with her and broke all communication. My mom couldn't afford daycare, so she had to drop out of college. He tried to reach out to me this year, after our game against Tennessee." We'd won, and I had arguably my best game of the season, earning me placement on highlight reels for several weeks. "But," I shake my head. "I had no interest."

"What a jerk. I'm sorry."

"What about you? Do you know your dad? Your biological dad, I mean."

She shakes her head. "I never met him. I don't even know his name."

The light turns green for us to walk, and we're halfway between the intersection before I ask, "Can I ask why you went into foster care?" I glance at her, trying to read her expression. "I don't want to come across like an insensitive asshole, so if I'm... You can..."

Mila shakes her head, a tight but sincere smile marking her face. "My mom was a drug addict when I was born. I didn't go home with her until I was eighteen months old."

"What happened?"

She lifts her shoulders. "I lived with her for about six months, and a neighbor called for noise complaints because they heard me crying. CPS put me back into foster care for another year. I lived with my mom again, and she was trying really hard to get clean and stay sober, but she had no money, couldn't afford daycare, and had been fired from her job, so we were living out of her car. Someone noticed we hadn't moved from a parking lot for a few days and called the cops, and I went back into CPS. I lived with her one final time before I was adopted.

Her words are a laceration to my chest as I imagine Mila as a child, bouncing from house to house, stranger to stranger, sleeping in the backseat of a car.

"I don't remember most of it," she quickly adds, swiping at a piece of hair that the wind drags across her cheek.

"They stopped giving her chances?" I ask as we stop again, the college's track ahead of us.

Mila blows out a breath and tucks her hands into her vest pockets again. "She was arrested, and a few years later, she overdosed and passed away."

My heart breaks, and everything inside of me demands to pull her into a hug, but as she leans back on her heels, I know that's the last thing she wants. "I'm so sorry."

She shakes off my apology. "A few months later, my social worker met Alex's brother and found out how hard Alex and Jon had been trying to adopt, and she reached out to them. A lot of people have opinions about whether gay couples should adopt, which is shameful because they offer the same loving and stable environments as straight couples, and statistically, they adopt more kids like me than straight couples do,"

"Kids like you?" The words don't sound right on my tongue, worse in my head.

Mila stares at me for a moment, imploring me to read between the lines, but I shake my head because I can't. The space is blank. I can't even begin to guess what she's referencing.

"Undesirable," she says.

I pull back, feeling the word brand my skin as another piece of her comes into view, one that doesn't fit with the fiercely confident and stubborn woman before me. "What? Mila, no."

"People want to adopt babies and toddlers who will acclimate easily, not kids who have abandonment and trust issues and require years of therapy."

"But you were seven. Still a young kid."

Her lips quirk to one side. "Those formative years are pretty damn important."

The light turns, and Mila looks both ways before crossing the street. I follow her, wanting to ask a hundred more questions, each more personal than the last.

"I don't want you to feel sorry for me or think differently of me because of this. I hate pity, which is why I don't tell most people about this part of my life. Alex and Jon are amazing parents, and I literally want for nothing except to know how to punch someone in the face." She lifts a shoulder and quirks her lips with a smile I know isn't genuine.

"How long do you think it will take before I can beat you around the track?" she asks.

I scoff. "I run four miles a day. Minimum."

"That doesn't mean I won't be faster than you." Challenge shines in her eyes.

"Your legs are still sore," I point out as I begin stretching.

"Less sore."

I smirk, shaking my head.

Her confidence wavers, but only for a second. "Okay. I'll bet you that in a month—"

"You'll need more than a month if you plan on standing a chance."

She rolls her eyes. "In a month, I can beat you taking one lap."

I shake my head. "I'm not betting you."

"Don't you want to hear the stakes?"

I raise a single brow.

She places a finger against her chin and purses her lips.

The need to kiss her feels like a barbell against my throat, suffocating me slowly. Painfully. "You have to invite your Highgrove friends over to meet us."

"And *when* I win..."

She makes a show of rolling her eyes.

I smirk. "You have to stop referring to me as an acquaintance."

Her blue gaze narrows, and I know the look is caused by doubt rather than sarcasm. "Are you accepting the bet?"

I shake my head. "No, but I want you to stop referring to me as your damn acquaintance. If you ever call or text, I'll be there. Not because I'm Hudson's friend but because I'm yours."

Her eyes cross my features again, and then she offers her hand to me.

We stretch in silence and then run the same two-and-a-half-mile stretch we've built up to.

"Let's cool down with the walk back, and then we can stretch upstairs. I've got a jump rope for you to take home."

Mila staples her hands to her sides, her breaths heavy. "Jump rope? How much longer until you teach me how to hit someone?"

I grab her wrists and pull her hands to the top of her head. "This helps open your lungs." She looks up at my hands wrapped around hers, the motion stretching her back and pushing her chest out slightly. Suddenly standing this close, holding her like this feels dangerous, erotic ... tempting.

I release her and step back. "You're not ready to shadowbox yet. We haven't even started working on balance." I turn toward campus.

Mila walks beside me, hands shoved into the pockets of her vest again. "Is there an expeditious training cycle?

"This is it. Trust me. I will get you there."

When we make it to the dorm building, my blood is still too

fucking hot, and it burns hotter as we step into an empty elevator together.

I've learned over the years that I have a Mila scale, which allows me to be around her for durations of time and not act on impulses that would challenge my friendship with Hudson or the rest of our group. That scale should have a couple of days left before I'm so distracted by the ache left by lust and arousal that I have to avoid her for several days.

Perhaps it's that damn cursed kiss or the way she's slowly showing me sides of her I've only been able to see from a distance, or the flush of her cheeks as she stretches her neck and closes her eyes that has me swallowing and imaging her astride me, under me, her knees pressed up as I bury my face between her thighs and feed this hunger that has been gnawing at me, at my bones, for years.

I've ignored the desire and never tempted it until kissing her.

Mila pulls up the sleeves of her sweatshirt and unzips her vest.

Because it's hot, I remind myself.

The doors open on the fourth floor, and I lead Mila down to my room, where I unlock the door and flip on the lights.

Mila steps inside, returning her hands to her pockets as she peers around. Camden made a significant investment with this building, providing dorms that are bigger than most one-bedroom apartments, equipped with a living room, kitchen, dining room, bedroom, and private bath. I have a corner unit, giving me the benefit of a bigger living room and additional windows.

I have a lot of pride in my space, knowing how damn hard I worked to get here.

"It would look better with a black wall," Mila says, a sly smile curving the corner of her lips and making me consider an entirely new challenge involving how quickly I could transform that tease into a plea and then pleasure.

I smirk and grab the plastic bag with the jump rope that I'd meant to bring downstairs this morning and hand it to her.

"After you stretch tomorrow, jump rope for five minutes, and then do your run."

Her shock is barely visible, a drawn brow and beat of hesitation as she accepts the bag. "We're not meeting?"

I shake my head. "I'm going to Highgrove for a few days."

She nods as she takes a step back, her teeth catching the inside of her cheek, and I swear I see disappointment in her blue eyes. "To visit family and your friends?

I nod. "Cole has a fight tomorrow, and I need to fix a window at my mom's."

Mila nods a couple of times. I can smell the vanilla scent of the lip balm she applied while we walked here, and my gaze sits heavily on her lips for several long seconds, the desire to lean forward and kiss her that same damn barbell suffocating me.

I take a step back, and Mila does, too. I run a hand over my hair and glance at the clock, realizing I'm going to be late meeting Cole again. "We're still on for Topgolf?"

Mila licks her lips and then bites that damn spot, though she doesn't allude to what has her nervous, and a part of me wonders if it's me. If she feels the same damn fire under her skin whenever she's near. "Yeah."

"Thanks for the jump rope."

I don't move, knowing that if I do, I'll do something stupid like ask her to stay and lose today to bliss and pleasure. "I'll see you later this week."

Mila nods, and without another word, she leaves. I can't help but think that later isn't soon enough.

Chapter 21

Mila

I call a greeting as I open the front door. The scents of cinnamon, sugar, and scrambled eggs fill the air.

"Morning," Alex calls.

I set my new jump rope beside the door and head into the kitchen, finding Jon with an apron that says "#1 Dad" across the front, flipping french toast. "You made it just in time for breakfast."

Alex looks up from where he's seated at the kitchen table, working on his laptop. "You left early."

I angle my head in the direction of the door. "I had to meet Grey."

The ghost of a smile crosses his expression. "I like him."

I roll my eyes and try to stop his words of approval from attaching to my straying thoughts. Jon presses a kiss to the side of my head. "Ignore him."

"I plan to." I pick up a piece of sliced pineapple and pop it into my mouth as Alex makes a wounded cry.

"Why are you breaking the rules and working at the breakfast table," I ask, trying to change the subject.

Alex removes his glasses and rubs his eyes with his pointer finger and thumb. "Contract deadlines. Complaints. Proposals." Stress punctuates each word. Alex's creativity is more than a drive. It's his sustenance, and when he's in the midst of a project, it's difficult for him to surface except in small bursts.

I lean forward, pressing a kiss to his cheek. "Well, maybe you should get some work in today. I have a ton of things I need to get done to prepare for the semester that I've been putting off, so I was going to spend most of the day in the basement anyway."

Jon slides a plate filled with French toast drizzled with cream cheese frosting, crispy hashbrowns, scrambled eggs, and fresh fruit in front of me, along with my favorite coffee.

I've been taking care of myself and cooking for the better part of three years, but being home and pampered by my parents turns my heart to soft goo, making fears like Julian feel as far away as Pluto.

"Maybe we should head to the beach later this week," I suggest. "It's supposed to get nice again."

"Great idea," Jon says. "I love everything about California, but our beaches here are impossible to compete with."

"That's what Evelyn says, too," I say, grabbing the ketchup and drawing a pattern across my hashbrowns.

"And maybe today we could..." His words trail off as Alex glances at him, a silent request to help him today. Jon is twice as fast at typing and is often Alex's sounding board for ideas as well as communications.

"Don't worry. I have loads to do."

After breakfast, I head downstairs to the basement, which we converted into my own personal apartment. It wasn't necessary, but my parents gifted it to me as a surprise, having it professionally made over. It's beautiful, warm, and artsy. I love the space and planned to stay here rather than move into an apartment, but Jon hated the idea of me being alone, and Alex thought I'd enjoy my college experience more if I was closer to campus.

I spend the next two hours watching self-defense and fighting videos online and eventually cuddle up with a book and a fresh cup of coffee. I'm considering ordering something for lunch when my phone dings with a message. If someone was here, I'd be embarrassed by how fast I reach for it, hoping it's Grey reminding me to do something tomorrow or asking me another question.

My heart sinks a little, seeing Hadley's name.

> Hadley: I'm obsessed with this month's book. I was telling Hannah we should make you the official selector of books.

> Me: I'm obsessed, too! I've read it twice.

> Hadley: How are things going?

The last time I saw Hadley was at the booster event last week, following Silva insulting me and Grey kissing me. I'm not in a much better head space now than I was then, and I struggle to answer the simple question.

> Me: Things are going pretty well. My parents are in town, so we had a belated Christmas yesterday.

> Me: How are you?

> Hadley: Fun! I'm searching for flights. My sister scheduled her induction to be in two weeks.

> Me: Congratulations! That's exciting.

Hadley is close to her siblings in a way that reminds me of my relationship with Hudson.

> Hadley: Yes! She's nervous, so I'm hoping things work out and I can arrive before the baby and then stay a couple of days.

I don't know what else to say as a minute and then another ticks by. I mastered small talk years ago, a requirement of shuffling homes or perhaps a product, but similar to Hannah, Hadley and I are past the stages of small talk, on the fence of friendship, which requires opening up and sharing—trusting. My thoughts drift to Grey and how much I've recently shared with him.

Embarrassment paves a path for regret and rejection to crash over me, recalling how I'd told him about how uneducated I was when moving here. I think of how I've shared things with him that likely have him seeing me in a new light—one where he pities me or realizes exactly how many rips and tears exist beyond my exterior that often make me feel a sense of brokenness beyond repair. Reasons mount in my thoughts for why he didn't kiss me this morning when my body language clearly asked him to.

I groan in the silence of my room, wishing I could go back in time to that damn self-date and cancel.

> Hadley: Do you have plans for today? Hannah and I were planning to binge-watch Twilight. She only saw the first movie, and I feel like I'm failing her by not making her watch all of them.

Hadley: She also didn't read them, so I'm looking forward to her reaction in movie 5 when Carlisle ... well ... you know 😉

She's doing the heavy lifting and inviting me though I've made little attempt to reach out since Florida. Briggs claims I keep everyone at arm's length because I'm afraid they might hurt me. He even has a fancy diagnosis, calling it anxious and avoidant attachment, which is why my friend circle remains at three.

I type out three excuses for why I can't come and then think of book club, of how much Evelyn likes Hadley and Hannah, of how Nolan looks at Hadley like she's his reason for existing, and slowly, my fingers glide over the keys.

Me: That sounds fun. What can I bring?

Hadley: Tortilla chips, if you don't mind. I'm going to make some dips.

Me: Sounds good. What time?

Hadley: As soon as you can get here.

Me: I'll see you soon.

The thought of Julian Holloway following me has me taking the most indirect route, ensuring no one is following me. I arrive with two bags of tortilla chips, a bag of jalapeno chips, and three other flavors because my aversion to attachment is from fear, not because I don't care.

My heart beats a familiar race that has me recalling what it felt like as a kid on a new family's doorstep, hoping for the same thing I am today—acceptance.

Hannah opens the door with a smile that grows into a laugh as her gaze lowers to the bags in my hands. "You might be Hadley's soul mate."

I step inside with a grin, trying to find my confidence. I've only been here a few times, but each time I come, I fall more in love with their house. The charm and rustic appeal feel like a warm hug, like I should be walking around in sweats and fuzzy socks while sipping coffee and making myself at home.

Hannah leads us into the kitchen. It's half the size of the one in our apartment but holds twice the charm. An array of scents greets us, spices, cheese, popcorn, and chocolate. Hadley's at the stove, stirring something that smells of candied sugar and vanilla.

"Hey! I'm almost done," Hadley says.

"Mila's channeling your same go big or go home energy," Hannah says, taking the bags of chips and laying them on the counter.

Hadley grins. "I thought it would be fun to have a popcorn bar."

"Five flavors of popcorn," Hannah says. "To go with our four dips and four desserts."

Hadley merely grins. "Would you like anything to drink?"

"If you have some coffee, I would love some."

"Hot or chilled?" Hadley asks, quickly becoming my favorite person of the day.

"Chilled would be amazing." Iced coffee has always been my vice.

She grins. "You can help yourself. They're on the bottom shelf."

I open the fridge and take a second and then a third look at the fruits and vegetables with varying googly eyes staring at me.

"Don't ask," Hannah says.

I glance at the orange next to the green bell pepper and

smile. Hadley and Nolan are notorious for pulling pranks on each other, and I have no doubt this is one of them. "How have things been since getting back from Florida?" I ask, grabbing a chocolate-flavored coffee and taking a final glance at the milk carton that stares at me with six eyeballs.

Hadley nods. "Nolan and I just returned from Philadelphia yesterday."

"I'm surprised you didn't freeze," I say.

"Oh, I did," Hadley says, taking the pot off the stove. "But it was worth it. What have you been up to?"

I watch with curiosity and fascination as she pours the hot contents over a bowl of popcorn.

"Not much. I began working out with Grey because apparently my coffee and binge-watching diet isn't sustainable." It's a half-truth. I have gone up a pant size this year.

Hadley raises a brow as she stirs the mixture, long threads of sugary sweetness bridging clumps of the popcorn.

"What kind of workout?" Hannah asks.

"Right now, we're doing cardio, which only makes me feel stabby every other day."

Their laughter seems more than just courteous.

"He's not making you do their football routine. Is he?" Hadley asks. "Because I've watched that, and it's brutal." She signals to the bowls. "These are ready. Let's take them to the living room."

I grab two of the bowls and shake my head as I follow them to the living room. "No, his friend is an MMA fighter, so we're supposed to be doing some of that stuff..." I want to tag on an excuse, tell them it's to release anger and stress or because it's supposed to be a good workout, something—anything—that will prevent me from launching into my fears.

"An MMA fighter?" Hannah asks, taking a handful of the cheesy popcorn I set down. "Is he single? I refuse to date any more football players, but an MMA fighter..." she fills her mouth with popcorn as she tilts her head with consideration.

"I have no idea," I tell her, grinning.

"Do you have a picture of him? How do we see my potential future husband?" Hannah asks.

I chuckle. "I've never seen him. His name's Cole something." I forgot his last name nearly as soon as it was spoken.

"Is he a professional fighter?" Hannah grabs a laptop. "Maybe we can find him."

"I think so. He has a fight tonight."

Hannah's eyes grow wide, and she looks from me to Hadley. "Are you guys thinking what I'm thinking?"

"That you really want to watch Twilight and stuff yourself full of popcorn and dips?" Hadley asks hopefully.

Hannah doesn't respond, turning to the opened laptop. "Do you know where the fight is?"

I shake my head. "They're from Highgrove, but I can't imagine it's there. There's nothing in Highgrove but farmland and a couple of factories." I hate the itch of hopefulness scratching at my subconscious.

Hannah continues sleuthing while Hadley tells me about the popcorn flavors she made, butter toffee, marshmallow, cheese, and rosemary parmesan.

We sample each delicious kind while recapping the first movie, recalling details I've forgotten.

We barely make it past the opening scene when Hannah sits up. "I found it." Her brow furrows. "Or ... I *think* I found it." She turns the laptop around to show me the screen. "Have you heard of a place called Better Days?"

I shake my head. "I've only driven through Highgrove."

Hadley leans closer. "Are you sure this is it?" There's scarce information, yet Hannah's already pulling up Google Maps and searching for the address.

"I think it's a bar," she says.

I shake my head. "It can't be there. Can it?"

"Maybe we should go," Hannah says, hope bleeding into her words as she turns to Hadley. "We haven't been out on a Camden tradition in weeks. I need a little excitement and adventure."

This past quarter, Nolan took Hadley to multiple Camden traditions, some secrets, and others far less. It was how I initially knew he liked her as more than a friend.

Hadley slides her gaze to me. "What do you think?"

I shrug, trying to look indifferent. Apart from the videos I watched this morning on YouTube, I've never seen a fight. I want to see what Grey is training me for—what I might be capable of doing eventually. "What time does it start?"

"Nine," Hannah reads.

The idea of Grey seeing us and thinking we're there to see him keeps me from letting my previous thoughts take flight. "I don't know," I say, shaking my head. "I'm pretty content with dip, popcorn, and fictional men."

"Don't make me play the edible cookie card again," Hannah says, determining our plans with the simple reminder.

We park at an old bar appropriately named Better Days because it's certainly seen its better days. Several of the letters in the neon sign are burned out, so from a distance, it reads, BeDs.

"Is this it?" Hannah asks from the back seat of my car.

I look from my GPS to the single-story white brick building.

Hannah skims over her phone and then looks at the bar again. "I guess we go in and check it out. I mean, if it's not here, they can probably give us directions."

"There are a lot of trucks here," Hadley points out. "Something has to be going on."

"Is that a chicken?" Hannah asks.

We turn to see a chicken crossing the road, confirming we're in small-town Southern America.

"I think the joke's on us, chicken friend," I murmur.

"Come on. Let's go." Hannah opens the back door and slides out of the car. My nerves are my shadow as we cross the parking lot and open the front door.

The bar is empty except for a lone bartender who looks at us for a split second before turning his attention back to his phone.

"We must have the wrong address," Hadley says quietly from where we remain unmoving just inside the front door. The lighting is dim inside, and I can only think it's so people don't stare too long at the worn interior where pictures, dollar bills, and posters cover the walls.

"Maybe we should go follow the chicken," I suggest.

Hadley laughs as Hannah turns to her phone, but before she can load the website again, a door opens near the back, and noise floods the space as a guy our age steps out, pressing a phone to his ear. "Say that again? I was down in the fight and couldn't hear you."

Hannah grabs our hands and heads for the door. A wooden staircase without rails sits beyond it, leading into a basement. Warning bells blare in my head, suggesting we go back and finish the dips, desserts, and the final Twilight movies as I follow them down. We step into a basement filled with people.

I stare down a man who looks at Hannah like she's his new plan for the evening. "She's not interested," I tell him before pressing a hand to Hannah's shoulders, encouraging her to keep walking. Like upstairs, the basement is poorly lit. It stinks of beer, sweat, and tires, making me glad I didn't eat too much. I'm not sure it would stay down.

"Why do I feel like we just fell down a rabbit hole?" Hadley asks, peering around at the crowds of mostly men.

The mood is deceivingly light. Money and bets are being passed while others talk easily, showing their comfort with both the location and those around us.

We follow Hannah, weaving through the crowd to get a better view. A man wearing a baseball hat low over his eyes stops in front of me, greeting a friend before turning and acknowledging me with a slow plunge of his gaze. "I haven't seen you before," he says.

I stare at him, debating whether my inclination to be sarcastic will get us into trouble, and then recall Grey's comment about keeping his head down while in Highgrove. The thought propels me to question if Grey knows him—if this guy knows Grey. Are they friends? Enemies? Acquaintances?

"We're here to watch Cole," I say.

The stranger's smile is a slow crawl that reveals perfect white teeth. "He's up next." He leans back, allowing me to see through the next few layers of spectators, where steel crowd barriers keep everyone from the middle of the room.

"Are you friends with Cole?" he asks.

I shake my head as Hannah says, "Yes."

The stranger looks between us, his eyebrows raised.

I don't try and clarify. Sometimes confusion is the best ally.

The guy slips his eyes from me to Hannah and then Hadley. "Well, enjoy the show." He waves us forward, and we move past him.

"I see Grey," Hadley whispers.

I do, too. I saw him the moment the crowd parted. He's across from us, standing in the front row against one of the barriers, his hand on a man's shoulder who's a few inches shorter than him, whose hands and wrists are taped. I assume he's Cole. He's leaner than I expected.

Grey tells him something, brow drawn, face serious as he draws a hand across the crude area designated for fighting.

Maybe he's not more easygoing with his friends in Highgrove.

"Is this legal?" Hadley asks.

I shake my head. "I don't think so."

Hannah looks torn, glancing around the fight and then at the stairs. "Maybe we should—"

"All right, all right!" a man calls, rounding one of the barriers and stepping into the middle of the room. He's dressed entirely in black, even his baseball hat, which is sideways. "Are you ready to feast your eyes on Cole Stephens and JB Wright?"

Everyone whistles and cheers as they shift forward, pinning us in place as they pull out phones that they direct toward the mat.

"It can't be *that* illegal if we're allowed to record it," Hannah says.

"Is that really a trustworthy barometer these days?" Hadley asks.

More announcements are made, but the crowd is too loud to hear most of the details. It's evident that most are here for Cole, though, when he steps out and the crowd roars in response.

"Where are their shoes?" Hannah asks. "They're going to need a rabies shot after this."

A guy next to us gives her a bewildered look that has Hadley clearing her throat. We don't stick out based on our looks alone, it's our wide, stunned eyes and judgment that make us stick out like sore thumbs.

"Are we too close?" Hadley asks. "How well do you think these things will hold if the fight moves this way?" The moment

203

the question leaves her lips, Cole punches his opponent so hard, it's like hearing a rubber mallet connect with a board.

My stomach rolls.

"Ouch," Hannah says.

The opponent moves surprisingly quickly and kicks at Cole. Cole shifts, almost lazily, avoiding him easily.

With every hit, the crowd surges, and when blood spills, it becomes nearly earsplitting. They're bloodthirsty.

An internal war is taking place in my head, the desire to be able to inflict this kind of pain and the utter horror at the notion.

I sag back, ready to tell Hadley and Hannah we should go when a set of icy blue eyes stop in front of me, and my body hums with familiarity as Grey appears.

"What in the hell are you doing here?"

Chapter 22

Grey

Mila's eyes shine with defiance, but I recognize an underlying edge of panic from the hotel that keeps her silent.

"Hey, Grey," Hadley says.

"Is Nolan here?" I ask.

"He's at an outreach thing overnight."

He and Corey were roped into going together, fielding questions, and talking with high school students. "He's going to lose his shit if he finds out you're here." And want to punch me in the face. Repeatedly. "Come on," I say.

"We're leaving," Mila says.

I shake my head. "You can't. The doors are locked until the bets are paid."

"What kind of fire hazard idea is that?" Hadley asks.

I jerk my head again, indicating for them to follow me back to where Dustin, Abe, Bryant, and Sonny, a girl from Highgrove who's been trying to get Cole's attention for the past six months are watching the fight.

Dustin raises his eyebrows, looking from the girls to me

before lowering his bottom lip with an expression that says, *Not bad.*

It makes me want to punch *him* in the face. Repeatedly.

"Hey," Sonny says, scooting over to make room for them before glancing at me. "You guys are here to see Grey?"

Mila stares at her for a moment. "We came to see the fight."

Dustin elbows me. "Rejected."

"I'm Sonny," she says, ignoring Dustin.

"I'm Mila. And this is Hannah and Hadley."

"What has you guys coming to see the fight?"

Hannah shrugs. "I'm dealing with some anger issues. My ex drugged me with edibles a couple of months ago, and I thought coming here and watching guys beat the shit out of each other might help."

Sonny raises her brow. "Is it working?"

Hannah nods. "A little."

The crowd cheers, but I miss the move. I've been distracted since spotting Mila in the crowds. I want to ask her what in the hell they're really doing here but focus on the fight. Or I damn well try.

Every time one of the three moves, my eyes follow, ensuring no one gets separated when there are so many strangers tonight, with JB being in the ring from West Virginia.

Abe looks at them and then at me. "Tell me you're not getting involved with one of them. I can smell the classism from here."

Mila turns, looking over her shoulder at him, her eyes nearly silver in the darkened space. "That's just soap."

Dustin howls out a laugh.

Abe's face contorts with anger, a sore loser even outside of the ring.

Mila stares at him, not a threat but an assessment, or maybe she just refuses to flinch.

206

I stab Abe with my elbow. "Focus."

He turns to face me with a disgruntled look, and as he does, Mila shifts to look at the fight. "You know what happens if they tell someone," Abe says.

"They're not going to say anything."

Abe gives me a doubtful expression.

Thankfully, the fight is brief. We expected it to be. Untrained fighters are eager to compete, and more often than not, they're willing to put a hefty sum of money on the fight, making an easy rake.

Cole comes to our corner with a cocky smile, wide from his mouthguard. He spits it out and fills his mouth with the water Mackey hands him before spitting it into a bucket.

Hadley blanches.

"You were slow with that uppercut," Mackey critiques him.

Cole chuckles, the adrenaline preventing him from feeling the cut above his right eye. "He brought a full crowd. I wanted them to feel at least like they got a few minutes for their hard-earned cash." His eyes glitter with humor as he sweeps his gaze over Hadley, Hannah, and Mila. "Who in the fuck are you?"

"Grey's friends," Dustin says.

Cole's eyebrows jump, and he looks across them again before connecting with me. "Well, shit. Introduce me."

I do.

"Congratulations. It was nice meeting you all," Mila says, offering a wave.

"Aren't you going to celebrate with us?" Cole asks.

Abe mutters something under his breath that has Dustin laughing.

Mila doesn't turn to acknowledge them. "Maybe another time."

"One drink," Cole says. "On me."

"We can stay for a drink," Hannah says.

Sonny's gaze shifts to Hannah. "We'll meet you up there."

Any other night, I'd stay down here and ensure the smooth distribution of monies, but with Mila and the others here, I leave Bryant, Dustin, and Abe with Cole.

"Blair!" Sonny calls as we enter the bar. A woman with white blonde hair tipped pink, and red lips turns to face us. She smiles when she sees Sonny and quickly makes her way over to us. "I'm so glad you made it. This is Grey, the guy I've been telling you about."

Beside me, Hadley's eyes grow round, but she quickly tucks the expression away. Hannah's not half as discreet, turning an accusing look on me and making me feel like a complete asshole. Mila, however, is once again unflinching, shoulders back, face impassive.

"It's nice to meet you," Blair says, smiling at me.

I nod, trying not to scowl at Sonny. She's notorious for trying to set me up with everyone she knows.

I suspect she believes Cole will want to date her if I date one of her friends. It wouldn't matter.

"Let's get a table," Dustin says.

Sonny threads her arm through Blair's, leading her to the back of the bar, where they slide into an extra-long booth.

The rest of us join, and Sonny introduces everyone for a third time.

Minutes later, the others join us from downstairs and crowd into the booth as cigarette smoke fills the bar, prompting yet another round of introductions.

Cole looks at me, a butterfly bandage holding the cut above his brow closed. "Oh shit," he mutters, leaning back in his seat. "For not dating, Grey's got a whole goddamn buffet."

"They're friends," I growl. "Hadley's dating one of my teammates."

"*Friends?*" Abe asks with a smirk. "They came out to

fucking Highgrove unannounced. Clearly one of them wants your nuts."

Hadley's brow flattens, and if Nolan didn't want to hit me for them being here before, he would for subjecting her to Abe's judgment.

"Thank god a man finally understands women," Mila muses.

Easy laughter fills the table, but I wait for Abe's biting return. So does Mila, though she doesn't hold his stare this time.

My two worlds are crashing together with the grace of a fucking linebacker.

"What did you guys think of the fight?" Cole asks them.

"Was that sweeping thing you did with your foot hard?" Hannah asks.

Cole grins, and Dustin laughs.

"Revenge against the ex-boyfriend?" Sonny asks.

Hannah shakes her head. "I have a younger brother who's a pain in my ass."

Laughter chases her words.

"I've used that move more than once on my pain-in-the-ass brother," Cole says, eliciting new laughter and a half dozen jabs aimed at Abe, who flips him off.

Cole's eyes shift to Mila. "How do you guys know each other?"

"My best friend plays on the team with Grey."

"Best friend as in fuck buddies, or he won't pay attention to you?" Dustin asks.

I have to hold my tongue from the automatic instinct of telling him to shut the fuck up. This is how my friends talk to each other, and I told Mila these parts of my life were different, played by different rules. But if I jump in, it will only make things worse.

"Of the platonic variety. We've been neighbors since we were kids," Mila says.

Bryant smirks. "That doesn't mean much. Cole chased his neighbor for what? Three years, was it?"

Cole runs a hand down his face. "Will you ever let that story die?"

"Remember how many yards you mowed that summer, trying to save up to buy that necklace?"

Cole shoots Bryant a warning look as a stack of cups and two pitchers of beer are dropped off at the table, followed by Mackey.

"I'm just saying, girl next door is every dude's wet dream and the cause of tented pants," Bryant says, taking a glass.

"She and Hudson are like brother and sister," Hannah says.

"Hudson?" Abe asks. "Hudson McKinley? You two are neighbors?"

Mila squares her shoulders and nods. I know she'll come across the table if he insults Hudson.

"That dude's fucking loaded. His dad played in the NFL." Abe looks over her again, likely seeking signs of wealth that are subtly apparent with the gold chain around her neck where three rings interconnect and a slender gold ring around her middle finger. If he saw her Audi, he'd hate her on the spot.

"The NFL?" Sonny asks. "You know people who have been in the NFL?" She turns to me.

"My coach was in the NFL," I tell her.

"Damn. Is he rich, too?" she asks.

I shrug. Peters is disgustingly well off, making over two million a year plus bonuses for the past thirty years, but I have no idea what Krueger makes or how good his contract was while he was in the NFL, only that he was injured and forced into early retirement like so many players are.

Cole also assesses Mila through a new lens. "Welcome to our little hell hole. What do you think so far?"

I imagine Mila sleeping in the backseat of a car—a thought that has refused to leave my brain. I stare at her, wondering if she'll tell them she was poor—poorer than all of us.

"I'm in a bar with a secret room with nefarious intents." She raises her eyebrows. "Color me intrigued."

"I think she called us interesting," Dustin says.

Cole raises his glass and tips his chin to her. "I'll drink to that." He takes a long pull from his glass.

"So you guys are all *just* friends?" Sonny asks, her eyes stopping on Hannah, who asked the most questions during the fight.

Hannah nods. "Yeah. Grey's been training with Mila, so we just wanted to see what a fight looked like."

Cole sputters, beer dribbling down his chin that he wipes away with the back of his hand before turning to me, laughing. "You're training a chick? Bring her to the gym. Mackey, it's your dream. You can finally have a girl fighter."

Mackey shakes his head. "No offense," he says to Mila, "but no way in hell."

"Wait. You want to fight?" Dustin asks her. "Color me interested, now."

"No," I say, "She's not training to fight."

Cole doesn't look at me, though. His attention is locked onto Mila like the jaws of a pit bull, waiting for her response—reading her.

"I want to learn how to punch someone," Mila shares.

"Did you date her ex, too?" Dustin asks, pointing at Hannah.

Laughter bubbles from the table.

"Come by the gym. I'll teach you how to punch someone."

Cole pulls out his wallet, slips out a business card, and slides it across the table to Mila.

I want to intercept it like a pass on the field, not because I care about her seeing Cole again but because half the guys who train in Mackey's gym don't note gender when they take a swing, and I'd lose more than Mackey's respect if one of them goaded Mila into the ring.

I swallow. "We're still working on conditioning. She doesn't need to go to a gym for that."

Cole's eyes shine with amusement as he looks at me. "On second thought—" He reaches for the card, but Mila's faster, clasping it in her fist like a secret.

"Grey, Blair is obsessed with football, and she's hilarious and so much fun. I can't tell you how many times I've told her you two would be perfect together. You're the grump, and she's the sunshine." Her smile is radiant, and her accent is thick.

Beside her, Blair smiles nervously. She's pretty, with two deep dimples, light brown eyes, and swaths of brightly colored hair that hints at her being up for a good time and not caring about societal norms.

"She's totally your type," Sonny says.

"Being a grump is probably my best attribute. I'm gone and busy all the fucking time, which is why I don't date."

Cole raises his eyebrows and takes a long drink. "Grey's type is fucking football."

Sonny frowns.

"What is your type?" Hannah asks, looking at me.

I motion to Cole with my glass. "Football."

She narrows her eyes. "Everyone has a type."

"I can be a grump," Dustin says.

Sonny laughs. "You're all assholes."

"I'm pretty busy, too," Blair says, her accent even thicker than Sonny's. "I'm not really looking for anything serious."

Hannah yawns. "You know, I'm kind of getting tired, and we have a long drive, maybe—"

"I haven't finished my beer yet," Hadley says, gripping her drink. "So, do you all know how to fight?" She looks across my friends.

Abe shakes his head. "Bryant got fat and lazy." Half the group smirks.

"I used to whoop your ass," Bryant objects. "But now I have to work full time because I have two kids and a wife. You know, this was once proof that a man could feed his family. Women thought it was hot." He pats his stomach.

Dustin scoffs.

Cole sets his drink down. "Grey would have made one hell of a fighter, but he chose football. Abe does mostly underground. Once he can learn to rein in his temper, he has a chance of getting into the business."

"Fuck you," Abe bites.

Cole waves a hand at him to prove his point.

Hadley looks at Dustin. "Do you fight?"

"Not anymore." He points to his left eye. "I took a cheap hit and am mostly blind on this side."

No one makes a joke, not even Abe. The accident was serious and caused a financial debt Dustin's still working to pay off.

"I'm sorry," Hadley says.

Dustin shakes it off. "It wasn't meant to be. I'm working toward becoming an electrician, now."

"You don't like our beer?" Abe asks, still focused on Mila. She's the only one not drinking.

My resolve to remain silent and neutral withers as my fists clench in my lap, wanting to hit Abe and tell him to back off.

Mila slides her gaze to him. "I'm driving."

Hadley drains the rest of her beer and sets it down with too much force. "I'm kind of tired, too. We should go."

As they stand to leave, I do, too.

"Where are you going?" Dustin asks, looking at me.

"I'm going to walk them out."

"No one's going to bother them," Sonny says.

"Yeah, we're fine," Mila says, pulling her coat tight. "Congratulations on your win tonight," she tells Cole.

"Nice meeting you guys," Hadley says with a wave.

I follow them, ignoring Abe's inappropriate remarks at my back.

The air is again cold, and there aren't half as many lights outside as there should be. "What in the hell were you guys thinking?" I ask, turning on them.

Shock and confusion paint their faces.

"This is not where you guys belong," I tell them.

"*Where we belong?*" Mila spits my words back at me.

"These fights can get dangerous," I say.

"Whose fault is it that women can't go somewhere alone?" Hannah asks. "Not ours. So be mad at all the brutes who poison the well."

"Trust me, if I could pick out every asshole who was a dick like your ex, I would pitch them to an island so it would be safer, but that's not the reality." I glance back at Billie's bar, where we've been participating in underground fights for the past few years.

"But if it's not safe and it's not legal, why are you here?" Hannah asks.

"Because the world isn't black and white." Is the best and only explanation I have.

Chapter 23

Mila

"That was..." Hannah doesn't finish her sentence.

"Yeah..." Hadley says.

"What was with Abe?" Hannah asks. "He needs an attitude adjustment, stat."

"He was a dick," Hadley confirms.

"He wasn't that bad," I say.

"Not that bad? He was shooting you devil eyes," Hannah says.

I noticed. "He's me."

Hadley whips her head to look at me from the passenger's seat. "He's *you*?"

"In our friend group, I'm the suspicious one who doesn't open up easily, resists change, and is the most guarded. I'm more refined, but I'm Abe."

"No, that role's filled by Katie," Hannah says.

Hadley giggles, and I can't stop my own laugh from leaking out, though I shake my head. Katie has a tougher exterior, but she warms up. My suspicions never rest.

"You're nothing like him," Hannah tells me.

But I am.

"Okay, girl talk. I hereby invoke an NDA that whatever is said tonight in the car doesn't leave." Hannah leans forward, gripping the headrest of my seat. "Do you like Grey? Because I can usually spot these things, but you two have me thoroughly confused."

I shake my head. "No."

Hadley stares at me. I can feel the doubt emitting from her. "He wasn't at all interested in that Blair chick. As soon as Sonny introduced her, he was looking at you."

"He wanted you to be jealous," Hannah says.

"I don't date football players."

"You and me both," Hannah chimes.

"Why not?" Hadley asks me.

Telling her my real reason would be cruel, so I give a plausible excuse instead. "It would make things weird with Hudson being my best friend."

"That makes sense," Hannah says.

"Or..." Hadley says. "Maybe it would be seamless."

"Valid point," Hannah says.

"Grey doesn't date, so it's a moot point."

"He's *never* dated anyone?" Hannah asks. "Like *ever*?"

I shake my head, realizing once more that there's a lot about Grey I don't know, including this detail. "Not since I've known him."

"Since neither of you wants to date, you could always do a friends-with-benefits situation," Hadley says.

I side-eye her. "Like you and Nolan?"

Hannah howls with laughter.

Hadley raises her hands. "What's the worst that could happen? You guys catch feelings for each other?"

. . .

Her words fester in my thoughts after I drop them off and lie in bed. My bedding is too hot, too cool, too heavy, and not heavy enough. I'm restless, and more than once, my thoughts stray to Grey, wondering if he and Blair hit things off once we left. Is he kissing her the way he'd kissed me? What else might they be doing?

The thought of Grey naked makes that pressure between my legs grow as I trace my finger along my bottom lip, allowing the memory of that damned kiss to resurface. I recall the bite of his teeth, the graze of his tongue, and imagine him doing that along my breasts, my neck, and between my legs. The heat and roughness of his hands against my thighs, my ribs—everywhere.

These past couple of weeks are wreaking havoc only because we're spending so much time alone due to our friends being busy from the holidays along with this stupid and crazy deal we struck. Maybe it's also the fact I haven't had sex for over a year, and Grey is undisputedly one of the most attractive guys to walk the earth.

I roll over and stare at the pages of my book, but I can't focus on the words. I close my eyes, but the image of Grey kissing Blair, running his tongue across her, and driving inside her makes my stomach uneasy.

I growl with frustration, hating that we went to Highgrove to watch the fight, and that Evelyn planted this seed of me being with Grey in my thoughts, which Hadley watered tonight with the suggestion that Grey could be mine in all the physical ways.

The sound of my phone vibrating stirs me awake.

Five people call me. Two are on the second level of the house, two are in another state, and Griff is across town. All of them should be asleep, which has me scrambling for my phone.

Grey's name on the screen is the last thing I'm expecting.

"What are you doing?" I ask.

"I didn't know if your parents were asleep."

"Of course, they're asleep. It's five."

"Five thirty."

I pull back the covers. "Are you here?"

"You're supposed to be warming up."

My brows furrow as I ascend the basement stairs and open the door that leads out near the front door. I pull the curtain back, exposing the window beside the door, and peer out at Grey, standing on the front porch.

I hang up, disarm the alarm, and pull open the door.

"What are you doing?"

Grey's eyes flash to my Disney's Stitch pajamas that I received as a birthday present last year. They're so thin you can practically see the outline of my breasts, certainly my nipples. I cross my arms over my chest.

I swear, his scowl deepens. "Why aren't you dressed."

I return his scowl and search for signs of a night of unadulterated bliss: a hickey, scratches on his neck, swollen lips. I want to be angry with him, the impulse so intense I have to hold my breath and remind myself he hasn't done anything to warrant my anger before I can respond. "For what? Unless there's an alien invasion, I'm going back to bed."

"It's five thirty."

"Exactly."

"You're supposed to be warming up," he says again.

A gust of cold wind rifles my hair and has goosebumps coating my skin. "And you're not supposed to be here. You said you were spending the week in Highgrove."

"Are you quitting?"

"Hello, judgment. It's so nice to see you again. Won't you please come in?"

Grey's eyes flash with silent objections, but he passes me and steps into the house. I'd like to have this conversation here, next to the front door, so he can leave, but Jon is a notoriously light sleeper. I cross to the basement door, swing it open wide, and point for Grey to go downstairs.

He hesitates.

"It's this or you leave," I tell him.

His jaw clenches. I don't think he's used to being told what to do. He moves forward, though, silent on the stairs that lead down to my personal space.

I close the door and follow him.

Grey's peering around as I reach the bottom step. "Why do you rent an apartment?" he asks.

"Why are you here?" I counter.

"So you can trust me to answer your question, but not if I'm capable of training you?"

I'm undercaffeinated, exhausted, recovering from multiple near panic attacks, and struggling with more inse-curities and jealousy than I've experienced in the past several years—maybe ever. The combination is making me incapable of sparring with Grey, even with words. "Are you that upset that we came out last night?" My eyes pinch. "Are we *that* embarrassing? Or is this because we ruined your blind date?"

"It wasn't a date."

"A hookup then."

"We didn't hook up. Nothing happened. I left an hour after you did. *Alone.*"

I hate the relief that slides through me, potent as caffeine, easing my muscles.

"If you wanted to see a fight, why didn't you just ask?"

It takes me a second to recall we're still arguing and why. "Would you have let me come?"

Grey stares at me, a resounding no clear in his clenched jaw. "It wasn't safe."

"Sonny was there. So were other women."

"It wasn't safe for *you*."

I shake my head, emotions snarling in my stomach—anger and offense with sharp thorns of regret that leave me wishing I hadn't told him about my past. "I've been taking care of myself for a long time."

Grey takes a step closer to me, anger dancing in his eyes like flames in a fire. "It kills you to ask for help. Doesn't it?" He takes another step and then another.

I stare at him, pride thrumming in my chest like a shield, one Briggs has warned me against hiding behind. "I didn't need help." I can't tell him the real reason we went last night because selling out Hannah would make me a jerk. "We were just there to see the fight. After two weeks of working out and not even teaching me how to shove someone, I wanted to see what it was all about. See if your friend was as good as you claimed."

Grey swallows the rest of the space between us, so close I can feel his erratic breaths and the warmth radiating from his body. "Or maybe you just wanted to see me."

His arrogance gives me whiplash that has my anger spiking. "I—"

Grey's hand encircles the back of my neck, hauling me toward him so fast and hard I have to raise my hands to brace myself as I collide with his chest. Before the shock can settle, he's kissing me. His mouth is hard and urgent, a declaration of war as his lips rove across mine without the same introduction I'd felt with our first kiss. Instead, he kisses me as though he knows me, like he's punishing me as he tips my neck back and runs his teeth over my bottom lip. He doesn't allow me to meet his rhythm as he takes complete control of the kiss, greedy and purposeful as though he's memorizing me—marking me.

220

He pulls away just as suddenly as our kiss began, his chest rising and falling with heavy breaths, his eyes as bright and piercing as the stars I'd stared at last night—the stars I think too much about, like him. The coldness sweeps over me with the loss of him pressed against me as my heart bleats in my chest.

I should be asking him what in the hell he's thinking and why he's here. I should tell him this is likely a terrible idea that we'll both regret, but instead, I'm gripping his shirt and sealing my mouth over his again.

Grey envelops me, sliding one hand into my hair. His fingers span around the back of my skull, angling my head with the slightest of pressures before his tongue invades. He sweeps into my mouth as his other hand wraps around my lower back, ensuring he's in complete control.

I run my tongue along his, matching the savage and unforgiving tempo he established, losing myself in the heat of his mouth, the pull of his fingers, and the demands we both work to develop and then establish.

Grey's hand dips under the thin barrier of my shirt, and I match him, sliding my hands under his sweatshirt and discovering hot, sculpted flesh that I rake my fingertips over. He groans, and I take the point, kissing him harder.

His hold on me tightens as his fingers fist my hair and compress against my back, pressing me so close I feel his heart against my chest and his desire pressing into my stomach. A sound between a gasp and a moan catches in my throat, and I know Grey feels it, maybe hears it, because his lips pull into a smile against mine for half a second before he plunders my mouth with his tongue, taking this point.

Fury has me kissing him harder. I want his pleasure more than my own. It's a game—a dangerous, reckless match that leaves me feeling wanton.

I slide my hands down his chest, each muscle contracting as

I pass over it until I'm gripping the band of his sweatpants and underwear and slipping my hand inside.

Grey's moan mixes with mine as I wrap my hand around his length. My body aches, an empty feeling that has my heart racing and desperation making me clumsy as I tug at his pants, forgetting the rules and the points as the need to feel him inside of me becomes my only thought.

"Mila," Grey says, encircling my wrist before I can move further.

I'm breathless, my heart pounding painfully in my chest, reverberating in my core with one focus—him.

"This isn't why I came."

I shake my head. "I know. And I know you don't date, which is perfect. I don't want to date, either. Relationships freak me out, and I suck at them." The words pour out of me with conviction. I've always been terrible at relationships. I don't trust people, which makes me cagey to let people in, so I always date guys who are like Green-eyes from the football game or guys too burned to care or ask.

Grey's eyes bore into mine, and I see his lust slipping away, sense reminding him who I am—who we are. His restraint is impressive, hinting at how strong his morals are. There are a million things I don't know about Grey, details I would fail if quizzed about his preferences, but time has sewn knowledge about his honor, character, and loyalty.

Grey's sapphire eyes track mine as I take a step back toward my bedroom, and I don't think either of us knows if I'm inviting him to follow or trying to escape. The rules of our game are too new, too unknown.

He steps forward, reaching for me fast as a strike. He wrapps his hand around my hip, the roughness of his skin is so much better than I'd imagined, promising the friction I've imagined so many times. His lips land on mine like he feels the same desperate need and holds the same hope that this will quench whatever desire burns between us.

I pull away before things go too far, wordlessly leading him to my room, where I close the door and try not to allow the intimacy it offers to fester as I turn to face him, hating how fast the brazenness that had me kissing him eddies.

Grey steps beside me and reaches for the hem of my shirt. With a gentle tug, he pulls me closer and kisses me. His hands make purchase on my waist, giving me the illusion of feeling small while he continues kissing me, trailing his fingers up my torso, across my ribs, so light, it's nearly ticklish, and then over the swell of my breasts.

Heat swallows me a second before he pulls away and reaches down, grasping my shirt in his hands again and stripping it off with one tug. My nerves and desire soar as he watches his thumbs brush across my nipples.

His eyes snap to mine as I sigh, studying my reaction as he rolls my nipple between his fingers. He slides his other hand over my chest, neck, and jaw, and then skates his thumb against my bottom lip. He slips his thumb between my parted lips, pressing it against my tongue. I close my mouth around the callused skin as he rolls my nipple again, harder this time, resurrecting the rules.

I run my tongue over his thumb and suck. Grey groans, a long and intoxicating sound that has desire pooling between my legs. I rake my teeth against his skin, and Grey bends closer. Anticipation that he's going to run his tongue over my nipple as I'd imagined last night has my breath stuttering, but then his mouth comes down on my neck, kissing up to my jaw where he nips me at the same time he pinches my nipple again. His tongue soothes the spot, and then he's kissing down the column of my neck, across my collarbone. Goose bumps chase every kiss, lick, and taste while he teases my nipple into a stiff peak.

I run my hand over his pants, and Grey's hips shift forward, his breath catching, encouraging me to do it again. This time, I press firmer as the ache in my core increases.

He sinks lower, grazing his tongue over my untouched nipple. My back arches, and the need to feel him inside of me is so damn consuming I'm shaking with want.

"I need..." I start to say.

Grey gives my nipple a final flick of his tongue and then straightens, the bulge in his pants proof that he knows exactly what I need.

He moves us to my bed with a hand on my waist and pulls the rumpled bedding lower. I reach for his pants, but Grey catches my wrist. "I need to taste you first."

I shake my head. "It's just sex."

The ghost of a frown mars his brow, but before I can study it, he bends down and places a hand behind both of my knees, knocking me on my back without an ounce of grace. He doesn't give me a second to recover, discarding my pants and under-wear with one clean swipe.

"God, you're beautiful." His hands go to my thighs, and I hate that my thoughts wander to that man in Orlando telling Grey he hoped he had a bag.

Grey spreads my legs, each palm pressing down on my thighs, and though embarrassment lingers in the back of my thoughts, the reverent way he stares down at my exposed sex quiets those nerves. Grey pulls me to the edge of the bed, then drops to his knees, and before my next breath, he runs his tongue across me. My back arches again, and my plea sounds too much like his name as I slide a hand into his hair, trying to remind myself that blonds aren't my type.

Grey runs his tongue over me again, lazily, exploratory, reminding me of our first kiss. Every time I arch or gasp, his grip constricts, and he hums in response, an appreciative sound that

I get drunk on. I'm lost to the sensations of sharpness from his unshaven face and the way his tongue goes from teasing to demanding, marching me straight for a release and then stopping, leaving me on what feels like a cliff.

"Grey." My voice is no longer a plea but a warning as I tug at his hair, trying to direct his mouth back to where I need it so I can tumble into the abyss.

He chuckles a dark and mirthless sound. "You're so damn wet. So responsive," he says, flicking his tongue across me again.

I shiver as my eyes slam shut and my heart beats a needy and separate tune. That throb between my legs builds as he leans back again, determining his next move. With his mouth still inches away from where I want him—need him—he brushes his fingers over my sex, rubbing that bundle of nerves and then drawing his finger down to my entrance, and slowly— so damn excruciatingly slowly—he presses inside of me.

I groan, barely managing to keep my eyes open because observing Grey watch me has become my new favorite hobby. His eyes flash to mine as he withdraws his finger and presses it back inside of me. He adds a second finger, and my hips surge off the bed. Grey shifts forward ans seals his mouth back over me, working me with his tongue and his fingers like a musician plays his favorite instrument until I feel the tremble start in my spine and spread to my thighs and down my legs. My entire body trembles with need as Grey's pace becomes a torturous demand, and then I'm coming apart, panting and whispering his name as stars flash behind my eyelids.

He runs his tongue over me a final time and then stands, his chin wet with my arousal. I expect to see a smirk, proof that I lost this first round that he dominated and wrung me out with, but instead, he's staring at me like I was the one on my knees.

I fist his sweatshirt and pull him toward me, but he remains still, forcing me to sit up to meet his mouth. I kiss him, tasting myself on his tongue, a heady and wicked taste that makes my head spin.

Lust and panic vie in my chest as I realize I nearly slept with the guy I've been convinced only tolerated me.

Briggs would say this was a terrible way of proving my self-worth.

"Get dressed. It's time to go running." He stands, and heads back out to the main area of the basement, leaving me in a cloud of bliss and confusion.

Chapter 24

Mila

"You seem distracted today," Briggs says, leaning back in his chair, pen relaxed in his hand rather than poised to write.

I scrub a hand over my face. "I almost slept with Grey," I blurt out.

Briggs crosses his legs, and though he tries to hide his surprise, I see it. We've worked together for too long for me to miss the way he blinks faster and his lips part without a word. He turns down to his notepad, flipping back a couple of pages. "Grey's Hudson's best friend...?"

I nod though he's still distracted, searching through his notes. "We got caught in the moment and..."

Briggs stares at me, waiting for me to finish my sentence.

"It was a mistake."

"Are you saying that because it *was* a mistake or because you think it *should* have been?"

"He's leaving next year."

Recognition has Briggs leaning back in his chair. "That's

why you've been keeping him at arm's length all this time." It's not a question.

"I really didn't think he liked me."

"And now?"

I shake my head. "I don't know. He doesn't want a girlfriend, and Grey's not casual. I've told him a lot, and if I told him more..."

Briggs stares at me with eyes too kind and caring. Despite our relationship remaining professional, he sometimes looks at me with a level of affection parallel to my parents.

Tears flash in my eyes, unwanted and unbridled. I don't want his sympathy right now or for him to think about the years and experiences I lived through that make letting people close to me so damn difficult.

"It was a mistake," I say firmly.

"Next May is a long way off. You and Grey might date and realize you're better off as friends or decide you want to try long-distance. Or maybe he won't leave. Maybe he stays here."

"He's too good of a football player. He'll be drafted for sure."

Therapy is different than talking with a friend who immediately jumps in with assurances and hopeful promises. Briggs makes me sit with my words and realities.

"Are you afraid of him leaving or afraid he'll get too close?"

My throat remains too tight. "You already know the answer."

"And you know that's not how this works."

He wants me to tell him because we're never supposed to make assumptions in therapy. "Both."

Briggs is silent again. He's waiting for me to look at him, but I can't. Not yet. One hint of pity and these tears will fall, and I'm not in the mood to cry today.

"Mila," he says, voice soft and calm. "Have you been on any more self-dates?"

I blink back my surprise at the question, and my throat loosens. I shake my head.

"I want you to go on a date this week with yourself. Remember, no tech, no books, just you being present with your thoughts. When you get home, I want you to look at yourself in the mirror and tell yourself some positive affirmations."

I hate mirror meditation and nearly remind him of this, but I don't because it only reveals how insecure I'm feeling. When I first moved to Oleander Springs, my insecurities and fear of acceptance led me to codependency. I didn't know who I was or what I wanted, only that I desperately wanted to stay. It took me years to shed those habits and even longer to believe Jon and Alex wanted me, not because they were stuck with me but because they liked me as a person, as an individual—as a daughter. I stopped trying to be who I thought they wanted me to be: polished, classy, smart, and worldly, and began discovering who I was and what made me happy. It wasn't easy. It still isn't always easy.

"Remember to recognize that when you feel like pulling back, your brain is trying to protect you because of old patterns and past traumas." He shakes his head. "You've come a long way, Mila. You have the tools and knowledge to know when a relationship is safe and healthy, whether it's friendship or more. Trust yourself, and trust that Grey—your parents, Evelyn, or Hadley—want to be there for you because you're a good, kind, funny person, deserving of love and friendship."

Tears burn in my eyes again as he silently stares at me, willing the words he's said a hundred times to imprint on my brain finally.

"Mila..." he says again.

This time, I can't stop a tear from sliding hot and fast down my cheek. Even without looking at him, I hear his pity.

"Your past and those who failed you don't determine your self-worth because it's inherent. They failed, not you. You didn't fail them."

More tears slip past my defenses. "Will you please stop?"

He does.

Doubt is intrinsically hard-wired in my thoughts and reactions. Even deeper is the self-loathing I've been trying to escape for the past thirteen years. It's like trying to swim to the surface, and they're my shipwreck, but every time I try to escape, they pull me back, forcing me to paddle against the same damn tide. Time and time again.

Some days I feel more hopeful that I'll be able to leave the wreckage behind. Other days, like now, I worry it will eventually drown me.

I mute my thoughts and fears and stare at a blank space on the wall. "I'll go on a self-date," I tell him, keeping my voice steady and calm.

"You're numbing yourself." It's not an accusation but a reminder.

I turn my gaze to him, my tears finally controlled like my emotions.

Briggs looks defeated.

"I can't do this today, Briggs. It's too exhausting."

"Hating yourself is the exhausting part," he tells me.

"I'm pretty sure it's the liking myself that's so damn exhausting."

Briggs pulls in a deep breath—his version of a sigh.

"My parents and I are heading to the beach after I leave here. I have lots of time to date myself at the beach."

He gives a wry smile. Sometimes I think Briggs also fears

my past will eventually drown me. "What are you going to do about Grey?"

"Pretend it never happened and move on."

"You know that never works. Burying what happened between you won't make it go away."

"It's already done."

"Did it mean something to you?"

I know he's asking if there was intimacy because we've talked about intimacy a lot over the years. I once believed intimacy meant sex, but Briggs taught me intimacy is much more than that. It's sharing beliefs and ideas, allowing yourself to be vulnerable, holding hands, and cuddling. Intimacy makes me uncomfortable, another reminder of why I've always been attracted to men like Green-eyes who don't care and those so emotionally damaged they don't dare look in my closet because they've soldered theirs shut.

I swallow, recalling how Grey had looked at me with something more than lust, how his touches were a methodical and intentional mapping of my body. "I don't know." It's as honest of an answer as I can give at this moment because I don't want it to mean anything, know it can't mean anything, but I also feel the hint of melancholy that threatens to sink into my bones when thinking it won't be anything.

"Yes, you do," Briggs urges me.

"He's focused, Briggs. It would be unfair of me to ask for more when I know he doesn't want to give it, especially when we both know I might not be capable of reciprocating it."

Briggs sits up in his chair, eyes growing round. "You're wrong." The silence stretches, and as I stare at him, waiting for him to tell me what I'm wrong about, he stares back, eyes hard with determination. "You're capable of giving and receiving whatever you want to give or receive. It's your choice. That's why we're doing these self-dates. You're depicting your worth, Mila. You get to decide how much you want, how you want to be treated, and what you're willing to give in return, not just to others but to yourself.

"We talk about forgiveness a lot, and you've done a damn good job of forgiving others, but you must forgive that little girl inside of you and your future self that you blame. Forgive yourself, Mila."

Tears crest over my eyes again, blurring the room. As much as I hate the emotions, I'm grateful they exist, reminding me I'm not entirely broken. I still have the balance that keeps me from falling apart—the push and pull—determination and creed.

When I get home, my thoughts are in a million places.

"Ready to go?" Alex asks, handing me a Starbucks. "We got road snacks."

"Aren't we supposed to stop and get these?" I ask.

"Oh, we will," he says with a smirk that slips as I remove my sunglasses.

"I'm okay," I assure him, feeling the puffiness of my eyes. Years ago, I would have concealed all signs of my emotions. I remind myself this is another sign of my growth.

Alex's shoulders sink. "Rough day?"

"Rough therapy session."

He presses his lips together, his eyes gentle, before he takes my coffee back and sets it down on the dining room table. He wraps me in a hug, one hand on the back of my head and another on the middle of my back. When I was younger, past the point when I tried to conceal everything from him and Jon, they both rushed to solve my problems until realizing they often weren't tangible issues that could be resolved. Most of the problems I struggle with reside in the recesses of my memories and thoughts—in my judgments and perceptions of myself.

"We have to get going, or we're not going to get there until —" Jon's words and footsteps stop somewhere behind me.

Alex nods at whatever silent inquiry the two share, and then Jon's footsteps echo softer and slower as he crosses to us.

"Is everything okay?" Jon runs a hand over my shoulder.

I think of telling them that it's not. Telling them about my encounter with Julian Holloway, how much I'm struggling with their long absences, how I can't fathom Hudson leaving next year, and how I may be growing attachments to Grey, who will also leave, has me feeling like I'm floating on an iceberg that continues breaking off into smaller pieces. They would stay. Jon would come home more frequently or propose that I move with them and transfer to California. They would try to fix it because they have always been willing to go to the ends of this earth for me.

"I'm okay. I'm just ... tired."

Alex squeezes me before loosening his grip. "Why don't you ride with us? You can nap in the backseat. Nothing good comes from being exhausted or hungry."

I nod, reaching for my coffee. "I probably will. Maybe not sleep, but just rest."

Jon nods. His gaze is even more inquisitive.

"Everything's packed?" Alex asks, reaching for his iPad on the counter and scanning a list or email that has him missing Jon's assurance.

Jon gives me a rueful grin and slides his arm over my shoulder. "Do you have a jacket?"

I nod. "I packed two."

He grabs the turquoise-colored throw from the back of the couch and a pillow that he tucks under his arm. "Set the alarm, and don't forget your coffee, babe," he calls to Alex. Outside, he turns his attention to the clear blue sky. "It feels like California today." He sounds relieved. "Want to talk about what's making you so tired?"

"Sometimes it feels impossible to be normal."

Jon crosses his arms, looking at me under heavy brows as he leans against his silver SUV, waiting for me to elaborate.

"I've been going to therapy for thirteen years, and making new friends still makes me itch."

"Grey?"

I shake my head. Grey is a different dot in the pointillism painting that makes up my life. "Do you remember me telling you about book club?"

He nods.

"Four girls joined in addition to Evelyn and me. Hadley, Hannah, Katie, and Brielle. Hadley dates Nolan, Hudson's teammate, and Hannah's her roommate. Hadley and Hannah are really nice. They're sweet and kind and funny, and they want to be friends, but they have no idea how..."

Jon's brow lowers, and his lips purse as he stares at my tear-filled eyes. "How what?"

"How..." I hate the word crazy. It's offensive and hurtful, and for years, I labeled myself with the derogatory term. "Difficult it is for me to trust and let people in. How easily I can be triggered and how fast I can withdraw."

"Have I told you about when I came out to my family as gay?"

I shake my head.

"As you know, they're devout Christians, and I was so worried if they knew that I was different—that I was attracted to men—they'd see me as unworthy or broken, and we'd become estranged. My parents used derogatory terms for gay people my entire childhood, laughed at gay-bashing jokes, and heckled any marches or movements. But when I finally came out to them, they realized I was still me. Nothing about me had changed except that I could finally be unapologetically me. Everyone thinks everyone else is normal, but the secret is, *no one's* normal. No one's better. We're all just trying our best."

His eyes glitter as they cross over my face. "You don't owe anyone your full story, but you should never feel like you have to conceal who you are." He nudges me with his elbow. "Let them see how stubbornly loyal you are, how fiercely protective and committed you are to honesty, and how strong your determination for equality and fairness is. Let them see you're Mila Fucking Atwool."

A tear skates down my cheek as I smile. "I'm going to fire Briggs. You're a way better shrink."

Jon laughs, tugging me forward into his embrace. He knows I'm kidding. Briggs has taught me more about myself and life than maybe anyone. But something is different in the reverence and faith that comes from Jon—someone who didn't have to love or care for me but chose to—that makes my heart soar as high as the stars.

Chapter 25

Grey

I show up at Mila's apartment at five. I haven't seen her since Tuesday morning when pretenses went out the window, and I dove on her like a man depraved and starved. I couldn't help myself, couldn't go another day without kissing her. I've wanted to feel, taste, and consume her every minute of every day for the past two and a half years, and since the booster party, my resolve to remain single, prioritize my relationship with Hudson, and allow Mila to keep me at a distance all slipped away the second she kissed me back.

I've spent all week obsessing about tonight, trying to tire myself and my thoughts. But nothing has calmed me despite extra weight sessions, golf lessons with Corey and Palmer, and going toe to toe with Cole in the ring multiple times.

I'm fucked.

Evelyn opens the door. "Hey, Grey. Come on in. Mila's just finishing getting ready."

Hudson jogs down the steps, and I find myself on the defense, waiting for him to strike. "Hey, man."

I wasn't expecting the guilt in my chest to grow in strength and size like a fucking tornado, yet it does. Hudson's been warning the entire damn team away from Mila since day one—another contributing factor for why we thought there was more between them than just friendship—and I wrapped her legs around my neck like a scarf and made her orgasm on my tongue hours after allowing her stay at an underground fight.

If there's a hell, I earned myself a first-class ticket.

Before I can ask him how his trip was or plead for his forgiveness, Mila descends the stairs wearing jeans, a plum-colored sweater, and dark tennis shoes. That same barometer in my chest that warns me when I'm around her too long—eases at the sight of her. Similar to being around her too much, an unease grows when I'm away from her for too long. I don't remember when it started, only that it's a constant balance.

"What is Topgolf?" Evelyn asks.

Mila's silver-blue eyes spear me for half a second before going past me to Evelyn.

"It's a driving range with fancy lights and music," Mila says.

"When's the last time you hit a golf ball?" Hudson asks her, his lips crooked with amusement.

"If you're asking if I'm going to embarrass myself, the answer is probably. But let's be honest, I'm just there to give Grey the semblance of a balanced life."

"At least this booster seems nice," Evelyn says. "Hopefully, he doesn't prove to be a shrew."

Mila slides on her coat. "Here's to hoping.

Hudson turns to me. "How was the week?"

I swallow. "Good. How was your trip?"

"Crazy," Evelyn answers.

Hudson grins. "We had a good time."

"Tell him how you slept on a bunkbed," Mila says.

Hudson chuckles as Evelyn's face turns scarlet.

237

"Aren't you guys going to be late?" Evelyn asks.

"Mila." Hudson's voice turns serious. "Be careful tonight. If anything weird or—"

"I know. I've got it," Mila says, tucking her hands into her pockets. "We'll see you guys later."

Hudson nods once.

"What was that about?" I ask as we step outside.

"What was what about?"

I wave a hand toward the closed door of her apartment. "Hudson warning you to be careful."

"Nothing, just Hudson being Hudson. It had nothing to do with you, just safety in general."

I know she's lying, but I don't know how to call her out on it without sounding paranoid. "How was the beach?" I ask. "Where did you guys stay?"

Mila smirks as she slides her hands into her pockets. "Do you think I made it up to avoid you?" Her smirk spreads into a smile. "Because I would have thought you were lying if you told me you were going out of town." She laughs.

I had. I questioned if she was stewing in regret, too embarrassed or angry to see me again. "I was just making small talk."

Mila raises one brow. "You never make small talk."

I stare at her, working to place her tone that tries to imitate sarcasm. Mila matches my stare, lifting one brow. For a second, I think she's daring me to talk about what happened between us, label it, and advise on how we will move forward.

"Blair would be so disappointed if you lost that prize-winning grumpy and cynical personality. How will she be your sunshine?"

My brow flattens into a glare.

Mila laughs as we stop beside my truck. "Oh, good. You're not broken." She flashes another smile, and I'm pretty damn sure it's relief this time in her gaze. "We stayed at Corolla

Beach. It's Jon's favorite. He loves the wild horses, and Alex loves that some of his favorite sappy movies were filmed nearby." Her voice is the soft melodic tone I've begun to recognize as the one she uses when opening up.

I open the passenger door.

Mila looks from me to the open cab. "And I worked out every single day as promised. I'm officially ready to learn how to punch someone."

I flick my chin in the direction of the truck. "You're not ready yet."

She maims me with a glare. "It doesn't have to be perfect."

For a second, I debate if her annoyance is because she's hoping our arrangement ends sooner than later. It probably could. Despite her claims of disliking and avoiding organized sports, she's a decent athlete. I could teach her where and how to strike someone to at least shock them.

"How many more weeks of conditioning until the next step?" Mila's question breaks through my thoughts.

Mandated team practices begin on March first. I'll be back to waking up before dawn and pinching every hour to continue working on the field and off. With more time, I could train Mila to do so much more than just stun someone. I could teach her to evade a hit, read body language, and knock a grown man on his ass.

We have four weeks left, and I want every one of them. "Until you're running four miles daily and your balance improves."

"I have great balance."

"No, you don't."

Her brow flattens. "How would you know?"

"You favor your right side. Most do." I close her door and round to the driver's side.

"People take boxing classes and start shadowboxing on their first day."

"They shouldn't." I start the truck.

Mila glares at me.

"Be glad I'm not making you do all the mental shit Mackey made us do." I wait for the gate of her apartment to open and pull forward, heading for downtown.

"I've been in therapy since I was seven. Mental shit I can do."

I glance across at her.

She catches me and raises both eyebrows. "You've seen me naked. Why do you still hesitate to ask me questions?"

"Are we ready to talk about that?"

"What's there to talk about?"

My expression turns incredulous. I haven't been able to forget the taste of her, the sounds of her release, or the way she looked at me.

"What were you going to ask me about therapy?" she asks, skirting the conversation.

"I don't know if my questions will be offensive," I tell her honestly. "I don't know anyone else who sees a therapist; if I do, they don't talk about it. I don't know where the lines are with these subjects."

"More people should go to therapy. In my utopian society, everyone would attend therapy at least once a week."

"Why?"

"Because as humans, we're full of conflicting thoughts and feelings that we rarely understand or know how to work through, and we suppress them, forcing them into tangles that grow and fester." Her gaze is on the windshield, and traffic's too busy to wait for her to turn to me.

"What do you talk about in therapy?"

"We talk about all kinds of things. Initially, it was a lot of untangling things that happened during my childhood. We still work on untangling some of those knots. Childhood traumas are a bitch."

Trauma. The word has that faded and pixelated image of Mila come to the forefront of my thoughts. My throat is dry as I try to swallow. "What kinds of traumas?"

Her gaze slides to mine. "That's a little too deep for Topgolf, don't you think?" We stop at a red light two blocks from the address. "Do you need a crash course on the clubs or jargon?"

"I've been practicing with Corey and Palmer this week."

Mila nods distractedly. "I bet we could get Barnhardt to double the amount he offered you."

I scoff. "He's offered me a lot."

"He owns a private yacht and jet. I doubt he offered you enough."

Corey talks about spending summers sailing. It's a life I can't imagine. I spent summers camping in tents, building bonfires and forts. When it got unbearably hot, Cole's parents would drive us into Oleander Springs, and we'd find a neighborhood pool, pretend we lived there, and go swimming. I know next to nothing about golf, but a goddamn yacht is so far outside of my wheelhouse that I'm worried the forty thousand Barnhardt is offering me may slip off the table when he realizes I'm a redneck hick who didn't step foot outside of North Carolina before playing for Camden.

Chapter 26

Mila

This location is Gerald Barnhardt's newest and largest. No doubt he invited us here to show off a little. It's huge, swanky, and impressive.

"Damn," Grey says, looking awestruck.

"Don't get distracted," I tell him. "In a few years, you'll be worth so much, you could buy this place. Or hell, build one in Highgrove." I'd been nervous about tonight, but things seem normal between us. I don't know if I'm disappointed or just relieved. Regardless, I'm happy to be here and take my mind off the fact my parents returned to California this morning without a planned return date.

Grey's gaze drops to mine, and he smirks.

My stomach drops, recalling the way he'd made a similar expression in reaction to when he pinched my nipple. Before the thought can settle, he looks sideways at the long lines again, his unease a fading shadow I only recognize because I've known him so long.

"You have a hell of a lot to offer, Grey. Just because you don't have a million dollars in your bank account yet doesn't mean you're not worth a million dollars. Alex has to attend stuff like this all the time to get funding for scripts. It's all part of the game. You're here to get paid because they want your face on their brand. Don't think they're doing you any favors. This is all business."

Grey's gaze sweeps over my face, reading me for sincerity. I don't know if it's my desire to assure him or his trace of vulnerability that makes this moment feel more intimate than his face between my legs. "They want *you*, Grey. Don't forget that."

"Are you Grey Meyers?" The question pulls our attention to a stranger twenty feet away. His shock is visible with wide eyes and dropped jaw. "Dude, check this out. Grey Meyers is here!" he says, turning to a friend.

I want to roll my eyes, but instead, I smirk at Grey with a silent, *See? I told you so. They all want you.*

They do.

They've all become increasingly popular and recognizable, and no one hesitates to ask for autographs and pictures as this man does.

"Greyson!" Mr. Barnhardt appears, smiling proudly. "Thanks for coming tonight. I'm so glad you guys could make it." He shakes Grey's hand and then mine. "Lovely to see you again, Mila."

"You as well. This place is amazing," I tell him.

His smile broadens, confirming his reasoning for inviting us here was to flex his wealth. "Let's head upstairs. We'll wait for the others and get something to drink."

The stairs lead to a narrow hall that has bays extending the length of the building. The course spans so far into the distance the net is nearly invisible.

It's another obnoxiously warm night that feels like early autumn, perfect for Topgolf and terrible for snow that has me slipping out of my coat as Mr. Barnhardt proudly tells Grey about the amenities of the building before instructing us to follow him to the area he's reserved for us tonight.

I move to follow when Grey pulls me back, his arm a bar around my shoulders, pressing me against his chest. Cedar and sandalwood tease my nose as a golf club swings in front of me so hard, I feel and hear the air turbulence. If I hadn't stopped, I'd likely be on the floor with a broken leg or ankle. Maybe worse.

Grey shifts, positioning me at his back, one arm tucked around my waist as he faces the man who swung the club. He's visibly inebriated, barely standing upright as he drives the club into the tiled floor with enough force to make it snap.

"Hey," Grey's voice is a growl. "What are you doing?"

The drunk man looks at us with glassy eyes, smiling like Grey complimented his swing. He's a little older than us, his cheeks tinted red from the alcohol.

"Sorry, man. He didn't mean to. He's had a rough week," the guy's friend says, coming to his side.

"I couldn't care less," Grey says. "Get a handle on him or leave."

Mr. Barnhardt quickly approaches us, gaining the attention of a nearby employee. "Get these guys some pitchers of water, coffee, and some breadsticks on the house." He turns to us, eyes on me, as I slowly unwind from Grey's touch. "Are you all right?"

I nod, trying to shake off the unwanted feeling of being a damsel in distress.

"I'm sorry for the scare. Let's get you over here so you can take a seat."

Grey walks beside me, a wall to the bays, with his hand between my shoulder blades.

We stop at the last bay, where the upbeat pop music and bright lights make tonight feel like a real date rather than my being here as Grey's fake girlfriend to help him secure a binding deal.

"I took the liberty of ordering some of our most popular dishes, but please, let me know what I can get you both to drink?" Mr. Barnhardt says, tapping one of the large touch screens near the tee.

"Iced tea would be great. Thank you," I say.

"Is sweet tea okay?" he asks.

I grew up trying to drink my iced tea like Jon, wanting to hate sweet tea as vehemently as he does, but I've slowly begun realizing I feel relief rather than disappointment when they only serve the sweetened variety. "Even better," I tell him.

His smile is approving because here in the South, people who don't like sweet tea can't be trusted.

"I'll have the same," Grey says, glancing at the golf clubs and then the green ahead of us, his body shifting away, allowing enough space for another person between us.

Mr. Barnhardt enters our orders before turning back to us. His wealth is displayed almost overtly, rings with channels of diamonds on both ring fingers, clothes made of rich fabrics in designer brands, and shoes a supple leather.

"Tell me, Greyson, how do you feel about deciding not to enter the draft?" he asks, turning to Grey.

Grey's confidence is a mask that he wears so damn well. "It was the right decision. We'll have the advantage next year, making us unstoppable."

Mr. Barnhardt's eyes gleam as he grins. "Let's hope so. If your face is all over my businesses, I need you to be a winner."

I wince but recover before he can see it, pasting a smile on my face. "Grey's one of the most sought-after wide receivers in the country, not just our conference. Everyone recognizes his face, and he's practically a god here in Oleander Springs. Did you see how quickly people recognized him in your lobby?" I don't know the proper etiquette or details for a sponsorship meeting, but I do know it's vital to establish that we know Grey's value.

Mr. Barnhardt's gaze turns to mine, hints of surprise or maybe shock visible for a second before he nods. His gaze flicks to Grey, and they continue discussing football: the team, Coach Krueger, and the new offensive plays—all subjects that have Grey's deep-seated knowledge and dedication shining, making him look every bit the star.

When Mr. Barnhardt's colleagues show up, I'm a little disappointed to see all five are men. It makes me feel even more like a trophy.

"Are you a model?" the man who was introduced as Jeremiah asks. The question is shockingly common from men who are shorter than me.

I shake my head and take a drink of the iced tea they put a pink straw in to mark as mine.

"She should be," Mr. Barnhardt says, eyes lingering on me, dancing a fine line of being inappropriate.

Grey glances at me from where he's talking to the COO, and though he didn't hear the exchange, he seems to read my body language and excuses himself before coming to stand next to me as Mr. Barnhardt and his colleagues make small talk, catching up on their weekend.

Grey's brow lowers a fraction. Once more, his eyes contend for being brighter than the stars as he studies me. "Everything okay?" His voice is a smooth and deep sound that slides down my spine like a caress.

I nod, allowing the façade of intimacy to continue as I tilt my face toward him and smile.

Grey rubs his thumb softly across my back. "Thanks for being here."

At least two of them are watching us. I lean forward and

press a kiss just above his jaw. "Shine for them, Grey. Show them you're worth a million bucks."

He turns his face, and my heart skips, certain he's going to kiss me again. I want him to so badly my breath catches. His nose, lips, and chin gently press along the right side of my face, breathing me in before kissing my temple. It feels like I ordered an ice cream sundae and was given a single sprinkle as disappointment careens in my stomach.

We begin the game, three of the men going first before it's my turn.

"Do you need help?" Mr. Barnhardt asks. "Do you need someone to show you how to swing?"

Sarcastic retorts form on my tongue, but I swallow those with the reminder that this is about Grey's payday. I'm not about to jeopardize it due to a stranger underestimating me. Besides, I've always been a fan of actions speaking louder than words.

"Should we get her some ladies' clubs?" another of them asks.

"She's as tall as you," one replies.

Grey clears his throat and looks at me. "If she needs anything, she'll let us know. Mila's more than competent."

I select the pitching wedge and move to the tee. I only took up golf because Alex loves the game and bribed me by allowing me to drive the cart and later because Hudson plays. I hear both voices as I line up and draw my driver back. I swing, crushing the ball down the green. I won't admit it to Grey, but my recent workouts have made me stronger and aided in hitting the ball harder.

When I turn around, one of the men assesses me. I know he doesn't think I'm half as pretty as I was thirty seconds ago before hitting the ball farther than him.

Pride shines on Grey's face as I return the club and resume my seat beside him.

"Don't worry. I'll take it easier on them with the next shot and let them win. I just needed to flex for a second."

Grey's fingers thread through my hair as he leans close. "Don't you dare take it easy on them."

"Like attracts like, I see," Mr. Barnhardt says, gazing at us. "That was impressive, Mila."

"That hit barely scratches the surface of how impressive and amazing she is," Grey tells him.

With the excuse I'm supposed to appear like his girlfriend, I find every excuse to stand closer, finding myself so damn present that the end of the night shocks and disappoints me.

Chapter 27

Mila

"How are you today?" Briggs asks, sitting across from me. "How was the beach?"

"Briggs, do you think my attachment style could change?" Multiple professionals and studies confirm they won't, that the traumas and inconsistencies I faced as a child will shape the rest of my life, making me always suspicious, distant, anxious, and painfully independent.

"Do you want them to?"

I hate when he answers my questions with another question, and I remind him of that with a silent glare. "Yes."

"I believe you can do anything you put your mind to. The mind is a powerful muscle. Like your workouts with Grey, practice will make you stronger. You know what you want, and I'm here to help you achieve those goals and overcome every hurdle you're ready to face. But, Mila, you're already a formidable force. Don't lose sight of your accomplishments."

Silence sits between us. Classes began yesterday, and despite my anticipation for the new term to start just a couple of weeks ago, I've found ways to fill my schedule, so I don't miss the routine of classes. I don't want to talk about this, though, or about my parents leaving and my uncertainty about when they'll return. Instead, I turn to a subject that takes the microscope off me. My heart thumps, and my nerves crackle. "I saw Julian Holloway."

Briggs blinks, visibly surprised. "When?"

"Last Sunday."

He blinks faster, and I know he's wondering why I didn't bring it up. It was because what transpired between Grey and me felt far more urgent, or because I needed more time to digest the situation, or because staying home with my parents made me feel safe and protected, regardless of the potential threat. "What happened?"

I trace a line over my chin. "He said something strange."

Briggs waits with rapt attention.

"He said I've been ignoring him for years."

Briggs leans forward, eyes stretched round. "Was there any more context?"

I shake my head. "Do you think he meant it metaphorically, as if society had ignored him for years, and I represent society?"

The chair creaks as Briggs leans back while shaking his head. "It's not a good idea for us to try and speculate what he meant. Did you tell anyone? The police? Your parents?"

"He said he wants to talk to me."

Briggs shakes his head again, faster and more determined. "No. It sounds like he might be mentally unstable. Engaging with him would not be safe." He stares at me.

"Nothing about it makes sense. I haven't heard a word or seen him in months." Nine months, nearly to the day.

"You, of all people, know things rarely make sense." He jots something down on his notepad. "Where did you see him? What happened?"

I tell him about the incident, how I felt his presence before seeing him, how he gave Evelyn water, and my error in insulting him.

"You need to contact the police," Briggs instructs, running a hand down his face as he does before launching into an avalanche of advice. We talk for the next forty-five minutes about what I need to do to remain safe.

"I haven't seen him since. What if it was just fate testing me?"

"Testing you?"

"To see if I'm over my fears."

Briggs shakes his head. "Don't mistake coincidences for fate. He was there because he was working. You were there because you were jogging, and Evelyn needed to sit down."

"I was running," I correct him. "Grey snaps at me if I jog."

Briggs doesn't crack a smile. I knew he wouldn't.

"You need to tell your apartment manager, the university, your friends, and the police. And you need to change your route." He's already told me all of this. Twice. But I nod again.

"I will."

"Mila," he says in a stern voice. His eyes are determined and intense, but that edge of gentleness and care that prods at my emotions is visible. "You deserve to be and feel safe. You deserve happiness and peace. What you don't deserve it suffering."

Briggs has repeated these words to me a hundred times. More. Over the years, Briggs has pointed out numerous times how I've constructed and clung to emotional patterns and destructive limiting beliefs that convince me I deserve pain—deserve to suffer. It's common for people who've experienced trauma, he's assured me.

He stares at me, pleading with me to do more than just hear the words this time.

Tears form in my eyes, pleading with him to understand how much I wish I could and how badly I try.

This was not the therapy session I was expecting. I planned to discuss my fake date with Grey at Topgolf and how difficult of a time I'm having with the ruse being over. How I don't know where we stand because, apart from my jokes about him seeing me naked, we still haven't talked about what transpired. Julian Holloway has been a bubble in my thoughts, though, and I knew it would eventually pop.

I pull in a deep breath. "I'll contact the university and the police," I promise him since I can't say the words he wants me to.

Briggs nods. "If you need anything, reach out. Continue your positive affirmations, and remember, you can do this. You can do anything you put your mind to."

I nod as I stand, pulling on my coat.

"I'll see you next week," he says.

I nod again.

The skies are darkening when I leave, the air cold and damp. This morning we had sleet, the closest thing we've seen to snow since last March.

"Mila," the sound of my name interrupts my thoughts. Before I can look up, my blood turns cold, and my heart races.

Julian Holloway stands beside my car, less than ten feet in front of me. Nausea hits me like a blow to the stomach, and I freeze.

He raises both hands just as he had when I saw him last week, gaze beseeching rather than angry as he takes the position of innocence. "I just want to talk to you."

"Are you following me?"

I've been seeing Briggs every Thursday since September. It's the most stagnant and dependable part of my schedule.

Julian takes a step forward, lowering his brow as though

he's offended by my question. "Why didn't you respond to any of my letters?"

I somehow find enough self-preservation to step back, widening the gap between us. "I don't know what you're talking about."

He laughs, a cruel and sardonic sound that I know will live in my brain and haunt me for years to come. "You could have helped me. You could have changed everything. I had to miss my mother's funeral because of you."

Fear feels like a weight on my shoulders, holding me in place and defying Briggs's claim that I deserve safety and peace. He's clearly crazy, and I should already be inside the office, yelling for help. "Stop following me."

His eyes narrow on me, and he takes a step forward.

I counter him with a step back and then another.

"Do you know how many years of my life I lost because of you?" He shakes his head.

"I found you. I will always find you."

A man wearing a thick wool coat steps outside, a cell phone pressed to his ear, and I move to him, fast as lightning. "I need your help. This guy's following me." I point at Julian.

The stranger looks at me with stricken eyes and turns to look at Julian. "I've got to go," he says to whoever he's talking to. "I need to call the cops."

Julian's gaze turns panicked and then frenzied. For a second, I think he's preparing to rush us. My training with Grey has not prepared me for this. Bile burns my throat.

The man beside me starts talking into his phone, and Julian gives me one final look before retreating to his truck, the same white truck with a rusted fender and Phillies' bumper sticker. Relief tickles my senses that it's the same truck he drove before. I was terrified I might have been looking for the wrong vehicle for the past nine months.

Julian accelerates as soon as he turns out of the office building and drives out of sight as the stranger recounts what happened twice before nodding and hanging up. He turns to me. "The police said you can call or stop by and file a police report if you want."

If I want? As if this is an option.

"Thanks for stopping."

He doesn't reply, his ashen face confirming he didn't do it out of choice.

I hurry to my car, slip inside, and lock the doors. Briggs and I have discussed emotional responses at great length. The amygdala is the part of our brain responsible for keeping us safe from real and perceived dangers. He and other professionals refer to this as the guard dog and opossum portion of the brain because people will either react to the adrenaline by fighting back like a guard dog or freezing like a opossum.

I always thought I'd be a guard dog, but it turns out I am one-hundred-percent opossum.

My muscles are tense and unmoving.

I wasn't prepared. I didn't react. I wasn't even watching for him despite having just talked about him.

I force a slow breath in through my nose and out through my lips three times before realizing how painfully cold I am. I start my car.

The clock on the dash confirms Grey and Hudson are at practice and Evelyn's in class.

Despite my precaution and preparation, I feel woefully lost and uncertain about what to do.

Is Julian waiting for me? Will he follow me right now?

I search for the nearest police station.

With jerky, tight muscles, I arrive at the station ten minutes later and wait for another two to ensure Julian hasn't followed me before darting inside.

A receptionist asks me to wait, and before I've managed to regulate my breathing, an officer in his forties with thinning hair invites me to follow him to the back of the station. We stop at his desk that's cluttered with papers, half-drunk coffee cups, and a dozen bobbleheads. I stare at them as I clear my throat and gloss over the details of why I'm here. When I tell him Julian broke in last year, the officer pulls up the file and cuts me off so he can read the notes.

I skip ahead to last Sunday, when Julian approached Evelyn, and how he was there today, waiting for me.

"Did he threaten you?"

I blink. "Yes! He's following me. I think he might be stalking me."

The officer taps his pen, retracting it a dozen times before he shakes his head. "Did he say he wanted to hurt you, that he would hurt you...?"

"He might be stalking me," I say again.

"It's not illegal for him to talk to you. You were both in a public space."

"What about following me?"

"Can you prove he's following you?"

My piqued anxiety has caused a rush of adrenaline and cortisol that has me forgetting half the conversation. "He said he found me, that he'll always find me. And he broke into my apartment last year."

"And he was charged."

"For trespassing."

"Listen, I see this has you shaken. But this comes down to burden of proof." He sighs. "Unless you can prove he wants to hurt you, he's not doing anything illegal, and our hands are tied." He presses his wrists together as though pretending he's cuffed.

I stare at him for a long moment, feeling a sense of déjà vu that sours my stomach.

"Listen. We tend to see this most often after a bad breakup. Did you two date? Sleep together? Did you lead him on?"

His words are a slap in the face. "I barely knew him. He worked at the apartment building I lived in."

His stare is judgmental. He doesn't believe me.

"I *wasn't* dating him. I didn't know him."

"You said you haven't seen him in months. If he's really stalking you, he's doing a pretty lousy job, if you ask me..."

I thank the heavens that Jon and Alex aren't here. Tables would be flipped.

Resentment nests in my thoughts, poking at my fears and questioning whether he's right.

"Do I leave the same way I came in?"

He climbs to his feet, looking relieved I'm willing to leave. He escorts me outside, where the cold licks at my skin. My heart is beating faster now than when I arrived, my chest tighter from the lack of answers or help.

I drive around town for forty minutes, going through neighborhoods and taking random roads to see if I'm being followed. Two hours later, I arrive at my parents' house. It feels so different—so empty—without them. Julian's words replay in my head over and over again. I'd rather be at the apartment, fixing dinner with Evelyn, talking about our days, and discussing what book to choose for February's book club, but the very last thing I want to do is lead Julian straight to those I care about most.

I lock the door and set the alarm before meticulously checking that every window and door is secured. Then I flip on all the lights, trying to create a faux warmth.

My parents keep the utilities on when they're gone in case I ever want to come by, but I know without looking that the fridge is cleared and the pantry empty to prevent the multitude of bugs they'd draw.

I text Hudson and Evelyn, so they don't worry.

> Me: Trying an experiment for Briggs tonight, so I'm staying at my parents' house. Don't forget to set the alarm.

Guilt spears me. I pride myself for being honest. Sure, I have my secrets—who doesn't—but this is the first lie I've told my two best friends in all the years I've known them.

Hudson will be furious I didn't contact him right away, and Evelyn will give me a look of disappointment that will fester in my thoughts like a stain, impossible to forget or ignore.

Evelyn texts me back almost immediately.

> Evelyn: Is everything okay?

It's not. Not even a little. The park was a coincidence. I'm fairly sure of that. The lawnmower and uniform attest to the fact, but today wasn't. I had looked up the nearest park while waiting to speak with the police, and it was ten minutes away. Julian didn't notice me and wander over. He'd followed me or knew how to find me.

I don't know which alternative is more disturbing.

I glance back at Evelyn's message, uncertain if I'm keeping them safe by staying away or putting them at risk by not telling them.

Distance is safer.

> Me: Yeah. I'm going to eat my weight in pizza, and I'll be home tomorrow. Be sure to lock the doors.

I warm up a frozen pizza I find in the chest freezer.

Stupidly, it makes me feel a little better that not everything I shared was a lie. I even plan to host a self-date and do the positive affirmations Briggs asked to stave off my guilty conscience. Though, justifying my actions only deepens my guilt.

I lock the door leading down to the basement and my bedroom door. A nightlight glows in the corner. I couldn't sleep without it for years, but now, light is a nuisance when I sleep. When Evelyn and I moved into our apartment, I used three layers of painter's tape to fully conceal the tiny green light that flashes on the smoke detector in my room. I welcome all the lights tonight as I hold on to a very thin idea that might be even worse than staying here alone.

Chapter 28

Mila

I park and stare at the red brick building. It's bigger than I expected, located at the end of a strip mall. It's not at all what I was expecting for a boxing gym.

I slowly get out and try to ignore how my heartbeats turn erratic from the combination of lack of sleep and nerves. One of the highlights of working out with Grey has been sleep. I've struggled to fall asleep and remain asleep most of my life, but since working out with Grey, the exhaustion or the idea of becoming physically stronger has lulled me to sleep and allowed me to remain asleep.

Last night, paranoia made every sound feel like a bad omen. I spent hours online, psychoanalyzing and attempting to diagnose Julian Holloway, despite Briggs warning me not to. I couldn't help myself, after all, I'm a big fan of the adage that knowledge is power.

Researching the brief encounters was akin to scouring WebMD and other medical websites for symptoms. Everything got scarier and increasingly convincing that I was going to die.

I wasn't sure if he was stalking me or delusional. Possibly both.

It took me hours to fall asleep, and I woke up a dozen times before giving up on the idea of sleep, dressing, and braving the house. The exhaustion isn't just from sleep, though. It's mental and emotional.

I lift my chin a little higher as I grab the door and pull it open.

A string of bells hanging on the inside jangle loudly, announcing me as the scents of bleach, leather, and the faint traces of cologne settle in my nose. Three sets of eyes turn to me from where they're working out on nearby equipment, curiosity visible in their varying expressions.

"Are you lost?"

I recognize the voice immediately and turn to find Abe, his hands and wrists taped.

I swallow, recalling my plan. "Is Mackey here?" I ask.

He shakes his head.

"He's on his way over," Cole says, stepping up beside his brother with similar tape patterns around his hands and wrists. His brow is still yellowed from the bruise he received in the fight Hadley, Hannah, and I watched. "Mila, right?"

I nod.

"Did you change your mind?"

I stare into his curious and playful brown eyes. Unlike his brother, I can't tell what he thinks of me being here. "I don't want to learn to fight. Not professionally," I correct myself. "But I want to know where and how to hit someone."

"Isn't that what Grey's teaching you?" he asks.

"He's busy." And he's going to be busier. In a few weeks, spring season starts, so his practices will be more frequent and longer.

Abe laughs. The cruel sound tries to rattle my determination, but it holds nothing against Julian's evil laugh.

I flick my eyes to Cole, already knowing Abe won't accept me. I inherently know because we're too much alike. His eyes scrutinize me for several beats, and then he nods.

"You're not fighting anyone," he says, glancing at the ring in the back corner.

I nod, accepting the condition easily.

Cole blows out a breath and points to the back wall, where a rainbow of colored jump ropes hang on a giant peg in the back. "Get in fifteen minutes of jumping rope, and then Dustin will work the bags with you."

Fifteen minutes sounds short, but I'll be winded regardless of all the cardio I've been doing these past few weeks. It turns out jumping rope is highly underrated for its intensity.

"Who do I pay?" I ask.

Abe scoffs, making a joke under his breath.

"Mackey will sort that out ... *if* you stick around," Cole tells me.

I nod, and my determination to prove myself grows by the second. I spent years studying harder than my classmates, continuing my therapy sessions, and reversing some of the most basic tendencies that kept me safe during my early childhood to prove to people who thought I'd end up as another statistic wrong. I'm so damn tired of feeling inferior and physically weak. Abe doesn't stand a chance of intimidating me or insulting me to change my mind.

I select a red and white beaded jump rope and begin jumping before I even find the clock to track my time.

When fifteen minutes pass, I hang my rope up. A sheen of sweat covers my pink face reflected in the mirror across from me. Dustin and Mackey are with Abe and Cole, huddled near one of the wide cylindrical poles that run from floor to ceiling. I cross to them, feigning bravado.

Abe claps a hand on Dustin's shoulder, noticing me before the others.

Dustin looks at Cole and then Mackey, shaking his head as he swears. Mackey laughs, and Cole grins before he peels away from his friends and approaches me, running his palms over his thighs.

I follow him to a punching bag, where he lays a white strip of tape on the ground. "Are you right-handed or left?" he asks, skipping introductions or small talk.

"Right."

He nods. "Before we start, you need to work on your stance. Have you and Grey been working on any balancing exercises?"

"A few."

He grimaces. "You need to work on it a lot. One of the fastest ways guys get hurt in the ring is by having shitty balance. If you can't recover when you hit someone or take a hit, you're going to go down, and the last place you want to be is on the floor."

He moves closer to the tape line he made, dragging his foot over the edge where it doesn't lay flat. "You're going to have your left foot forward, pointed at one o'clock, and your back foot at two."

He demonstrates for me, his knees slightly bent and hips loose as his feet straddle the line. "If your knees are straight, you'll be fucked. But you don't want to bend too far, or you'll be fucked. Then you want to twist your upper body sideways, protecting yourself and making less of a target for your opponent."

Again, defense seems more crucial than offense, as Dustin orders me into a fighting stance. I feel silly, certain my lack of participation in organized sports is shining bright as the August sun as Dustin walks around me, tapping my feet apart with his, moving my elbows and fists until he's content. Then he directs me to move while maintaining the stance, correcting me at every turn.

He's a hardass.

My thighs and calves ache. Sweat makes my shirt stick to my back and mats my hair when he finally tells me to take a break and get some water.

I wish I'd thought to bring water, but the nerve to come required all of my attention.

"Over there," Dustin says, pointing at a water cooler.

"Thanks." I grab one of the tiny paper cups, sparking a forgotten memory of one of the foster care families I lived with. They only had these cups, and everything they cooked was burned. The strange acrid scent of the cup hits my nose as I take a sip, and I swear I taste char in the back of my throat.

I drink the rest in one gulp and wipe my mouth with the back of my hand.

The bells on the door hit like rocks rather than jingles as the door pushes open. I turn to find a pair of sapphire eyes pinned on me, with a scowling Grey behind them.

Chapter 29

Grey

Mila's look of surprise is quickly replaced with a look of determination before she turns her glacial eyes to Cole.

He dismissively rolls a shoulder. "Did you really think we weren't going to call him?"

"I can find another gym," she says.

Abe's brows arch, surprised by her response. I wish I were.

"We'll give you a minute," Mackey says, whistling to catch everyone's attention before directing them to the opposite end of the gym.

I return my focus to Mila. "Did you bring a bag?"

"I'm not leaving."

I glance around, looking for something that might be hers.

"This isn't part of our deal. I told you, if you want to do this, we do it my way."

"Then the deal's off." She throws her cup in the garbage and turns on her heel.

I shift, intercepting her before she can make it more than a foot. Animosity shines in her gaze. "You're not working out here."

"Why not?"

"Because one or more of these assholes isn't going to hesitate to punch you, and likely it's going to be fucking Abe."

"They already told me I'm not allowed in the ring."

Thank God Cole was here. I have a sneaking suspicion that Abe would have led her into the ring like the mother fucking Gingerbread Hag. When Cole texted me she had shown up, I was heading to the facility for a weightlifting session. I skipped it and drove straight here, fearing all the ways this could have gone wrong.

"Let's go." I point at the door.

Mila glances at the others, who aren't even trying to hide the fact that they're listening. Her shoulders fall, recognizing they're not going to come to her defense before she pivots and passes me, shoving the door so hard the bells swing and clang violently against the door.

I follow her, though my reflex is to stay.

"Why did you come? Why didn't you call me?" I ask.

Mila refuses to look at me, continuing to her car.

Shit like this, drama and the silent treatment are two factors that make avoiding relationships so goddamn easy. But my anger is too concentrated, and my list of questions is too damn long, directing me to follow her. I press my hand against the driver's side door of her car before she can reach for it.

"Mila, why in the hell did you come here?"

Her gaze pierces mine, offense and anger on full display, but my attention quickly shifts to her mouth, noting she's biting the inside of her bottom lip again.

"What happened?" I ask.

Her eyes bounce between mine, and through the veil of her anger, I see the vulnerability she's working to hide.

"Talk to me," I implore, taking a step closer to her.

"I..." She shakes her head, eyes glittering with tears. "I didn't come here to cause issues or to piss anyone off." She swallows. "I know you're about to get a hell of a lot busier, and I don't want to put the weight of my impatience on you."

I blow out a breath, searching for level ground. It feels like I'm dangling from a peak, the same damn peak I've been suspended from for weeks—longer. "I'll still work with you every day. You have my word. But this place isn't safe for you to—"

"I need to learn how to hit, Grey. Today. *Now.*"

A tear slips from her eye, eliciting an ache in my chest that nearly brings me to my knees. She hastily brushes her fingers across her cheek, trying to rid the signs of her emotions.

"You don't have to hide from me," I tell her.

She looks away as two more tears slip down her cheeks.

I wrap an arm around her shoulders and pull her against me, her face meeting the crook of my neck. She's rigid but doesn't make a sound or movement to object as I hold her, my palms pressed to her back as I feel the frantic race of her heart and stilted breaths.

Minutes pass before her muscles loosen fractionally. She doesn't melt into me, doesn't even lean her weight on me, but the slight shift is enough to tell me that she needs this contact.

"I saw the guy who broke into my apartment yesterday."

I try not to let her words reflect in my posture, feeling regret wash over me for not being there. "Where? What happened?" I want to ask a dozen more clarifying questions but force myself to stop.

She shakes her head and for a second, I think she doesn't want to answer, but then she shudders, and I realize she's trying to keep her shit together. "He was waiting for me."

"What?" The word explodes from me as I step back,

needing to look at her again to verify I didn't overlook any bruises or injuries.

Mila stares at me with so much naked fear it disarms me.

"Did he touch you? Hurt you?"

She shakes her head.

"I think he's crazy. He claims I've been ignoring him for years. Letters or ... something. And how I made him miss his mother's funeral..." She shakes her head. "I don't know. I can't remember." She wets her lips.

My breathing stops as my thoughts tumble down a hill of dread as the number of questions I want to ask her triples. This scenario has become so much bigger than needing to learn to strike someone, bigger than self-defense, but I know firsthand how imperative it is to have control over your future. I can't take away her past or erase these fears, but I can give her this ounce of control. "We'll set up a schedule. Cole, Dustin, Mackey, and I will train you, but I want to be clear, this isn't for you to engage with him. If this guy approaches you again, you get as far away from him as you can. Do you understand?"

Mila stares at me with so much hope, she could ask for the world right now, and I'd find a way to give it to her.

She nods.

"I have two rules: no training with Abe, and no getting in the ring with anyone else."

Mila's appreciation and relief are tangible, reflected in her bright eyes as she nods. "Deal."

I tip my head back toward the gym, considering the rules I'll be setting for my friends as we walk across the parking lot. Mila's eyes are wide, her nerves still visible as I reach for the door.

"Keep your head up and your shoulders back. If it becomes too much, let me know."

Mila looks at me and then tilts her chin up, eyes becoming walls of indifference, oozing confidence.

I pull the door open wide and follow her inside. Cole meets my gaze with a grin. Abe snickers. "She has a good stance," Cole remarks. "Dustin was planning to work the bags with her." He nods toward the heavy bags.

I glance at Dustin, who gives a nearly imperceptible nod of assurance, and then at Mila.

"Let's get you wrapped," I say.

She maintains an air of indifference as she follows me to the pole where screws are drilled into the concrete, holding rolls of gauze and tape. I grab the gauze as Mila holds out both hands.

"Wrists straight," I say, pinching the joint to raise the palm on her right hand.

"Do you guys always wrap your hands?" Mila asks, watching me wrap the gauze around her wrist several times.

I nod. "It keeps your wrists from getting hurt, your knuckles from splitting, and the small bones in your hands from breaking."

When I finish, Mila stares at her hands, and though she doesn't voice how strange they feel, I know that's what she's thinking.

I grab a roll of red tape and rip off a large piece that I gently slap just below the neckline of her shirt.

She looks at it. "What's this?"

"It means you're not allowed in the ring."

She frowns. "So you've just marked me as the sacrificial lamb. Awesome."

That red tape means she is off-limits, and anyone who dares to engage with her will get kicked out of the gym. "Sit tight for a minute," I say. "I need a word with Dustin before you begin."

Mila shakes her head, cutting me off before I can move.

"He's already taking it easy on me."

"I need to make sure he's on the same page and—"

"This falls within your two rules."

"Those are the rules I have for *you*. I have an entirely different set of rules for them."

She maims me with a glare. "I need to do this, Grey."

It goes against every damn instinct in me. Still, I manage to nod. "I have to get to practice. Tomorrow, we'll meet here at six instead of at your apartment."

This time, anticipation glitters in her gaze rather than tears before she agrees and goes to where Dustin waits for her.

I head to where Mackey and Cole are reviewing notes on a clipboard. They stop talking, looking at me with matching expressions of humor and know-how.

"She's got spunk," Mackey says.

Cole smirks. "Is this what all the girls at Camden are like?"

I scoff. "No."

His grin grows. "I didn't think so. What's her story?"

I glance over my shoulder to see Mila following Dustin's instruction, her gaze focused on him alone. I turn back to Cole. "You'll have to ask her."

He raises an inquiring brow. "Does it involve you?"

Mackey taps his clipboard and walks away.

"You've caught feelings for her," Cole says.

"We're friends."

"How long have you been telling yourself that line?"

Too long.

Cole winces like he hears my thought. "I'll keep my eye on her."

"Just so we're clear, I expect her to leave here in the same condition she's in now."

Amusement has him cocking his head. "Sixteen fucking years."

269

I lower my brow.

"It took sixteen fucking years to find your weakness." He grins, but it's not predatory or cruel. Instead, he looks joyful. "This will be interesting."

I scratch my brow, unamused. "She's going through some shit. Keep an eye out for anyone who doesn't belong here, and if she starts acting cagey or nervous, don't let her leave. Get her in Mackey's office and call me."

The humor drains from Cole's face, and his gaze flicks to the glass door before returning to me. "What kind of shit? An ex?"

I shake my head. "I don't know all the details yet."

Cole's cheeks round before he blows out a breath. "Shit. Okay. Yeah." He nods, running a thumb across his chin. "I'll talk with Mackey. For her build, she's going to have the most strength in her legs. We can teach her the Triangle Choke and—"

I shake my head before he can finish his thought. "No fucking way. If someone bothers her, I want her to run like hell and call me and then the cops."

"You want her to be able to defend herself."

"A Triangle Choke puts her on her back. If she doesn't have him positioned right, it puts her at risk."

"She doesn't have the upper body strength to use her arms. Not yet."

I shake my head again, my discomfort for leaving her here growing by the second. "This is to build her confidence and teach her how to strike and stun someone as a last resort, not to actually fight."

Cole raises his brow. "If you're worried that someone's going to show up here looking for her, it sounds like he's already started the fight."

My blood runs cold. "I have to go figure out what's going on."

He nods. "Want Abe to go with you?"

I almost take him up on the offer just to keep Abe away from Mila. "Can I trust him to be here?"

Cole grins. "He'll only taunt her."

I want to believe him. Hell, I do believe him. I've known Abe my entire goddamn life, but I also know what a hothead he can be and how callous his words can be. "She'll swing at him."

He laughs. "I'm sure he'll deserve it."

"I didn't say he won't." I glance over at where Abe is running a private session. He's been pulling shifts here for Mackey since last year.

"I'll keep her safe. Including from Abe."

I tamp down my words of concern and doubt and extend my fist to his. "I owe you."

Cole winks.

I take a final glance at Mila before heading back to Oleander Springs.

Chapter 30

Mila

I take another drink of Sprite, replaying the conversation in my head again as I wait for Hudson and Evelyn to meet me. I stare blankly at the menu for the tenth time, Mariachi music playing in the background as I munch on a tortilla chip.

"Hey," Evelyn greets merrily, stopping at the table. I stand and wrap my arms around her, my lungs filling. I sent her three texts last night and two more this morning to ensure they were okay, and I didn't leave them like sitting ducks.

"We ran into Grey, and I kind of invited him to come," she whispers guiltily in a rushed voice.

I glance up, spotting them just a few feet away. Knowing Evelyn, *ran into* means they texted him, inviting him to come.

I can't believe I cried in front of Grey. On my intimacy scale, crying is a ten. I haven't held his hand, but Grey has brought me to orgasm and now seen me cry. I don't want him here because I'm going to be opening the intimacy gates to Hudson and Mila, apologizing and delving into all things Julian Holloway, which include my fears and insecurities.

"Hey," Hudson says, greeting me with a loose hug before he slides into the booth across from me. Evelyn sits next to him, forcing Grey to the seat beside me. I scoot over to give him extra room, but he moves with me, his thigh grazing mine, just close enough to feel the heat of his skin and wish he were closer.

I consider postponing this conversation and pretending I just wanted to see them to catch up, but my last class will keep me out until after eight, and the chance of Evelyn being home alone makes delaying this conversation impossible.

"Yesterday, after meeting with Briggs, I saw Julian Holloway." I rip the Band-Aid clean off.

Hudson's gaze snaps to mine. "Again?"

"Again?" Grey's hand drops to the table, and he goes still, eyes pinned on me, making my face heat. I know if I turn to look at him, I'll find accusation staring back at me.

Hudson looks from me to Grey and back again. "You need to tell him. We should have told him last year."

"I did. I told him about Julian breaking in when asking him to train me."

Hudson doesn't look half as shocked as he does proud and relieved.

"When did you see him the first time?" Grey asks, eyes critical as he turns to look at me, his thigh pressing against my knee.

"Last Sunday."

Recognition has his sapphire eyes blazing, realizing that was the same night I came and watched Cole fight at Better Days.

I turn my gaze to Hudson as he asks, "Why didn't you call me?"

"You were in practice, and Evelyn was in class when it happened."

"Where did you see him? Did he talk to you again?" Evelyn

273

searches my face. "God, Mila. Are you okay?"

"He talked to you last Sunday?" Grey asks. Evelyn and I take turns telling him about our first incident.

"We run through that park every day," Grey says.

I nod. I've wondered how many times he might have seen me, no less than a dozen times. I pull in a breath. "I think he might be following me. He was waiting beside my car yesterday."

"Jesus fucking Christ," Hudson mutters, dropping his menu. "What happened?" His gaze rakes over me as Grey's had, taking inventory of my features like he's searching for wounds.

"He was talking about a bunch of nonsense." I shake my head, still unable to recall all the details of the conversation. "Something about ignoring letters and missing someone's funeral."

"Letters? We need to go to the police," Evelyn says.

"I did, and they said he wasn't doing anything illegal. That unless I can prove he's following me or wants to hurt me, there's nothing I can do."

"What about a restraining order?" she asks.

I shake my head again. I read extensively about restraining orders last night after terror led me down one too many rabbit holes online. "Same situation. To get one, I'd have to prove he has the intent to harm or kill me, and it would still have to be reviewed by a judge."

The guys have to abide by stricter rules to play college football.

"Did he ask for anything? Make any demands?" Grey asks.

"No, but our conversations have all been pretty short. Yesterday, we were only alone for a couple of minutes when a guy came outside, and I stopped him. He called the cops, and Julian left."

Hudson runs a hand over his hair, jaw strained. I know he's mad at me and, even worse, disappointed. "Mila, he's already broken into your apartment. Why in the hell did you think going to your parents' house alone last night was a good idea if you think he's following you?"

Grey bristles beside me, but I can't look at him to know if Hudson's tone or something else puts him on edge because my emotions are shuffling like a deck of cards. It's anyone's guess which one is going to be flipped over first.

"I didn't want him to follow me to the apartment."

Hudson's gaze hardens. "That was stupid. You put yourself in danger."

"I refuse to put the two of you in danger." I swallow as my throat thickens and my face grows warm.

"Mila," Hudson's voice turns soft. I quickly shake off his impending apology. I can't hear it right now. I want his anger— need it to help me flip over a new card that won't entail me sobbing over our tortilla chips in a restaurant filled with strangers.

"Do we think he's a stalker?" Evelyn asks. "What do we do about a stalker?" She reaches for her phone, ready to devise a plan.

"I don't know." My voice is raspy from the emotions I work to swallow again. "It doesn't make sense. He's been gone for months. I haven't seen him since he broke into my apartment. Nothing about this makes sense." This line is becoming my catchphrase, and in my head, I hear Briggs reminding me again that it doesn't have to make sense.

Evelyn shifts her water glass and sets both hands on the table. "The apartment's safe, though. We have an alarm system, and to get in, you have to stop at the gates and be let in by the guards."

"There's no gate to walk in," Grey says. "We run the green trail every morning."

Hudson leans back. "We should stay at the dorm." He turns to Evelyn and then me. "It's a locked building. He'd need a key card to get in, and there are cameras and security everywhere. Plus, a hundred guys are on the same floor and would be happy to put him at the bottom of a dogpile."

I hadn't even considered the idea. Fear has made me tunnel-focused, but the thought surprisingly calms my frazzled nerves. As safe as our apartment has felt these past few months, knowing Julian is a mile away any given day sends ice into my veins. Plus, Hudson's right, the dorms are secured, filled with people, and he's on the fourth floor, ensuring Julian won't be staring at us through any windows.

"You guys can have the bedroom, and I'll sleep on the couch," Hudson says.

"I'm not taking your bed," I tell him.

"You could stay with me," Grey offers.

I turn to Grey.

He presses his thigh against my knee a little harder. "That way we could get some extra training sessions in."

Despite the cradle of fear I've been cocooned in all day, his words elicit filthy thoughts that make my face flush. "Are you sure? I know you need to focus and…"

"I'm positive," he says. "I wouldn't offer if I weren't okay with it."

"We'd still be close. I could walk to classes with you," Evelyn says.

Hesitation fills me as I stare at Grey. Staying in his hotel room for one night was way different than moving into his dorm for a week—maybe longer. "For how long?" I ask.

"Until we figure this shit out," Hudson says, sealing our deal.

Chapter 31

Mila

I f life came with rules, there would undoubtedly be one about not staying with the guy you thought didn't like you a month ago, whom you struck a deal with and are currently trying to avoid catching feelings for.

Everything about this feels like a bad parody as we carry my bags into his dorm five hours later.

I clear my throat as he flips on the lights. Staying here crosses that intimacy line again. This is his space. It doesn't just smell like him, it's a reflection of him. "Thanks for allowing me to stay here. I owe you."

"You don't owe me anything." He carries my bags toward the bedroom.

"Where are you going?" I ask.

Grey doesn't stop or answer me, which has me following, leaving a wide gap between us. He sets my bags down at the foot of his king-size bed, where a dark green comforter stretches across the top. I take in the minimalist space for a second. A dresser is along the wall beside the door with a TV, and next to the bed is a single nightstand with a simple lamp. A large, framed black-and-white map of the world hangs on the wall beside me.

"What are you doing?" I ask.

His expression is intent, hinting at annoyance. "You're not sleeping on the couch."

A month ago, I'd be firing off a sarcastic retort asking where he plans to sleep if I'll be sleeping here, but now, vulnerability has me afraid to ask, dreading his response will be anywhere but here.

"Do you have any more classes tonight?" he asks before I can process a response.

I shake my head. I skipped my evening class to pack, reasoning that it's the first week, and will likely only be a syllabus review.

His jaw flexes. "I want to take you to Highgrove. You should talk to my mom. A guy used to stalk her. He'd show up at her job and sit in her section, so she had to serve him. Follow her home..."

Panic rises in my chest. "What happened?"

Grey lifts a shoulder. "We'll talk about it when we get there."

"I don't know if going is a good idea..." Staying with Grey and meeting his mom all within a couple of hours has an entirely new wave of panic inching into my thoughts.

"Cole's going to meet us at the gym afterward," he says, turning and heading back to the living room without giving me a chance to tell him I don't think that's a good idea, either. Despite all my conditioning, the muscles in my arm, shoulders, and chest hint at being sore from working out with Dustin.

Grey returns with my remaining bags.

"I should change," I say.

"She won't care what you're wearing," he says, taking the bags to his room. "But grab some workout clothes."

Everything about my childhood was first impressions, a habit I haven't been able to lose fully. Whenever I met a new family, I was meant to be presentable, polite, and silent. I rummage through my bags, trying to recall where I'd put my nicer casual clothes. I pull out a green sweater and clean jeans and head into the bathroom to change before shoving some workout clothes and shoes into a gym bag.

A handful of guys from the team call out to Grey as we walk toward the elevator. There will be rumors, just like last year when I stayed with Hudson.

I nearly tell Grey, but something keeps me silent. I don't want him to think that's why I'm staying with him or why I hesitated.

Doubts are teasing my insecurities as I follow Grey out of the warm confines of the lobby and across the parking lot while texting Evelyn, letting her know where I'm going.

"How was the gym this morning?" Grey asks as he starts the truck.

"Good." My voice is too high, and my nerves are too thin, and it has absolutely nothing to do with having a potential stalker.

"Dustin's a good teacher."

"He doesn't talk much."

Grey sniggers. "Only when he's working. Otherwise, he never shuts up."

"Mackey claims my hamstrings are too tight, and I'm going to have back issues when I get older if I don't learn to stretch."

"He's not wrong."

"I stretch four times a day. I just have tight hamstrings."

"You need to buddy stretch."

My thoughts jump to the last time Grey helped me stretch, and my entire body flushes.

We take backroads into Highgrove, crossing two train tracks

and passing a dozen crop fields before he pulls into a gravel driveway and turns his truck off.

The outside lights flip on, and the door opens.

Grey's gaze flashes to mine as he climbs out. I wonder if he's also freaking out that I'm crossing yet another line into the privacy he's maintained for so long.

"You guys made good timing. Traffic must have been light, or you were driving like a maniac," his mom says. "Please tell me it was the former." She's stunning, with light hair, bright eyes, and an inviting smile that lights up the dark.

"We left earlier than expected," he tells her.

It's cold again tonight, my breath stretching before me as I follow Grey to the front steps, where his mom waves us inside.

Warmth seeps into me as I step into the house, where the savory scents of chicken noodle soup lend to the welcoming space. A couch is adorned with a fuzzy throw, and the kitchen has bright white cupboards and a light countertop where pops of marigold yellow and burnt orange brighten the space with rooster-themed decorations. The space feels comfortable and inviting, like a long, unhurried hug. It reminds me of Hadley, Katie, and Hannah's house.

"Mila, this is my mom, Colleen. Mom, this is Mila," Grey says.

Despite seeing her picture and knowing she was young when Grey was born, her youth still surprises me. She could pass as a college student.

"It's nice to meet you," I tell her. "Your house is lovely."

She smiles affectionately before taking a step closer and surprises me by wrapping her arms around me. "It's so nice to meet you, Mila." She holds me tightly and then steps back and smiles at me. Nothing is threatening or judgmental about her. I was expecting her to be cold

or indifferent, similar to how I still sometimes think of

Grey, but she is the definition of sunshine, glowing with warmth and happiness.

"Please, make yourself at home. Can I get you something to drink? I'm making chicken and dumplings for dinner. Is that okay?"

"Chicken and dumplings is one of my favorites. Thank you for having me. I really appreciate it."

Her smile stamps deeper again. "It's one of my favorites, too."

A wave of emotions catches me by surprise, thickening my throat and blurring my eyes as I stare at her as though she's a unicorn that will fade at any second.

Colleen cocks her head, her gaze softening into a maternal look that makes my chest throb. It's rare that I miss my mother, but there are times when the pain of missing what might have been, is so great, it renders me speechless.

I smile and avert my gaze to the living room where plants are strewn around. I focus on a plant in a yellow planter, then a picture of Grey giggling as a young kid with wavy hair that reached his eyebrows, a soft red blanket, and finally the book on the coffee table. Next, I listen to the soft boil of dinner, Grey's voice as he visits with his mom, the wind hitting the side of the house. Lastly, I focus on the scents of the chicken and dumplings, thyme, and roast chicken making my stomach grumble.

My heart slows, and my lungs fill.

"How's the roof?" Grey asks.

"You fixed it," Colleen says. "I thought for sure it needed to be replaced, but I think you bought another couple of years."

"It was an exposed nail. The tar should keep it from leaking again," Grey tells her.

The smile she gives him is filled with affection and love.

A timer goes off that has her moving into the kitchen. She

turns it off and lifts the lid off the Dutch oven. Steam billows out, carrying a punch of rich aromas to my nose.

"It smells so good," I say.

She grins. "I hear you and Hudson are best friends. That you grew up together."

I nod, wondering if she and Hudson have met.

Once again, her smile feels genuine. "Do you have other siblings?"

I pause, the question catching me by surprise. The past twenty-four hours have had me on the emotional rollercoaster from hell—maybe longer if I consider my parents leaving. Emotions scratch at my throat once more. I clear it. "I had a sister," I tell her.

Colleen's smile fades, regret and anguish creasing her brow. "Oh, Mila. I'm so sorry."

I force a tight smile and nod. It's all I can do.

Emotions last for just ninety seconds. It seems impossible. Psychologists claim that any feeling that lasts longer is our thoughts restimulating the emotion, keeping us in a loop.

I've been stuck in this loop for over a decade, and it's barely become more tolerable. Society has deemed it my responsibility to now say something to ease the moment, assure her that it's been a long time, that I don't need her apology, that I'm okay—but I believe society is wrong. We can't hide from pain, and if we spent more time empathizing with others, perhaps we'd spend less time critiquing and criticizing.

Grey steps closer and then pauses. He reads me better than most, seeming to understand I need a moment to allow gravity to press against these still raw emotions and find some semblance of balance, so I don't become the black hole I've always feared becoming.

"Life can be cruel," Colleen says.

It can, but as Briggs has reminded me so many times, I don't have to suffer to experience the pain. I can still be grateful for Jon and Alex, for meeting my best friends, and for obtaining a future that my life in Oklahoma would not have provided.

"Are you from Highgrove?" I ask her.

Colleen shakes her head. "Virginia."

"Really? What brought you here?"

Another timer beeps, and she shuts it off. "I followed my best friend. She moved down here when she met a guy. Two years later, she moved to Tennessee, and I stayed." Colleen removes a tray of cornbread muffins from the oven. Here in the South, we love our carbs and our cornbread. "Grey mentioned someone's been bothering you," she says, tipping the golden muffins onto a cooling rack. "Tell me what's going on." Her response is so maternal it replays in my thoughts a second time.

I hadn't intended to share my story again, rather expected to hear hers, but I find myself wanting to tell her, explaining all the little dots that are faded and don't make sense.

As I do, Grey moves around the kitchen with her, filling bowls with the chicken and dumplings, gathering silverware and drinks, and refusing my offer to help. I like watching him here, seeing his familiarity and comfort, precision to detail, and competence.

Competence is sexier than a sports car or chiseled abs, and Grey has it in spades. Football, martial arts, training, and even this insignificant moment where he doesn't ask how much we want or where anything is because he already knows.

"I'm so sorry this is happening to you," Colleen says as we sit at the dining room table. It's big enough to seat six, the wood surface stained and lightly dented in areas, showing years of use. Some wish walls could talk, but I'd give my eyeteeth to hear the stories this table could tell of birthday cake candles being blown out, homework sessions, and dinner conversations. If the walls are the skeleton of a home, the dining room table is the heart.

"This guy sounds like a big red flag," Colleen says, adding pepper to her bowl, and I note how Grey had placed it in front of her, anticipating her needs. I inwardly swoon. The romantic in me gives meet-cutes the middle finger. I have to stuff that romantic voice inside my head down, remind her we have more pressing issues, and Grey's mother is beside me. Now is not the time to outwardly swoon.

My first bite of dinner is an explosion of flavors, warm and comforting. "This is so good," I tell her.

"She's a fantastic cook," Grey says.

Colleen smiles. "So is Grey."

I glance across the table at him, my surprise likely evident.

"You haven't cooked for her?" Colleen asks.

"I barely cook. I eat all my meals at the facility."

She waves off his excuse. "He makes a baked feta pasta that is out of this world. Seriously. He could sell that recipe for a million bucks. It's so good. And his fettuccine alfredo is perfection in a dish."

"I had no idea."

Colleen nods. "He's also a great carpenter and handyman. He and my dad made all these cabinets, built the deck off the back, redid the bathroom, all the insulation..." She glances around. "They basically rebuilt this place. He's always been very intellectually curious and takes it upon himself to learn new skills. He constantly amazes me."

I love that she brags about Grey. I love it even more that it makes his cheeks bloom red.

"Back to the point," Grey says. "We're trying to figure out if he's stalking her."

"None of it makes sense," I echo the words for what seems

like the hundredth time. "I feel paranoid even thinking he could be following me."

"You have to be paranoid," Colleen tells me. "You have to be mindful of every detail. Predators are patient. The guy who bothered me would come to the cafe where I worked every day, even on my days off, because no one would tell him my schedule."

Predator. Hearing her refer to Julian as a predator feels almost relieving, as though the concerns I've struggled with for nearly a year are valid and accurate.

"Did he talk to you?" I ask her, wanting to draw more similarities.

She nods. "It's imperative you don't engage with him, though. If he starts calling you or sending you messages, keep them, but don't reply. If you encounter him in person, be firm and clear. Tell him you're not interested, and you want him to leave you alone." She sets her arm on the table and leans a little closer. "Don't apologize to him, and don't sugarcoat anything. They'll twist everything. And be sure you're keeping a log of everything he says and does. Every time you see him, every time he contacts you, you need to record it and call the police."

I try not to frown, thinking of my encounter with the police last night and how helpless I felt when leaving.

"They didn't do anything when he broke into her apartment but a fine and a misdemeanor charge," Grey says.

Colleen sighs as she shakes her head. "That's ridiculous." Her lips purse with thought. "You need to be careful. I wish there were strict laws to keep you safe and protected, but right now, you need to watch your back. It's so important you're with someone all the time right now. When walking to class or heading to the grocery store, always be with a friend."

"She stayed with Hudson last year after he broke in, and

we're wondering if that deterred him since he didn't contact her," Grey says.

Colleen shrugs. "Maybe? There are so many possibilities. Stalking is underreported and understudied. Many mistake the actions to be flattering or nonpredatory, and as you've experienced, little is done even when they cross the line, even when they break the law. That's why it's so important you keep track of everything that happens." She looks at me with eyes the same noteworthy blue shade as Grey's. "I know it can make you feel silly or paranoid, but he's a threat, and you need to treat him as one."

"How were you able to get the guy to stop stalking you? Was he arrested?" I ask.

Colleen shakes her head. "I think he got tired of me pulling a shotgun on him every time he drove by and probably found a new victim." Terror and pride are visible in her gaze, and she doesn't hide either.

"Mila's learning self-defense. She trained with Dustin this morning," Grey explains.

"Good for you. Even without having someone completely terrifying in your life, I think it's great you're learning to defend yourself. Too many men don't understand the word no."

"You don't see him at all anymore?"

Colleen shakes her head. "No. But I'm still careful. I'm always paying attention."

"I'm sorry you had to go through that. I'm sure it was terrifying."

She gives me a knowing smile, and I appreciate she doesn't work to brush off the trauma she experienced, either. "Did you grow up in Oleander Springs?" she asks me.

It's a loaded question. Typically, I'd say yes and not second-guess my response. I did grow up in Oleander Springs, but something about Grey's mom wants me to be more transparent.

"I moved there when I was seven." I reach for the glass of water in front of me.

"That's quite the scar." It's not an accusation in her tone, but something similar. A polite prompt for an explanation. Briggs and Jon share a similar tone. I don't know how she noticed; few do. The scar is so old, a mostly silver line against my fair skin, except for near the top, where the skin is always red. Usually, my watch covers it, but I took it off this morning when training and forgot to put it back on.

"Sorry if that sounds nosy. I'm a medical assistant for an orthopedist's office," she explains.

I shake my head, refusing the apology. "I cut myself on a piece of glass when I was little."

"It's amazing how resilient kids are. Grey was a climber when he was little. I couldn't turn my back for more than a second."

I fill myself with chicken and dumplings as she tells me how Grey loved hanging from the trees and how much he loved helping his grandpa. Then I tell her about my parents, and when I mention living beside Lake Oleander, she shares how much she loves the area, and I find myself extending an invitation for her to come anytime.

"I will take you up on that offer," she says. "We'll have a girl date."

It sounds a thousand times better than a self-date.

We clean the kitchen together before Grey shares we have to get going.

Colleen gives me a tight hug. "If you need anything, please feel welcome to reach out. I'd be happy to go with you if you need someone or just talk through things. And if you need an advocate for talking to the police, let me know. I'll go with you."

My throat thickens once more as I nod and thank her.

The outside air is a welcomed reprieve, stinging my skin and drying my eyes as the wind hits me.

Grey starts his truck and waits until his mom closes the front door before backing out of the driveway.

"What's wrong?" he asks.

I glance at him, the darkness of the cab cloaking his expression.

"Nothing."

"Are you worried about Julian?"

"I like your mom."

He stares at me.

"I struggle trusting people, but I particularly struggle trusting women, especially mothers. A condition of my childhood, I suppose. But I really liked your mom." The admission is high on the intimacy scale, but I can't bring myself to care.

Chapter 32

Grey

"We aren't taping our hands?" Mila asks as I instruct her to remove her shoes and join Cole and me in the ring. While she changed, I filled Cole in on all things Julian Holloway.

Cole's eyes have lost the goading that was present this morning. Instead, he's all focus and discipline.

"No. We're going to shadowbox and practice some holds."

Mila slips between the ropes, joining us. She looks tired, and a part of me wants to call it a night and reconvene tomorrow, but a bigger part of me is glad she's exhausted, knowing this is when mistakes are made.

Cole runs a hand over his hair and leans against the ropes as I approach Mila. "First things first, if you can avoid a fight, avoid it. If that means running away, hiding, or asking for help, do it."

Mila nods, but her gaze drifts to Cole as he circles me.

"Most people won't try and hit you. They'll grab you, usually from behind." I pause as Cole demonstrates what I mean, his arm wrapping around the front of my neck. "We'll teach you moves, but one of the fastest ways to make him let go will be to poke him in the eye. Use your nails, knuckles, it doesn't matter. Someone sees something coming toward their eyes, they're going to recoil, and it will give you that gap you need to get away."

Cole nods, and moves to the front of me, turning to look at Mila. "If he doesn't flinch because he's like Dustin and has a blind spot, dig your thumb into his eye socket, and believe me, he'll let go."

Horror flashes across Mila's features.

I don't allow the thought to settle, continuing. "If someone comes at you from the front, you can also use your knee. A knee to the groin will make any guy drop." I slash a hand through the air definitively. "Eyes and groin hits will make them release you, and then you run like hell."

Mila turns, her face inches from mine. Hesitation is etched across her brow. "What if someone grabs me, and I freeze?"

I nod. "It's normal to freeze. Adrenaline makes you lose motor skills."

"Like a opossum," she says.

Cole shakes his head. "That's why we're here. We're going to teach your reflexes to behave like a goddamn grizzly. You won't even have to think."

Mila stares at him, gaze critical. "This isn't teaching me how to hit someone. I understand that defense is important, but what about offense?"

"We'll get there," I tell her. "Tonight, we're going to prac-tice on you getting free when I grab you."

Cole flashes me a grin. "Don't be afraid to hit him, Mila."

"You guys can't be serious—" She looks from me to Cole, and then her breath catches as I grab her leg, nearly tipping her over before steadying her.

"Get ready," I tell her, pacing a few steps back.

I go at her again, wrapping my arm around her shoulders. "You're tall. A guy's likely going to grab your waist or shoulders. If he takes you by the waist," I move my arm to her middle, "you go limp. Make yourself as big and heavy as possible, and then wiggle. Make it hard for me to hold on to you."

We practice again and again, walking through each scenario until Mila declares she needs a break.

I glance at the clock, realizing it's already past ten. "We should call it a night. We'll come back tomorrow."

Mila blows out a long breath and slips out of the ring, going to where she left her shoes.

I turn to Cole, offering him my hand. "Thanks for coming."

He nods, taking my hand and reeling me in for a hug. "Anytime. She's a quick learner."

"I'll send you and the others this clown's mugshot. If he comes around here, let Abe go to town."

Cole grins. "Are you coming tomorrow?"

"I have three classes, practice, and a meeting with that booster I was telling you about. Hopefully to sign a contract."

"We'll take care of her."

I glance in Mila's direction as she ties her shoes. "I want you to be sure to put red tape on her."

"She might have fun. She seems scrappy."

He's goading me, and I know it. Still I react, growling out a swear.

Cole slaps me on the back. "God, this is more fun than I anticipated."

I shake my head and offer a final goodbye before scooping up Mila's bag and leading her out to my truck so Cole can lock up.

We drive in silence for several minutes, my gaze on the rearview mirror, ensuring no one is following us.

"How did you guys learn all this stuff?"

"Everywhere we could. Cole does mixed martial arts because he learned multiple fighting styles, and this allows him to combine them."

"What got you guys interested in fighting?"

"Cole got jumped one day at school. They kicked the shit out of him, and the school didn't do a goddamn thing. They said there were no witnesses to prove who had started the fight. So we decided since the school wouldn't do anything, we would."

"That's terrible, but it's also kind of amazing. You guys trained how to kick ass while I was trying to beat crazy world records by eating the most slices of pie in a minute."

I chuckle. "We did other kid stuff."

"Yeah? Like what?"

"Legos, sprinklers, campfires, riding our bikes..."

"I never learned to ride a bike."

"You never learned to ride a bike?"

Mila shakes her head. "I've never slept in a tent, either. And until you gave me that jump rope, I'd never done that."

"Even after you were adopted?"

"They would've in a second if they knew. I was kind of like a twenty-five-year-old, shoved into the body of a seven-year-old when I moved here." She gestures with her hands as though compressing an object.

"It must have been hard coming to a new state and a new family."

She's quiet, and I think I must have said the wrong words. "Not because they weren't good parents, just that would be a lot of change. Hell, half the guys on the team had a hard time adjusting when they were eighteen."

"Do you want the nitty gritty or quick and vague?"

"I want all of it."

Mila's eyes flash to mine. Silence stretches between us for a full minute. "Jon and Alex saved me. Most people wouldn't have been willing to adopt me. I acted like a twenty-five-year-old because I'd seen so much, but I was also a bit like a feral cat. Malnourished with trust issues, depression, and anxiety."

I'm silent as guilt hits my stomach, quickly chased by the bitter taste of panic.

"Do you still experience anxiety or depression?"

She nods. "It's like an illness. It doesn't completely go away, but I've been fortunate, and through therapy and lots of trial and error, I've found techniques and different things that help me keep it all together when I start to feel the desire to fall apart."

"I'm here," I tell her. "If you ever need anything ... to talk or to..." I shake my head, feeling completely useless and uncertain. "I'm here."

"Training with you helps a lot—more than I expected. Briggs has been basking in an obnoxious ray of vindication. He's been trying to convince me to pick up a physical hobby for years." She pauses. "Maybe clinging to my stubbornness is how I show my claws?" She flexes her fingers, her tone light.

"Does it help to talk about those years before moving here?"

"That's a complicated question, and the answer is even more complicated."

"Why?"

"My childhood wasn't entirely bad or tragic, but it's like a minefield. Some of the memories trigger my depression or anxiety, so I have to tread through them carefully. And I don't usually talk with anyone about them aside from Briggs and sometimes my parents."

"Not even Hudson or Evelyn?"

"Some stories can't be unheard."

It's my turn to feel haunted.

When we pull onto campus, my gaze sweeps across every

dark and lit space, searching for anything out of the norm. I find a parking space in the front row.

Mila follows me to the doors, which require a keycard because of the late hour. A few student-athletes are in the lobby, studying. We ride up to the fourth floor and go to the end of the hall, where I unlock my door. "I'll get you a spare key tomorrow."

Mila nods, following me inside.

"Do you want to shower first?" I ask.

She nods, avoiding eye contact. "Sure. Yeah. Let me just get my stuff." She pauses for a second as though working to recall where her things are and then heads for my room.

Moments later, she reappears, clutching a small pile of clothes and a pink bag. "I didn't pack any towels. Do you have an extra I can borrow?"

The thought of Mila naked is something I've been wrestling with for weeks now, and the realization she's about to be naked in my shower has my cock aching.

I nod. "I'll show you where everything is." I cross to the small hall closet outside the bathroom without daring to look back at her and point out the extra towels and washcloths. "There are spare toothbrushes and toothpaste in the bottom drawer of the vanity, too."

"For your overnight guests?" Her tone is teasing.

"I don't have overnight guests. I don't bring people here."

Panic sketches across her features. "Ever?"

I shake my head.

Mila clutches her clothes to her chest. "Maybe I should stay with Hudson. I don't want to impose."

"Mila, go shower."

"I'm serious."

"So am I. And I need to take a shower, too, so unless you

want to make some kind of pledge to save water and shower together, you need to get in there."

Challenge flashes in her gaze, and I reach for the hem of my shirt.

She shoves me before I can get it above my navel and disappears into the bathroom.

The water turns on as I text Hudson. I'm not in the least surprised when he texts me back with a link to a shared spreadsheet with my name and other guys from the team, their schedules and availabilities blocked out, so someone is always available to walk Mila to classes or anywhere else she needs to go. She's going to hate it.

Mila steps out of the bathroom ten minutes later, her hair wrapped in a towel. "I'm going to blow dry my hair in the living room so you can shower." She looks tense.

I nod, filling in the final slot of my schedule for the week before pocketing my phone and grabbing some clean clothes.

Under the shower stream, my thoughts return to Mila's haunted words that some stories can't be unheard.

When I get out of the shower, Mila's still drying her hair. Her eyes catch on me, darting across my bare chest before she averts her attention to the wall. She's going to hate my proposal even more than Hudson's spreadsheet.

I brush, floss, and fill two glasses with water before Mila finishes.

"You can leave it under the sink," I tell her as she starts to put her hair dryer back into her suitcase.

"I think I should sleep on the couch," she says, shoving it into her bag.

I shake my head. "We already talked about this."

"Actually, we didn't. You just had a supreme bossy moment, and I chose not to argue because I got the impression you weren't in a good place to negotiate."

"You think that was a supreme bossy moment?"

Her gaze strays to my chest, and her cheeks flush.

Heat slips along my spine as a sense of urgency flows into my veins.

Mila takes a step back, stumbling when she hits the open door with her elbow. She gazes at the floor, bed, and bags—avoiding me at all costs. "I was going to sleep on the couch at Hudson's anyway. I'm—"

"If you sleep on the couch, I'm sleeping on the couch. We'll fit a lot better here."

This gives her pause. "Why would you sleep on the couch?"

"Because I'm not sleeping in a separate room."

"This is just a ... precaution. An extra precaution. It's not as though he can get into the building."

I shake my head. "Brush your teeth and get into bed."

"I—"

"I will pick you up and put you in this bed."

It's likely the wrong thing to say to her. Mila tends to dig in her heels the same way I do.

"Is this your way of showing me you can be bossier?"

I don't answer.

Mila takes another step back, and I mirror her this time. She raises both hands. "I'm just going to brush my teeth." She crosses the hall, leaving the door open a crack as she proceeds to brush her teeth.

She returns, her pink shower bag in hand, lingering by the door. "For the record, I think we should discuss this tomorrow after I maul you in your sleep."

"Is that a threat or a promise?" I tease.

"Has Evelyn told you stories? She compares me to a giant man-eating squid." Mila puts her bag into her suitcase and slowly approaches the side of the bed I usually sleep on. I don't mention it as she pulls back the covers, her pajama pants and matching tee covering too much of her and exposing entirely too much at the same time.

"It's a king-sized bed."

"You say that like it will save you."

I laugh and flick off the light, a million dirty thoughts rushing to the forefront. "Do your worst," I tell her before climbing in on the opposite side.

She lays at the edge of the bed, her back to me, leaving enough room for two people to fit between us.

"What time is your first class tomorrow?"

"Ten."

"We'll do cardio here and then head to the gym at six. You can stay and work with Dustin while I'm at practice."

She groans. "I knew you were a morning person, but I didn't realize you were *that early* of a morning person."

"Do you need anything? Are you warm enough?"

She rolls her upper body, so her shoulders are flush against the bed and turns to look at me. It's so dark I can barely discern the outline of her jaw.

"Have you ever hit someone? Not in football, I mean."

"A few times."

"Did you ever freeze?"

"The first time I did. I wasn't expecting it. It was a guy my mom was dating. I was sixteen and hit his bumper by accident. He clocked me." I trace my finger across my cheekbone as if still able to feel the sting.

"What happened?"

I release a long breath, recalling that afternoon. "I wasn't expecting him to hit me, so I took the full impact. I was still stunned when he moved to shove me, but my reflexes kicked in, and I put him in a rear-naked choke hold. I told him if he ever came around or talked to my mom again, I'd bury him in the backyard."

"I can't believe he hit you. What a jerk."

I raise a hand to hers, brushing my thumb across her knuckles. She doesn't pull away, so I do it again. "I was fine. It barely bruised."

"Is it really called a rear-naked choke hold?"

"It is. Want me to show you how it's done?"

In the silence, I catch the bright reflection of her eyes. "No! But I need to know why it's called that."

I chuckle, letting my hand relax over hers. "It's a Jiu-Jitsu move, and it's called that because, unlike other strangulation techniques, it doesn't require the opponent to wear a gi training uniform."

"We need to work on your pillow talk. Telling a girl that you know how to strangle someone before she sleeps with her back to you is strictly off the table."

My fingers curl around her hand. "You're always safe with your back to me."

It's silent again, my need to pull her closer nearly outweighing the warning in my head that I could fuck things up if I push this too fast.

"We'll see if you're singing this same tune in the morning." She slips her hand free and rolls to her back. "No rear-naked choke holds."

She falls asleep nearly instantly.

Chapter 33

Mila

I wake up to Grey trying to extract himself from the full body hold I have on him. My legs are tangled around his, my arms twined around his waist, and my breasts are plastered to his biceps.

I wince, retracting and slipping to the opposite side of the bed. My muscles protest, sore and cold, as I move away from Grey's heat.

"I think I get the squid reference, now." Grey's voice is husky with sleep.

I hate how much I like it. "I warned you to let me sleep on the couch."

He stands. "I wasn't complaining."

I swallow thickly, grateful the room is still pitch dark. "What time is it?"

"Time to get up." He flips on the bedside table, and I whimper like a vampire exposed to the sun as I sink into the pillows.

"What time is it really?"

"Almost five."

I groan. "I might have to learn how to do a rear-naked choke hold today, so you'll sleep in."

Grey snickers as his palm connects with my butt with a firm slap, making me jump. My head snaps up in time to see his side profile and the impressive bulge that his sweatpants do little to conceal.

He moves to the closet, his back to me. Each muscle is a piece of art as he tugs a shirt free from a hanger and slides it on. A Camden hoodie goes over it. "Wear layers. We're going to the gym after we go running, and it's cold out." His hair is beautifully disheveled, reminding me of that morning he came to my apartment, and lust took over my brain.

"Food. Coffee."

"It's on its way. Get up."

"On its way?" I release a final groan of protest and slip out of the warmth of the covers. I push the door shut with my foot and get dressed.

Grey's greeting a freshman player I barely know holding a paper bag and a drink tray as I step out.

"Thanks," Grey says, closing the door.

"Is this from the facility?" I ask.

Grey turns to face me and nods. "It was this or cereal this morning. Every time I tried to move, you stirred."

My cheeks heat, wondering how long he was awake trying to get free.

He withdraws two creams and a single sugar from the bag, placing them in front of one of the coffee cups, reminding me once more of all the little details we know about each other. He pulls out two plates with covers, and we sit in amicable silence, eating scrambled eggs, toast, and a small mountain of fruit.

"Are we going to go running at the track or the facility?" I ask as we clear our dishes.

Grey shakes his head. "If he's watching you, I want him to see me. See us."

I lace up my shoes, my heart a sticky beat of *us. Us. Us.*

Outside, the ground is frosted white. I blow into my hands, my eyes stinging. "It's dark and freezing. No one's going to see us because no one's crazy enough to be outside."

Grey nods as the doors to the dorm open behind us, and three guys appear, nodding toward Grey, respect in their gazes.

"The football team doesn't count," I say. "You're all nuts."

He grins, catching my hand with his and lacing our fingers. His hand is warm, the skin on his fingers and palms rough with calluses. It feels remarkably nice, and I try to recall the last time I held a boy's hand. It's been a long time. Like kissing on the lips, holding hands is intimate, requiring a level of closeness I often avoid.

The groundskeepers have already sprinkled deicer across the sidewalks that lead us to the track, where a handful of people are crazy or devoted enough to their sport to be running.

Everything is normal, and I can't help but wonder if we're overreacting.

A blonde girl wearing leggings and a sports bra calls out to Grey and waves. Her gaze falls on me and then our joined hands, and I wish I could say it didn't encourage me to stand a little closer to him as though I'm making some kind of claim.

"She's going to get hypothermia," I muse.

Grey's lips quirk with a smile. "Ready to stretch?"

"I'm sore," I admit, as our hands slip apart, and we move to stretch. The muscles under my armpits are particularly tender, as is every other muscle in my arms and over my ribs. "I didn't realize hitting took so many muscles."

Grey gives me a knowing look.

When I sit down on the cold ground to stretch my

hamstrings, Grey hunches down in front of me. "It will be a deeper stretch if I help."

Innuendos line my tongue, and I have to bite them back because every one of them involves him being deep inside of me, stretching more than my hamstrings, providing a relief my body has been craving.

I lie on my back as Grey gets into position above me, resting my leg on his shoulder and leaning forward. "Tell me when."

Despite getting stronger and building endurance, my hamstrings are still pitifully tight.

"Hudson put together a spreadsheet that includes everyone's schedules. We need you to add your classes."

"Someone should be with Evelyn. He talked to her," I remind him.

"He was showing you how close he can get. The guy who stalked my mom used to drop off gifts for me. We don't know if he was trying to taunt her or if he really thought that would change her opinion. Sometimes these people are sick and need help. But Hudson's already added Evelyn, and Nolan added Hadley, Hannah, and Katie. We'll have someone from the team with you guys at all times."

"For how long?"

Grey moves, and I swap legs. This time, he keeps a hand on each of my thighs, his knee so close to my center I have to focus on not moving to press myself against him. "We'll see," he says vaguely. In my experience, vague responses are used to eclipse ugly truths.

My independence claws at my chest as we remain silent. I want to refuse. I don't want to hide and change my life for Julian fucking Holloway, but I already have. I did a year ago and haven't been able to readjust to normal since, regardless of my attempts and desire.

"We're going to do a couple more stretches together," Grey

says, lowering my leg. "Put your feet together and bend your knees." He pats my knees.

I move to follow his instruction.

"Lie back," Grey says, resting a hand on the inside of my knees as my back presses against the cold ground again. Grey rises on his knees, and without warning, my thoughts shift to when he was in a similar position between my legs, and I was naked. Desire and heat curl low in my stomach, and the way I ache for him is nearly painful.

"What if he gets mad and tries to do something? What if he goes after one of you guys?"

He smirks, but it's dark and mirthless. "Let's hope he tries."

"No," I say, shifting out of the stretch, my heart straining.

Grey lifts a single brow as he stands, extending a hand to me. I want to refuse and bat his touch away, but I slowly accept his hand. "This is a bad idea." I shake my head and try to pull my hand free, but Grey tightens his grip before I can.

"What's wrong?"

"If me being around others deters Julian because he realizes I'm involved with someone else, cool, but if this is a risk, we're not doing it. I'm moving back into the apartment, and I'll track things and report it, but I'm not letting you or anyone else get involved."

Grey's broad shoulders block the track from my view as he steps closer to me. "Nothing is going to happen. Everyone will be safe ... everyone except those who have to walk Katie to class."

I scoff, but my guard is raised, a panic attack on the fringes of my actions threatening to possess me. My gaze skitters, trying to find something to focus on, but everything looks like a threat. My chest burns, my thoughts are fuzzy, and my breaths are loud in my own ears as Grey says my name a second time.

Warmth enrobes me as Grey presses his mouth to mine.

He's kissing me softly, gently, as though he senses how close I am to the edge, and one wrong move will push me over.

His thumb grazes my cheek as his other hand sinks into the back of my hair, near the base of my ponytail. He angles my head and steps closer, his chest pressing against mine so hard it forces me to lean into him, so we don't topple over. His lips part, and I taste the mint of his toothpaste before my body melts against him, pliant and wanting. His tongue brushes the seam of my lips, and his fingers constrict in my hair, deepening the kiss as though sensing the transition of my thoughts as they veer from dread and fear straight to bliss and desire.

His thick erection presses against my stomach, and a sound between a moan and a whimper leaves me as my back arches. Desire has never felt like a need—until now. I press my hands to his waist, grappling with his shirt to feel his bare skin under my fingers, hot and perfect.

Grey hums an approval, swiping his tongue against mine, purposeful and slow, and my body sparks with recognition, recalling the way it felt to have his tongue between my legs. A voice cuts through the lust that has me feeling drunk on him, and I slowly pull back and find Emma Kemp.

My emotions take a one-eighty.

Again.

Deceit cuts the same lines lust just laid. "I thought that was you," Emma says, ignoring me with more than her singular word as she stares at Grey. "You're right. The track *is* empty at this hour."

I try to take a step toward the track, but Grey wraps his hand around my waist, pulling my hips flush with the side of his thigh so our bodies are a 'T' shape.

"Emma stopped by the facility because her dad knows we have great trainers, and I was getting taped up." The explanation is intended for me, or maybe for Emma. Grey was offered multiple sponsorships but still hasn't signed with Linus Kemp or Gerald Barnhardt.

I recall Hadley's words from the booster meeting, how vicious Emma has been, and lean a little closer to Grey, playing my role since meeting her. "It's nice to see you, but you'll have to excuse us. We have to get in our cardio before classes. We like to work on our endurance."

Her gaze shifts to me, understanding clear as her smile grows tight.

I feel the gentle rumble of Grey's laugh as he prompts me forward. We hit the field and fall into a jog.

We run with focus—Grey because he's an overachiever and me because I don't know if he just kissed me again because he wanted to or because Emma was here.

When we do our cooldown stretches, Grey tries to make small talk, asking about my classes today, how I slept, and even compliments my pace of the run. When my answers remain polite but short, he stops trying, and we stretch in silence.

The silence follows us back to the dorm, into the elevator, and up to his room.

I refuse to sit and get comfortable. I don't want to get used to his space. Instead, I stand beside the couch and check my email while he packs a gym bag.

I don't want to talk to him, realizing whether it's impractical or just, I'm mad at him.

"Don't forget to input your schedule into the spreadsheet. Any time our schedule overlaps, mark them one color."

I'm already reviewing the spreadsheet, trying to tamp down the horror and embarrassment at seeing row after row of schedules that have already been entered. Hudson's recruited the entire damn team.

I discover a section filled with colors and find Katie, Hadley, Hannah, and Evelyn's schedules have already also been added. Guilt reminds me I need to reach out to them and apologize, not because this is my fault but because it's impacting them.

I enter my classes and times but don't color code where Grey's and my schedules overlap. I don't even look because lately, every time I test fate, it tests me right back. Knowing my luck, Grey will be available to walk me to every class of every day, and Emma Kemp will be in all my classes, and we'll have to continue this inane lie.

I feel Grey's stare, hot on my neck.

I don't look up to acknowledge him.

We managed to coexist for two and a half years, toeing the line of being friends. It was comfortable, easy, reliable. This new space where he insists we're friends, and I'm sharing stories about my life, and he's training me, and kissing me to deter another girl, introducing me to his mother, and holding my hand to successfully breach every line of intimacy I avoid has me bristling. I want to yell and scream. I want to say hateful words, so he knows it all means as little to me as it does to him. But more than anything, I want that comfort of being acquaintances back.

"What's wrong?" he asks.

"Does it really matter what Emma Kemp thinks?" I snap, my gaze finally narrowing in on his.

"I don't care what Emma Kemp thinks."

"Then why did you kiss me?" The question explodes from my chest—from my pride, from somewhere that makes kissing Grey feel different, and loathing the fact because I've been terrified for the past several weeks that it doesn't feel different to him. That this is entirely unrequited.

Grey's eyes are hard, his brow furrowed. He looks like he

wants to yell at me, too. Remind me the premise of our deal. That he's helping me and has invested way more time into this bargain, and that he's only kissed me a fraction of the times she's been around.

He walks toward me, pure stealth and grace.

"I had no idea she was out there. Did it look like I was capable of paying attention to one damn thing but you?" he asks. "No." His voice is an eruption of anger. "I was between your goddamn thighs imagining things I shouldn't be imagining, and then you looked so starkly terrified, and I didn't know how to find the right words to assure you, so I kissed you."

I stare at him for a second, my anger evaporating too fast. I want to cling to it, bathe in it, allow it to protect me because anger has always felt like the safest emotion.

"I know you feel this, Mila." He steps closer.

I pin him with my gaze. His words feel like a trap, a slide straight into the fiery pits of vulnerability hell.

Grey strikes then, his mouth on mine, hands on my waist— forgoing words.

We're both terrible at words.

His tongue pummels mine savagely, his hands dipping beneath the layers he instructed I put on, finding my skin greedy for his touch. I sigh the moment his fingers press against my bare skin. He gets the first point.

I kiss him harder, meeting each thrust of his tongue as I scrape my short nails through his hair that is decidedly more brown than blond. I try not to lose myself in his touch as his hands skate up and down my sides, inching my shirt higher, my joggers, lower. I catch his bottom lip with my teeth, nipping the flesh as I grip his cock through his sweats. He's hard and so damn big, flexing his hips into my hand as he emits a low groan worthy of two points.

I stroke him as he reclaims my mouth, and for a several

minutes, we allow lust to settle between us, not hurrying to the next step as we bask in the perfect unison of our mouths.

Grey roams to my breast, his fingers shifting my sports bra high on my chest to free both breasts, and as his hands glide over each aching globe we sigh together.

I tip my head back, willing to lose a point to feel this, to allow him to worship my breasts as he had last time, teasing, licking, pinching until I didn't know what would come next or what I wanted more. His thumbs graze over my erect nipples and his hips grind against mine, a ghost of pleasure where I so desperately need to feel him.

I strip off my shirts, and he rewards me by pinching my nipples. His gaze is on my face, on my mouth swollen from kissing him, my eyes drowning in lust. I wrestle off my sports bra, and lean against the coolness of the wall, prepared to forfeit the game.

Grey surges forward, capturing my lips with another heady kiss as his hands swipe and roll my breasts.

"I love your breasts," he says, kissing me again as he flicks one hardened peak and rubs the other. Like Grey, everything he does is a near confliction.

I reach for him, shoving my hand beneath the barriers of his waistband and underwear and wrapping my hand around his girth. We release a shared moan, his at relief, and mine due to the ache that intensifies in my core.

I pump him in my fist twice, and then his fingers still me as he slides against my wet heat, and I practically orgasm out of anticipation.

"Fuck," Grey says, a tortured sound as he leans his forehead against mine.

Neither of us moves, aware we have two distinct options, we can stop and walk away or allow this to change everything between us.

I want him to choose. I want him to be sure.

My determination hangs by a thread. "God, Mila. Tell me you want this. Tell me you want me, and I will give you the goddamn world."

My hand tightens around him, stroking him as I kiss him frantically.

Grey thrusts two fingers inside of me and I gasp, writhing on his hand as he kisses me harder, more urgently, trying to absorb every gasp and moan I release as I lose myself to each thrust of his fingers that eases the incessant ache for him.

"Grey, I need..."

He twists his fingers, and my spine grows weak as he slides his fingers to my clit where they glide lazily along my flesh.

I groan, a sound of annoyance and pleasure. It feels so damn good I can't stop myself from imagining an entire day spent naked, laid out before him while he strokes me like this, an orgasm just out of reach but not caring because it feels so good. Like something forbidden and perfect.

"What do you need?" he asks, running his nose along my cheek.

I shake my head. "Don't stop."

He doesn't. He tunes me like an instrument until everything in me feels aligned, perfect, and right, and that orgasm that felt a mile away comes barreling down my spine, blindsiding me and making my knees weak. My breaths fall out of me in gasps. He doesn't lessen his strokes, if anything he goes faster, harder, wringing out every ounce of my orgasm until I place my hand over his, the stimulation too much.

He kisses me, and for a second, I fear this will be like last time, and he's going to tell me it's time to go, but then I'm airborne. With me over his shoulder, Grey crosses to his room.

My back hits the mattress, and with my next breath, he's stripping off my pants and underwear.

"Do you have a condom?" I ask.

Grey reaches into his nightstand and pulls out a sealed box. I take it from him, using my teeth to rip the plastic and hand him one of the foil packets.

"Lose the clothes, Meyers."

He chuckles, stripping out of his sweatshirt first, exposing his perfectly sculpted everything. His thumbs hook into his sweatpants and boxer briefs next, drawing them down, releasing his long, thick cock, the head tinted purple with his own desire.

The ache that was sated seconds ago returns at the sight of him.

Grey rolls the condom over his length, and I stare at him, debating where to go. "Lie back." His voice is gravelly and soft as he runs a hand over himself.

I lean back on my elbows so I can watch him. Grey smirks, running his hand over his length again, allowing me to admire him. Then he grabs my thighs and tugs me to the edge of the mattress. He props one of my feet against his chest and moves his hand to his cock. He rubs the tip over each swollen and desperate inch of me twice before slowly pressing against my entrance.

I sigh a breathy moan, and Grey presses in a little further. He's so large pain licks at me before pleasure chases it away. He eases into me until half of his length is buried inside of me, the fullness of him stretching me, making me want to beg him to move. But he pauses, lifting his eyes from where our bodies connect to my face.

He made the first concession, and I don't hesitate to make the second, realizing for the first time the purpose of the hundreds of hours spent on self-worth and what I want. I want this. I want him. I reach forward, running a hand over his jaw, it's a lover's touch, something as intimate as holding hands, and then I lie back, my hand still cupped around his jaw, inviting him to cover more of me—all of me.

He leans down, kissing me, his fingers gently rolling my nipple. I moan, a breathy sound as I arch my back. "I want you so bad."

His sapphire eyes darken, drinking me in, and then with one hard thrust, he's seated inside of me. Pleasure steals my breath as it settles over my muscles, and down to my bones. The fullness of him is too much, yet not enough. I need him to move, need to feel him thrusting inside of me until this desire burns out.

Grey resumes kissing me, remaining obstinately still as I adjust to his size. I try to shift my own hips, but he presses down harder, kissing me fuller. This time, I deliver the declaration of war and advance, biting his bottom lip. He snickers quietly, kissing along my jaw, taking his time, and maintaining the upper hand.

"Grey." My voice is throaty to my own ears, frantic with an underlying edge of a threat. "I..."

"I know," he says.

I shake my head. He has no idea how it feels as though my body is screeching with demands of friction. How my heart feels as though it's been creeping outside of my body for weeks —years.

Grey leans down, his body blanketing mine, so warm, so wide, so impossibly strong. Then he's kissing me again, drowning out the need for him to move as he sets a new demand with his mouth, and as soon as our pace is set, a rhythm of teeth, tongues, and lips, he moves, and I forget how to kiss, how to breathe, how to exist as he slides out and then presses back inside of me.

I forget about scores as he moves above me, every move smooth and deep, filling me in a way I never imagined possible. I wish for a second orgasm, and in the same breath, pray it doesn't come so he never stops.

His breath mixes with mine, his blue eyes dancing above mine, reading my every gasp and moan.

"Harder," I say.

That smirk returns to his lips, accepting the challenge as he sits up, gripping the back of my thighs, sinking deeper inside of me, and then he moves faster and harder, each thrust slapping our bodies together.

His gaze is on our bodies, his grip firm but not tight enough, his movements too measured. Just as I'm about to ask him to go harder again, wanting him to get lost in this with me, wanting him to burn out with me, Grey slides a hand between my legs, and I clench around him.

He makes a sound low in his throat, his movements becoming less measured, more frenetic. And as I do it a second time, his gaze flashes to mine. "Fuck, Mila."

Our war resumes: my determination to make him lose composure and his will to maintain it.

Sweat beads along my hairline, and his thumb moves over me so damn deliciously I don't even feel the warning of my orgasm before it shatters me. Then Grey pumps harder still, his movements becoming faster and less controlled before he unravels with a long groan. His chest falls against mine, a mountain of warmth.

My breaths are as uneven and heavy as when we complete our morning conditioning, my entire body sensitive, as the temperature drops and I sink a little deeper into the bed, a sense of satisfaction radiating all the way to my toes and fingertips.

Grey slowly slides out of me, and I open my eyes to find him already staring at me.

My arms feel weak as I scoot myself over, making room for him to lie beside me, and I'm a little surprised when he does, his hair disheveled and eyes gleaming brighter than I've ever seen them.

Chapter 34

Mila

"Can we just stay here all day?" I ask, running my hand over Grey's, mesmerized by how good his skin feels against mine, even like this.

"Sunday, we can," he tells me, kissing my shoulder. "Cole's expecting you." He doesn't move, though, just as reluctant as I am to leave.

"Are you ready to talk about this?" he asks.

I look at the alarm clock. "Don't you have a class this afternoon?"

"Forget the class."

I shake my head. Grey's been working his ass off for nearly three years. The only time he skips a class is when the team travels for games. There's no way in hell I'm going to let him start now and prove that dating is a terrible distraction. "We can talk Sunday."

"Sunday?"

"I'm willing to talk when you give me my break."

He stares at me a moment, then smirks as he shakes his head.

"What? I'm being reasonable."

Grey trails kisses up my arm, across my shoulder, and along my jaw. "Keep telling yourself that." He gives me one last hard kiss and then stands, moving to his closet. Naked Grey jumps in the standings, passing both sweatpants Grey and tux Grey to become my official favorite.

I tell him as much as I pull clean clothes from my suitcase and slip into the bathroom to take the world's fastest shower with my hair bundled on my head to save time.

When I get out, Grey's ready to go.

"Do you want to shower?" I ask.

He shakes his head, eyes dark with amusement. "I want to smell you on me all damn day."

My blush runs all the way to the roots of my hair, and he grins, sensing it.

Once we get in his truck, Grey passes me a bottled coffee from his bag, and my heart does a ridiculous spin.

"How do our schedules align this semester?"

"Tuesdays and Thursdays are terrible," I tell him.

I study his schedule again, realizing he has a class this morning that I overlooked. "How are you going to be in two places at once? You have a class that starts in an hour."

"I won't be able to stay at the gym. Cole will drive you back into town."

I quickly shake my head. "We're taking this too far. If you guys decide I can't walk alone, live alone, or drive alone—I'll go crazy. Literally."

Grey releases a heavy breath. "I know." An entire conversation is tagged to those two little words as we pull up to the gym.

"I'm safe driving myself. I'll take different routes, change my time, and pay attention. And I want to walk to classes alone. I'll stay with other people, avoid dark areas, but I need this."

Grey doesn't look even a little surprised or angry, like he

was expecting my response. "I want you to text me when you leave and arrive."

"Deal," I say without hesitation.

I can tell he's not happy with the situation, but he accepts it.

The skies are blooming with soft pastels, resembling an oil painting as we cross the parking lot.

"Hey," Cole says, turning as the bells announce our arrival. He's shirtless, his torso covered with a sheen of sweat that draws my attention. I get distracted by the multitude of tattoos covering much of his skin. When my gaze meets his, his smile confirms he caught me looking.

"So you're mine for the next two hours." Cole moves to grab the gauze.

Grey moves forward, taking the roll from Cole. "Where's Dustin?"

Cole flashes a triumphant smile.

Grey ignores him, hanging the gauze again. "Did you get the picture I sent?" he asks, glancing at Cole.

Cole nods. "I sent it to everyone. That guy won't get within ten miles without me knowing."

"Julian?" I ask.

Grey nods, his gaze lifting to mine.

"We aren't allowed to do that," I tell them. "It's actually illegal. Jon got in trouble for harassment when he distributed his photo last year."

"Fuck that," Cole snaps.

I turn to Grey, hoping he'll be more reasonable. "If he were to press charges, it would impact your eligibility. We can share it among close friends but can't post it on the internet or give it to others."

"Make this make sense," Cole says. "He's acting like a crazy ass motherfucker, and *still* has us by the balls?"

It's my turn to release a mirthless laugh. "If you think this is a joke, you should see how skeletal and scarce the laws to protect children are."

Grey's gaze shifts to mine, a silent question visible there as it is each time I mention my past. It's not intrusive, and no more attentive than he is any time I speak, just that edge of a question that sits there.

Abe steps forward, appearing from the back room I'd changed in last night with Dustin at his side.

"Political bullshit doesn't have a place in the gym," Abe says.

"Political?" I ask, smiling like I'm in a pageant. "That's such a nice and convenient label to put on shit we don't want to address, isn't it?"

"Oh, please. Preach to us. Let us hear how your marginalized ass has had it so damn bad." Abe crosses his arms over his broad chest.

Grey shifts subtly at my side. "Enough."

"No. No. She wants to enlighten us." He lifts an arm. "Enlighten us."

"But you know everything, right?" I taunt him.

Abe takes another step, eyes glacial as he stares me down. "If you—"

"I said enough," Grey says, stepping forward.

Cole grips his brother's shoulder. "Abe's heading to work."

Abe's gaze remains locked on mine, tight as a Pitbull's jaws. I ignore him, knowing that avoiding his gaze will anger him further. If he wants a pissing contest, he's met his match.

"Are we going to have a problem?" Grey asks, squaring up with Abe.

My sails lose their wind. These guys have been best friends long before I knew Grey—his own version of Hudson, Evelyn, and Griffin, and the idea of harming that has my pride rescinding.

"No," I say, shaking my head as I take a step back. "I'm here to learn. I'll keep my thoughts to myself."

I know Abe thinks he's won, and while that burns something deeper than my pride, I'd do it again in a second to preserve this relationship for them.

Dustin raises his eyebrows, looking at me as though I've grown a nipple in the middle of my forehead.

"When did my gym become a place to fuck around?" Mackey asks, stepping out of the office, carrying two large boxes that he shoves into Abe's arms. "Get this shit out of here." He

turns to Cole. "Your ass is supposed to be on the bags." His gaze turns to me. "And you've been here for five minutes and haven't warmed up yet." He turns to Grey last. "And what are you doing besides distracting everyone?"

No one responds.

Mackey claps twice. "Get moving before I kick all of your asses."

"I'd like to see you try, old man," Cole says, picking up his gloves.

"We'd hogtie you and hang you by your fucking ankles," Abe says. "Give that back of yours a break." He moves toward the door.

Cole laughs. "Your own personal inversion table. We'll even give you a good view." He moves to the heavy bag.

Mackey gives each of them a hard stare and then cocks his head. "Come on. Let's look at the schedule." He and Dustin head for his office.

"Is jump roping all I'm supposed to do?" I whisper to Grey.

His gaze is filled with uncertainty and reluctance as he looks at me, and I know he's debating staying or taking me back with him.

"You need to go," I remind him. "I'll be fine. I'll text you as soon as I get back."

"I'm calling Corey. He'll come and get you."

I want to object on principle alone. Wasting another person's time makes me feel supremely uneasy, but riding with Corey would be a hundred times more comfortable. "Tomorrow, I'm driving myself," I remind him.

"If you need anything, call me. I'll leave my phone on."

"I just need to know what a warmup constitutes."

"Stretch and then jump rope."

I nod, feeling a similar note of hesitancy for him leaving. I bury the thought. "I'll text you later."

Grey nods, releasing a shallow sigh before turning toward the door. I move to the back wall, shedding my sweatshirt before I grab a jump rope and begin.

"Ready?" Dustin asks twenty minutes later when I walk with purpose back toward the ring.

I nod.

"Let's get you taped. We'll do more punching and then work on kicking." He points at an old metal folding chair. "Sit backward on the chair, and rest your forearms over the back."

I do. Dustin wraps his hands around my forearm and begins massaging, catching me off guard.

Dustin's gaze jumps to mine, feeling me tense. "Boxers hurt their hands and wrists due to impact," he explains. "Or you can get carpal tunnel and other issues. Massaging helps. We all do it." He proceeds to point out which joints and muscles can flare up and cause the most issues, turning my hands so palms face up. "This is..." He points at my wrist, and his words catch, staring at the same scar Grey's mom had noticed. His gaze bounces to my opposite arm, finding a series of scars at my wrist. His gaze lifts to mine. "These are old."

I can't tell if it's a question or not, so I nod. "I got them when I was seven."

"Do they impair your mobility?"

I shake my head.

As though challenging my confirmation, he moves and bends my wrist and each of my fingers before resuming the quick massage, his gaze tracking each of the scars. Though he doesn't ask about them, I feel his curiosity.

"Let's go."

Chapter 35

Mila

"This is terrifying," Hannah says, admiring the raspberry pink toenail polish as the nail tech adds a second coat. Katie is on her left and Hadley on her right. It's Saturday, and the first chance the five of us have had to get together since the Julian incident. I just finished recapping everything again, though they heard the story from the other guys. Hudson brought up a solid point that the others need to know so they can watch out for him and remain safe.

"Have you seen him since?" Hadley asks from her chair across from me, her toes shining purple.

I shake my head. "Not a sighting or a word."

"So, is he the worst stalker in the world, or did he already move on?" Hannah asks.

"It's only been a few days," Evelyn says.

"Hopefully, it's done, and having the police called scared some sense into him, but I'm sorry that you're all getting the security detail craziness."

"I don't hate it," Hannah says. "The guys always carry my bag, and I've been asked out on two dates, simply because of association. Guys I never knew suddenly want me because they see me with football players."

"What does that say about them?" Hadley asks, blinking through her train of thoughts.

"That they're disgustingly shallow, and the guys you want to avoid," I say.

Hannah nods, looking bereft. "But the real question is, what's it like living with Grey?"

Hadley spears her with a look. "That *isn't* the priority of this afternoon."

"But we *are* curious," Katie adds.

Evelyn flashes a smile that eases something in my chest. She's been so worried. The two of us exchange a dozen texts a day, accounting for our whereabouts.

It's only been a few days, and already I've learned sleep habits and cleaning habits of his along with a dozen more details I'd never thought about like his favorite flavor of toothpaste is peppermint, he drinks herbal tea every night before bed, and he makes his bed every morning. He's neat, but not obsessively, and all of his underwear are black. "He doesn't like to watch TV," I share.

Hannah sits forward in her seat. "Tell us this a prelude to something dirty. That he doesn't watch because he's busy doing something else that involves nakedness. Primal nakedness."

"He studies a lot."

Hannah leans back in her seat and sighs with visible disappointment. I almost feel guilty for not admitting that Grey and I slept together, but since nothing has happened since and I'm not certain where things stand between us, mum's the word.

At least, for now.

My nails and toenails are a happy, bright shade of teal as we head to lunch, asking for a table in the back of the restaurant where we can see if anyone approaches us.

Lunch is filled with stories and laughter, discussions of books, classes, boys, and clothes—normal things that don't include Julian Holloway or the gym until I announce I have to get going.

"Are you going to show us these moves you're learning?" Hannah asks.

"No. I look uncoordinated and awkward, but I actually kind of like it. It's hard, but in a good way. You guys could come with me. We could train together."

"I'm considering it," Evelyn says. "Ever since seeing Julian, I can't help but wonder how many times another creep has managed to get that close to me without my even realizing it."

"It would be fun to do it together. The gym needs more estrogen, and maybe we can gang up and take Abe down."

Hadley cackles. "No way. That guy has vindictive tattooed across his forehead."

I slip my purse over my shoulder and grin. "But with five of us, he can hardly do a damn thing about it."

"One battle at a time," Evelyn says. "Be safe. We'll see you tonight for book club. Text me when you get to the gym."

I hug each of them and head for Mackey's.

I expected the gym to be empty, people spending their Saturday anywhere but working out, but it's busier than I've ever seen it. It's even busier an hour later as Cole and I finish shadowboxing. The majority of people are men, some familiar, going to their stations while others look uncomfortable and new, like me.

Cole slaps a long piece of red tape to my chest and a second to my back before I can protest.

"I'm not going to get in the ring with anyone," I say.

"We've seen the way you rise to a challenge," Cole says. "It stays."

I frown. "What did I do?"

He merely raises his brows.

"If you're referring to Abe, I diffused that situation."

Mackey scoffs from beside Cole, his expression condescending. "Cole needs to work on his jabs. Go get on a bag before they're filled and work on your right kicks. Focus on your extension. I want to see at least two of these pretty nails broken by the time you're done."

Every day, I understand a little more why they all mouth off to Mackey. He's ruthless, persistent, and gives Grey a run for his money when it comes to being bossy. But my determination to be a good student has me walking toward the bags.

"Atwool, get your ass in gear, or you'll owe me fifty pushups," Mackey yells.

I scowl, but my pace increases. I go to the far end, hoping to gain space and not draw the attention and critique of Mackey or Cole. I stand in front of the heavy bag, imagining a line on the floor as I square my shoulders as Dustin has taught me. Grey was supposed to be here thirty minutes ago. His absence has me on edge.

I concentrate on my stance and form as I punch the bag with my left fist, and then kick it with my right foot. Grey wasn't exaggerating when telling me balance and stamina are crucial for fighting. I likely needed several more weeks of cardio and balance before moving on to these steps, but I'm managing. Mostly.

I continue moving around the bag, counting the steps in my head, focusing on my extension as Mackey had instructed.

"Nice," a guy with dark hair and deep dimples says, resting a hand against the bag beside me. "You have great technique."

He's lying. I look as new and uncoordinated as I feel—Mackey and the others will attest to the fact.

"Thanks." I use the back of my forearm to wipe the sweat from my brow. I think I've sweated more in the past month than I have in my entire life combined.

His smile grows as his eyes drop to my tight tank and leggings.

I ignore him and hit the bag again, resuming my counts as a second guy joins him. This one has a series of tattoos along his forearm and dark auburn hair he has pulled back in a ponytail.

My focus falls to the bag as my muscles tire and my lungs plea for a breath, making it harder to maintain my balance and form.

Both men chuckle, and in the reflection of the mirror beside me, I see one of them make a lewd gesture with his hand and tongue.

I wonder how Mackey would react if I knocked them over with the heavy bag like a couple of bowling pins.

"What's your name?" the guy with dark hair asks as the bag moves, forcing me to turn. Mackey would be correcting me, telling me my hit was too low.

"I'm just here to work out," I say, punching the bag.

"So are we. Does that mean we can't be friends?" He looks at his friend, who moves closer.

"We could help you work out, *as friends*," the guy with auburn hair says, taking another step closer to me. "We could help you on your technique. You need to get lower. I could show you." His gaze drops to the red tape on my chest. "What's that for?"

"It means you leave her alone because she's property of the gym," Abe says, appearing behind me, arms crossed over his chest.

"She doesn't seem to mind our attention," the one with dark hair says.

"Don't make me kick your asses," Abe says.

The guy with auburn hair laughs outright.

Abe's eyes go scary dark, and then he rotates, landing a series of punches and kicks against my bag with flawless precision.

The guy with dark hair nods and takes a step back. "Message received. Red tape means off-limits."

The two drift down to another unoccupied bag without another word.

I turn to Abe, still impressed by his moves, and shocked he came to stand up for me. I'd bet a hundred bucks Mackey asked him to, but the fact he came still surprises me a little. This week, I've gotten the impression Abe would rather push me in front of a moving car than train with me. He never offers tips, critiques, or encouragement. Rather, he treats me as though I'm a virus and avoids me. "Thanks," I say, my voice soft but genuine.

"Work on hooks," Abe says and walks away.

At five, the bells on the door catch my attention and I turn to see Hudson with Grey. Panic nests in my thoughts, painful in my chest.

"You're not done," Abe says from where he's perched a dozen feet behind me. Just as quickly as that narrow olive branch was extended, he snaps it in half.

I want to object and make sure everything is fine, but instead, I deepen my squat and work on hooks as instructed. I run through the drill for a solid ten minutes before standing, my muscles strained and burning.

"You could have gone longer," is all that Abe says, following me over to where Grey is introducing Hudson to Cole and

Mackey. Grey's attention flits to me, eyebrows drawn with question.

I give a smile through shallow breaths and nod with assurance.

"Good to meet you," Cole says, shaking Hudson's hand.

Hudson nods, his gaze finding me for a second before noting Abe behind me. "You, too. I appreciate you guys helping us out."

"It's not for your benefit," Abe says.

Hudson arches a brow.

"This is Abe," Cole says. "Ignore him. We all do." He looks at Hudson, a silent dismissal to Abe that makes Abe silently seethe.

Guilt pinches in my chest. Abe's rude and unrefined, but the way the others talk to him bothers me on a fundamental level. I know I can't stand up for him, know my pity would only make him loathe me. After all, we're two sides of the same coin. Every day, I'm more sure of the fact.

Cole gestures to the gym. "If you want a tour, we're happy to give one. This place is open seven days a week, just pop in." I don't know if he's trying to sell him on the overpriced workouts I've learned they package to those who come down from Oleander Springs because of their earned reputation and Cole's fighting record or if the offer is earnest.

"Sounds like the facility," Hudson says.

"Pretty damn close," Grey says.

"If they can teach me how to punch someone, they could probably teach you to be lethal," I say to lighten the mood and cement his invitation here.

Hudson grins. "I never thought I'd see the day that I'd be driving to a gym to pick you up. A bookstore, yes. Coffeeshop, for sure. Jail, potentially—but a gym..." He shakes his head, humor bright in his eyes.

I scoff.

Mackey grins. A real grin.

I roll my eyes at him and head to the large pole where the rolls of tape and gauze hang along with multiple pairs of scissors. I grab one of the pairs to cut off my tape. Grey follows, taking the scissors and flipping my hands to face upward. "How was today?"

"Good. How was your day?"

The ghost of a smile crosses his features as he nods and cuts the tape off my right hand and wrist, tossing the sweaty and dirtied pieces into the nearby trash. He slips the scissors into the tape of my left side, high on my wrist, and cuts down to my palm before pausing, his gaze taking in my scar for a beat and then continuing.

As he turns to throw it away, I note the way Dustin stares at Grey, a silent confirmation passing between the two that assures me Dustin told him or asked about the scars. Old habits to pull back have my thoughts spinning to staying with Hudson and Evelyn or my own apartment, relying on the multiple safety precautions.

"See you tomorrow, Mila," Cole says, snapping my thoughts back to the present.

"Tomorrow's Sunday," I say.

"We only take breaks the day after a fight," he says.

Which would theoretically mean I'd never get a day off. His eyes gleam. He may not be as overtly obnoxious as his brother, but he's just as adept at provocation.

I don't bother with a response.

Mackey's lips tip higher.

"We'll see you tomorrow," Grey says.

"Where's Evelyn?" I ask as we step outside, the air so cold it steals my breath.

"Class. She gets out in ninety minutes. Your book club got

moved to my dorm, so we're supposed to go pick up snacks and drinks." We stop at Grey's truck, and I climb into the backseat, sitting behind Grey.

This week has been busy. Between training and classes, the only free time I've had was spent doing video chess with Griffin and homework. At night, when I would normally read a few chapters, I lie in bed physically exhausted and so sexually frustrated I can't focus on reading. Now that I've experienced Grey, I want more and I'm pretty sure he's waiting for me to talk through things before we sleep together again.

It's forced me to think a lot about what I want—both to give and receive.

We pull up to a grocery store on the outskirts of town, the store and parking lot both bigger. Most students drive here because the prices are a lot less than those near campus.

"I'll get drinks," Hudson says.

"We'll meet you in the frozen food aisle," I say.

Hudson disappears with a cart as Grey trails me to the frozen snacks. "Are you okay with Hudson meeting everyone?" I ask, realizing when I shoved myself into this part of his life, taking Hudson and Evelyn was an inevitability I hadn't considered until today.

Grey looks at me with those depthless blue eyes that always take in more than I intend. "Sometimes a belief or an idea is wrong. You were right about this. Cole and those guys are like brothers to me, but the team has become a second family to me. They need to know each other, especially now when I need to call on both to help."

"What if things get ... prickly?"

Grey smooths strands of my hair that fell from my ponytail behind my ear, humor glinting in his gaze. "It's not an if. It's a when."

329

"Exactly." I think of Abe's quick judgment and reaction to Hudson.

Grey grins. "It's not my problem to solve. The only way Abe is ever going to improve as a fighter is if he stops underestimating his opponents and popping off, and we both know Nolan's ego sometimes needs checked."

I shake my head, laughter sticking in my throat because he's making this all sound so simple—too simple. I decide not to point this out or question him, realizing that today was a first step toward bridging these parts of his life. He may change his mind, and he has that right.

"Did you get distracted?" Hudson asks, pulling up beside us.

I take a step away from Grey, feeling as though I've been caught doing something I shouldn't. I peer at his cart, filled with juices, coffees, bottles of wine, cookies, crackers, and bags of fruit. "Damn, I trained you to be a good boyfriend. You know the five of us can't eat all this though, right?"

Hudson pulls out his phone to check the time. "The guys are coming, too."

"To book club?" I raise an eyebrow. "Do you know what we read last month? The details that we'll be discussing?"

"We're going to play poker."

I think about last month's book club, and how we discussed the plotlines and characters before giggling over the idea of having twenty orgasms in an hour. We indulged in cookies, and it was the first time in a year I found myself wanting to open the lines of friendship, allowing more people into my small circle because the night was so fun. The interaction will be completely different with the guys there. A wave of resentfulness hits me, dark and ruthless, that a stranger has and continues impeding my life.

I grab a dozen different appetizers, each one sounding better than the last because I'm starving and bitter.

"You want me to help you guys carry this up?" Hudson asks twenty minutes later as we pull into the dorm parking lot. He checks his phone again, his nerves contagious.

"No. We've got it," I tell him. "I've been working out." I flex, though my sweatshirt is too baggy to show the outline of muscles that are slight but visible.

Hudson grins. "I'll be back in ten."

Grey and I wrangle the bags into the elevator and upstairs to his dorm. "We're going to have to rearrange the freezer to fit this stuff," he says.

"I could eat it all right now," I say, opening his freezer. I pull up my sleeves and am about to reach for a bag of mixed berries when Grey's thumb slides over my exposed wrist, tracing that damn scar that's caught too much attention. His fingers gently fold around my arm. "This is the scar my mom saw." His touch has chills dancing across my skin, followed by a rush of warmth. "Why have I never seen it?"

"My watch covers most of it."

His jaw is shaven, but the shadow of stubble along his chin and jaw emphasizes his masculinity as the clean and fresh scent of cedar and sandalwood hit me with each of our breaths. "You got them when you were seven?" His blue eyes hold mine, filled with a plea and note of desperation that puts me on edge. "How? What kind of accident?" His tone is gentle but firm as he takes my other hand, holding my wrists up to reveal the series of scars that I refuse to look at. I don't fight him. I don't want to. I'm beginning to like showing Grey my ugly sides a little too much.

But this isn't one of them. "There are some stories you can't unhear," I remind him.

"Did someone do this to you?" His voice is haunted.

I shake my head.

Relief doesn't slip into his gaze. Instead, his brow furrows further. "What makes scars like this?"

I smirk. "A pet mountain lion would make a good story."

Rejection has his gaze shifting over my shoulder.

"Trust me, Grey. It will change things. It will change everything." A tear rolls down my cheek.

"Maybe I want everything to change."

I'm torn between definitions of what he's saying—could be saying—when a heavy knock on the door echoes through the room.

Chapter 36

Mila

I want to ask him to ignore the door and focus on our conversation so my past doesn't cause a rift between us.

Another knock and Grey strides to the door, pulling it open.

Palmer and Corey are on the other side. "Did we..." Palmer asks, gaze skirting from my face to Grey.

"We can come back." Corey takes a step back.

"Yeah." Palmer nods.

Grey doesn't object, letting them go before he closes and locks the door.

I move around the tiny island, hating the defeat visible with Grey's rounded shoulders. Another tear slips down my cheek. I brush it away, but it's replaced by more, determined to carve paths down my cheeks as I feel that pull for everything to just come apart. "Ask me something else. Ask me anything, and I'll tell you, just not ... this."

"It won't change the way I see you."

"It will." Tears flow thicker.

Grey shakes his head. "I've spent the past two and a half

years trying to change the way I see you. You could tell me you were from another planet, and it wouldn't change what I feel for you."

Warmth spreads through my chest as my mind wars with his words. "That I'm stubborn and headstrong with a healthy dose of opinionated?"

"Among other things," he says, holding my gaze. His hypnotizing stare draws me closer without a word. "Tell me you think about me. Tell me you can't stop thinking about the other morning. About me being inside of you."

A blush that has nothing to do with embarrassment and entirely to do with desire flushes my cheeks. "Constantly."

His head angles back a fraction, his relief palpable. "Mila," my name is a prayer on his lips. "It's you."

"What?"

"My type is you." His lips come down on mine, the wall at my back. The kiss is urgent, hopes and fears merging into a symphony of bliss as his tongue parts my lips and plies my mouth.

He grips my waist, fingers slipping under my shirt, finding purchase on my skin, and just that simple touch is enough to undo me. It is every time.

I slide his hand to the apex of my thighs, and he groans.

"Grey," I'm pretty sure I'm begging.

He kisses my jaw as he slides his hand into my underwear and leggings, his breath a hiss as he discovers me wet and hot as his fingers part me. He presses his fingers to my clit, and I gasp. My vision goes dark for a split second before I close my eyes and lean my face into his neck, losing myself in his scent, warmth, and strength as his fingers work over me.

His hand slips out of my pants, and panic has my eyes flashing open, waiting for Grey to tell me this is wrong, and we can't. That he doesn't want me, can't because he has goals, and a dozen other reasons I've heard him recite for why he doesn't date.

Grey's eyes are pools of desire as he stares at me. "You're mine. You have been since the first day I saw you, painting that damn black wall in Hudson's dorm." His hands run the expanse of my waist, fingers digging into my clothes as though he's considering shredding them, and I'm pretty sure he could. "You're mine. Your secrets, your pain, your fears—they're all mine."

Tears dance in my eyes, unwanted, especially now. "You don't date."

He shakes his head. "I don't."

My heart throbs with the confirmation, hating how off-balance I feel.

"Dating can imply temporary or casual. What I feel for you is neither of those things." Grey leans forward, capturing a tear with a kiss.

Thirteen years of therapy spent learning how to identify and label my feelings and emotions hasn't prepared me for this moment.

He leans into me, caging me against the wall, his hips sinking into me as his mouth challenges mine. With each hungry lash of his tongue and nip of his teeth, I hear his intention, feel him claim me—mine. Mine. Mine. His hands also mark me, slipping around to my back, stroking, tracing, and clenching in matching tandems.

We kiss like it's a sport, like we were made to kiss each other.

Grey leans back, staring at me with lustful eyes, but the adoration in his gaze burns even brighter. He looks at me like I'm something to marvel at, something priceless and rare, eliciting more of my tears. "I'm really bad at this stuff. I have commitment and trust issues that nearly rival my abandonment issues."

"You're not bad at this, Mila. You're just scared."

"Terrified," I admit.

"Do you trust me?"

With every fiber of my being. "Yes."

The edges of his lips curl with a smile. "I've waited two and a half years, and I'll wait longer. We'll do this at whatever pace you want. If you want to call me your boyfriend or your friend —it doesn't matter. As long as you're with me, the rest is inconsequential."

I lean into him, kissing him as another tear slips from my eye.

Grey presses a kiss to my mouth and then lowers his face as he lifts my shirt, revealing my sports bra. He kisses between my breasts, along the fabric, and down my stomach as he lowers to his knees.

"I haven't showered." My objection is weak in my own ears, but I was a sweaty mess when leaving the gym, and a part of my brain warns I'll regret this once the fog of lust clears.

Grey looks up at me as he pulls my laces free and removes my shoes. "Good. You're about to get a whole hell of a lot dirtier." He hooks his hands into my pants and underwear and drags them down my legs, so they pool at my ankles, where he threads them off, and tosses them carelessly behind him.

Cool air hits my most sensitive area, but the goose bumps covering me are attributed to the way his eyes turn into liquid pools of fire as he licks his lips and lowers his gaze to my center. He leans forward, pressing his nose against me, and takes a long, deep breath that should make me feel embarrassed but, instead, only makes the desire become an ache.

Grey grabs my leg and hooks it over his shoulder before repeating with the other side, ignoring my objections as I become entirely reliant on the wall at my back and his shoulders. Every comment ever made about the size of my body flashes to the forefront of my thoughts on a wave of panic.

Grey fits his palms against each globe of my ass, lifting me, so I'm level with his mouth, and then his long fingers spread my folds, and his mouth seals over me, obliterating every memory and thought.

His mouth is possessive, the long hard strokes a tease that awakens every nerve in my body, coiling and desperate for a release he seems intent on prolonging. His soft groans, my breathy pleas, and his tongue sliding against my wet flesh become my favorite soundtrack.

"Grey," my voice is a warning and a plea.

He moves to my clit, grazing his teeth over the nerve endings and making me choke out a sigh before he lavishes the same spot with his tongue. I feel my orgasm building at the base of my spine at the exact moment he pulls back.

My skin is on fire. I'm burning from the inside out. My bones are jelly. I curse.

Grey slips my legs down so my feet touch the floor and staples his hands to my waist, knowing I need the support.

"I want you to come on my cock," he rasps against my ear, kissing my jaw.

I nod, wanting that, too, so goddamn much, I can't think of anything but how empty I feel. I move toward the couch, but Grey's hand on my wrist stops me. He reels me in, and then I'm in his arms, being carried to his bedroom.

I'd be fine with the floor at this point or the couch or the counter, but Grey deposits me on his bed, the woodsy scent of his cologne warming me as he makes quick work of stripping out of his clothes. He wants me just as badly as I want him.

"That shirt needs to come off," he says, running a palm over his length.

Heat swallows me as I watch him, studying the way his fingers clench and move over himself.

"Mila," his voice is a growl, a warning that has my eyes snapping to his face, working to recall what he'd said. "Your top."

I grab the hem of my shirt and tug it off with the same sense of abandon he had with my pants, as though I don't want to see them again, ridding everything that keeps me from feeling him against every part of me.

Grey leans forward, gripping the band of my sports bra. He pulls the garment over my head as his mouth closes over my left nipple. My sigh is a guttural sound as my back arches into the heat and friction of his tongue. I drag my fingers through his short hair, never wanting him to stop and at the same time, desperate to feel him everywhere.

He pinches my opposite nipple at the same time he slides a wide finger inside of me. It's euphoria.

Pleasure radiates through me with so much intensity my lungs tremble.

"God, I love the sounds you make." Grey's voice is silk against my skin. I didn't even realize I'd made a noise. Grey adds a second finger, and my moan is so loud I take note. The neighbors probably take note.

His fingers thrust inside of me again as he reaches for his nightstand, grabbing the box of condoms.

I take the box, and he rolls my nipple as his fingers curl inside of me, adding his thumb to my clit. Stars. I see stars as the box dents under my fingers as I squeeze it.

"You're so goddamn beautiful. So perfect." His breath is a cool breath against my flaming skin.

I drop my head back, grinding down on his fingers, forgetting my task until I feel his erection, thick, hot, and hard against my thigh. I rip at the box with my teeth, and Grey strokes at my clit, a reward or a bet to see if I can remain focused. It doesn't matter because I want to feel him inside of me, or I'm going to fall apart.

Condoms spill across the bed. His only reaction is a crooked grin. I drop the box and kiss him as I grab a condom from beside my knee. Then Grey finds that spot—the one that makes thoughts and breathing and existing seem impossible, much less doing them all at the same time.

"Don't stop," I beg, pressing my eyes shut.

"Never." Grey kisses my chest, my neck, and my shoulder as I come apart, moaning and gasping as he pulls every bit of pleasure out of me, spreading my wetness over my folds and across my thighs.

I'm hollow. I'm liquid. My muscles are buzzing from the intensity of my release.

Grey kisses his way down my jaw and then my mouth, where the taste of me lingers on his tongue.

I feel like I could nap for the next month, but Grey's release is at the front of my thoughts. I kiss him as I stand on shaking legs and sink to my knees.

Grey's breath is a hiss as I lick the length of his shaft. I do it a second time and his hips tilt forward as his head falls back, his breaths becoming labored. It makes me feel so damn empowered. I smile as I take him into my mouth. He releases a deep moan, and weaves his hands into my hair, likely making a wreck of my ponytail. Even with him hitting the back of my throat, I can fit a hand around the base of his shaft.

I study him, memorizing each reaction and breath as I suck him deeper, run my tongue over his length, and discover how his control weakens when I run my tongue over the head. This time as I slide my mouth over him, I twist my hand, wet against his shaft from my mouth, and Grey growls. The sound feels like a prize.

I'm about to test it again when Grey's hands slip under my arms. He hauls me up and onto the bed. "I want to finish inside of you. I need to feel you." He brushes his fingers over me, ensuring I'm ready as he rips open a condom. He rolls it over his erection and climbs on the bed, pulling my leg across my front.

Anticipation has me holding my breath and arching my back. He slides inside slowly, the ache so sweet and good my breath leaves me with a groan. His hand around my thigh tightens as he growls, thrusting fully into me. I moan.

He's so deep, and I'm so full, bliss surges through me. Each of his thrusts transforms my breaths, turning them into pleas and pants as I clench around him.

"Fuck, Mila," the words drag out of him, filled with need and ecstasy, as he pins me with his gaze. His stare is more intimate than our actions. Instinct encourages me to drop my gaze and focus on the pleasure, but I don't. I let him witness how he makes me come undone—how desperately I want him—allowing the intimacy to spike my blood and make each thrust carry me to the edge of breaking.

Grey reaches between my legs, pressing his fingers against my swollen clit, and with a final thrust, I cry out my release as wave after wave of pleasure rolls through me. Grey erupts a moment later, his forehead against mine as he slowly shifts his hips, reeling through his orgasm.

Chapter 37

Grey

Euphoria consumes me. Everything seems within reach and plausible as Mila wraps her arms around my shoulders, her breaths fast and hard.

I kiss her temple and roll to my back, taking her with me so she lies across my chest.

She makes an amused sound and tucks her face against my neck as I smooth her hair. "What are we going to tell Hudson?" she asks.

I run my hand over her hair again. "Depends on what you want him to know."

Her fingers trace a pattern across my chest. "If we're not dating, what are we?"

My relief at her question is so great it feels as though my entire body sighs. I lean forward to kiss her forehead. "We can call it dating, but the way I'll look at it is that we're together. A team."

"A team can consist of a lot of people..."

My arm around her waist constricts. "Exclusively a duo."

She shifts and pushes up on her arms, her breasts pressed

against my chest. It takes everything in me not to glance down and marvel at her nakedness against me. Her silver eyes hold a note of hesitance before she swallows. "I just want to be sure you don't feel obligated. That sex hormones and this ridiculous Julian Holloway mess isn't making you feel like you have to—"

"Don't finish that thought," I tell her, shaking my head. "I meant every word, Mila. You've been mine for the past two and a half years, and fuck knows I've been yours."

Questions or maybe doubts flare in her eyes.

I spread my hand around the back of her head and kiss her, knowing I won't be able to convince her now, maybe not even in a week or a month, but eventually, she'll know how damn hard it's been to remain away from her and not push her when I knew she wasn't ready.

"What about football and being too busy?" she asks.

"You make me want it even more. You will never be a distraction but a reason. My reason."

Understanding shines in her eyes. "I wasn't lying to you, either. I have abandonment and trust issues. They can make me feel jealous and insecure, and…"

"I want you," I tell her. "I want you just the way you are."

"How does this change things?"

"For starters," I say. "No more falling asleep on the opposite side of the bed, as far away as possible."

She laughs, laying her cheek against my chest. "As if that matters. I wake up plastered to your side every morning."

I grip her thigh, and pull her leg up, draping it over my waist. "And your pajamas are staying in that damn suitcase."

Mila chuckles. "We're going to have to figure out the rest of the details later because book club starts in ten minutes, and I need a shower." She presses a chaste kiss to my chest and slowly slides off my body, getting to her feet.

Her cheeks flush for half a beat, and she moves to her bag,

digging through her things to get what she needs before she peers back at me. "You can join me if you want. We don't have time for ... but if you need to shower..."

I'm out of bed in a second, following her into the bathroom.

Mila steps into the warm shower. I dispose of the condom and follow her. The water scalds my feet, but it doesn't faze her as she tips her head back, wetting her hair. Her back arches, her breasts on display, rose nipples soft peaks. My cock twitches, and my blood thrums, hot and needy.

As she straightens, her gaze drops to my erection, and she catches her bottom lip between her teeth. Her eyes are dilated and bright with desire. "Grab a condom."

"I thought we don't have time for..."

She slips a hand down her front, dipping it between her legs.

"Don't you dare stop," I tell her. Wet footprints mark my path to the bedroom, where I grab a condom from the floor. I have it on before reaching the shower.

Mila's standing under the spray, back arched and lips parted as she looks at me while she thrusts her finger inside of her.

I move closer, and as her finger sinks inside of her, I rub my thumb over her clit.

She gasps and the sound is quickly chased by a moan. While she has a finger buried inside of herself, I slide one of mine in as well.

We work in unison for several minutes, the scene so perfect and erotic I know it will consume my thoughts for weeks. She slips her hand free and turns around, placing her hands on the wall.

I cover her left hand with mine, and her back arches, ready for me. In one hard thrust, I'm inside of her.

Her cry of ecstasy vibrates in my chest, and I grip her waist.

My thrusts are hard and deep, my pace matching her breaths. I want to draw this out, enjoy having her hot, wet, and needy, but the reminder of our friends waiting for us has me dipping my hand between her legs as my pace increases. The slap of our skin, the tightness of her, and Mila's gentle cries as she orgasms have me quickly following her release.

I kiss along her bare shoulder as I slip out of her heat, knowing I'll never get my fill of her but looking forward to trying.

Two hours later, I'm holding a hand of cards I should have folded, my attention straying to Mila for probably the hundredth time since we arrived at Hudson's dorm.

"Any news on the psycho?" Corey asks.

Hudson and I exchange a look, and both shake our heads.

"What are we going to do? How long do you think the university will be cool with us having them stay here? Someone's going to say something. And in a couple of weeks, it will be March, which means longer practices and gym time..."

"We do this as long as we have to," I say. "We'll figure shit out and make it work. If Hudson and I have to move off campus because they won't allow them to stay, then we'll do that."

"Mila stayed with me for over a month, and no one said a damn thing," Hudson says. "If someone has a problem with the situation, they can talk to me."

Over on the sectional, the girls burst into laughter, and I glance up to see Hadley nodding and Evelyn leaning into Mila, who rests her head on Evelyn's.

"Yeah," Palmer says. "Or me. Because we're not going to let a goddamn thing happen."

Corey nods. "Agreed. This is coming out wrong. I'll walk Mila to class every goddamn day if that keeps her safe. I'm just asking what our next steps are. How do we ensure that next year when we have away games, nothing will happen? Is there someone we can talk to? Something more we can do?"

"Not yet," Hudson says. It's a waiting game at this point, and it leaves us uneasy because we're the offensive line, used to forcing our will and advantage.

I nod and fold my cards, making the excuse I need to get something to drink because the conversation leaves me feeling restless and useless.

Nolan follows me into the small kitchen, grabbing one of the tarts Hadley made. He leans against the counter beside me as I fill a glass with water. "Are you going to tell her?"

"Tell who what?" I ask.

"Mila."

My gaze jumps to his.

"You've had feelings for Mila as long as I've known you. You should tell her. Something good should come out of all this shit."

I give him a blank stare.

He smirks. "You think I missed how you looked at me like you wanted to feed me my own scrotum last year when I flirted with Mila." He takes a bite of the tart and raises a brow. "You should tell her."

I nearly admit I did, but Hudson joins us. His expression relaxed. "They're talking about working out with Mila," he says, tipping his head to the girls.

I scoff as I shake my head. "Mila's idea?"

Hudson grins. "Of course."

"Katie already excels at bringing guys to their knees. Just ask her to teach them." Nolan gestures to his sister.

Hudson and I chuckle, but the idea is already percolating in my thoughts, wondering what Mackey's reaction would be to find a gym full of women wanting to learn self-defense. Abe would lose his shit.

"Mila and I are still doing cardio every morning. Anyone's welcome to join." A part of me regrets the invitation as soon as it leaves my mouth. I like having that time alone with Mila. The secrets she entrusts me with. The private smiles.

"Hannah and Hadley don't get out of bed before ten unless there's a fire," Nolan says.

"Let me know," I say.

We stay at Hudson's for another hour before Mila turns to me with bleary eyes.

"You look tired."

"You're not supposed to tell women that," she reminds me, pointing at me.

Evelyn grins. "You do look like you're ready to fall asleep."

"I am," Mila admits, laying her head on the arm of the couch.

"I bet we know someone who could carry you to bed," Hannah chimes, looking at me.

"Indeed," Hadley sings.

Nolan's elbow finds my side.

Mila's gaze swims with amusement as she slowly unfolds from the couch and stands.

"This was fun," she says, gathering a handful of cups. "I'm glad we did this."

"Me, too," Hadley says, helping Mila gather and carry the last cups into the kitchen. "Who wants to pick the next book? Or do we just make Mila the designated librarian?"

"In Mila we trust," Hannah says.

Evelyn beams like a proud sister.

"Rather than wait another month to get together, I think we should do a Galentine's next week. We can do it at our place or a restaurant?" Hadley says.

"What in the hell's Galentine's?" Nolan asks.

"A celebration of friendship," Hadley says. "And Valentine's Eve, so you have plenty of time to prepare for Valentine's."

Palmer prods him.

"I'm in," Mila says.

Evelyn nods. "Let's do it."

When we return to my room, Mila barely has time to kick off her flip-flops before I tag her around the waist, pulling her back against my chest. "They already know. We should talk to Hudson tomorrow."

"Are you nervous?"

I shake my head. "No. Are you?"

"A little. You're Hudson's best friend on the team."

It was a contributing reason for avoiding her my freshman year. I bury my nose in her hair, pressing my lips to her temple. This simple gesture, the ability to hold and touch her as easily as breathing, is how I know we were inevitable.

I also knew it when I couldn't bring another woman into my bed, and I had to avoid Mila whenever she brought a guy around.

I kiss her temple. "Let's get ready for bed."

"Are we really going to the gym tomorrow?" she asks, spreading toothpaste on her toothbrush. "I thought we were taking a break?"

I nod. "We are. It will be a light day."

"That's not a break."

"We should work on holds again."

Her eyes find mine in the mirror, and I see hesitation shine in her reflection. She doesn't like the holds, but since most attacks begin with one of three holds, it's one of the most crucial lessons for her to learn right now.

I set a reassuring hand on her back as we brush our teeth.

As we climb into bed, Mila's phone chirps.

"Everything okay?" I ask.

"It's Alex. He's asking if I like this jacket." She twists her phone to show me the screen.

"Is there a story about you and coats? My mom loves handbags, but is your thing coats?"

Her lips tip into a smile, but I know it's fake. I know her too well.

"When they came and met me in Oklahoma, it was March. It had been a record cold month, and I didn't own a coat. They couldn't take me the same day, so they left their coats with me. It's one of those things they can't unsee." Her eyes are filled with a worldly glint, a reminder of my question earlier regarding the scars on her wrists.

"Do you keep in touch with anyone from Oklahoma?"

"I have an uncle who reaches out occasionally, but I've only met him once. He asked Alex and Jon for money, and they gave him some. I don't know how much, but he didn't reach out again for like a year, and it was to ask for more money."

I frown, hating him already.

Mila prods me with her elbow. "Dustin said you're one of the only people who can beat Cole. Did you ever do underground fights?"

I nod. "I did. I probably would have stuck with it, but it requires being in the gym even more than football. School or a job are next to impossible, and I wasn't willing to take the gamble. I wanted a contingency plan."

"Do you miss it?"

"I've always loved football more, but there are days I miss the ring. Fighting, especially MMA, requires a lot of physical and mental strength. Getting into your opponent's head and anticipating their movements and weaknesses can be intoxicating."

Mila moves her leg over to rest between mine. "I'm glad you chose football since it brought you to Camden."

My hand around her shoulder constricts, drawing her closer. "Me, too."

* * *

The frost is so thick when we wake up, we skip the track. Mila doesn't object. She sips her coffee from the passenger seat, quiet like she is most mornings.

Abe and Cole are already working out when we arrive.

Cole takes one look at my hand on Mila's shoulder and grins. "What do you want to start with today?"

Mila strips off her sweatshirt and heads to the back of the gym to grab a jump rope to warm up.

We work on breaking out of holds for the next two hours before heading to the café where Evelyn works. Hudson's in the back, working on homework, a cup of coffee and a sandwich in front of him.

"Hey," he says, moving a textbook over so we can join him. "How was the gym?"

"Good." Mila's voice is high, her nerves palpable.

Hudson looks from Mila to me, and then back at her.

Mila drums her fingertips against the table. "I have a confession to make."

Hudson leans back in his chair.

"I kissed Mila," I blurt.

Hudson's gaze shifts to me.

"I kissed him back," Mila adds. His eyes jog back to her. "I assumed something was happening when you didn't knee him in the balls after he kissed you at the booster event."

I assumed no one had seen me kiss Mila because no heckle or comment had been made about it.

"You should tell Evelyn. She's been dying to talk to you about it." Hudson inclines his head to the counter where Evelyn's helping a customer.

Mila gives him a final glance before getting in line.

"Are you okay with this?" I ask.

Hudson picks up his coffee. "I wouldn't have let her stay with you if I didn't trust you." He takes a drink.

"No warning or threat?"

Hudson gives a crooked grin. "Mila's been letting you in little by little for a while. You mean something to her, and I'm not going to ruin that. Mila's experienced enough loss. She deserves people in her life who want to be there for her and care for her, so as long as that's your intention, we're cool."

I nod. "You have my word."

Chapter 38

Mila

G rey's face is ghost white. "What happened?" He freezes in the way he does. I've realized he does this when assessing a situation, a result of his MMA training.

My hands feel sticky, my skin too tight. I glance down to see I'm covered in blood. It marks my hands, arms, clothes—everything is red. It smells like stale cigarettes and the pennies my sister and I used to stack and play with, sorting for specific dates that one of our foster family parents was always looking for in the buckets of coins he'd accumulated over thirty years. Pain sears me, razor sharp. I didn't feel the pain until looking down, but seeing the blood sends a warning signal to my brain.

"I think I cut myself..." I look up, but Grey's gone.

Panic fills my chest. I'm too hot and too cold as my heart races.

I call for Grey as I struggle to recognize where I am. A hide abed is made into a bed, and a brown bear with a pretty blue ribbon sits atop it.

I walk across the dirty and worn carpet, to a broken window

above the bed. Blood paints several jagged edges and a bloody handprint is stamped to the corner. I raise my hand to it, noticing my palm dwarfs the bloody print.

"Grey?" I call out the window. My chest hurts and I can't breathe. It feels like I'm having a heart attack.

A purple shoe outside in the yard catches my attention. I step onto the bed, trying to get a better look. The bed wobbles under my weight, and I reach out to steady myself. My arms aren't cut anymore. They're healed, but blood still covers me.

"Mila?" Evelyn calls from somewhere inside the house, opposite of the window.

I turn away from the window, eyeing the closed door. Intuitively, I know it's locked. "Evelyn, I'm stuck! I'm locked in."

"Mila, help!" Evelyn's cry is frantic.

I want to stay and look for the purple shoe, but I jump off the bed and race across the room in three bounds. The gold doorknob jiggles but doesn't release. It's locked, just as I knew it would be.

"Evelyn!" I scream. "I'm coming!"

I slam my shoulder into the door as I've seen happen in a hundred movies, but it doesn't give. I repeat the move several times, and then turn, searching for something that will help me escape.

"Mila! Help!" Evelyn's voice moves from the house to outside. I scramble back to the window, climbing onto the back of the couch so I can get as high as possible. The panic in my chest insists I hurry as I grip the window and pull myself up, but the glass is old and cracked. It splinters under the pressure. The inside of my wrist catches on a sharp edge, slicing through my skin.

I scream as blood runs down my wrist, warm and ticklish as it forges a fresh path, over the patches dried blood.

I glance out the window and see the purple shoe on the foot of a woman lying on the ground. It's Evelyn.

"Evelyn!" I scream through tears and panic as I smash out the remaining pieces of glass that tear open my arms. "I'm coming!" I reach forward and lose my balance.

I'm falling—

I open my eyes, my heart beating the same painfully fast rhythm it was in my dream. The room is dark, and I still can't breathe. Disoriented, I sit up and yank my arms out from under the covers, the razor-sharp cuts still burning my skin.

"Mila?" Grey's voice is thick and groggy with sleep. "Are you okay?"

I nod as I get out of bed, my stomach roiling and skin damp with sweat.

The pungent scents of blood, cigarette smoke, and mustiness are in my nose as I cross to the bathroom. I close the door and flip on the lights. Under the bright fluorescent lights, I inspect my arms and hands again, shocked there's no blood, though I know it was a nightmare. Tears streak down my cheeks, as hot and ticklish as the blood had felt.

I clutch my wrist, the pain still so intense it feels real.

Grey knocks softly. "Mila?"

When I don't respond, he opens the door. I don't see his reaction because I can't force myself to look at him.

I wait for him to ask a dozen warranted questions, but instead, Grey closes the distance between us and pulls me into a secure embrace. I keep my arms folded in front of myself, one hand still pressed to my wrist as his warm skin engulfs me. Sandalwood, cedar, and a hint of orange chase the smells of cigarette smoke and must, but the scent of blood lingers just as real and intense as the pain on my skin and in my chest.

I tuck my face in the crook of his neck, trying to sort through what I saw, and what happened. But as soon as I think of the room, the broken glass, and Evelyn on the ground, I sob.

I cry for what feels like hours until my nose is congested, my head aches, and my lips and eyes are dry.

Grey rubs a hand over my back.

"It was a dream," I say, shaking my head. "It felt so real."

"Do you want to talk about it?"

I don't. Not even a little. But the idea of holding it all inside of me makes me feel the threat of breaking, that there won't be enough gravity to keep me together.

"I dreamed you and I were at the house my sister died in. But we were the ages we are now. I wasn't seven." I run a hand across my cheek, sticky from crying. "Evelyn was there, too, calling for me, but I couldn't see her. I couldn't find her. I didn't get to her fast enough." My voice cracks.

"Mila," Grey's voice is barely above a whisper.

Tears fill my eyes again. "I didn't save her."

His grip tightens, pressing me against him with a fierceness like he doubts gravity will be enough, as well.

Grey

Mila cries until she throws up, and then she clutches her head while I retrieve ibuprofen and a tall glass of water.

She takes them and downs the water, glancing at her wrist where she's stained her skin red from gripping her arm so tightly.

I want her to talk to me, tell me about the dream, but the way her eyes close and her fingers dig into her temple assure me now isn't the time.

"Come on. Let's lie down."

Mila shuffles to the bedroom, her entire body dragging before she collapses into bed. She doesn't bother with the blankets, curling into a ball on her side. I tuck her in and climb in beside her. It's just past four thirty, still dark out.

Mila cuddles close to me, head on my shoulder. Her breaths are ragged and occasionally she wipes a stray tear away as I hold her close.

To my relief, she falls asleep faster than I expected.

I grab my phone and enter Mila's name and Oklahoma into an internet search. Nothing from the past pulls up, but Jon's social media is in the mix of results. Mila shares their last name. She must have changed it when she was adopted. I have no idea what it was before. Like much of her life before Oleander Springs, it's a mystery to me.

I turn off my alarm to go running and lie back, doing the only thing I can right now and hold her.

Mila stirs just after ten. Thankfully, it's Wednesday, and neither of us has an early class.

"How are you feeling?" I ask.

"Kind of numb."

She looks numb.

"Talk to me, Mila. I swear, nothing you tell me will make me change my mind about you—about us."

"You'll look at me like I'm broken."

The sun seeps in from the corner of the window shade, just enough to highlight her face as I roll so she can see the sincerity in my eyes. "Not a chance." My voice, too, is filled with sincerity. "I already know you're a badass."

She forces a smile, but it barely hits her lips and certainly doesn't touch her eyes as she stares into the distance as though her thoughts are in a different place, a different time.

"My sister's name was Mallory. She was bossy, and head-strong, and stubborn, and my idol. She was my constant. In a world where nothing remained static, Mal did. We had plans, huge plans. Mal was an artist, and we were going to move to

Paris. She was going to paint, and I'd sell her art, and we were going to live with ten cats near the Eifel Tower and eat french fries and french toast in France." A tear rolls down her face. "Every night we were together, we'd sleep in the same bed, even if it was on a towel on a bathroom floor. We didn't care. Maybe because we didn't know to care or because kids know how integral hope is for survival."

She pauses, biting that spot on her bottom lip.

"The last time my mom had custody of Mal and me, she was trying to get sober and clean again, but my mom could never say no. She'd go a week or a month—longer—and the first offer for a drink or a line of coke, and she'd accept. In her mind, anytime she went a day without drinking or getting high was her overcoming addiction. She thought she could choose to stop, but she never could. A sip would turn into a glass, and that glass turned into two, and then three, and then a bottle. It was the same with drugs.

"Sometimes I wonder if she battled with depression and anxiety, like me, and that was her way of self-medicating or maybe she just..." Mila shakes her head as her eyes shine with more tears. "I don't know. I just know she couldn't stop, not for Mal, or me, or even herself."

I thread my fingers through her hair, coaxing the strands out of her face, wishing I could siphon off some of her anguish.

"We were staying in this really old rundown house. It smelled, the carpets were filthy, and it was always freezing. Mal and I stayed in a room together upstairs, and there was a lock on the outside of the door. They said it was to enforce bedtime. But they would forget about us, sometimes all day."

Anger races agony as her words run through my mind, imagining Mila cold and hungry.

Her face reddens as tears spill over her lower lashes. "Sometimes it's really hard to remember her. Like every day, every new memory threatens to replace ones of her. But that day...," she shudders, "we were so hungry."

She shakes her head, anger visible in her eyes for a second. "Mal thought she could sneak out the window, and back into the house and let me out. So we pushed the hide abed over so she could climb on the back to reach the window. The windows, like the house, were old, and it was sticking from being painted, and the handle was broken. Mal was pressing on the window, trying to grip it, and it broke. All at once, she lost her balance and fell out headfirst."

She sobs, the sound of her heart fracturing. Mine fractures for her.

"I couldn't reach. I was too small. I could only see over the edge of the window."

I know without her explaining that's how she got her scars —why telling me about them was too hard.

"A neighbor heard me screaming eventually, but it had been hours. My mom was arrested that night, and I never saw her again."

I pull her close to me, tucking her into every part of my body, understanding with absolute certainty she's a hundred times stronger than she realizes to survive that and continue trusting, and smiling, and loving as she does.

Chapter 39

Mila

"I'm proud of you, Mila. And I hope you're proud of yourself. How did you feel sharing Mal's death with Grey? Talking about her again?"

My eyes are itchy and red. It's Friday morning. Briggs and I now change the time we meet every week. It's a pain in the ass for both of us, but he does it without complaint.

"Relieved but also a little embarrassed. I puked."

"Is that why you feel embarrassed?"

"It made me remember how weak I'd felt. How useless I'd felt."

"Mila, you were barely seven. You weren't weak. You were a child. What if that was Grey's story? What if he lost a sister? Would you look at him differently? Would you think he was weak?"

I don't respond.

Briggs nods as though he knows my answer, sees it in my eyes or pursed lips. It wouldn't. "Giving him all the pieces of the puzzle will allow him to understand your boundaries and triggers."

"I just wish I could be normal."

His gaze lacks sympathy, instead determination fixes on me. "No one's normal. Everyone is fighting their own battles. You're a warrior, Mila. Never forget that. Now that you've shared this trauma, it's a good idea to spend time taking care of your inner child. Remind her that she's safe and loved, and assure her she didn't do a damn thing wrong." His eyes fill with tears.

My emotions mirror his, blurring my vision, though my jaw flexes obstinately. I hate exercises that require working on my inner child.

"You were seven, Mila," he reminds me again, more adamantly.

I sniff, wiping at tears with my fingers.

My dream has haunted me since Wednesday. It's been difficult to fall asleep because I fear I'll have the same nightmare. Even awake, I think of my bloody handprint on the glass, the smell of that house, Mal's purple shoes, and the stained walls.

"My dream felt so real, Briggs. I could remember the way the house smelled and how the carpet was always rough and dirty against my feet. I could picture it like I was there. Details I had forgotten about."

"Several people had asked about your scars. It probably wrestled the memory loose."

I nod and try to ignore the restless feeling that consumes me each time I think about the dream. I can't understand why I couldn't see Mal. Why she wasn't in the memory, considering I'd stared and screamed at her until my voice went hoarse.

"I didn't come today just to tell you about Mal and this mini breakthrough that happened because of you."

Briggs wipes a tear from his cheek. "This was all you, Mila. All I can do is teach you. You took the steps. Don't forget it."

Watching him fight his emotions makes more tears form and my throat to tighten. Briggs isn't the first grown man to shed tears over my story, though I'd prefer he be the last.

"I have a friend date next week. It was supposed to be tonight, but Katie got sick so we're rescheduling."

His grin turns authentic as he dries the corner of his eyes. It makes me more uncomfortable than it should. Emotions always do.

I glance at the clock on the wall, realizing we're a couple of minutes past time.

"Are you doing something special for Valentine's tomorrow?" I ask, sliding my coat on.

"Mila," Briggs says, not moving. "I'm proud of you, and I care about you, and I think you're amazing."

Positive affirmations from others have always been difficult for me, which is why Briggs peppers them into our sessions.

Tears warm my eyes again. "Thanks, Briggs."

He nods.

My emotions have me feeling more exhausted than my past couple of days of gym workouts, where Mackey has seemed nearly vicious. I have a hunch he's waiting for me to admit I can't or won't. Little does he know my stubborn flag has a concrete base buried so deeply even I can't always find it.

I step outside and turn both ways, taking in the parking lot, the street beyond it, and the sidewalks.

Mackey has been drilling into me that I need to be aware of my surroundings. I always thought I was aware, just like I thought I'd be a guard dog—or an alley cat—if someone ever bothered me. But I've realized our conscious and subconscious minds aren't always on the same page or in the same chapter or even the same book.

The parking lot isn't as full as Tuesday evenings when I sometimes have to park at the opposite end of the building.

Nerves and adrenaline spike my blood as I cross to my car, my head on a swivel as Mackey instructs, paying attention to everything that moves.

I slip into my car and lock my doors before I'm situated. The leather seats are warm, easing my racing heart. Earlier this week, everything was frosted, but this morning, it's nearly seventy. Locals joke it's normal for snow to wash away the pollen at least once during the spring.

For a long time, I refused to see any faults in Oleander Springs, appreciating everything it offered and gave me. Recently, though, my thoughts have been drifting to what I want after graduating and where I want to live. It has my thoughts turning to Grey, wondering if he has a preference for where he plays.

I release a heavy sigh and grab my phone so I can send an update. It seems like I have a dozen group chats now, half of which are used to check in and update each other on our whereabouts. Already, we're using them less.

I open the one with Grey, Hudson, and Evelyn. All three are in class, but I text them anyway, per our agreement, letting them know I'm leaving and am stopping at the store for socks and granola bars. I go through socks twice as fast since I began working out.

I ease my car onto the main road, vigilant about noting every vehicle around me.

I drive to Target, where I park near the back. Parking at the rear of a parking lot is a habit that formed shortly after my parents gifted me my Audi, and I parked in the front row and got door dinged—twice.

The sun is warm on my skin. Evelyn will appreciate the warm weather when we go running later with Hudson, and I know her asthma will, too.

Inside of Target, I grab the couple of items I came for and

some additional things I'll need if I stay at Grey's much longer —extra shampoo, conditioner, face wash, as well as a waffle iron I plan to put to use tomorrow for Valentine's Day. As I head to the front to checkout, anxiety flares in my body, triggered by the waffle iron and items for Grey's.

I have no idea how long we'll continue staying at the dorm. Last year, I stayed with Hudson until summer began. My parents had wanted me to come to California, and I'd been considering it until Evelyn arrived. Seeing her every day helped shove the shadows fear casts over my thoughts and convinced me to stay. But it's February. I can't stay with Grey until May—or I shouldn't want to. The reality is his dorm feels comfortable, warm, cozy, and familiar. I miss my apartment, but I like the security the dorm lends, like that it smells like Grey, and that I wake up every morning tangled around him like a bedsheet.

I check out, return my cart, and head for the parking lot with the fierce determination to stop focusing on the future and be present. If I show up to the gym distracted and gloomy, Mackey and Cole will ensure I regret it.

I pop my trunk and am just about to set my bags inside when a flash of white lurches to a stop behind me. I turn as Julian jumps out of the driver's seat, leaving his truck running and door open.

My opossum wants me to freeze.

"What are you doing?" I ask, realizing my car is already between us, my bags on the ground.

"Get in the truck," he orders.

"What do you want?"

"My life back. Compensation for everything you took." He moves with me, circling the car.

"I'm not whoever you think I am."

"You're Mila Phillips. I know exactly who you are."

His claim is like a bomb detonating in my head, causing so much shrapnel I can't make sense of the mess. No one in North Carolina aside from my parents and a handful of people know my last name was Phillips before my adoption.

Julian gains several inches on me, causing me to sprint to a nearby car to put a cushion between us. My guard dog is awake, nudging my opossum with its nose, telling me to run, scream, and hide. But I'm trying to grasp how he knows me, why he blames me.

He sneers, and recognition nearly blinds me. "You dated my mother."

"And you sent me to prison."

Anger explodes in my chest, nearly eclipsing my panic. I've read how adrenaline gives people superhuman strength in emergencies, and if there were ever an emergency, it seems like vengeance for Mal, for Julian Holloway blaming me, making me fear every dark space and corner should warrant an emergency, but as I shove at the car in front of me with both hands, it doesn't flip over and crush him. It doesn't even sway.

Emotions grip me with arguments, vindication, and an entire warehouse of questions starting with how in the hell he could blame a seven-year-old for his negligence.

"I was going to be out in four years, but your parents petitioned the judge to keep me there for *eleven*. Eleven years of my life because they said you were traumatized. Do you know what trauma is, bitch? Trauma is losing your entire life overnight. Trauma is sleeping in a cell meant for cattle for *eleven fucking years*. Trauma is guards watching you take a shit every goddamn day and having to watch your ass every second, so someone doesn't rape or kill you. You know *nothing* about trauma." He slaps the top of the car from where he stands across from me, and I see the glint of zip ties in his hand.

Mackey told me most guys aren't used to getting back up

after they take a hit, but I fear Julian might get up even if I were to hit him with my car, much less a strike to the face.

I glance toward the store knowing I need to be near people. As many people as possible.

"Try it. Try and outrun me." Julian moves toward the rear of the car, anticipating my move.

My heart thunders. God, if there were ever a time I didn't want to make a bet, it would be now.

I grip my purse, and turn the opposite direction, and sprint across the parking lot entrance and down the sidewalk, not daring to look back to see if he follows me. I run like my life depends on it, certain it does. I push myself and every limit and weakness as my legs, throat, and side ache.

I turn into a parking lot, aware that I can't maintain this pace, and spot the red letters of Costco. Relief has me speeding forward. My shins and lungs burn, but I don't dare slow down or stop until I reach the door, where I finally look behind me. Julian's a few hundred feet away, hands on his knees, staring at me.

I quickly dig out my Costco card and slip inside. The familiarity and busy aisles do little to ease my duress. My heart is still careening in my chest as my thoughts cycle like a slot machine—my past, my future, his anger, the police, hide, run, Grey, the gym—everything is going too fast, preventing a complete thought.

I head down an aisle, peering over my shoulder every few feet. I go down two more aisles before stopping where something hasn't been restocked. I slide into the empty space, tuck my knees against my chest, and try to will myself not to fall apart as I call Jon. I need help and answers, and Jon has been giving me both for nearly fourteen years.

It goes to voicemail, and I consider hanging up but don't. "Dad, I have some questions I need you to answer. Waylon

Klein is here in Oleander Springs. He's Julian Holloway now. God. I had no idea. I didn't recognize him. He's furious. He feels like we owe him for the time he spent in prison. I don't... I don't know what to do." I try to stop the building sob, but it tears out of my throat. "I'm sorry. I'm not trying to scare or worry you guys. I'm fine. I just..." I want to tell him how Julian chased me, how I think he'd planned to kidnap and zip tie me and use me for ransom. "I love you. Call me."

I sit for a moment and consider the questions I was asked the last time I went to the police station. Did Julian hurt me? Touch me? Threaten me? Can I prove he wants to kidnap me, or is this another game of he said, she said where he could claim he was stopping to help with no malintent?

I scroll down to the numbers Grey made me add and dial the first one.

"Mila?" Cole answers after the second ring.

I'm silent. I wasn't expecting him to answer.

"Mila?"

"Can you come and get me?"

"Where are you?"

"Costco in Oleander Springs."

"What happened?"

My throat thickens. "Julian pulled up while I was putting grocery bags into my car, and I ran."

"Where's your car?"

"In the Target parking lot, a couple of miles away. I don't know if he's waiting for me."

Cole's voice is muffled as though he's covering the mouth-piece. "We're coming," he says, a second later. "Where are you now? Are you where people can see you?" In the background, a car engine revs.

"Sort of."

"Sort of?"

"I need a minute."

He doesn't push me.

After a few minutes, I tell him what happened and where I'm hiding.

It should take him thirty minutes to reach me, but Cole arrives in half that. "I don't have a membership card, but I'm right out front. Black SUV."

I extricate myself from my hiding spot, my body stiff and fatigued. I look at everyone like a threat as I make my way to the exit.

I spot the SUV immediately, half pulled onto the sidewalk. I remain frozen in the exit, searching for Julian and his truck when the passenger window of the SUV lowers, and Abe calls out to me.

I dart for the back door and throw myself inside, all semblance of calm gone.

"Are you okay?" Cole turns to face me from the driver's seat, raking his eyes over me, searching for physical wounds.

"I need a Valium and some fucking tacos." I release a deep breath.

I sense Abe's relief that I don't burst into tears.

"Let's go see if your car's okay," Cole says, inching back into traffic.

"You're going to my car?" Alarm slips into my voice.

"Hell yeah. I'll let him get in one cheap shot, then pummel his ass and wait for the cops to drag him in." It's such a macho male response.

"What if he has a gun? He spent eleven years in prison. I don't think we should underestimate him."

"I thought you didn't know him?" Abe lowers his visor and looks at me in the small mirror.

I want to flip him off. Instead, I look away.

"Mila, a little information would be good right about now. I need to know what we're walking into," Cole says.

"He served eleven years in prison," I repeat.

"For..."

"Manslaughter charges for killing my sister."

The car falls silent as Cole stops at the entrance of Target, his turn signal on, blocking traffic. He remains there for several minutes, ignoring the few who honk at us.

"If he's there, we'll keep driving," Cole says.

I'm nauseated as I direct them to my car, where the trunk is still open, and my purchases are spilled across the ground. I don't move. I don't want to get out of the backseat. The tinted windows and locked doors of the SUV offer a sense of security I'm desperate to cling to.

"There has to be something on me or my car," I tell them. "It's too coincidental that he's been able to find me this many times, and I never see him coming. I know that sounds paranoid, but..."

"It doesn't sound paranoid. Every asshole with twenty bucks can track someone these days by buying an Find-it Tag. You're supposed to use them to track your own shit, but people can use them on anything. We suspected the same thing when you called."

"Do you see anything?" Abe asks, turning to Cole.

Cole shakes his head and turns around to look at me. "Sit tight. We're just going to see if we can find a tag."

I nod.

The two slide out of the car and look every direction before Cole picks up my things and sets them in the trunk. He closes it as Abe circles my car, scanning his phone across it. He stops at the back and calls Cole over.

Abe ducks out of view as Cole peers around. Abe stands a minute later with something pinched between his fingers.

Abe glances toward the SUV as Cole says something. The brothers talk for a few minutes, though it feels like hours. My unease is growing by the second. I find four items to focus on, three sounds, and two scents, but it does nothing to nullify my nerves.

Cole comes to the back door and opens it. "We have to make a little pit stop by the police station."

We ride in silence to the police station—the same one I went to the last time Julian approached me.

Inside, Cole greets the receptionist and explains our emergency and we are immediately paired with an officer. I'm grateful it's not the same one as the last time I was here.

"Tell me what's going on," the officer says, looking across the three of us.

I take a shallow breath and launch into the story.

I wonder what Briggs will say next week when I tell him I had to share the hardest parts of my past with Abe and Cole as my audience.

I self-numb, a tactic I mastered years before, but it rarely works when discussing Mal. Today, shock, fear, or stupefaction allow it to work. Mostly. I still shed some tears. Abe passes me a tissue box, and I consider throwing it at him. I don't want him to accept me or be kind to me because he pities me.

The police officer finds Julian's file easily, and explains they knew his past charges from when he went by his birthname, Waylon, it was my last name being legally changed that prevented the dots from being connected last year or even a few weeks ago when I'd come to report him following me.

The officer looks embarrassed and almost ashamed when he tells us that stalking, even with proof, is a misdemeanor charge, and without having anything more concrete, the best we could likely hope for was a restraining order.

"Is this a joke?" Cole asks, pointing at the Find-it Tag. "He was carrying zip ties, and this is the second time he's pulled up on her. Someone's going to get hurt!"

"Careful," the officer says, pushing his chair back as he looks around the station.

I hold my breath and grab Abe's hand. I know he's going to hit something, just not what. I don't think he does, either. "Let's go," I say.

"We'll do everything we can," the officer says. "I'll reach out to his parole officer and see if we can up the charges, but a lot of times, we can't even track who registers these tags because people use VPNs, and we can't track it back to a person's IP address."

"He's found her twice, officer," Cole says tiredly.

The officer nods. "I'd suggest searching the rest of your things."

As we leave, Abe offers to drive my car back. I'm relieved. I can't navigate my own brain right now, much less four thousand pounds of steel.

Cole drives the speed limit with me in the car, winding down the same backroads Grey uses to take us to the gym.

When we arrive, the red brick building feels more familiar than it should as he parks in the front.

Mackey looks relieved when we step inside, but his expression fades in a second. "Get changed."

A part of me is relieved he doesn't want to discuss the details or allow the panic to sink in. I need the distraction of being here.

I head for his office and close the door to change. One of the most fascinating details about working out for me has been the transition in how I see my body. Over the past few weeks, I've been amazed at how much I'm able to endure, and how hard I can push myself. How there are times I mentally want to give up and my body refuses and vice versa. It's created a sense of pride and gratefulness—emotions I've never felt toward my own body.

When I finish changing, I head toward the jump ropes, but Mackey stops me. "In the ring."

I pause.

"This is when fighters fuck up," Mackey tells me, pointing at the ring for emphasis.

I stare at him and wonder if it's written all over my face how I froze, how I'd forgotten every single piece of advice down to my stance and lost all confidence in myself for fighting. I would have been the girl in the movie everyone screams at.

I kick off my shoes and climb into the ring.

"Abe, get in there," Mackey instructs.

My thoughts skid to a stop. Abe never shadowboxes or trains with me. The only minor exception was those lone ten minutes where he watched my back when those guys were creeping on me. It's one of Grey's two rules.

Abe looks equally confused as he pulls off his shirt and shoes and slips between the ropes.

"Are you—" I start.

"You can work, or you can leave," Mackey says.

I get into position.

"He grabs your arm. What do you do?" Mackey nods at Abe.

Abe hesitates but grips my wrist.

I break out, and Mackey barks the next order. Abe grabs me again and again and again, but rather than find the rhythm I normally do, each hold feels more difficult, my muscles more fatigued and my mind weaker.

"He's trying to see how far he can push you," Abe's voice is barely above a whisper as his arm bars across my chest, gentler than Cole—a fact that surprises me. "Don't break now—not for Mackey, and certainly not for that asshole."

Chapter 40

Grey

Cole, Abe, Dustin, Hudson, Palmer, Corey, Mila, and Evelyn fill my mother's house. Nolan only stayed in Oleander Springs because Hadley and Hannah were in class.

The guys from the team and I arrived here an hour ago after receiving a series of texts from Cole warning me things had gone awry. *A*-fucking-*gain*.

Mom sets a mug of hot chocolate in front of Mila and stares down Cole. She's pissed at him, Mackey, and Abe for making her work out, certain Mila's in shock after running three and a half miles from a lunatic, and the cops informing her there was little that could be done.

Again.

Mom's been at the stove, making hot chocolate while drying her eyes as Mila recounted her past.

I hated that Mila had to tell the story again, and watching her pain cut up our closest friends only made it harder. Evelyn cried, and Hudson had to wipe his face more than once.

"She needed to work out," Cole insists. "She needed to clear her head."

Mom glowers.

"I'm okay," Mila assures us all. "I just wish we had better answers for next steps."

Palmer sets his hands on the table. "It sounds like best case scenario is the cops issuing a restraining order."

"A fucking misdemeanor charge." Cole glances at my mom. "Sorry, Colleen."

Mom doesn't even blink.

"He can't track her anymore," Abe says.

"But depending on how long he's been tracking her, he already knows her routine and everywhere she goes," Corey points out.

"Including where the gym is," Mila adds.

Cole sits straighter in his chair. "Let him come to the gym."

Mila shakes her head. "I don't want you guys to get involved." She looks across the group. "Any of you."

Evelyn places a hand on Mila's shoulder. "I can't understand why our only options are sucky or suckier?"

"She could stay out here in Highgrove," Cole says. "It might be the safest place for her."

"She's not staying out here," Hudson says.

"Why?" Abe asks. "Our town isn't good enough for you?"

"Because she has classes and friends," Palmer shoots back without faltering.

"And a guy wants to kidnap her and hold her ransom." Cole stands.

Corey moves to stand beside Palmer.

Hudson tucks a wide-eyed Evelyn behind him.

"Enough," I say, moving between the two parties that naturally divided to opposite sides of the kitchen when they arrived.

"The amount of testosterone in here is going to all of your

heads," Mila says, abandoning her chair and blocking the open route between Abe and Palmer. "We're all on the same team."

"I don't know them," Abe says, shaking his head.

"But you know me," I tell him.

"This is going to involve all of you," Mom says, leaning against the fridge, arms crossed. "Mila is safest when she's around others. This will require you all to get along."

"And you guys would like each other if you were meeting under better circumstances," Mila says.

Abe laughs viciously.

Mila looks ready to try out the left hook she was working on when I arrived at the gym on Abe's face.

Thankfully, the alarm on the microwave goes off, alerting us the frozen lasagnas Mom brought home are ready.

"Dustin, Cole, you two get drinks. Hudson and Corey, grab some plates." Mom turns to me. "You and Abe get the card table and chairs."

Abe follows me to the back addition that Grandpa and I built on. Neither of us speaks until I pass him four of the eight chairs. The table isn't a traditional card table but a folding buffet table that we use to play poker and other card games during the warmer months when Mom hosts barbecues and birthday parties outside so the house isn't so cramped.

"Is this serious? I mean, she's hot. I get it, but—"

My fist is balled in Abe's shirt so fast he doesn't have time to drop the chairs and defend himself.

He arches his brow, and grins, proving he'll never shy away from a fight or show fear. "A simple yes would have sufficed."

I release my hold and shove him back several inches. I've never hit Abe, and I know if he remains too close right now, that streak will end. "I should have introduced you to these guys two fucking years ago," I admit. "They're good guys, guys we would've been friends with."

Abe shakes his head. "They've had their lives handed to them on silver platters. They have no idea what it's like."

"Hudson's had to be a parent for most of his life to his little brother who has autism. Their mother was a sorry drunk for most of their childhood and their dad traveled around the country playing football. And Corey's parents have never watched him play a single fucking game. They're strangers to each other. And Palmer lost his mom six years ago. Money can do a lot, but it doesn't make you invincible."

Abe loses a breath.

"If you give them a chance, they'll grow on you."

"So will mold," Abe says.

I glare at him.

Slowly, Abe sighs. "We'll consider things neutralized until shit gets settled."

I snicker and grab the other four chairs, leading him back to the dining room where we set it up, blocking entry to the living room.

Mom calls names and hands each of us a plate filled with lasagna, garlic bread, and salad before assigning us a seat like we're in fucking grade school, ensuring she mixes the two groups.

"I can't get past the fact this guy feels like you owe him." Dustin shakes his head as he covers his salad in ranch dressing.

Mila shakes her head. "I can't get past the fact I didn't know about the sentencing or my parents petitioning the court."

"It doesn't surprise me," Hudson says. "I would have done the same in their shoes and kept you out of it. What if they'd lost?"

"I wasn't looking for revenge," Mila says.

Cole pulls his head back like he's been slapped. "You didn't want revenge?"

Mila's eyes glitter with raw emotions. "My list would be too long. He was one of too many who failed Mal."

"What about the letters?" Evelyn asks. "Did Jon know what Julian or Waylon or whatever his name is was talking about?"

Mila nods. Jon had called moments after I arrived at the gym, and Mila set the call on speaker, allowing me to hear both sides from the cab of my truck. He was enraged, upset with Mila for not telling him about Julian sooner, livid at the police and how they handled it, and enraged that Julian Holloway was still traumatizing her all these years later. After telling Mila about the letters and their part in keeping him in prison, he assured her he would handle it. "Jon said he sent a few hundred to a PO box they set up for court correspondence. He said they sent them all back without opening them."

"So how in the hell did Julian find you?" Hudson asks.

Mila shakes her head. "I have no idea. I mean, he would have learned about my last name from the letter my parents sent, I suppose. I have no idea when he moved here or how he found me once he did. I also don't know where he's been for the past several months."

"I kind of liked it better when he was a crazy, delusional stalker," Evelyn says. "I hate that this is so personal. I hate that he's making you go through all of this."

"Yeah, me too," Palmer says.

Corey nods.

Mila pulls in a deep breath and holds it. "In case anyone is interested in the rest of my life story, I can eat an entire whipped cream pie in under ninety seconds, and have an unhealthy fear of zombies and tight spaces. I'm also terrible at chess, despite playing several hundred games, and I've tried to beat a few hundred world records."

Evelyn smiles. "I bet it's close to a thousand world records."

"And you haven't beat one?" Palmer asks.

"Technically, we beat one, but you have to do it a second time and have someone come out to witness it," Evelyn explains.

The conversation eases into jokes and stories. Occasionally, silence hangs a little too long, but everyone except for Abe works to fill them.

Regardless of Mila's strength and persistence, something else is bothering her. I can sense it in the way her gaze passes too quickly over mine, and she remains out of arm's reach as we collectively help clean up the kitchen. She's trying to create distance, and I have no idea what to do about it.

"I see why you like her so much," Mom says hours later as I hug her goodbye.

The rest of the guys are already in their cars, getting ready to part ways for the night. Corey offered to take Mila's car.

Mom folds her arms. "This will pass. I'll talk to my friend at work. Her husband's a cop. Maybe they can tell us something we don't know."

"Anything's better than the advice she got today."

Mom nods. "Drive safe, Grey. And watch your back."

"I always do."

She hugs me a final time. "Love you."

I make my way to my truck where Mila's waiting in the passenger seat.

"How are you?"

She turns to look at me, and slowly releases a sigh. "I'm okay."

"It's okay to tell me you're not."

"I'm going to be okay, but I'm feeling overwhelmed. I just need a little time to process."

I nod and put the truck in gear. The moment I move

forward, the team moves with us, like a formation on the field, keeping us in the middle as we drive back to campus.

When we make it up to my dorm, whatever is bothering Mila becomes more noticeable as she maintains a gap between us. "Do you mind if I shower?"

"You never have to ask."

She nods without looking at me and heads to my bedroom where she gathers her things that are still tucked away every day. I wait until the shower turns on, then head to the bedroom to plug in my cell phone and pack my duffel bag for tomorrow. Mila's still not out when I finish, so I move onto homework, though it's the last thing I want to do.

I finish nearly all my homework before Mila appears, wearing sweatpants and a long-sleeved shirt, her hair blown dry. She puts her things away and then stands at the end of the bed, hands clasped in front of her, drawing that restlessness feeling to the forefront of my thoughts.

"I think we should talk about our options." Her voice is soft and deceivingly diplomatic.

I close the heavy textbook for my finance reporting class and drop it to the floor, giving her my full attention. "What options exactly are you referring to?"

"What if Julian sees us? Sees *you*?"

I shake my head. "Who cares if he sees me."

"What if he tries to hurt you to hurt me?" She takes a step back that I protest by taking a larger step forward.

"Together," I tell her. "Remember? This means the good *and the bad*. We don't get to pick and choose. He wants you to feel isolated, but fuck that and fuck him."

"I want you to be safe."

I grin humorlessly, refusing to admit just how badly I've been hoping Julian approaches me, how I've already imagined him stepping onto campus, trespassing, and giving me the proverbial green light to defend myself. Each strike would be payback for every moment of peace he stole from Mila.

"Like you, I only go a few places. The gym, practice, class, and here."

"What about the track? Maybe we should stop going?"

"We could run at the facility."

Hope and approval greet my offer. "Really? Are you sure?"

"If it makes you feel safer, absolutely."

She nods.

"Then it's done."

Mila blinks. "Just like that?"

"Just like that." I reach forward, tracing my thumb along her bottom lip in an attempt to make her stop biting the spot that reveals she's nervous. She does, her warring emotions visible in her silver-blue eyes.

"We'll be careful. We'll continue changing our routine and reporting anything that happens. You're safe here."

"I never would have been able to outrun him today if you hadn't made me do so much cardio."

"You did such a good job, Mila." I shake my head. "I don't think I told you this yet, but I am so damn proud of you. Running away was the right move, and you are so fucking strong and fast he didn't stand a chance. And we're going to continue training and we're going to make him leave you alone."

She maintains my stare for a lone second. "But what next? Now that he knows I can outrun him, he won't try and chase me again."

"I think Jon's right." He called again while dinner was cooking, and said his lawyer would be drawing up charges, but they felt confident Julian would leave after his plans were so badly foiled. "If he's bitter about prison, he won't want to go back."

"That didn't stop him from trying to kidnap me today," she points out.

"He won't. We'll keep you safe."

"We should get some sleep. It's late."

I nod. "Get tucked in. I'm going to brush my teeth."

When I return, Mila's reading a book on her phone.

"How are you doing?" I ask, stretching out beside her.

"I'm okay."

"How are you really doing?"

She sets her book down and looks at me.

I would give my right hand to hear her thoughts right now. "What would Briggs say right now?"

"He'd probably ask how my inner child is feeling?"

"How is your inner child feeling?"

"I've replayed the day that Mal died so many times in my head—hundreds, thousands of times. I always think how it could have gone differently if we had waited, or the couch had been at a different angle, or I had been holding on to her, so many things could have changed the outcome. I've been blaming myself for so long, and it took this guy blaming me today to realize it wasn't my fault. He didn't push her out the window, but it was his fault and our mom's that she was so desperate she was willing to try and climb out that damn window."

She goes silent as her hand tangles in my shirt.

"And I hate that I've carried it with me this long almost as much as I hate that he was the one to ease this mountain of guilt I've been carrying for so damn long."

Chapter 41

Grey

Growing up, my mom always insisted on making every holiday special. Valentine's Day was no exception. She would splurge on doughnuts and decorate the house with paper hearts. A few years, she insisted on us making a nice dinner together and dressing up. She's always been big on manners, and I think going through the dating circuit and meeting some of the jerks who concealed that they were assholes, and the deadbeats who never even tried to disguise being assholes, had her working to ensure I didn't turn out like them.

This is my first Valentine's Day with a date, and it's not just anyone. It's Mila, the woman I've cared about for so damn long. She's become an integral part of my life even without her realization.

Yesterday, Jon insisted on flying home to Oleander Springs today, but Mila convinced him to wait with promised concessions she won't go anywhere alone, would keep her phone and mace on her at all times, and would scan her car daily to ensure no new Find-it Tags are added.

I slide out of bed, turn off the alarm, and silently close the bedroom door so Mila can sleep in. She tossed and turned last night, and more than once, I woke up and found her reading a book. When I offered to talk about things or assure her she was safe, she told me reading helped settle the myriad of feelings she didn't know how to process or wasn't ready to face.

My phone vibrates with a text as I grab a glass of water.

> Hudson: How is she? Are you guys taking the day off?

> Me: She had a pretty rough night. She's still asleep now. I'll let her decide if she wants to work out, but I'll suggest we take the day off.

> Hudson: I don't think any of us slept well. Jon's already texted me this morning, and it's 3 am there. I was going to give him your number. Is that cool?

> Me: Yeah. No problem. If we go to the gym, I'll let you know, but I think we're going to stay in. I'm going to change the plans I had for today.

> Hudson: Corey spoke to his dad, and he suggested they might be able to charge Julian with extortion. Apparently, the laws are pretty damn serious—it's a felony offense and comes with 4 years of prison.

My jaw clenches, anger surging through my body at the disparity in charges.

> Me: That's such bullshit.

> Hudson: I know, but at this point, I don't care what he's charged with as long as he's arrested and behind bars because I'm ready to turn the tables on him and see how well he likes being threatened and chased for 3.5 miles.

It's like he picked the thought straight from my damn brain.

> Hudson: Anyway, keep me updated.

I spend the next hour prepping the living room. With Nolan living with his sister, Hannah, and Hadley, thanks to the exception in the rules, allowing him to live with a family member, his dorm has become a multi-functional space for the rest of us. I stored what I need for today in there for the past couple of weeks. I'm not sure what Mila's reaction will be, especially after yesterday, but I know if anyone deserves love and care, it's her.

I'd planned for us to go tent camping this weekend so Mila could cross it off her list of things she's never experienced. The weather is unusually warm, and it would have been the perfect weekend, but instead, I set the four-person tent up in the living room and put the air mattress inside to make it comfortable.

I know from stories she and Hudson have shared that Mila loves card and board games. I stack a pile of borrowed games on the coffee table along with an assortment of snacks. Next, I get to work on breakfast, putting blueberries, sugar, and a little water in a pot to boil into syrup while making pancake batter.

My phone vibrates with another text and then a second. The first is from Jon.

> Jon: How long has this been going on?

I don't know if he's referring to Mila and me or Julian Holloway. Either answer seems dangerous. Few people in my life intimidate me. Perhaps it's something I should thank my mom for because she never made me feel like I was better or less than anyone else, but Jon Atwool makes me shake in my proverbial boots. Mila adores her parents and respects them with the same reverence I do my mom. I know his opinion of me matters more than anyone's.

> Jon: If you see Julian Holloway again, I want you to let me know. Immediately.

My relief comes out as a long sigh as I text him back.

> Me: It's been going on longer than it should.

The dots appear as soon as I send my text.

> Jon: Got a minute to chat?

> Me: Yeah

My phone rings in the next second.

"Hi, Jon."

"How's Mila doing?" He sounds exhausted.

"He dredged up a lot of tough memories. It's been a rough couple of weeks for her."

Jon sighs. "What kind of a monster hunts down a person after destroying their childhood?" He pulls in a breath. "I never expected this. *Never*. She must be going through hell."

"She was, but last night, she said she realized Mal's death wasn't her fault. I know it doesn't make things easier, but after taking so much from her, I'm glad Mila finally took this back, because..." I pause and hear the sharp intake of breath on the other line followed by a quiet sob.

"Nearly fourteen years." His breath shudders.

"Hudson and I are going to her apartment tomorrow to ensure there are no additional Find-it Tags." The batteries on those damn devices last an entire year.

"Thank you," he says. "And thank you for being there for her." He sniffs. "If she needs anything, Briggs is always on call. He'll do virtual visits or phone calls. And if you need anything, money, food ... *anything*, let me know. I can wire money now."

"I don't."

He releases another long breath. "She must really trust you." His assurance feels like an award that I want to hang as a focal point on my wall to remind myself that the greatest achievements in life never have a damn thing to do with money. Money isn't why I met Mila, and it didn't make her trust me. She and I built what we had with time, effort, and care. Money also didn't make my childhood great. My mom did. My friends and grandpa did. Learning to play football and fighting did. But I've also seen how poverty eats people alive, strips their self-esteem and confidence, and buries them in debt when they get sick or injured. It's so hard to find a middle ground when one isn't visible—may not even exist.

"She'll be safe. I swear."

"I have a meeting with my lawyer at noon. In the meantime, if anything happens, weird calls, strange messages, whatever—call the police and then me."

"I will."

"And, Grey, we're in your debt." He hangs up.

I pull the syrup off the stove, add the zest and juice of a lemon. I pour a ladle into a small bowl to sample it as Mila steps out of the bedroom.

"What is all this?" Her eyes dance across the room, wide and bright as a smile forms on her lips.

"Happy Valentine's Day."

"You set up a tent."

"You said you've never been tent camping."

She laughs, and it's the best sound I've heard in the past twelve hours. "This is the best surprise ever." With eyes infectiously bright, she walks toward me. I wrap my arms around her waist as hers encircle the back of my neck, and kiss her.

She leans back with a faint smile, keeping her arms locked around my neck as she takes a deep breath through her nose and turns to look at the stove. "I was planning to make you waffles." A shadow of disappointment crosses her features. The waffle iron had been broken, run over by Julian fucking Holloway. "But this smells even better."

"Do you remember the first summer we went to the beach together?" We stayed at Corey's family's beach house, a literal beachfront mansion with the other guys.

Mila nods.

"We had breakfast at that small restaurant the first day because we hadn't gone grocery shopping yet, and you ordered pancakes with blueberry syrup."

Her eyes shine with recognition. "I'd forgotten about that place. Why didn't we ever go back? I practically licked my plate."

I grin. "I'm making you that same breakfast, and this time, when you get whipped cream on your lip," I skate my thumb over her upper lip, "I plan to lick it off."

Her pupils dilate with lust. "Tell me we're taking the day off."

I nod. "We are."

She presses closer. "Good. I think we can find better ways to get in our cardio."

"So many better ways," I agree, stripping off the tee Mila

385

wore to bed. Her breasts are bare, and her nipples are already peaked.

I slip off her sweatpants and underwear next.

She chuckles. "You always just fling them across the room."

I nod and, without warning, lift her onto the small kitchen island.

Mila squeals as the cold connects with her skin, a challenge for me to make her forget, just like I hope to make her forget all the pain Julian has caused. I spread her knees with my waist and grab the small bowl of blueberry syrup I'd set aside to sample. I dip my finger into it to ensure it won't burn her, and when I discover it's safe, I smear the purple syrup across her breast and nipple.

Mila arches her back, a soft moan gathering in her throat. I lean down and lick the stiff peak, and she hisses as she wraps her fingers around the counter. I lick her again and then seal my mouth around her nipple, lavishing my tongue across the taut peak until her thighs spread wider with a silent invitation. I dip my fingers into the syrup again, painting more of it across her stomach and thighs.

I lick it from her stomach first, overjoyed by the giggle she releases. Then, I lower my mouth to her thigh, licking and caressing her skin there while bringing my clean hand to her middle and stroking along her core.

She moans, bringing one hand to my hair and raking her nails across my scalp.

I slip my fingers into her, knuckle deep, and she writhes, leaning back on the counter, forgetting the cold or simply not caring.

Mission accomplished.

I spread her thighs wider and drag my tongue across her again and again until she's breathless. Then I slide my fingers inside her and devour her clit, greedy for her orgasm.

Mila's thighs tremble as she lifts her knees, breathing my name again and again. I slide a second finger inside, curling them to that spot that makes her breaths labored, and worship her with my mouth and fingers until she falls apart.

Chapter 42

Mila

"Faster," Cole says, slapping my hand away.

"If I go faster, you'll tell me my form is bad." It's been two and a half weeks since Julian chased me. I haven't seen or heard a thing from him, but I haven't allowed his absence to lull me into believing this mess is over. Rather, I've focused my efforts even more on working out and time at the gym, practicing with precision and focus that Mackey, Cole, Abe, and even Dustin demand from me.

They're quick to tell me when I'm too slow or my form's wrong—which is still a lot, much to my displeasure.

"That's why you have to keep working. Keep practicing."

Mackey lingers at the side of the ring, offering instruction and the occasional jab at Cole when he doesn't block me well enough or on the rare occasions when I exceed their expectations and land a hit. Those few instances, Cole smiles so wide and proudly, I swear something is wrong with him.

"Don't worry about making a direct hit to his nose," Mackey says, climbing into the ring. "If you get a little cheek or upper lip; it will still burn."

The bells on the door ring, and we all turn to see Grey. My heart races as it does every time I see him.

Cole takes my moment of distraction and tackles me.

* * *

"Why didn't you tell me about your mom?" Palmer asks as I pick out items for our belated Galentine's celebration.

The flu spread to Hadley and then Hannah, delaying the celebration. I don't mind, though. March is still a great time to celebrate friendship.

I pause and turn to Palmer.

He shakes his head. "I didn't realize you knew your mom. Since you never talk about her, I assumed she was never in the picture."

My heart squeezes with emotions I can't place topped by a hefty layer of sorrow and guilt. Palmer's mom committed suicide, a tragedy he rarely discusses. "Because you cared deeply about your mom and miss her." I shake my head. "And I don't have those emotions about my mom."

The doubt in his expression awakens my defenses. "Losing a parent, regardless of the reason, leaves a mark."

I turn my attention to the *Tart Apple* red nail polish, and *I'd Rather be on Vacation* teal in my hand, my thoughts static as I try to recall what I'm doing rather than the emotional scars from my childhood. I pick out four more colors before turning to Palmer, one of the kindest, funniest, and most loyal people I've ever met. "If you ever want to talk about your mom, I'm here for you."

He nods. "I know."

"Is it hard for you to trust people?"

Palmer folds his arms over my shopping cart. "No, but caring about people sometimes fucks with my head."

Palmer has casually dated a string of cleat chasers the group knows are placeholders. Like Grey's aversion to dating, I assumed it was because he was too busy with football, but doubt and his solemn eyes blow that theory to pieces.

Maybe Jon is right, and we're all trying to navigate through life, feeling like everyone else has the secret sauce when none of us really do.

"Me too," I admit. "But I also suck at trusting people and a short list of other things you all keep crossing off."

He chuckles and wraps an arm around my shoulders. "It's about damn time." He checks his phone. "Speaking of time, we need to wrap this up. It's time to hit the gym."

Today is Palmer's first day of working out at Mackey's, and while I initially suspected it was because he didn't trust Abe and the others to watch out for me, I realize when we arrive that Palmer's doing his part in bridging these two sides of Grey's life, and now mine.

Three hours later, I'm showered and rushing with Evelyn to the Italian restaurant Hadley made a reservation at to celebrate Galentine's.

A year ago, I didn't have any female friends. A few acquaintances, yes, but no one I'd call after a particularly rough day or even a great one. I thought I was okay with my friend group consisting of Griffin and Hudson, two people I'm privileged to rely on and trust, unlike so many who have promised to do so. But, when Evelyn moved back last May, she filled a void I didn't know existed. She sparked my addiction to romance novels, listened to every whim, thought, and fear like it was her own, and became a safe space. Now, as the hostess takes me to the table filled with our book club, five women gathered to celebrate our budding friendship, I can't help but hope this becomes a tradition for years to come.

The colorful bags in my arms aren't the only gifts.

Katie bought everyone a paperback of the next book we're discussing. Hadley passes out fuzzy socks adorned with hearts and lips along with bath bombs. Evelyn gifts us each an adult coloring book with positive women affirmations, and Brielle hands each of us a gorgeous bouquet of flowers. Hannah's gift is a box filled with gummy bears, herbal teas, and a Golden Girls sticker that has us all laughing before I pass out the presents I brought, which contain a bookmark, various beauty products, and a journal filled with prompts in case others struggle like me to get out their thoughts.

"We're celebrating us tonight," Hadley says, raising her glass. "I was dreading this year." She looks at Hannah and then Katie before turning to the rest of us. "I didn't think I had any friends, and now I'm sitting with five of the funniest, kindest, most accepting, and wonderful women I've had the pleasure of meeting. I'm so damn proud to call you all my friends."

We stuff ourselves on pasta and garlic bread and laugh over romance novels and plans for this spring—plans that aren't exclusive to book club.

We're stuffed and giddy from our evening of girl time as we leave the restaurant, arms filled with gifts. The energy and happiness that consumes me is even better than the warm *zeppoles* we dipped into rich chocolate for dessert. That strange space between acquaintances and friendship is a distant memory as we say goodbye and confirm plans to meet at Hadley, Hannah, and Katie's next week for fondue and facials.

"Oh my God, is that snow?" Evelyn asks as we step outside. "In March!" she exclaims.

I grin, that magical feeling of wonder and beauty shocking me like it does every time I see the snow.

I give a final wave to the others as they head for their cars, and link my arm through Evelyn's, leading her to where I parked.

"I've never seen snow," Evelyn says. "Will we get enough for it to actually cover the ground?" She reaches out, palm open, staring at the snowflakes that melt against her skin. She smiles, wonder and amazement bright in her eyes. It reminds me of Mal, who loved the snow so much her passion became addictive and made me love it, too.

"Maybe? We'll see. But I bet we get a snow day." Oleander Springs is allergic to snow. "I'm amazed the restaurant didn't kick us out." I glance back at the restaurant and around the parking lot a final time as I unlock my car. Despite not hearing from Julian and scanning my belongings for Find-it Tags—twice—my paranoia is still strong. But as I look around, the only thing I see is snow and people's mixed reactions—hating or loving the frozen water crystals.

"Check Camden's website. I bet they already announced classes are canceled for tomorrow," I tell her as we slip into my car. The idea of being locked up with Grey all day feels like the best gift imaginable. We haven't taken a day off since Valentine's. "I need to call Grey and let him know we're leaving. Did you text Hudson?"

"I will right now. Do you think it's snowing at the dorm?"

I nod while calling Grey. As my car starts, it directs the call to speakerphone, and I usher a quick apology to Evelyn.

He answers on the second ring. "Hey. I'm just getting ready to leave Mackey's. Are you back at the dorm? Is it snowing there?" His voice a warm caress through the speaker.

"It just started. It's coming down fast."

"You know what this means?" he asks.

"You're on speakerphone," I remind him.

Evelyn giggles.

Grey clears his throat. "I was going to say, you might get a second day off."

"But not a day off of cardio, right?" My smile is so big, I'm sure he can hear it in my voice.

"Definitely not," he says.

I slow to a stop at the red light, mesmerized by the snow falling on my windshield. "We'll probably beat you back to the dorm. Traffic's pretty light, so we—"

The impact of something hitting us barely registers before I slam against the airbag. Metal and screams fill my ears. It takes me a few seconds to realize the screams are mine.

The airbag begins to deflate nearly instantly, and I shove it away, trying to look at Evelyn.

"Evelyn!" I yell, reaching for her. "Are you okay?" I grab her shoulder. The movement has pain firing off in my collarbone, but I barely notice it as Evelyn turns to face me, eyes stretched with terror. "Are you okay?"

"Mila?" Grey's voice repeats loud and demanding through the speakers of my car. "What happened?"

Evelyn's face pales. "Go! Drive!" She shoves at the wilting airbag in front of her. "Mila, go!"

I look over my shoulder and see a white truck reversing, and like that day he approached Evelyn at the park, I know it's Julian Holloway without seeing him.

I run the red light, my tires screeching, and my dash flashing about my rear tire being low.

"Call the police," I tell Evelyn, pressing the gas pedal to the floorboard. Behind us, the truck accelerates, seemingly undeterred by the crash, unlike my car.

"Mila!" Grey barks my name.

"Shit," Evelyn gasps as the truck connects with my bumper,

causing the car to swerve. "Hello. I have an emergency. Someone just ran into us with their car and he's chasing us!" The edge of hysteria has her voice louder and higher than usual.

"Mila!" Grey barks. "What's going on?"

"Julian just crashed into us with his truck. Evelyn's calling the cops, and I'm about to get on the highway and head north."

"No. Come to Highgrove."

I shake my head. "Grey—"

"Head south, Mila. You can lead him right to the police station. We'll meet you there."

"No. He's behind us. He's following us," Evelyn says to the police dispatcher. "We've been trying to report him, and no one has done anything and now he just rammed into us. Twice!" She's spiraling, anger thankfully in the driver's seat rather than fear, or maybe her amygdala is the guard dog unlike my opossum.

"I got you. I found you. We're coming," Grey says. We downloaded apps to follow each other after the first Julian incident, something I am eternally grateful for as Grey tells me which exit to take.

I grip the steering wheel tighter, my gaze shifting to the rearview mirror as I manage to get a car between Julian and us. The tire gauge on my dash turns red, the pressure in the teens. The road is turning a soft shade of gray from the thin layer of snow that continues falling, harder now, creating a kaleidoscope appearance.

"Something's wrong with my tire," I tell him, fear an echo in my chest. "I'm losing air. Fast. He hit the back. I don't know if the wheel is bent, or broken, or..." There's nothing between Oleander Springs and Highgrove but sleepy neighborhoods, woods, and farm fields.

"Cole, grab Abe and Mackey and whatever weapons Mackey keeps in his office."

"They have weapons?" Evelyn asks, eyes wide with shock as she looks up from her phone where she's texting. I know it's Hudson without asking.

Another time, the same words might catch me up, but right now, I have two things to focus on, how to evade Julian and keeping Evelyn safe. "What did the police say?" I ask her.

"The dispatcher put me on hold," she says.

"You're on hold?" I cry.

"You're twenty-five miles out." Grey swears.

The dark road I've traveled daily seems unfamiliar, the details escaping me as I glance up and see Julian's white truck, which has stalked too many of my nightmares, speeding up.

"Just keep coming this way. Your car will be harder to maneuver with a flat tire. Make sure you have both hands on the steering wheel. It will want to pull."

I could already tell the difference. "Hey, Grey." Tears itch at my eyes.

"I'm here."

"I love you."

"Mila, no. Not like this."

I sputter as a tear skates down my cheek, pressing the car to go faster still. "But I do, and I should have told you sooner. I should have kissed you two years ago because I wanted to kiss you the first time I saw you."

"Go. Go!" Grey yells, and I hear the anger and regret in his voice. "It's going to be fine. *You're* going to be fine."

Evelyn's breaths are becoming wheezing, too high and pitchy.

I turn to her. "Do you have your inhalers?"

She nods with tight jerky moments.

"I need you to take your emergency inhaler."

She gives another tight nod and reaches for her purse, withdrawing her inhaler with a trembling hand.

"You're getting close to fields," Grey says. "How's your tire pressure?"

"It says eleven."

"Shit." In the background, I hear Cole say something that makes Grey swear again, his tone vicious. "Mila, you're not going to make it. The tire will blow out if you go much farther. You'll be safer near a forest or a neighborhood, somewhere you can hide until we get there. You don't want to be stuck out in the goddamn crop fields. The forest you're passing is only another mile. It might be your safest chance."

I glance in my mirror, spotting Julian barreling toward us.

"How are you feeling?" I ask Evelyn.

"I'll be fine."

"You need to take another hit of your inhaler. It's cold." I glance at the woods beyond her that appear dark and menacing as I consider us running through them.

Evelyn nods as she slips the inhaler between her lips again and takes another pull.

"We'll stop here," I tell him. "Which direction do we run?"

"Drive as close to the tree line as possible, and then run a few hundred feet and find somewhere to hide. The cops will be there soon. Abe's on the phone with them now."

I place my arm across Evelyn's chest. "Hold on." I turn the wheel so sharply, the tires screech with protest. The weight of the car shifts dangerously to the right side for several seconds before we land on all four tires with so much impact, we bounce in the air, nearly hitting our heads on the roof of the car. The dash is flashing and beeping as I drive straight for the trees. Behind us, Julian skids to a stop on the highway.

"Mila?" Grey's voice is strained, every ounce of control that usually consumes him gone.

"I love you," I say again. "I'll see you soon." It's a promise. An oath.

I silence my phone, and zip it into my pocket as I duck out of the car not about to be the idiot in the movie who leaves every way of being tracked or calling for help behind. Evelyn meets me on the other side, eyes filled with determination and fear.

I grab her hand and we sprint for the dark wall of trees and vines as Julian drives toward us.

A sharp popping sound echoes behind us. We don't turn around. Brambles and branches snag our clothes and scratch every fraction of our exposed skin.

"He has a gun," Evelyn whispers, frantically.

I thought a gun would be louder. It's another thing Hollywood has lied about.

There's a scraping sound in her lungs, a warning that has her shoulders heaving and her skin pallid. Her stress or the cold —both—are too much even for her inhalers.

The sounds of moving grass and breaking twigs alerts us that Julian's not nearly far enough behind us.

"You need to hide," I tell her urgently, tugging off my coat.

Evelyn bats me away as I open it for her. "He's too close. We need to keep going."

"You can't run. You need to warm up and hide. The cops will be here soon. We just need to buy some time."

"Then we're hiding together."

I search for a hiding place. "I'm going to lead him the other way."

Evelyn shakes her head as her fingers become talons around my wrist. "We're not separating."

"He'll hear you," I say, hating myself for making her feel weak. But her breaths are louder and more ragged than our shared words. "You need to take your medicine, warm up, and stop running."

Defeat has a tear slipping down her cheek.

"I'll be fine. I swear. I'm going to distract him and then hide. I'll come back as soon as the cops arrive. Don't move until then." I help her into my jacket. The black coat conceals her, allowing most of her to fade into the dark forest. I motion toward a fallen tree and point to the slight indention that allows her enough space to crawl into.

Evelyn's shivering as she clutches her inhaler. "Are you sure?"

"Positive," I say with a nod. Her breaths are too loud and distinctive. I know I only have minutes to lead him far enough away.

"Swear you'll be okay," Evelyn says.

I nod. "I swear." I can't tell Evelyn how much I love her, how our friendship has slowly been healing wounds in my chest for the past thirteen years, allowing me to overcome and better myself in ways many of my past therapists didn't think I could be healed.

Tears streak down her face, and I know she's refusing to say the same words. "Go. Hide."

I drag a fallen branch up to further conceal her, and then remain still. I strain to listen over Evelyn's heavy breathing and my pounding heart.

I can't see him, but the sound of breaking branches taunts my nerves as I consider a safe route to cut away from Evelyn without getting too close to Julian.

I curse my light blue sweater that makes me stand out, and boots that make running uncomfortable and difficult before sprinting to hide behind a nearby tree. I dash to the next, and then another, working to get far enough away from Evelyn before making a sound.

Once I'm far enough away, I stop behind another tree and rummage around on the ground until finding a rock. The forest has gone silent. Julian's listening for me, now.

I throw the rock away from me, in the opposite direction of Evelyn, as far as I can, then run like hell. I tear through bushes and trees, ignoring how my ankles sting and ache as they roll while trying to find purchase on the uneven ground and protruding stumps and rocks I can't see.

Rustling behind me tells me Julian's running too.

I stop behind a large bush, trying to silent my heavy breaths.

For the first time in my life, I curse the snow as it breaks through the canopy overhead. It won't be deep enough for tracking, but everything will be slick.

My heart and breaths feel amplified as I try to listen for Julian's whereabouts.

A stick breaks in the distance, and fear nearly cripples me. He's not following me; he's heading straight for Evelyn.

Chapter 43

Mila

I stumble over a stump and slice my hand open as I reach out to catch myself. Adrenaline has me climbing to my feet and listening carefully as I hop over a fern. I silently thank Mackey for making me work on so many damn lunges and jumps and Dustin for constantly making me work on balance exercises.

I run as fast as I can, my hands out in front of me, trying to gauge where anything dangerous is. I'm terrified I'll fall into a ravine and break my leg or impale myself on one of the broken trees.

I hiss as brambles tear at my neck, then, sprint forward as the canopy thins. A thin layer of snow that covers the ground, brightening the section of forest to allow me to see almost clearly. I stop at the other end and listen.

Branches snap, and Julian swears, no longer trying to be silent as he edges closer to Evelyn.

"Hey," I yell. Sprinting toward him, still too far away for us to see each other.

Something cuts my arm, and a branch breaks as my calf

drags across it. In the back of my head, I know I'm going to be bruised and sore tomorrow. I try to bring that thought closer to the surface. I want to cling to the pain, embrace it because it means I'll be here. I'll endure the pain, wait for the bruises and cuts to heal because I no longer need a series of self-dates to remind me how desperately I want to be alive or how I want to be treated. I already know how desperately I want to feel Grey again, see my parents and friends, beat a world record, and continue to work on accepting and loving myself as much as I love life. As much as I love Griffin, and Hudson, and Evelyn.

As much as I love Grey.

I yell again to catch Julian's attention, louder this time.

I don't know where he is, and it's so damn dark, I'm not even certain I'm near Evelyn as I move behind another tree so I can listen.

I've always loved the forest. Growing up in Oleander Springs, next to the lake and woods, the forest was a second home, a setting Hudson and I navigated often, but it's eerily silent and dark tonight.

A noise nearby has me crouching lower. Fear has my opossum peeking its nose out, unsure what I heard or how far away it was as adrenaline makes it difficult to think or focus. Another rustling tells me I'm still not close enough.

"Hey!" I yell again, running faster.

A pop, followed by the sound of splintering tree bark nearby has me falling to my hands and knees.

A bullet.

A mothertrucking bullet.

At this rate, Briggs will be able to retire to Tahiti, thanks to the additional trauma Julian is inflicting.

Bushes and branches snap with movement and I realize Julian's moving and this time, he's coming directly at me.

Finally.

I turn around and scurry across the soaked ground on my hands and knees, terrified he'll see me if I stand.

"You can't hide," Julian yells. "Haven't I proven that to you?"

A thorn catches my cheek as I turn to look over my shoulder, wondering if it's safer to remain down where I might be a smaller target or get up because I'm faster on my feet.

"Do you know your mother never even mentioned you? I dated her for four months before I even knew you and your sister existed." He stops talking, and another bullet pops.

I freeze.

This would be a great time to know how many bullets a gun can hold. How many times he can shoot before I can stop being terrified.

"Your mother locked that damn door, not me, and she still got out sooner. I didn't even know you, didn't want the two of you living in my house." Bushes rustle again, and I scamper another ten feet so I can hide behind a stump.

"Do you know what I had left when I was released from prison?"

I slink forward, hearing the rage in his voice. I remember next to nothing about him, barely even his face. We only lived with him a couple of months before Mal died, he and my mother were arrested, and my life changed forever. I huddle behind a wide oak tree, where I pull my knees to my chest.

"Nothing!" he screams. "I lost my house, my car, every goddamn thing I owned because I let a slut and her two idiot kids live with me."

His words should anger me. Another day, they might, but right now, I focus on the rustling of bushes that tell me he's drawing closer.

"They kept you hidden for so long. Adopted to your rich

Hollywood dad. They changed your name, and pretended you weren't the trailer trash you were..."

He stops, and my heart thrums, wondering if he'll shoot again. I pray his visibility is as terrible as mine.

"Your uncle offered me everything he knew for forty bucks."

Hearing this is like stepping on a nail, causing me to mentally buckle.

"Forty bucks," he repeats. "That's all your life was worth to him."

Another pop. Another splintering of tree bark.

I huddle tighter.

"This could have been so easy. Things didn't have to come down to this. If you hadn't called to police, I would have taken it easy on you. I didn't want to hurt you. I just wanted compensation. I came to your apartment last spring with the intent of arranging a payment plan. You were supposed to tell your parents you wanted to buy a boat or a car or whatever in the hell you waste money on and pay me back for the hell you put me through. Instead, you got me fired and arrested. Again."

He's so close the ferns beside me shift. I try not to breathe.

"I tried to talk to you again, and you called me a fucking psycho."

I knew that insult dug at him.

"You want to see a psycho? Because I'm about to show you." He stops. "I know you're close. How long do you think you can hide?"

The ferns shift again.

"You came running at me. You didn't toss it, you..." He shifts, but the ferns don't move. He moves again, too fast in the opposite direction, back toward Evelyn.

I don't have a guard dog. It turns out I really am a feral cat.

I move out from behind the tree and lunge at Julian Holloway.

Grey

"Five minutes," Cole assures me, pressing the gas pedal down and accelerating, trying to race the clock.

Those minutes feel like a life sentence.

"How the fuck did he find her again?" Abe demands.

"There are lots of places to hide," Cole says. "Mila's fast, and she's scrappy when pushed."

"As long as she doesn't freeze," Mackey says.

"She won't," I snap.

Mackey spots her car first, pulled off to the side, as close the tree line as possible. She did a damn good job.

Cole crosses all four lanes of traffic and barely slows as we hit the shoulder of the road. He cuts across the grass, blocking Julian's truck as he pulls to a stop.

"Let's fan out," I say, opening my door.

The sound of a gunshot freezes my blood.

I'm going to rip him apart with my bare hands.

I hear Cole and Mackey devising a plan, but I'm already diving into the trees.

"You take the right side, I'll take the left," Abe says, moving next to me.

A scream pierces the air, and we break into a run, heading in the same direction. Snow offers the tiniest bit of light, but it's not enough to see clearly, slowing us down.

"Get the girls and get out. He's mine," I tell Abe.

"Mackey will take them. I'm staying."

A bellow of anger has us curving left followed by Evelyn yelling for help.

We sprint, branches and vines threaten to slow us down,

but the shouts have our adrenaline pumping and our feet racing.

We tear through the forest, running farther than I expected them to go, hearing shouts and grunts. I spot Evelyn first, holding a branch like a baseball bat. My heart careens in my chest, feeling relief she's fine and the panic that follows when I don't immediately see Mila.

"There," Abe says at the same time I notice the tangle of limbs on the ground. Panic and fear slam into me as I see Julian on top of Mila.

We rush forward as I try to take in the scene, realizing Mila has her legs wrapped around his waist and his head trapped in the crook of her arm, executing a guillotine choke hold.

It's not a complete hold. Julian's still conscious, but he's stuck, struggling in an attempt to get her off.

Abe releases a sharp humorless laugh. "I knew she had it in her." He pulls a gun from the back of his waistband as Mila's gaze sweeps to us, her eyes wide and frantic.

I drop to one knee and punch Julian in the kidney to make him stop fighting before wrapping my arm around his neck, near the carotid arteries Mila's missing. If I press hard enough on it, he will pass out.

I lock eyes on Mila, taking in the scratches on her face, the blood on her lip, and the absolute fear in her eyes as she maintains her hold on him like the absolute badass she has proven to be time and time again.

I want to hurt Julian Holloway in ways I've never wanted to hurt another person. Destroy him, one bone at a time. But I know that would only force Mila to remain here and experience more trauma. "I've got him," I assure her. I turn to Abe. "Help her out."

Abe doesn't move, keeping the gun trained on Julian. Luckily, Cole and Mackey are right behind us. They don't wait for instruction, grabbing Mila and dragging her out from under his weight.

"Look at you, champ," Mackey says to Mila as Cole issues a litany of threats to Julian, warning him if he moves, he won't leave here breathing.

Evelyn collapses beside Mila, pulling her into a full-body hug.

Cole pulls Julian's arm back into an armbar. "Where's the gun?"

"He dropped it," Mila says.

"He might have more," Mackey warns.

Abe pats him down.

"Don't touch anything," Cole says. "Just hold him."

"I want to make sure if he tries to move, he's not going to be reaching for a weapon," Abe says before tossing a switchblade to Mackey's feet. Once he's done, Abe positions himself over Julian, digging a knee between his shoulder blades. "I've got him," he assures me.

I release Julian and go to Mila, falling to my knees and kissing her hair, her face, her shoulder. Everything I can touch, I kiss.

Mila leans into me, closes her eyes and for the second time, she sobs in my arms at the hands of Julian fucking Holloway.

I want to destroy him and let her watch, assure her he can't haunt her again, but half a dozen police officers suddenly surround us, flashlights and guns raised as they announce themselves.

"Hands in the air," and officer says, pointing a gun at Abe.

"They helped us," Evelyn says, moving in front of Abe and Cole.

"Hands in the air," they repeat.

Cole reluctantly releases his hold on Julian's arm, and Abe

slowly raises his hands. "Everyone back. Keep your hands raised."

Evelyn, Cole, and Abe collectively move back, keeping their hands raised.

"Is she okay?" someone asks.

The moment he does, there's movement and a yell of determination.

Mackey steps in front of me, and a dozen bullets echo through the night before Julian Holloway falls to the ground.

Chapter 44

Mila

Our brains are like sieves.

The brain holds on to memories and facts believed to be important, discards details deemed irrelevant, and sometimes, our brains dispose or bury memories because they're too painful.

Most of this sorting happens at night while we dream.

Previously, I couldn't think of Mallory, even the sound of her laughter, without crippling guilt and sadness. I hate that it took additional trauma to help ease some of my past traumas, but as I lie in the hospital bed, listening to the doctor list off my minor and less minor injuries that include a fractured collarbone, fractured rib, and a slew of bruises, Mal's laughter fills my ears and heart, a presence I've ignored for so long, consumes me and makes me feel more complete than I have in too many years.

"These will need to be removed in a week," the doctor tells me, setting to work on stitching the cut on my biceps.

"And you're going to need to keep it bandaged the entire time. Don't let it dry—"

"We got it," a familiar voice in the hall says.

"We know," I think that's Evelyn.

"Yeah," a third familiar voice says.

The cacophony of voices carries down the hall, and I know they're coming for me before the emergency room curtain is pulled aside and Hudson appears with Evelyn at his side, Corey, Nolan, Hadley, Hannah, Palmer, Abe, Cole, and Mackey all joining them.

"We'll be quiet," Hadley says.

"There's no room," a nurse insists.

"We don't mind. We're close. We'll stand close," Cole tells her.

The doctor looks up at me, exhaustion mirrored in his gaze. "We're doing a sterile procedure here."

"Everyone, hold your breath," Palmer jokes.

The doctor rolls his eyes and points as he turns to look at the nurse. "It's a slow night. Open the connecting curtain."

She doesn't look happy about it, but she tugs the curtain open, doubling the space of my room, to accommodate the large group.

The medics who arrived after Julian Holloway was shot announced him dead on arrival. The words have been turning around in my thoughts for the past couple of hours, since the same medics insisted I ride in an ambulance to the hospital. I don't know how to process the news, only that I'll be talking to Briggs about it for weeks, months—maybe even years to come.

I stare at Evelyn, ensuring again that she's all right. "How are you feeling?" I ask.

She nods, but I see it in her large dark eyes that she's not. She was in a car accident, chased, and then watched someone lose their life. I have no doubt her mind is acting as a sieve currently, sorting through all the details, fears, perceptions, and holy shit what-if moments just as mine is.

"How did he find us?" I ask.

Evelyn holds up a small Find-it Tag. "It was in your coat pocket."

The coat I shoved her into. The coat that had him tracking her so easily.

I pale.

"Mila, I'm fine," she says. "He didn't hurt me. He didn't even get to me because you saved me." Tears pool in her eyes and it elicits mine to do the same.

"You came and saved me, too," I remind her. "That swing to his back was the only way I was able to hold him."

I don't know that my mind's sieve will replay the entirety of the events anytime soon. All I remember clearly is chasing after Julian with the determination he didn't touch Evelyn. I knocked him to the ground, but he rolled faster than me, punching me in the face. It stunned me. As many times as I've worked out with the guys and they've pushed me around, I realized in that moment they'd been taking it easy on me and never once had they hit me.

Evelyn had come out of her hiding space as soon as she heard me scream, grabbed the biggest stick she could find, and came charging.

"We never even taught you the guillotine hold," Cole says.

I scoff. "No, but you've used it on me a half dozen times."

Grey growls from his seat beside me.

Cole flashes a guilty grin and shrugs. "I was diversifying her training."

Mackey grins at me. "You did well, kid."

Grey

Hudson's dad, my mom, and Cole and Abe's parents showed up as the doctor finished stitching Mila's arm. The ER nurse took one look at our growing group, shook her head, and walked away.

Finally, at two in the morning, they discharge Mila, but rather than relief, everyone looks conflicted, not wanting to part.

"If you need anything—anything at all—call us. Morning, noon, night—we don't care," Hadley says as we leave the hospital as a large group. "And we'll stop over tomorrow."

Hannah nods. "We'll bring chocolate and ice cream. *All* the chocolate and ice cream."

Mila shivers beside me and huddles closer. "It finally snowed," she says. Three inches of snow cover the ground, making the night look unusually well-lit.

I press a kiss to Mila's temple and turn to the group. "I'll text you all when she wakes up."

They want to linger, but I usher Mila toward my truck.

Hudson and Evelyn follow behind us in his Jeep, and Corey and Palmer are right behind him. When we arrive at the dorm, Hudson asks Mila to wait a moment and the two hang back in the lobby. Before the elevator doors close, I watch the two embrace, tears marring their cheeks as Hudson says something and she nods, holding him tighter.

While I wait for Mila, I scan the rest of her things for a third time to ensure there are no more Find-it Tags because despite Julian being a nonissue, I hate the idea of her finding one in the future and it reminding her of being stalked like prey.

I don't find anymore, but I make a plan to search her apartment a second time as well. The coat had been in Evelyn's car when we searched the first time, and we never considered searching Evelyn's things, though I'm sure Hudson will be tonight.

When Mila returns, she showers, dresses, and then takes the Valium the ER doctor prescribed.

"How are you feeling? Do you need more ice? Something to drink?"

Mila shakes her head and crawls into bed.

"Even with the painkillers and Valium, I don't know that I'll be able to sleep," she says. "I don't know how you ever slept after a fight. I keep replaying the parts of the fight I can remember, thinking about what I should have done."

I want to remind her she wasn't trained to fight. We focused on endurance, cardio, and avoiding fights rather than participating in one. Instead, I open my arms to invite her to lie on me, wanting her tucked in as close to me as possible.

"You were amazing, Mila. Few would have been able to do what you did tonight. Don't overthink anything."

She gives a nearly imperceptible nod.

I don't turn off the light. On our ride to the hospital, I realized I waited patiently for two and a half years, believing I had enough time to figure things out. I could wait for her to date other guys and whatever else with the excuse it allowed me to focus on football and my degree to be the kind of guy she deserved. I wanted to end a cycle of poverty that would ensure my mom never had to question calling out of work when she didn't feel good in order to pay her bills.

I still want to break that cycle, still want to be the man Mila deserves, but I regret not taking advantage of every opportunity and every day I've had with her. I make a vow to myself I will never do that again. People don't choose to be poor. I know that firsthand. My mother worked harder than anyone I knew, and I will do everything I can to be the best son, the best boyfriend, the best wide receiver, and if I don't end up with a fancy house and new truck, it won't matter because I hit the goddamned lottery when it comes to love, and we will make it work regardless.

"Mila," I say.

Her silver eyes lift to mine.

"I love you so damn much."

She smiles, and it grips my heart. "I love you, too."

* * *

I can't help but feel as though I broke a promise as I pull into Mila's parents' driveway. I didn't keep Mila safe. Not entirely. The array of scratches and bruises covering too much of her attests to the fact.

Alex starts crying the moment he sees Mila's cut lip and bruised face. They flew in this afternoon, a direct flight from California that they booked last night when I called Jon to share what happened.

"Can you walk up the stairs?" Alex asks. "Should we carry you?"

Mila shakes her head. "I'm fine."

She's not, but she's amazingly brave, strong, and resilient.

Jon holds her hand as they walk up the front steps. I move to follow, but Alex turns and hugs me with a ferocity that stops me in my tracks.

"Thank you," he says. "We owe you more than you could ever know."

I shake my head. "She did the hard work."

Alex releases me slowly, wiping his eyes. "We were going to ask her to come live in California with us, but after hearing what happened and seeing you this morning, I have a feeling she's going to tell us she doesn't want to."

My heart feels like it's fallen into a blender. California would allow her to never have to relive these memories, and she'd be close to her parents, and I know she misses them terribly.

"You should give her the option," I tell him.

He stares at me. "I was hoping you'd say that."

His words take me by surprise and have me furrowing my brow.

"Her being safe and loved is all we care about—all we've ever cared about, and your willingness to sacrifice your happiness for her is the confirmation I need to know you love her." He smiles as he pats my shoulder. "Let's go inside."

Hudson and Evelyn show up a couple of hours later. Everyone's emotions are visibly strained from the mental and physical exhaustion of yesterday.

They order food, but no one eats much. The mood is somber with an edge of relief that has the occasional sigh being heard.

"It's getting late, we should probably go," Mila says.

"Why don't you stay," Jon says.

"I don't have anything here," Mila says.

"We can replace it," Jon says.

"Maybe tomorrow." She leans forward and kisses his cheek.

They walk us to the door with Hudson and Evelyn at our sides.

"Are you sure you don't need anything?" Jon asks.

Mila shakes her head. "I feel better than I look. I swear."

He hugs her gently and then moves to me, wrapping me in a tight hug. "Thank you," he whispers. "Thank you," he says again, tightening his grip before he releases me.

"I didn't—" I start to say, but Jon shakes his head.

"You did. The only person to blame is Julian Holloway." He shakes his head again. "Why don't you all come by tomorrow for breakfast. We'll make french toast, play games, and recover from this together."

Mila turns to me. "We can invite your mom."

"She'd love that," I say.

Mila gives a crooked grin that makes her wince as it pulls at the split lip.

"It's settled then," Alex says. "We'll see you all tomorrow at ten."

Our drive to the dorm is quiet, and our nighttime routine is nearly the same as it has been for the past several weeks.

I wait until we're in bed before turning to her. "If being here and having to remember Julian and everything he put you through is too much, I want you to consider your parents' offer. I don't want you to stay because you feel like you have to. You don't owe me or anyone else anything, especially not your mental health and sanity."

Mila turns to me. "Where you are is where I want to be. If that's here, or somewhere across the country, or somewhere across the world. You and me. Together. Remember? We're a team."

I remember. "I want you to be happy and safe."

She smiles. "Grey, you are what makes me happy and safe. Leaving you would break me. You're my gravity, keeping me together."

I shake my head. "I don't want to keep you together. I want to be your safe place to come apart."

Her eyes flash with recognition and then understanding. "Greyson Meyers, one day, I'm going to marry you."

I nod. "You're damn right because you are mine, and I am yours." I lean forward and kiss her like it's my last time, like it's my first time, knowing we've closed a chapter and begun a new one, this one entitled forever.

Epilogue

Two Months Later, Mila

I want to roll over and plead for more sleep but force my tired eyes open.

We survived Julian, spring season, and finals. Today is the first day of summer break, and it feels glorious.

"What time do you have practice today?" I ask.

"We're doing afternoon practices all week so the team can sleep in." They'll want to move them to mornings soon because the North Carolina heat makes afternoons insufferable. "So we have plenty of time to get to the track and go to the gym."

I pout. We've continued working out, maintaining the same strict regimen. I've found that the gym is a release I never knew I needed. It helps me just like my therapy sessions with Briggs.

Beside me, Grey sits up, his back against the headboard, reviewing his schedule as he does each morning. The sight of his bare chest and arms rid any residual exhaustion as my body hums, my breasts becoming heavy as that ache between my legs becoming a demand. I thought my unyielding desire for him would lessen, that all the time spent in the gym and running would make me exhausted, and that having Grey buried inside of me while against every surface of his room and mine would feed my craving for him. Instead, it's made it insatiable.

I reach beneath the blankets pooled at his waist, finding his cock already hard.

Grey's breath leaves in a hiss through his teeth as he drops his head back. I run my hand over his impressive length and then shift to my knees, pulling the blankets back to get a better image of Grey wearing nothing but his inked tattoos and underwear. That ache in my core intensifies, desperate to crawl into his lap and sink down onto him.

He watches me, need and desire darkening his eyes and weighting his eyelids. I'd give my inheritance to capture how he looks at me and make it into a mural on my wall.

I tug down the band of his underwear, freeing his cock as he remains still except to brush my hair back.

I grip him with both hands and draw my tongue across the head of his cock, loving the way his breath leaves in a groan, his hands fist in my hair, and his abs clench. I take him into my mouth and move one hand, so he goes all the way to the back of my throat before sliding back up, sucking him as I do.

"Fuck." His voice is guttural and deep.

I continue, changing my angle and flicking my tongue along his shaft and head with each pass.

Grey's thighs are hard as concrete as he works to remain still and controlled. It only makes me more persistent and determined to make him lose that orderly stillness.

This time as I lower my mouth over him and relax my throat, Grey's hips shift forward, his fingers knotting in my hair, wanting to fuck my mouth.

I smile around him, and he swears.

In one swift move, Grey pulls out of my mouth and rolls

me, pinning me to the bed. He grips my chin as his lips ply at mine, reinstating his control.

I kiss him back and invade his mouth with my tongue, seeking my own dominance or maybe encouraging his.

Before I can decide, Grey gathers my shirt in his hands and pulls it over my head, tossing it to the floor as he rises to his knees. He slips his fingers into my panties and slides them down my legs before dropping them near his pillow. I'm about to snatch them and toss them to the floor, but Grey's hands settle on my thighs, pressing my legs open.

He stares down at my sex with the carnal look of desire consuming his features and then falls onto my center like a starved man. He draws out my pleasure in waves that have my entire body tingling, hot, and entirely too tight before my release surges through me.

I've barely taken a breath when he props my legs on his chest, a pose that I know will forever ruin me from our partner stretches, and fills me so deep and full, I moan my relief.

Grey swipes a hand under me and lifts my hips off the mattress, shoving a pillow under my lower back and butt. The angle has him seated so deeply inside of me my eyes roll back. Without moving his hips, Grey skates his hands over the tops and insides of my thighs.

As soon as I open my eyes, his hips shift, a small roll that has my moan a breathy sound. He grips my thighs, a possessive touch as his thrusts grow longer, harder, faster. My breathing is ragged, my body pulsing with pleasure.

He reads me like a book, knowing how close I am to a second orgasm as he discovers the exact rhythm and spot that has my blood red hot. Then he slides his thumb over me, tipping me straight over the ledge where I never want to return from as he follows me right into the abyss.

"You're so goddamn beautiful," Grey says, pumping long and slow thrusts as my breaths rattle out of me.

"We could skip cardio and do this again."

He grins and squeezes my butt with both hands as he draws out of me. "We can do cardio and still make time to do this again."

He chuckles as I frown and then kisses the inside of my ankle before lowering my legs to the bed and getting up.

I take a weighted breath, never wanting to leave the confines of this room as the scent of his cologne and sex perfume the air.

"Are you looking forward to your photo shoot?" I ask.

Grey glances at me out of the corner of his eyes, disbelief colored in a question. Today's his first photo shoot for Mr. Barnhardt, a deal I thought I'd lost due to beating them all at Topgolf. But since Grey made national news along with Cole, Abe, and Mackey, everyone wants him. Barnhardt showed up at the facility two days ago with a contract and a cigar that he gifted to Grey to celebrate their budding partnership. Cole has been invited to Vegas. Mackey is bitter as hell that his gym is packed, but secretly, I think he loves it.

I'm so damn proud of Grey, despite feeling the nails of jealousy, knowing how many are imagining Grey in all the ways I do with his face and body covering them, exploring them—pleasuring them.

"Do I get signed copies for inspiration once the season begins?"

"What kind of inspiration are we talking about?"

"The kind where I'm wearing your shirt while my fingers are between my legs."

He hooks his fingers under my chin. "Only if it's while we're on a video call."

The idea of watching Grey pleasure himself in a foreign

hotel room with me as his audience has my blood thrumming with determination and anticipation.

"Tell me what you're thinking," he says.

"All the filthy thoughts."

He smiles fiendishly. "Fuck the track." And then he's on top of me, kissing me while making me giggle and moan as we find far more creative ways to get in our cardio.

Want MORE football romance?

If you loved Grey and Mila's story, there are more books in the **Oleander Springs Series**!

Check out:

- Evelyn and Hudson's story in The Return Play (Childhood friends-to-lovers!
- Hadley and Nolan's story in The Roommate Route (Friends-with-Benefits/forced proximity!)

Need More?

Dive into the completed series of **The Dating Playbook**. Set in Seattle, Washington, each book follows a separate couple.

- Bending the Rules and Breaking the Rules: Brother's best friend (PLUS SUSPENSE!)
- Defining the Rules: Coach's Daughter/Friends-to-Lovers
- Exploring the Rules: Enemies-to-Lovers

- Forgetting the Rules: Friends-to-Lovers (A hint of suspense in this one as well)
- Writing the Rules: Fake Dating/Best Friend's Brother
- Missing the Rules: Once you learn all the Rules, be sure to read this one! It follows the couple from Bending and Breaking 5 years later, and is a complete 46k novel.

Thank you so much for reading **The Fake Zone**! If you loved Grey and Mila's story, please take a moment to leave a review on Amazon.

There will be **more** coming in this world! Be sure to sign up to receive updates, as well as exclusive material, giveaways, and more! Sign Up Now!

KEEP IN TOUCH:

- Follow me on Amazon
- Email: mariah@mariahdietz.com
- Like my Facebook
- Join my Facebook Reader Group
- Follow me on Tik Tok
- Follow me on Instagram
- Follow me on Bookbub
- Follow me on Goodreads

Also by Mariah Dietz

Tangled in Tinsel, A Christmas Novella

Acknowledgments

First and foremost, I would like to thank you, dear reader. Thank you for taking a chance on Mila and Grey. Thank you for being so supportive and patient. You all are truly amazing and I can't tell you how grateful I am for you.

A special thank you to my kiddos who continue to share my headspace and heart with fictional characters who I love like real people.

Lisa Ackroyd, you are the dearest best friend and I appreciate you listening to the dozens of voice messages I send you at odd hours while trying to walk through a story or scene.

Laura Hidalgo, thank you for making this stunning cover and being so damn patient with me.

Carrie Ann Ryan, thank you for your endless support and friendship, and checking to make sure I was still eating and sleeping as I struggled with parts of this story.

Nicole McCurdy, I can't tell you how much I appreciate your content edits. You help me open my thoughts with every single book, and you allow me to fearlessly bound off the path. Repeatedly.

A very special thank you to Kassidy Hansen Rismon, Megan Klose, Lizzy Ganske, Brittany McEnroe, Jodi Lynn, Rachel Rumble, and Holly Bietsch for taking the time and work to read The Fake Zone before it was edited and before anyone else saw it.

Kyra Zörgiebel, AJ Marks, and Ruby Harrison Dodson, thank you for being my eagle eyes.

And last but certainly not least, a huge thank you to Jessica Rose for everything she does and all the sanity she brings.

About the Author

Mariah Dietz is a USA Today Bestselling Author and self proclaimed nerd. She lives with her husband and sons in North Carolina.

Mariah grew up in a tiny town outside of Portland, Oregon where she spent most of her time immersed in the pages of books that she both read and created.

She has a love for all things that include her family, good coffee, books, traveling, and dark chocolate. She's also been known to laugh at her own jokes.

www.mariahdietz.com
mariah@mariahdietz.com
Subscribe to her newsletter, here